If You Love Me, Come

Books by Claudia Moss

DOLLY: THE MEMOIRS OF A HIGH SCHOOL GRADUATE
IF YOU LOVE ME, COME
WANDA B. WONDERS SPEAKS HER MIND
WANDA B. TAKES THE CAKE
WANDA B. SINGS THE BAILOUT BLUES
SOFT TSUNAMI   (New Poetry Release)
NOT WITHOUT PASSION   (New Novel Release)

If You Love Me, Come

CLAUDIA MOSS

ISBN-13: 978-0-9832-6973-1
ISBN-10: 0-9832-6973-4

Cover designed by Lincoln Jude of www.ParcStudyo.com.

Printed in the United States of America

Acknowledgments

Muchas gracias to the Divine for the gift of life and the courage to live it. To my parents, Claude and stepmother Gladys Moss. My sisters, Diane Louise Moss McCall, Bernadette Stitts, Glenda Pearl Halcromb, Athera Everlener Pascascio and Katarina Moss, for listening to me 'talk this book into being.' My deceased Great-Aunt Josephine for giving me the freedom to write. My paternal grandparents, Willie David and Sophia Mae (Sinclair) Moss, the inspiration for Miz Too-Sweet and Mr. Will. My aunt Marion Young and my son Avery Monroe Sarden, II.

Many thanks to my beloved sisterfriends, Anita Contreras, Jaslyn Johnson, Brendolyn McCarty Jones, Shirley Majors, Gina Parks, Monique Jones and Nikki Rose, for loving the story. To Cora Lima and Counselor Malcolm Brown and Jean Bailey, for encouragement and friendship. To Fiona Zedde, for encouraging me to finish the novel. To Dr. Lisa West Norman, for always believing that I could and for voraciously reading the first drafts.

I love you all.

If You Love Me, Come

PROLOGUE

Techwood Homes was quiet that blanket-draped night in 1993, in Atlanta, Georgia. Unlike other evenings when the community was a blight of flashing blue sirens and amazed reporters on the eleven o'clock news or a whisper of Black Death strolling amongst its residents like a natural man. Which was why J.T. would have died and haunted a well-dressed woman in a grey Mercedes for the rest of her days had he known she drove the neighborhood's well-snubbed streets after ten p.m., telling herself she was looking for a new shortcut home tonight. She knew it was a lie. Fact was, she didn't know why she felt compelled to be in this tucked-away enclave where folks thrived in infected air and experienced different joys and sorrows than those who whizzed up and down North Avenue stiff-and-starch necked, as though merely glancing in the direction of the Techwood Homes Community Living Project might turn them into stone, causing massive traffic shutdowns in a profitable part of the city.

But the March evening was so peaceful and the bookstore's closing so lucrative and a killer flu's reputation so murky in pale-yellow streetlights, until the change of scenery proved a reprieve for the driving woman, accustomed as she was to bustling storefront shops, long noisy streets, milling nightlife, panhandled corners, and crowded eateries.

There weren't many residents about. Just short squat brick buildings, sitting like fat mortar ducks behind uneven sidewalks, disheveled and webbed with cracks. Graffiti-marked walls, with boarded-shut or empty-eyed windows, cast lonely shadows. Iron-winged gates surrounded courtyards hungry for grass and gatherings.

Atlanta's answer to housing low-to-no income families ten or twelve years ago, Techwood slid from a colorful development into a drab project in the 80's. Drugs and crime hurried its landslide, pressure-washing laughter from the units and leaving a stench of standing misery. In city hall, an SOS for renovation and social programs went up. For the young and the old. But those who could appropriate program funds closed their ears and hearts and tried not to be caught anywhere near the intersection of Spring Street and North Avenue, before or after nightfall. Most remembered Techwood's intolerance for white-to-bright skin and suspicion of strange dark ones, word on the walls and in the streets had it.

A teenage couple hugged up under a lamppost here and a knot of old folks congregated in a yard there fanned March mugginess like heavy flies. Of the eyes present, most
studied the stranger as intently as she them. And since they were neither glassed specimen nor caged wildlife, the woman slowed and waved. The scene before her could have been a Romare Bearden portrait on the walls of the High Museum on Peachtree Street or a flashback of smiling, country faces from her Alabama childhood. Thinking and driving, she marveled at it all. No one she knew ever considered visiting Techwood, yet here she was.

What a tragedy if the beauty of this street was never a triumphant feature in the **Atlanta/Journal &**

Constitution, in **Parade Magazine**, *on the news, or in folks' perceptions.*

Her thoughts splintered. One mind suggested she get on home, the other intimated she park, strike up a conversation. A nearby threesome looked interestingly innocent. Just as she cut the Mercedes towards the curb to park, something streaked from the dark into the white of her headlights. Jarringly, the idea of a collision eclipsed her breath.

Somewhere, someone screamed.

A searing shriek, the sound ripped through her, boiling her blood and pricking her skin. Her heart lurched. The reflex sent her right foot into the floorboards, practically forcing her bumper to kiss asphalt. Fear invaded her limbs, squeezing her windpipe, causing her body to shudder and tremble not to give up the Ghost.

Thank you, God! She shifted the car into park and leaped into the night, landing near the car's hood to lean over a child. A bronze boy of four or five, with large round nut-brown eyes, confusion at their core, nose running, face drawn in astonishment, as though the one thing he knew for sure was this street belonged to him and this person had no place on it. His jean shorts sagged and a dingy, striped T-shirt hollered to cover his middle. He clutched a frayed basketball.

"Hi. You okay?" The woman smiled a breathy smile.

The child didn't smile or answer, but his eyes twinkled. "Where do you live?"

He pointed to a dark unit on his left.

"What's your name?"

The boy remained close-mouthed, so the

woman bent low, lower. At his eye level, she'd appear harmless. Suddenly, they were caught in a paperweight of magically swirling time. The sweet way he studied her birthed a longing inside the woman to hear his voice. Their eyes caressed in silence, while the evening wind pin-wheeled playfully about them.

"Mooo-key! Mookey Man!" A woman's voice sliced the shadows.

Only then did he speak, his voice floating up to her---small, proud and unafraid.

"My name's Lewis Earl Reynolds."

The young woman grinned and reached out to him, but he pulled away and held one hand high. "I'm these many." Four stubby, grimy fingers wagged the air.

A current of warmth riveted them at the fit of his palm in hers. "Lovely!" she said in a honeyed tone. "I'm that and twenty-four more."

Not too far off, an older woman stood with her arms akimbo.

On cue, the March evening gathered itself, exhaled and yawned softly, its blue-black covers fluttering gently, nudged backward by the promise of dawn in the distant sky. Fate had accomplished her mission, unbeknownst to the people propelled toward one another like falling stars. Magnetized, they were unable to halt the inevitable if their lives depended on it, and since their lives did, thus began their story....

Chapter 1

I knowed something was on the wind tonight. Told Will and Preacher as much no sooner than I sat down in the front yard, after putting dinner away. Could feel it in my bones, in my knee caps, in the joints of my arms, and especially in that peculiar way this March wind over here in Georgia has of whispering in your ear, if you the listening sort, like me. Where I'm from, up round Lochapoka, Alabama, listeners about as ordinary as seers. Will say listening and seeing all the same to him. Then again what would a Georgia boy know? Every gift he has come outta 'Bama. Including me.

But it's a gift, this listening; though sometimes I don't do it well. Some listeners, like my Mama and her daddy, Grandpaw Hood, couldn't hear their own stories, just the stories of other folks' lives. Mama could only hear to listen at night, rocking on the back porch. When Mama Nature brought the Word in cricket songs and talk caught in grass blades and the language of swaying treetops.

But Grandpaw Hood heard best at the crack of dawn, in his sleep. And sometimes, unlike Mama, he heard things that left his cheeks moist and shortened his stride to a hobble, since what he heard he kept to hisself, it being too painful to share most times. A person had to bribe the telling outta Grandpaw Hood, arguing a suspicion needed nailing down. After the walk-down, though, he'd hand that sad news over to whoever, and then pray round the clock the person was strong enough to carry whatever.

Me. I can hear to listen only outdoors, most times. Sad and happy messages. Year round. Like today when the wind whispered, "She coming." I was hanging clothes on the line I had Will and Preacher to tie 'tween the trees out back. "A blessing," the wind murmured, "to many." All day I strained to listen, even ate my fried chicken, cornbread, and cabbage in the sunshine, chewing and listening, not wanting to miss a smidgen about this blessing of a woman. Had Mama been living, she'da said, "Gal, git up and do what-send-ever you gone do. No way you can miss a blessing created and sent to you, chile. God above loosing mail, sending it to the wrong box, getting held up in bad weather, being short on money and help, and plain sitting down on the job. Member what I told you: God don't aspire to be like us; we aspire to be Godlike."

Then, later, just when I forgot bout what I heard and went to laughin' and talkin' with Will and poking fun at Preacher in the glory of the evening after supper, up come Short Dog doing what he do best—passin' responsibility like he passin' me money for watching Mookey, being he know good and well Pinky expect him to spend quality time with his little brother. Yet he like a heap of men---woman foolish. Let the right gal stroll by and he loose his mind, leave everything but his wallet trying to make his feet fit her tracks. At fourteen, what he know bout stayin' off from home for days on end? Call hisself hanging with his crew or his gals, like he don't think grownfolks got scruples.

"Aaaw, Miz Too-Sweet, I got homework. A group project with the fellas. Be back soon, okay." Knowing he couldn't produce no class work, let alone homework, if his life jeopardized. That Mama of his is two steps from a gal herself, but she standing up to her responsibilities by stayin' and raisin' him and this lil one running cross our feet like a frisky puppy with a mouthful of sugar. Thank the Lawd that daddy of Pinky's only gal decided to take her with him or else the rest of these boys be beatin' down Pinky's door trying to set up residence and make babies, like there ain't enough babies to go round twice in every Techwood household. But I'm the Big Mama these younguns don't have, so I tell Short Dog to gone off and be careful. I love the slew of them, Will and Preacher, too. Preacher might never say a mumbling word, ever, but see if he don't get busy doing whatever that Pinky request.

"That her, Sweet?" Will ask, after I hush screamin'.

I nod, the wind humming a clear "Yes" and easing me to my feet. That car hadda hit my Mookey, I'da laid down for good. Imagine it'da made me question that ole wind, a thing I rarely do, and wonder if 'blessing' was the word I heard. That's when she bend down. Say something to Mookey and then walk him to the yard, where I scoop him up, slurp his cheek while he wiggle, and bump him atop my knees.

She pretty, voice and words smart enough to be anything she say she is.

A bookstore owner in the Spring Street mall, she say. Must be paid, too, 'cause nobody can drive the car she driving and wear the clothes she wearing and keep a store open on pennies. Say her name's Frenonia Roberts and her family and friends call her Free. I laugh inside myself, think if I was her, I'd be free, too, bout now. She tell Will the name of her business, the **WeAreFamily Bookstore and**

Coffeehouse, tell him he can read and buy books, eat and drink, and socialize all while he make his purchase. Will and Preacher feast while she talk, squinting to take in as much of her kind of pretty, a polished pretty that don't often walk Techwood streets. Can't much blame them. My eyes glued, too, and I ain't a man. She from a small family--sister here, Mama in Alabama. I know they on the same page she on; success.

"Get the lady a sitdown," Will instruct Preacher, who creak to life from his seat on the concrete steps of our unit, his attention so intent on this young woman, he blinkin' like he disoriented in deep fog. Will hopin' she gone stay and talk a spell longer. I knowed she ain't gone stand for that, if Will didn't. But the minute she sit down, her questions come and I go to talking, filling in the spaces she open.

"Yes, ma'am, Lewis Earl, our Mookey, got family. Half the time they just don't have him. Us do. His Mama, Pinky, the only name I ever knowed to call her, work at the new Waffle House at the intersection up the street. Bout your age, ending 20's, early 30's." Got another one, Short Dog, I say. His real names leave me like money. I mention Clemmy, short for Clementine, and then invite Miz Free to come back, meet the Mama on one of her off days. She smile, ask me bout Out Reach programs to benefit the neighborhood. I stare at her. Hard. Surely she could guess folks here ain't reaching out and folks outside sho ain't reaching in. And if they was, which would be nice and needed, it's to buy and sell what they shouldn't.

"Hmmm" is all she say, when I admit I never

heard tell of such programs, and then outta the blue, she ask, "How did you come to be called Miz Too-Sweet?"

Will clear his throat like she ask him, that half-chewed, palm-rolled cigarette bobbing between his tinted lips. "Came bout as a result of her not listening, the thang she born to do." He spread his legs and study the dirt on his brogans. I fold my big arms under my bosom, Miz Free's face shifting from a question to a period. She glance from Will to me, finally settling on me. Didn't take her long to realize Will's a one-line man. So I tell her how happen I come cross my name.

Buster D. Calloway give me that name, my second husband did. The first up and died. Left me lonely, so lonely I stopped listening for the first time in my young life—I was a little shy of twenty then, a married woman for coming up on six years, with two chillen. Instead of listening and touching the lives of folks round me, I went to tellin' God how much I needed a man to help out with the chores bout the place, help me tend to the chillen, sit side me in church, take me for Sunday rides, 'preciate my cooking, and, of course, tend to my womanly desires, which were many. It wasn't that I had it so fancy with Curtis Wilkes, my first husband, just that I ain't know me since he was busy making sho I knowed him.

"Abide in you" got hung up in the trees one morning when I was sweeping the front yard. Come evening it howled in from the backwoods as I strolled down to the pasture to cut wood and gather litter for the fireplace. Same words beat theyselves against my windowpane over in the night, rattling the window frame so they woke me outta a good sleep to make sho I heard.

But I was tired of me. I wanted to abide in me and him, whoever he might be. Didn't matter if the him swallowed me...again. I ain't knowed life any other way. Until the wind, a late-night silky wind, whispered, "Walk awhile with the next man who brings you flowers, then walk away again." Now wasn't that something? Was one of the most amusing things I'd heard in a long time, considerin' no man had ever give me flowers, unlessen they was for another woman. Time flew. Way after while, I was selling pole beans and onions and peanuts at the market on the square one Saturday, when the him that turned out to be Buster D. Calloway—and that D shoulda been for "Don't look at me" insteada David--moseyed up with a fistful of flowers, black-eyed Susans, to be exact. Told me I was the prettiest woman he ever seed behind a bushel basket and he bet I'd be prettier behind the one he was gone buy and prettier still before his stove, cooking them. Thank you, Lawd. If these ain't the sweetest words I been waiting on, let alone the flowers to pinpoint the right man.

I was so charmed I ain't realize he was blackening my eyes for the first year of our walk together, a walk that led through a short courtship and into a long marriage. Walked with Buster, I did, until he ended up dragging me, 'cause I was walking too fast or too slow. And all the while we walked, he told me I was too-sweet and he ain't never liked nothing too-sweet, not even lemonade. I sweetened the end result though, didn't matter what he did. And he did it all: whipped my chillen 'cause they was there, cussed my folks and banned me from them, took my extra market money, beat me to see how low I could cry, and swore the last thing he'd do was break me from being sweet.

But the morning came when I remembered the most important part of my message about the flower-bearing man, and, packing and praying, Buster at work, chillen before me, I walked away. All the way to my Mama's house, that sunny April wind sang, "Honor you and be." Being I don't hold grudges, I kept the name, Miz Too-Sweet. To remind myself I could never be too sweet being the world need sweet people, as long as some folks sour; us sweet souls balance life out.

Now that March wind hugging us like a Sunday shawl and laying cross Mookey's back soft and secure, near bout as precious as his Mama's palm. 'Tween the wind and Miz Free's chattiness, I can't decide who to listen to more, until Miz Free's last question won out. "The story in Preacher's name?" I parrot, sleep wrestling my eyelids. "I tell you on your next stopover. Our insurance you coming back."

"If you're a listener," Miz Free say, stretching, "I'm a holder. That story ought to be in a book for others to hold, too."

"That's mighty nice of you to say. Reckon I always pictured folks with lives way different from mine in books." I chuckle and keep bouncing Mookey. Miz Free shuffle her feet as if to keep them from walking towards that pretty car.

She get up and bow, like we royalty. "It's my pleasure to have stepped into your lives tonight.

Wouldn't have missed it for the world."

"The pleasure is mutual." My next part come butter soft, being I'm too old to hush myself now. "Most folks who don't live round here miss this world every day. How happen you here, and on a Friday night? You must work insteada court."

"I-I had a sensational day and the night seemed to suggest I ride so--" she flounder, pause to catch up with the rest of her thoughts, then say, "Miz Too-Sweet, I really don't know why I'm here. Isn't that the strangest thing? I don't have a single, logical explanation. I guess I was following a feeling, a hunch."

"That's usually what happen."

"Somehow I knew I was supposed to be right here. Wish I could stay longer, for you are a joy, Miz Too-Sweet, an absolute and utter delight." She bow to the menfolk, who nod and get two good eyefuls before she leave.

After Miz Free hug us, her words trail her, shadow soft, into the night, but not before they plant rows of gold nuggets in my mind.

I went to thinkin' what my Mama said years back: "You can't miss a blessing God mean for you." And in this case, God mean to bless I don't know who all.

Chapter 2

Who ever heard *of a preacher who never uttered a mumbling word?*

Free awakened to an exhilarating Saturday morning and probing thoughts of the people—such dear souls--whom she'd met in Techwood the night before. In particular, she couldn't stop thinking of the old man, the silent one, whose actual name might have been Preacher, with no reference perhaps to his occupation. Country folks, she knew, where like that. Mysterious. With names and nicknames riddled with meaning.

Moving in a languid rhythm that matched the easy day coming to life outside her upstairs bedroom windows, she tumbled out of bed to listen to birds twitter and traffic hum and silence still. She stood in the window and stared at the day, eavesdropping on the breeze's sultry slow dance in the tall trees around her spacious backyard.

Nothing happened that wasn't supposed to. No, she didn't know when, nor would she worry about it, but she'd return to visit with her newfound friends, the same hunch responsible for her being there last night assured her now.

On the way to the shower, she noticed the answering machine's persistent red button flashing on the nightstand. Fatigue had ridden her straight to bed when she got in, leaving time to answer Mother Nature's calls only. She pressed the machine's play button and headed to the bathroom to brush her teeth and wash her face.

"Hey, pussy cat, we still on tonight? Even

though your call came at the zero hour on Wednesday, when I was thinking you'd be hanging with the girls on a Friday evening, I stopped the world and jumped my ass off...'cause you know how much I brush my mane and roar when you call the shots, baby. Call when you get this."

Good Lord! She stopped splashing cold water on her face and stared at herself in the vanity mirror. Had she promised Junior Thomas they'd spend the evening together? Why hadn't he phoned the bookstore to remind her? She could see him now. Drying her hands, she reentered the bedroom, paused the tape, and dialed his home line. No answer. She tried his work number. Still, no reply.

Not one for leaving messages, she sighed. There was nothing she could do until he decided to call or drop by. *Whatever.* She'd try not to give him another thought.

The pelting spray of the shower caressed her skin, invigorating her from scalp to toes. So what if he didn't answer? She splayed her palms against the cool white tile and dropped her head under the blast. Maybe he was busy. Immersed in the moment. Like she ought to be. The thought slowly engulfed her in a sense of wellbeing. She focused on the racing droplets trickling through her permed auburn hair, plastering it to her face and neck. Fluttering like the gentle touch of fingertips along her shoulder blades, over her small saluting breasts, down the slope of her rounded belly, downward still to the soft dark hair between her thighs, supple now instead of taut like they were after a run through her neighborhood or around Stone Mountain Park—the water buoyed her sleep-weary limbs up, up, up to a joyous prickliness.

Hmmm. A mental masturbation began behind her shut eyelids.

She softened, felt him become her baby again, her J.T. What if he had answered her call with good loving on his mind---same as hers? She spread her legs and treated her clit to a slow, slow rub down under her middle finger, closing her eyes to better hold the delicious kneading. When she reopened them, she relished the scent of her arousal and the shivers of pleasure tingling in her slow-grinding hips. Satisfied for now, though she could have taken herself to ecstasy, she settled for watching hungry licks of water slick the sparse hair on her pruning legs. Then she rinsed her pussy's fragrance from her fingers and resigned herself to the sensuality of the fruity foam of her soap.

A half hour later, Free dressed in a white cropped tank and light pink jogging pants that made her hips resemble the sculpted backsides of Brazilian jeans mannequins, the pink and green AKA lettering down one leg of the soft material showing off her powerful hamstrings. In the vanity mirror, listening to the rest of her messages and smoothing globs of leave-in conditioner through her curls, she raked her hair around her head—her roller—to dry it for an hour or more under a hard-hat dryer to create "The Wrap," a popular, polished sweep of professionalism she loved.

"What's up, girly? What are you doing…screening?" Sharmayne's whine rolled out, slow and low, then purled into a giggle. "Listen. Give me a call so we can chat books. Oh, and don't let me forget You-Know-Who's latest. Ciao."

Free shook her head. What could she say? She and Sharmayne, friends for five years, were two years apart; at thirty, the sister had yet to part her lips and suggest a girls' night out. Only conducted herself as though she were a tired sixty, devoid of a zest for seeing and being seen. Free shrugged. She could wait to hear about Sharmayne's husband's latest repulsive word or deed. She'd call when she was under the hair dryer with a cup of green tea, an *Essence* magazine and a novel.

Had the tape split, she could've recited two of the remaining messages by rote.

"Hi, Aunt Free! It's me, Li'l Trevor, your favorite nephew! I'm calling to see if you need some weekend company, since I know you must have missed me. Oh, I got a good report card and kept my mouth closed for a decent conduct grade. I love you!"

Her nephew and only nephew. This weekend was out. His beloved aunt required "Me Time" with her man, but then the little darling took himself for her man, his big brown eyes suggesting what his well-trained mouth couldn't: "Why do we *need* Mister J.T.? Does he *really* like me anyway?" She added him to her call-back list. Her heart, he lent new meaning to precious.

A hang-up and a couple of telemarketers came next. Then Rhonda's elegant seductiveness. "Greetings, big sis! I know you're wonderful. Three cheers for the weekend! I'm calling, dear, to determine if Trevor received the Auntie Okay. Remember...no obligations. Any way you dish it, he'll have it. Peace and blessings."

She loved her sister, but there'd be no drop-and-dash this weekend. She placed her hair products under the vanity's white cabinets, grabbed an old portable dryer, her reading material, and headed downstairs to the kitchen.

Not fifteen minutes after getting situated, heat slowly warming her ears and hairline, the front doorbell chimed. Keys clicked. The door moaned. And a glaringly perturbed man in a Hawks jersey and jeans, sunshine glistening on his chocolate skin, emerged in the foyer. He was handsome---even as his features hardened into what resembled a wooden Ethiopian mask.

"Hey, Frenonia. Hope you don't mind me dropping in unannounced."

His teeth were straight, bright white, and clenched, the lips beautifully shaped.

Free grimaced at the unspoken bellyache in his voice and turned off the dryer.

"Of course not. Why should I?" She looked away not to concentrate on his face.

The square jaw, the goatee trimmed to perfection with three thin lines dropping from his bottom lip. Jet-black brows. Long lashes. That bedroom gaze. Just fine.

"So what were you doing you couldn't call me? I waited up. All night."

"Let's not go there." Free got up from the table and crossed her arms.

"You bring us here...every time."

"Right. So why didn't you use your key? You knew I'd be in sooner or later. We could've spent the night together and enjoyed breakfast. But no, we're fighting."

"You know how I hate wait---"

"That's your problem. Learn to do something

while you wait."

"Waiting is waiting…whether I do something or nothing; it's the same *damn* thing. I'm too considerate to make you wait for anything."

The way he growled the word damn triggered heaviness in her foot and she felt like kicking the hell out of something but she wanted everything in her kitchen, so she kept her mouth shut.

J.T. mopped his forehead with his palm, as though to wake himself from a bad dream.

"Whatever it was, whoever he was, he was more important than your man. I waited for hours, sitting by the phone like some love-starved teenager. Well, damnit, that shit ain't my cup of tea, baby girl."

"Again…your problem." Her irate eyes buttonholed his. "Don't come in here reprimanding me. I'm not your child. You could have called, not jumped to conclusions. And don---," she was about to check his profanity but her blood pressure shot sky high so her mouth went equally colorful. "---gotdamnit, why can't you ever ask me the how, when, where and why of a situation without barging in acting like an idiot? That's for starters! And why does it have to be about a man? Retire that tired-ass shit. Please. Who do you take me for…a whore? Like I don't have anything better to do with my time than hit the downlow with brothers with whom I don't have time to cultivate a legitimate relationship, let alone enjoy a fuck fest!"

"I'm sorry, but see…there you go now, talking like some bimbo." J.T. wavered on what to do, follow her to the kitchen windows overlooking the side yard or remain where he was near the center island. "Look who's passing blame." He determined it best to stay put. "This is about you, sweetheart? Not me. I always put you first, woman."

"Don't patronize me with that 'I'm sorry' mess. If you put me first, we wouldn't be strangers about now, darling. You'd treat me like you'd want to be treated and trusted. Hell, if you put me second, your language and tone wouldn't be so ready-to-hurt. You started the shit."

She intended her words to hurt, being her fists couldn't. Despite her intentions, her love for him consistently demanded she forgive, accept, and seek a turn-around, though she'd not been able to do so thus far.

"That's your ego, sweetie. Stop excusing yours and judging mine."

"I never feel your respect when I need it the most."

"That's you again, my lady. You have yet to answer my simple questions."

Free frowned. "It's not what you asked, but *how* you asked."

"Fuck the bullshit, Frenonia. Where were you? Who the hell were you with?"

He eyed her up and down, admiring what he saw yet unable to say it.

"And I hope you weren't dressed like that."

"Whatever this is isn't about me or my whereabouts. It's about you, Junior Thomas, and your perception of yourself, your insecurities, and your anger. The real question is, when are you going to stop resisting and face yourself?"

At best, cussing ticked Free off and left her in too many knots to unravel without a strong shot of rum, a martini, or a flute of wine. Something. She wanted to uncork whatever bottle she touched, swallow a long swig, re-cork it, bust J.T. on the back of the head, like fighters in the movies, and wipe her hands of the whole messy affair.

"Look, man, if you're so darn dissatisfied with my appearance, why the hell you still attracted to me? No, why are you still with me? Embarrassed men don't treasure women who leave a foul taste in their mouths; they don't desire women who lack a decent sense of self, do they?"

"You're so stubborn and self-centered, egotistical and judgmental. Grow up, girl. Cater to somebody besides yourself for a change."

Furious, she stormed about the kitchen in staccato steps, and he followed her, thinking, even in his disappointment—all he'd wanted was to hold her, since they both worked such long hours—and, staring at her butt, he realized how much he missed her graceful blackwoman's booty in sweats. Not to mention pink ones.

"You will not talk to me any way you choose. You can get out of my house until you learn how to address *this woman*." There was no mistaking the last part: she was her own woman, not his chattel on days like today, his woman on sweeter days.

J.T. swung his keys on the kitchen counter, the clanging startling Free.

"Is that a threat?"

"Take it however you please." He had finally located her last good nerve. So she came clean and slowly painted the portrait of her long night of inventory and how she'd come to be in Techwood and the people she'd met there. She left no stone unturned, serenading him with all the incriminating details he'd come for, from her closing alone to the near-fatal accident to her promise to Miz Too-Sweet.

As she guessed, J.T. seethed with indignation. "You stand me up for a rump through one of the most lethal neighborhoods in Atlanta, and for what? A car-jacking? Or so you can somehow loom larger than life in the presence of have-nots? You don't need to do that to be more of the dynamic Frenonia Roberts, young entrepreneur extraordinaire."

He threw up defeated palms. "Am I not giving you enough attention?" This woman could be exceedingly cantankerous when she took a notion. He eyed her with thoughts of shaking some sense into her pretty head, but she'd just misconstrue it as abuse. *Why did she harbor the desire to save the world?*

"I'm going to say this in the most loving way I know how." He walked over to her to leave nothing to her interpretation from across the kitchen. "Stay away from Techwood. In that Mercedes. You don't belong there, period. I love you, baby, but you're begging for trouble. Plain and simple. Watch a movie if you're itching to know how the other half lives."

Free stiffened, and then drew her body upright against the handle of the stove.

"I'm saying what I must in the most loving way I can, too, J.T. You are cynical, not to mention skeptical and overbearing---skeptical of everybody I meet and overbearingly jealous of anyone who deals with me. Your flaws run for miles, with paranoia leading. I'm not your precocious child or troubled teenager who snuck out of the house." She inhaled. In the silence, she could hear J.T.'s fear roiling, constricting his chest with regret, but she was already bound by fate. "Don't know why I let you treat me this way for so long, but I can't do it anymore. I love you, but most importantly, I love me, too. When I met you, I was already raised. Pastoria made certain of that. So understand now," she said, pausing for emphasis. "I want nothing to do with you until I know, from deep within, what to do with you. Don't call me; I won't call you. Absolutely no communication, please."

Free inhaled wearily. On her stroll to the front door, she cut J.T. a wide berth.

"If we never find our way back to one another, I'll always love you. But if we find ourselves *looking in one another's eyes*, as Paul McCartney sings in "Separate Lives," I hope we'll have changed enough to recognize and nurture the love that remains."

When the front door slammed shut---Free leaning against the decorative oak, J.T. standing dazed in shell-shocked sun---she bowed to the beauty and power of stillness, a space so redolent with peace, she knew one day J.T. would listen while she, too, like Miz Too-Sweet's Preacher, preached without uttering a mumbling word.

For her good, as well as J.T.'s.

Chapter 3

Sharmayne pulled away from him. His syrupy talk ineffective, pissing her off. She rose out of the covers, a Phoenix destined to survive, intact, despite hungry flames threatening her sanity. Indestructible, she was. No matter if his hand grazed her stomach, prompting her sable-colored belly to sink inward and flatten against her spine, her body persistent on making itself inviolable.

"Aww c'mon, woman. Why you gotta be so trifflin' all the damn time? And especially in the morning when I be tryin' to get me some good lovin'?" Her husband, Victor Naylor, glowered. It was all he could do to keep his trucker's fingers--- hard, knobby-edged numbers replete of tenderness--- from jerking his trying wife back down on the bed beside him.

They had been lying peacefully enough, until his yearning had awakened and his fingertips found themselves strolling down her skin on their walk to where they longed to be: skating across the fleshy, warm realm of her belly and thighs.

"Make me think you got a problem, Sharmayne."

Always suggestive, his tone. Of what, she didn't care, since he'd outright implicated her of every sin a wife could commit, from infidelity to lesbianism and everything in between. She watched him, studied the way he propped up on one elbow to add, "Shit. Had to rant and rave and carry on like a freakin' fool last night to get som'uh that stuff." Then, a bit more derisively, he wanted to know if she was saving it for Judgment Day, because if she was, the Lord wasn't going to do nothing but ask her why the hell she didn't fuck her hard-working husband like a good wife should.

But she had not spoken since she'd sensed his lust.

He laughed at the cornered expression in her posture, knowing the sound grated her nerves.

And how she'd come to despise it. How she detested the demeaning words he used when he spoke of the sacred coming together of lovers. She thought coupling, the display of love between two who swore to nourish one another until death bid them part, should've been pleasurable, rejuvenating against the trials of the world. For her, though, it meant waiting---waiting, languishing, marking time...

Buried under his cruelty, she accepted the realization that maybe she did have a problem. A concern. And maybe she was an intricate part of their problem. Yet what she suspected was proving to be more than she could deal with right now. So, when she could better turn it in her head, peek at it, and muster enough courage to share it with her best friend, she'd settle for it brazenly staring at her from a corner of her mind.

Waiting, too.

"So you gone completely deaf, huh?" Victor, tired of being stared at, decided to take action. Groped under the covers, his chest and shoulders suddenly in her face, his hands full of her ebony thighs and soft crotch. His breath came hot and fast on her neck; she closed her eyes to remove herself from the act. Lately, she found it more and more difficult. To remove herself. It might've hinged on his anger and passion sliding into a noisy release of desire. Whatever it was, she was thankful Victor wasn't a kissing man. She didn't have to contend with him in her face, with heavy breathing, an insistent mouth, and roughly nipping teeth. But she had to endure his gluttonous sounds: gulps, groans, chokes, grunts. They made her think of pigs routing in slop in the sties on her parents', Melba and Clyde Cooper's, farm.

Then he did it, and she froze. The dryness always shocked her into presence. Once inside her, he pounded away unmercifully, mechanically, monotonously. And although the skin of her thighs stretched taut to accommodate the pounding, the trucker's hands forcing her legs up and out, she moved elsewhere, conserving what he couldn't pound of Sharmayne Cooper-Naylor---well-read housewife, who longed to return to somebody's college to learn for the joy of it, to seek employment and become a productive member of society, to get out of this house and commune with others.

Was that too much to ask?

Absorbing Victor's sweat, she thought of her cherished friendship with Frenonia, her link to the outside world. Over the years, Free had made it easier to accept Naylor as a part of her eccentric last name--- Cooper-Naylor—a name, Free said, that should have inspired her to write in and of itself.

But right now she was slipping fast. And when she did this, this slipping outside of herself as Victor's body chastised hers, she discovered herself a girl back in Melba's kitchen. This time she sat on the floor, between Melba's feet, her mother sitting in a cane-bottomed chair, fingers dabbing into a jar of bluish-green Bergamot hair grease. She parted Sharmayne's coarse black hair into tiny, manageable sections and greased each well. The hair she finished gleamed in the weak glow of the kitchen bulb. Melba's voice was low, melodious.

"When you get up some size, 'bout the age to be married," she said, filling her youngest child, her only daughter, with the teachings that would follow her for a lifetime, "...remember that the wife hath not power of her own body, but the husband..." She never applied this teaching to the husband. Sharmayne had had to find this out for herself, years later. The attention her mother's gentle hands paid to her head made her sleepy, and Melba pecked her lightly with the teeth of the comb.

"Stay up, baby. This I'm telling you may help you keep your husband one day. 'Cause like my Big Mama always told me, 'Don't keep that li'l black hole between yo' legs from your man. Do and he be making tracks." Melba tapped her daughter's scalp again.

With Sharmayne's "Yes, ma'am," Melba went on. Told Sharmayne the Good Book said, "'Defraud ye not one the other.' You do, girl, the devil be at you, tempting you to fall." The words made Sharmayne shudder, planted a notion of a black hole being lost somewhere between her legs, where it frightened and amused her, making her think it had to be the soft indentation near where she peed. Had to be from that mysterious place from which blood trickled onto dainty white pads wrapped in tissue, which Melba handed her every month, for a week. But she never, with her own vision, laid eyes on the area. According to her mother, it was sacred. So sacred, she washed it. Protected it. But was forbidden to permit anyone, not even herself, to see or casually touch it, for any reason. Only a doctor. And that was in a dire emergency.

Yet her mother called attention to it often.

Truly it had to be a magical possession---or a wicked curse. "I'm raising you to be a virtuous woman, one whose price is far above that of rubies and that is more money than anybody round here will ever have." Melba braided the last tiny section of hair, leaving Sharmayne's face shiny under her crowning glory. Her teachings filled the kitchen and trailed a solemn Sharmayne out to slop the pigs: "It's alright to be pretty. But pretty is as pretty does and I ain't heard no man ask for pretty. He always ask for pussy, so safeguard both. They're for one man and that's your husband, whoever he be." All the way to the pigsty, the cockleburs tugged at her skirt and that P-word she'd seen on the walls of the girls' toilets at school tugged at her thoughts.

When her wayward spirit decided to ease back into her prostrate body, Sharmayne watched the morning light color the bedroom. She stared at his ejaculation in her pubic hair and across her thighs, knowing to leave it be; white wetness against her black skin his aphrodisiac. Too bad he couldn't leave it at that.

"I'd swear an affidavit if you don't have the best pussy this side of Kingdom Come."

Victor laughed a strident laugh and stretched bodily before rising to enter the bathroom. His Richard Pryor impersonation, "If you ever leave, baby, please don't take the pussy," imprinted the air like a scent. It never failed. Each time, that laughter, those words, became a huge howl, formed a fist in mid-air and socked her in the jaw, it flustered her so.

To hang on, she did what she did best---she waited. Seemed that was what her life, her virtuous existence, had come to, and she dared not think of tomorrow. That merely meant another day of biding time as Victor Naylor's ruby-bought wife. And she could not fathom the thought without hope—hope that at the end of the waiting, there would be someone who'd love her for her.

After her Saturday-morning meditations, she dialed Free's number.

Chapter 4

Frenonia walked into the **WeAreFamily Bookstore and Coffeehouse** on Monday afternoon, a brisk breeze hard on her heels. Being in the airy, brightly colored, roomy establishment imbued her with a characteristic lightheartedness. She walked around the tall, wide counter, eased her briefcase and purse to the back of its bottom shelf, and gave Reesa McMillan a pleasant sigh.

"Hey, Miss Lady, how's business?" Free came out of a tailored navy blue suit jacket, the skirt a pencil-straight charmer with the power to convert roving eyes to pinball marbles. Navy blue stiletto pumps accentuated her lovely legs.

Reesa was busily breaking open coins for the register drawer.

"What's up, Free? You know my motto: Business is great, as always." She glanced up from rowing coins, her almond-shaped eyes glistening with admiration. "Killer suit. Is it new? Haven't seen that before. The color and style scream sexy. Business sexy, honey, a sexy to which I aspire."

Free struck a pose and smiled. "Thank you, darling. I haven't shopped in a minute because my plate's full so a sister's long overdue. I love Miss Free."

The girl giggled. "Oh, that reminds me, how was the *NBAF* meeting?"

"Long, tedious, routine and testosterone charged. You wouldn't believe the clash of egos around a conference table of our leading politicians, clergy, artists and business leaders. Since our first organizational meeting back in January, it's been somebody or a group of some bodies vying to be the key player, muscling last year's steering committee plans in a direction of their choosing."

Free moved about the main showroom, dusting, straightening, and arranging books and magazines as she spoke.

"Uh huh," Reesa tsk-tsked, thinking of particular classmates, who, in different power plays, could vibrate air with high levels of estrogen. "I know what you mean. In my circles, there are Spellman women and there are *Spellman women*." She laughed, stressing the last part with her arms folded, her bottom lip puckered in sister-irked fashion.

They shared a comfortable merriment, feeling more like family than boss and employee.

"That's it. I've long harbored the idea I'd one day be an integral part of a *National Black Arts Festival*, but sometimes I rue the decision not to sit back and watch others lift the yoke and make it happen."

"Yeah, but you wouldn't be true to Frenonia Roberts. If there's a dream within you, a yearning, no matter how you might restrain yourself or procrastinate, eventually, it finds its way out. Why not just let yourself be, so life lives you? No more spinning your wheels unnecessarily."

Free wondered at this wet-behind-the-ear, college sophomore.

"And how did you come to be so worldly, my little love?"

Reesa swayed on the bar stool behind the counter. Fat Goddess braids bounced when she popped her fingers and jumped her shoulders. "My daddy, he's my hero."

"Hmmm. I'd love to meet your father, your parents, Reesa. What does your father do?"

The girl never spoke of her family, not even when they discussed families in books.

"Eddie Lee McMillan does whatever he wants. Some days he's a motivational speaker and a poet, on others he's a life coach, next month he'll be leading empowerment workshops in the Catskills, and at the end of the year he intends to celebrate the completion of the first draft of his second novel."

She stopped talking when three, young, professional-looking women emerged in the bookstore's doorway, in a gale of chummy conversation. They appeared to be on an extended lunch break. Reesa and Free greeted them before picking up where they left off.

"My mom, Marion McMillan, is his business partner," Reesa went on, perceiving Free's unasked question. "When they aren't together, which is rare, she's flying somewhere reveling in the art of making deals---powerful, big-money deals you'd never imagine her making."

"Aaaah." Free excused herself to answer a bubbly patron's questions about sandwiches and pastries. Then she directed the threesome to a spiraling staircase winding unobtrusively to the savory-smelling second-floor. There, Brendolyn Mason, whom everyone called "Bren," a twenty-one year old mother of four, operated the **Coffeehouse**, when she wasn't in culinary classes studying to be the chef of her own restaurant.

"Why wouldn't I imagine your mom cutting broker deals?"

"She's so unassuming. Mom, like daddy, doesn't prefer to wear wealth in public, but don't follow us home. By my friends' standards, we're all that and then some."

Reesa erupted in another bout of blissful laughter. "But Free, back to you. In July, when the *Black Arts Festival* jumps off, everything you're doing now will be well worth the journey, huh?"

Free nodded. "Please believe it. Despite the meetings and aching feet and amusing personalities, it's called enjoying each moment and making it count and trusting the next moment will take care of itself."

For one glorious week, the very pulse of Atlanta would drum with African-American creativity in art and culture. A cultural Olympiad, she'd come to think of the gala. Daily, it took on a life of its own.

The bookstore had a tendency to be crowded after one, and today was no different as the afternoon throngs filled the showroom. Their conversation fizzled in the rush, but Reesa's father's words lodged in the shiny auburn sweep grazing Free's shoulders: "Why not just let yourself be, so life lives you?"

Could life be living her now?

She had much to think about.

With Reesa preoccupied assisting another round of customers, Free surveyed the quietly humming showroom, basking in the glory of another stunning afternoon. Pools of chilly sunshine glossed the hardwood floors. The periodic music of the cash register pierced the silence. When soft, loving conversations about books fluttered the air, Free thought of Mookey Man.

She was facing a large Jacob Lawrence

painting—as though for the first time--on a wall at the back of the store. In it, multi-colored people in classic Lawrence style delighted in a feeling of community.

Flushed in warm thoughts, she walked to the children's corner, where she selected an armload of juvenile hardback classics and brought them to Reesa.

"Ring these up on my account, sweetheart." She watched as Reesa did so, slipping the selections into a pretty plastic bag that she deposited near Free's belongings under the counter.

"Has Li'l Trevor's reading diet changed? The last I knew it was up there with mine: **Madame Bovary**, **Heart of Darkness** and **Invisible Man**."

Free scanned a bin of comics near the counter, chose a Batman edition, and placed it near the bag of books. "There's a new little dude in my life."

Again, she divulged the details of her Techwood encounter, this time adding the tête-à-tête with J.T. and her meditating for the remainder of the weekend. No Trevor, no Sharmayne.

Through it all, Reesa sat consumed. "Wow! Now that's a weekend for you." She took a deep breath, and then exclaimed, "Hey, I know a girl from Techwood on scholarship at Spellman. She's cool, but I've never hung out with her."

"Perhaps this may be your opportunity to do so. Who knows what tomorrow holds?" Free gazed at her watch. Two o'clock. She'd made two promises in the past few days that she was bound to keep, come what may.

"Pass me the phone, please, sweetie."

"Sure." Reesa brought the small black phone up from the second shelf. "If you're heading to Techwood now, why not drive a car other than yours?"

The look Free shot Reesa was harder than a slap on the hand. "You can be car jacked anywhere. In Stone Mountain, here in Buckhead, in any Wal-mart parking lot in daylight, the Virginia Highlands, as well as in Techwood. When opportunity abounds, crime will knock. You know that."

"Right, but caution doesn't hurt either." Reesa smiled by way of apology.

And just as Free parted her lips to wonder aloud why poor people bothered to wake up in the morning, the front door swung open to a stout woman in a kiwi-green pants suit and two, tiny, harnessed and heaving girls. They were Free's cue to make her call, Reesa's to make a sale.

So, too, the breeze that trailed Free into the store and lost itself in the lofty space above the rows of towering bookshelves suddenly bumped into the gust of wind that rushed by the rosy-cheeked trio and, chasing one another, chilled Free's ankles and huddled about her calves, opening spaces within her she never fathomed.

Chapter 5

Ox tails and purple cabbage. I opened the windows over the sink this morning to chase the fried fish left on the air from last night's dinner and heard the words come pushing past the curtains like hardhead chillen still going when you done politely asked them to stop. Caught me off guard, being I ain't cooked no ox tails in so long, I near 'bout forgot how they eat. Will's dentures not what they used to be, I knowed he and Preacher ain't sweet on much outside of soft-fried chicken and fish and a skillet of turkey spaghetti. Maybe a meatloaf every now and then.

But ox tails and purple cabbage? Odd.

I put the thought in the back of my head and got a pot of oatmeal going 'fore Will could finish in the bathroom, where I left him shaving and trying to whistle. Said he didn't know if he was younger or his system just now adjusting to that vitamin syrup that doctor at Grady give him. You'da thought I was sneaking the stuff, being my eyes pop open round three or four every morning, wide awake and waiting for the dawn to sprinkle light through the blinds. Kitchen already spic and span, I'm in it wiping 'like somebody hunting dirt,' as Will can say, or more like the police hunting the crack these teenagers traffic. Half the time, I over clean cause I don't have nothing betta to do. Then, too, my Mama didn't put up with no filthy house, I don't care if it was a shack. The older I get, the more I know it's a privilege to look after yourself and yo man. A day gone come—you live long enough—when you gone hafta bow to somebody else's will, do what they say, when they say.

Till then, though, I'm the woman 'tween these walls.

Preacher come after Will set down, smiling and nodding his good mo'ning. While they eat, I step outta the apartment and stand in sunshine, taking in the blessing of Lovejoy Street coming to life. Don't need no wristwatch to know it's going on six.

There Pinky, waving at me and getting into her white gal friend's car, heading to work. Other folks piling in a piece of a car up the street, car pooling outta necessity---them Johnsons got the car and the others don't, so po' folks learn strength on the other side of church doors. Where two or more join together in one accord, money there, too. And the kids that go to school and those that play possum by-passing the bus stop at the front of the neighborhood trudge up the street slow, like they walking towards a whupping. Make me wonder what all they doing in schoolhouses nowadays.

I think on that too long, I be mad on such a blessing of a day. Whatever school they going to done lost Short Dog and Lord knows how many more. I take myself inside, laugh 'bout the wind's words, eat a helping of oatmeal and open the **Constitution** to the sale pages, where, get this, ox tails going for practically nothing at the supermarket round the corner. That's when I stop being hard-headed and tell Will where I'm going, yank on my wig hat and sweater, grab my purse, and tip out the door.

Over in the afternoon, Will's voice drift in from the living room, where he been enjoying a right good nap. "Sweet! Sweet! Door." Had me walking in circles. Wasn't expecting nobody, Mookey hadn't knocked on the backdoor, and Will was spry bout remembering to tell me if som'uh his folks planned to show up. But that wind whispered what it whispered for a reason, and nine times outta ten, that reason was knocking now.

True enough, I shoulda knowed the person standing before me was gone be on the wind's mind for a spell.

"Well, I do say! You done caught me wif my teef out."

That gal pay me no attention. Sail on in the 'partment like she been sailing in all her life, a bag in one hand, just comfortable. Kiss me on the cheek and smack a kiss on Will's and then Preacher's, the living room expanding to keep in that pretty voice singing, "Hellooo, everyone! It's so good to see you all. How is everybody?"

In a navy blue suit, she look like somebody cut her outta one of them magazines Clemmy read when she visit Pinky.

"Oh, fair to middlin'," Will say. "How you?"

"I'm fantastic, thank you! Glad to be here on such a beautiful day!"

Preacher glow like a 100-watt bulb.

I say 'Afternoon' into my palm.

She hand me a bag of books for Mookey and whisper in my ear, her scent what it must be to drown in a bottle of expensive perfume, skip the grave, and go nonstop to Heaven.

"Please put your teeth in and invite a sister to the kitchen, Miz Too-Sweet. How on God's green earth did you know ox tails and cabbage was one of my favorites? You are absolutely too sweet for sure!"

She swirl runway pretty then and go to telling Will and Preacher all about that big event set to happen in Atlanta this summer. Something call the *National Black Arts Festival.* Claim she gone escort us to some of the festivities though Will say, "I'll think on it, but I ain't never knowed books to beat life."

That's when I head down the hall to get my smile.

By the time I make myself presentable, that gal is serving the menfolk cabbage and cutting cornbread pones in her crisp finery, places set for me and her at the table, facing one another. Will in his usual spot at the head of the table, Preacher at the other end, eyes stitched to that gal tighter than I ever seed him stitched to Pinky.

Miz Free rare back in her chair and pat her still-flat belly. "That was superb. Thank you so much."

I grin so hard I can hear my teeth popping. "You welcome, baby."

Will grunt a compliment and jerk his head toward the living room. Preacher understand exactly what that mean and get in Will's footsteps.

"I'll clean the table and wash the dishes," Miz Free insist, getting up.

"No, ma'am. You darken my door for the first time you a guest. Next visit, though, you can wash and sweep and cook till you drop, just as long as you come back, okay?"

Her smile sweeter than cane syrup. "Yes, ma'am, when I do, I'll bring more books, including books for teenagers," she promise, winking, "because I've got plans to hook bigger fish."

"The size of Short Dog and his crew, I hope."
She nod and I thank God for her vision. "Yes, ma'am,
that be the best thing for them. They just killing time
now, though it beat killing folks. With your plan, they
can mark time and feed they brains, too."

Then, Miz Free state the real thing on her
mind so I get busy telling her Preacher's story.

Same as a man can walk across a woman's
flower garden and tear up roses and tulips like he's a
mindless puppy blind to beauty, same, too, can a
woman race through a man's mind like a polecat
chasing rats, her nails and sharp teeth scarring him for
life, leaving him unable to do the simplest things he
used to do. I swear 'fore God, I know.

Preacher that man.

He got me by ten years, Preacher do. Mate
with Will. And as such, I looked on the older boys
with interest, like most of the gals I come up with.
Seemed them older boys lived TV lives, when ya
people couldn't afford to watch the real thing. So
back in '48 when I was a tender sixteen, big-boned
and shy, I sat in my own amen corner of life to note
how grown folks lived, so when I got grown, I might
live a fuller life. Be a fine catch for a man whose
presence---a clean, 'make a home with you' presence-
--made most women, married or single, lovesick in
Lochapoka, Alabama.

Preacher is the quiet, strong type. No
reputation of boastful talk, like talking under a
woman's dress, saying what he gone do and not
following through, no, none of that for him. That man
let his work do his talk. And could he work. Had a
day job at the saw mill and held a night job at the

pool hall, where he did most everything. Say he kept the place clean, threw the trash out (the two-legged sort as well as the garbage), learned how to toss liquor, settled disputes, and, in general, made Mr. Roy Southhall, who owned the jook, a mess of money.

Life went without static for a season or so, until that Moore gal showed up.

Light-skinned, big-eyed, skinny, good hair, store-bought dresses—that gal was first cousin to one of the few, well-off black families in town. Gal sashayed around with a golden string in her hand; to it, she tied Preacher, quickly and neatly, and, without him knowing, I guess, half the other young men, as it was common knowledge she didn't go for boys. Her name, Reba Moore, sat on lips far and wide, but nowhere was the name uttered sweeter than from Preacher's mouth. The whole town listened to the praises that man sung that woman. To hear it meant you might as well been sitting in the Shiloh Baptist choir, washed anew under hymn after hymn.

"Have you ever seed a more beautiful woman?" he began most conversations.

"You don't see her type round these parts because the makin' of that type woman take decades of class and good blood and manners and money. Can't beat that mix. No, sir, nowhere," he swore over Heaven.

"Ya'll ain't got reason to be bad-mouthin' the likes of Miz Reba's pretty," he informed any gal who stared at him cock-eyed after he got to bragging in stores, in church, and on the street, "what with my future wife in town. She's what colored beauty is all about.

"You wanna talk about raisin' the quality of your offspring? Get a gal like Reba Moore, and every baby God send, I can feel it, will be a prodigy straight out the Golden Gates," he'd tell the menfolk. "So look to the North to harvest the juiciest fruit you'll ever taste."

He preached and sank deeper and deeper in love with Miz Reba Moore. And I reckon that was a blessing in whore's clothing. One night, his jewel sashayed into the pool hall on Roy Southhall's suited, old arm, and nine months later, she grunted out a pucker-faced, wailing youngun with a single light curl and Reba's face, pretty enough, I'll bet, to wreak a slew of lives. But I never knowed with certainty, as Reba and her baby left town on a midnight train, and Preacher's talking left with them. Her leaving dried his mouth drier than the parched-breath creek behind my daddy's, Mr. Sylvester Sinclair's, cornfield.

Hurt Preacher to his heart, that Moore gal's butcher knife so sharp it practically pierced his soul. After that, Preacher must have determined pride was too much in '48, when he was twenty-six and smelling his self. He let that be his lesson, as he ain't mumbled another word I heard or heard tell he uttered since. A walking motto of action speakin' louder than words, he reached down and picked up the work ethic he dropped for a woman and moved back into a silent room of a world he ain't long left to this day.

But through him, though, folks learned to mind they own business and be humble and watch Preacher preach without uttering a mumbling word.

Chapter 6

Up there, she and J.T. were back at it.

In her kitchen, reliving the Techwood confrontation. In his house, in the breakfast nook, feasting on one of his signature brunches. In the bookstore, laughing and talking and kissing. In her living room, playing and fucking. In the other's embrace, dreaming. In his screened-in sunroom, off the back porch, making love. In Piedmont Park, strolling and running with his dogs.

Somewhere it had to stop or else she wasn't going to make it to wherever her self-imposed separation was taking them. Since she wasn't a woman to rescind her word after making a decision, she banished Junior Thomas's name from her mouth and forbade it on the tongues of those around her. If silence didn't staunch his memory, she prayed activity would and promptly climbed out of her head.

Leaps and Bounds. Free had finally consented to check out the new kids' place after days of listening to her nephew's adamant pleadings, extolling its praises. Once she gave herself permission to get out more, the outing became the perfect opportunity for quality time with Trevor and Sharmayne, who undoubtedly spent too much time in her head and house also.

In the rearview mirror, she glanced at Li'l Trevor on the backseat, drawing.

"What are you working on, honey? Another comic book character?" That was all she recalled seeing in the notebook he kept stashed in his book bag.

The boy finished what he was sketching before looking up. "No, actually, I'm taking my characters a step further. These are new sketches of the futuristic world they'll guard and protect." He tapped the tip of his pencil on his nose. "Mom says characters have to live somewhere called a setting, Aunt Free."

Free caught Sharmayne's eye and winked, her raised brow indicating, Was that an answer or what? Sharmayne read the look and mirrored Free's astonishment then yoked her neck lightheartedly. Free suppressed a laugh. Sharmayne's sudden playfulness eased a bit of the deep silence that hung about her shoulders since she'd walked in the door.

"What's the matter, girlfriend?" Her voice lowered. "Victor?"

Gazing at passing cars and flat grassy stretches along Highway 78, Sharmayne was the embodiment of bottled angst. Dark eyes that moments before shared childish amusement now glistened with sadness, and Free, feeling its contagion, refused to be returned to the quicksand she'd just circumvented. "Talk to me, honey. I'm not like you and Miz Too-Sweet. I can't perceive what you can. I need words. Whatever it is, you should know I'm in your corner."

Sharmayne nodded twice, and then cupped her jaw despondently. "Later."

The building was encased in spotless glass. Tall, multicolored letters announced its name above the entrance. A short line of children and adults waited to enter its double doors. Behind them, Free and Sharmayne stood in line while Trevor speedily plastered his nose against the cool glass, gleefully watching droves of children crawling and milling and leaping like swarms of giant mice.

Free's earlier reprimand forgotten, Trevor let loose a wild whoop.

"Aunt Free, I told you! Look!" He pointed at signs mounted over a line of cash registers. "They've got food, snacks and soda. Wow! And look at those kids, they've got knee pads. O boy! How much longer do we have to wait?"

A blonde pivoted and flashed Free a *the-fun-has-yet-to-begin* smile.

Free reflected her enthusiasm. "Not much longer, sweetheart. But remember what I said when you get inside. Stay with me until you get to the play area, and follow the rules, okay?"

Trevor's okay evaporated in puffs of breath against the now-smudged pane.

She could hardly get the six-dollar admission out of her wallet fast enough, before Trevor was balancing a hot dog in one hand and dragging her with the other through a metal maze leading to the eating area and miniature obstacle courses. Wall-to-ceiling geometric shapes lined the walls and soft, colorful balls were everywhere.

"Girl, it's a good thing adults are free. I'd have taken Trevor to a park with a jungle gym before I paid twelve dollars to come in here and buy this pricey food, too."

"It's a change, a different experience." Sharmayne stooped to help Trevor untie his sneakers and pull on his knee pads. "One of the things we live for, unwittingly."

"Thank you, Aunt Sharmayne!" Trevor yelled, as though she were a million miles away. Then he crammed what was left of the hot dog down his throat, got Free's okay to play, squealed again, and disappeared into a surge of other jubilant youngsters.

Free and Sharmayne found the upstairs, glassed-in retreat for parents. Inside were necessary comforts: a pay phone, rows of cushioned chairs, concession machines, and two mounted televisions. An unobstructed view of the entire place gave Free a sense of added assurance, and she relaxed. Asked Sharmayne again what was on her mind.

Sharmayne winced, feeling herself a lock without a key. "I really don't know how to say this--" she started and stopped, unable to hold Free's stare.

Free gave her time to gather her thoughts. Before long, with perspiration soaking the armpits of her purple silk blouse, Sharmayne mustered the courage to speak.

"It's hard to say because to even think it is a sin. But I'm not happy, Frenonia. I haven't been for years now. It's just that lately I can't overlook it. Unhappiness refuses to be pushed under the bed or tucked in an already crowded closet. You know, slipped under an inconspicuous lid."

"Mrs. Cooper-Naylor, there's no sin in being unhappy."

Sharmayne sighed. Relieved they were out of earshot of a quietly reading, older couple.

"True. But not everyone thinks herself a lesbian, now does she?"

Once out, Free didn't know why the admission surprised her, but it did. She already speculated as much about Sharmayne. Hadn't the woman been growing more and more distant from the man she'd married, going so far as to admit she often slipped from her body whenever he desired sex? Didn't she recently have her order---not Reesa---books by Jewelle Gomez, Tee Corrine, Audre Lorde, and Becky Birtha, at different times, saying she was becoming more of an eclectic reader? Wasn't she forever yearning for Rhonda's freedom to have women friends without Big Trevor breathing down her blouse, like Victor Nayor scorching her neck whenever she left the house? And wasn't she keenly observant of women, aggressive women?

It was all as clear as the translucent tears on her friend's cheeks.

"Now who's silent? If you don't want to be friends anymore," her voice cracked and fell to a murmur, "I understand."

Free sucked her teeth, appalled. How could Sharmayne think her so vacuous, so ready to break friendship over the other's sexual preference? Was their bond that shallow? She could respond with indignation, but this wasn't about her. Besides, she loved this woman and that was all to it. She didn't know how to swim in such waters, so she asked, "Are you thinking you're a lesbian because you're no longer in love with Victor?" She pinched her nose. "You've never had a woman lover, have you?"

It seemed insulting to add, "Maybe you haven't met the right man, one who'll love you like you want to be loved," but she asked anyway.

Sharmayne welcomed the dialogue.

"I've been through the same questioning. Even cringed about what Melba would think, and you can imagine how she'll carry on when she finds out." Sharmayne grimaced. "For the past week, I've heard her inside my heart, hollering, 'I didn't raise no twisted woman! I raised you to love and cherish a man, heifer…do you hear me, Miss Sharmayne? A man! No where does it say in the Bible a woman who lies with another woman is worth her weight in rubies and gold. If it's there and I missed it, kindly show it to me. How can your spirits abide in a defiled temple with you thinking filthy thoughts?'"

Sharmayne rubbed her temples. "But, regardless of all that, the final analysis is the same. And no, Free, I've never made love with a woman, but I've longed for something different than what I've come to know bearing up under Victor. It's funny, but the man warrants some credit. He spoke my lesbianism long before I did."

Free turned, searching the crowd of jumping children. She spied Trevor leap-frogging across the room, doing his best to capture her attention. When she waved, he blew her a kiss and dove back into the rainbow balls.

"You get rid of ole Vic, the next man may knock you off your heels."

Sharmayne didn't laugh.

"I'm sorry. That didn't come out right, but girl, I've had some brothers I wouldn't wish on my worst female acquaintance---trust me. Yet I haven't closed myself off to men though."

"I love men. But as relationships go, I want to explore a softer side of loving. A knowing inside tells me to wait, that she *will* come, and soon."

Although curiosity opened a floodgate inside Free, she igged the reference to a coming woman lover. "So are you saying you're still attracted to men?"

"Put it this way…I can recognize and

appreciate male beauty. I see fine men wherever I go, and some approach me with interesting and not-so interesting come-on's. Some offer their business cards; others leave it at compliments, although the fact remains, I'm not sexually attracted to men." Sharmayne sat up in her seat and leaned forward, stretching her shoulders. "On the flipside, I've seen plenty of sisters with whom I'd love to broach a conversation if I were bold. And yes, some have moved me, awakening desires that make me soft and wet." The confession, evenly spoken, suddenly unnerved her. "Does that surprise you?" There. She retrieved a key she'd lost in the closet of her thoughts.

Free could only think to say, "Not really." She was more surprised at how flimsy her own voice sounded when she finally spoke. "What about your faith?"

"That part I'm yet battling. Leviticus 20:13 is hot-ironed in my brain. 'If a man also lie with mankind, as he lieth with a woman, both of them have committed an abomination: they shall surely be put to death; their blood shall be upon them.' But strangely, Free, my spirits, to whom I've listened since I was eleven, tell me that I've always known, that I'm whole and complete as I am, and that I shouldn't judge myself."

Enthralled, Free didn't bother to comment.

"I always knew I wasn't like other girls. I cared a great deal for females, connected more with them, loved being in their presence. But the strictures of my upbringing and my faith kept me from myself. Throughout my growing-up, though, I always knew, deep within, that everything would be fine."

Free nodded, understanding the last part, if

nothing else.

Beyond the glass, the Stone Mountain sky was a patchwork quilt of turquoise and azure and indigo squares, covering all traces of the day's fluffy white clouds, the curtains of evening fluttering down across the city.

"So where does this leave us, Frenonia Roberts?"

Free feigned a sneer. "I don't care if you're the last Black Woman newly arrived from Lesbos round by Venus. You're my girl and I love you and what the hell else matters?"

Hearing that, a grateful Sharmayne sighed, swung wide a door, and leap-frogged out of the musty closet inside her head.

Chapter 7

"**Next time I'll** factor the weather forecast into my personal leave." Rhonda Butler hung a rain-splotched red and white umbrella on an all-purpose stand in a corner of the **Coffeehouse**. "But rain or not, it's refreshing to be away from school. No bells. No Jomo Wyatt. No students. No Eiffel Tower of essays."

"I'll bet," Free said, "and who's this Jomo Wyatt? Must be a rough customer."

"You have no idea. Half the time I want to strangle him, but I---"

"Love all your kids if their names appear on your roll."

Free laughed and waited for her sister to rest the books she'd horded from the downstairs showcases on one of the small tables facing two enclosed glass counters filled with sandwiches, fruit bowls, salads, cookies and rows of cakes.

"I love it when you spend the day with me."

"With us," Bren Mason corrected. She was balancing a platter of freshly baked muffins from the kitchen. "Go, girl. Learn something new every day."

The sisters exchanged a questioning look, watching the younger woman row delicious-smelling muffins in a warmer on the counter.

"That umbrella--you're a Delta." Bren's full lips widened in a dazzling smile under a light-brown netted Afro. "So are my mother and aunts, but Frenonia here encourages me to heed the pearls and ivy if I'm to know true sisterhood."

"Hey, don't be starting no stampedes," Free

teased. "We are family, okay."

Rhonda laughed. "Cute pun, sis." Then to Bren, "Sisterhood has taught us elephants not to trample simply because we can."

"Touché." Free bowed genially and then curtsied.

The women shared sisterly laughter though Rhonda's dried faster than the other two, the thought crossing her mind that Free had only consented to one hour of Career Day at her school, Ida B. Wells High, in the last year.

"Are you ladies eating now or later?" Bren asked on her way to the kitchen.

"Nothing for me just yet, thanks," Free answered, pulling up a chair.

Bren waited on Rhonda, who perused the day's offerings, licking her ginger-tinged lips. She came to revel in the essence of the entire day. That meant breakfast, lunch and a Houlihan's dinner in Colony Square on Peachtree, with or without her sister. For two days, she'd anticipated blissful reading and congenial chatting to her heart's content. It wasn't like she took off in the middle of the week, every Wednesday, mentally relieved and dressed in jeans and a light sweater over a T shirt.

"Make it a banana nut muffin, fruit bowl and cup of decaf tea, please."

"My pleasure." This time Bren bowed before disappearing.

"That girl is going to make a divine restaurant owner one day. I can see her now, wooing her patrons with style and grace and a delectable menu," Rhonda said, sorting through the colorful hardback selections crowding the table. The smell of a new book, smooth covers, crisp pages, an undiscovered story, even the weight of the work in her palms thrilled her. Same as it did Free, still rapt in her sister's nearness.

"What caught your eye this time?"

Rhonda rowed Bebe Moore Campbell's **Brothers and Sisters**, Octavia Butler's **Parable of the Sower**, a poetry collection, **Life Poems**, by a local Atlanta writer, Kupenda Auset, **Just As I Am**, by another Atlanta author, E. Lynn Harris, Miriam DeCosta-Willis' **Homespun Images**, Walter Mosley's **Black Betty**, and Desmond Tutu's **The Rainbow People of God.** She stood the more provocative titles up---**In Search of Good Pussy**, **Sisters and Lovers**, and **The Serpent's Gift**.

"Now that's a line-up. And you even included our next book club selection. Cool." Free pointed to Harris' bestselling read. "You know Harris was in here the other day. He was being interviewed by a young writer with **Black Romance** magazine. Girl, I asked him about gracing *The Daughters of Isis* with his presence, but he's promoting his book on April 15th."

Rhonda sat in quiet astonishment. She would trade a month of school to be in Free's shoes for one week, perhaps Spring Break, if she and the Trevors stayed home.

"How was he?"

Free crossed her arms on the table and leaned toward her sister. "Handsome in a boyish way, so easy to laugh, and beams a 60-watt smile. Articulate and warm." Her eyes sparkled with mischief. "If he didn't write gay male romance, he'd make a great speaker for your senior writing classes or a writing assembly."

"Uh huh," Rhonda mused, "but the notoriety of a gay person or gay association enflames school folks with fear and rage and violence. You'd think the calendar read Dark Ages instead of April."

"That's everywhere. Wonder how the *Daughters* are taking it."

"On average, women normally crave romance, but we'll see, won't we?"

"Yes, ma'am. Was that the last one on the display? Reesa calls new orders for it every other week."

"There was one more."

"Good. I'm taking that to Sharmayne, who may be at my house for the meeting."

"Will Victor be out of the country in two weeks?"

Free laughed, startling a silver-haired reader moseying to a nearby table.

"No, girl, let's just say she's coming out in more ways than one." Free pooched her lips and lowered her head, peeking up through her lashes. "No further queries. Got to supervise Patty and Rodney's shelving and help Reesa unpack new arrivals." She sashayed a knowing strut towards the staircase. "Will join you in a moment."

When Bren brought her freshly prepared repast on a bright red platter and headed back to the kitchen, saying she had coursework to complete, Rhonda found herself enveloped in a delicious silence. She'd decided on Campbell's **Brothers and Sisters**. The cover art, the book flap, the author's face---all welcomed her inside. But she'd only read as far as the first couple of pages before the words blurred and old familiar feelings of self reproach rained down on her, leaving her uncomfortable and slightly disconcerted, as though she were wet to the skin, the result of a sudden spring shower from a cloudless sky.

Why couldn't she control that damn urge? After all this time.

A fever, it burned just below the surface of her skin, lying dormant sometimes, raging wild and grimly dissatisfying at others, though never totally out of control. And never voiced.

She was who she was, an educator; Free an accomplished entrepreneur. Since they couldn't exchange lives, Rhonda determined to bury her jealous sentiments. But, bedfellows, she and jealousy had been intimate too long. It hovered over her past; over her Easter Sunday dress that captured the light just so until she stood next to a sixteen-year-old Frenonia and the dress promptly lost its starch and fluff, as sure as motherhood droops the softened roundness in a youthful breast; over her high-school graduation when, unlike Free, the vale of her class, Rhonda had come within a hair's breath of being valedictorian just to have her hopes dashed against the suffocating walls of the counseling office when she learned she'd lost to a rival by one fraction of a point; over her big sister on those long ago occasions when she and Free partied together as teens, the boys pecking her shoulders like homeless parrots and asking after Free's whereabouts; and most devastatingly, over her when Free had been featured in an issue of the **Atlanta Magazine** for being a young, attractive, business-minded, African-American woman, who wrote her own meal ticket as the proprietress of her establishment, a popular spot for yuppies, the elderly, university students, her scholarly high school students, for crying out loud, and most of her literary-minded colleagues.

But then what had she done? Besides teach at the same school for more years than she cared to admit. Aside from constantly ferreting out opportunities for her students to—as she said--squeeze the richness out of life, without adopting her own advice. Other than postponing traveling, at home and abroad, for a more convenient time. She had to accept the truth---she was a master at living in the future, oblivious to her present.

Tacitly unaffected, or so she hoped, Rhonda endured it all.

Until she put herself first and carved time from her day, like now, to embrace a feeling of aliveness and joy. Hell, she was twenty-six. Their mother had said she could do anything, and it went without saying, she believed her…if only at certain times.

She had to stop her mind from raining why's. Why this recurrent remorse? Why not be satisfied with being Rhonda Butler? And if not, why not change?

"Nickel for your thoughts," Reesa proposed. "Is the novel that good or are you somewhere else?"

The girl's presence and words jarred Rhonda.

"What happened to penny thoughts?"

Reesa giggled. "Inflation."

Then she stared at the woman as if she were a museum portrait. "I can't get over how alike you and Free are, even in your differences." She shrugged, adding, "With carbon-copy noses and lips, you're pretty and cinnamon-colored; she's a mango pretty. Both of you could walk Spelman's campus and the guys from Morehouse or wherever would whistle and cut the fool, trying to get your numbers."

Rhonda found the compliments amusing and closed the novel. "Oh really."

"Yes, really." Reesa grinned. "And you're strong, intelligent, friendly, outgoing, fun, and active. You care about others, work hard, seem to think a lot, and you're both readers."

"Then how do we differ?" Rhonda expected the obvious M's: motherhood and marriage, Mazda and Mercedes.

The girl grabbed a braid and fingered its curly end in concentration.

"May I be honest?"

"Is there any other way?"

"Okay. Your posterior is flat, and your hair is like mine, thick-as-your-foot healthy. In addition, you impart knowledge; Free sells it."

Rhonda's eyes bucked and it took her brain a minute to connect with her mouth, giving Reesa the inclination to remind her she'd co-signed the honesty clause.

"Interesting." Rhonda marveled at youth. They were more perceptive than people gave them credit. She witnessed it daily. This girl might have culled other visceral differences, or similarities, had she the grace of time, but as it was she'd done a damn decent job. Maybe she and her sister were more alike than she thought.

"Rhonda, you know I love talking, although Mother dubs it psycho analyzing and claims, as a toddler, I could talk long before I walked. Anyway,

Free says to tell her Sisterlove she'll be up in twenty minutes."

Their lips came together, softly magnetized in the darkness.

She didn't refuse when the mouth, moist and lustful, demanding, kissed her so hard her lipstick smeared a sweet stickiness across her cheeks and chin, about her ears and down her neck, putting her nerves on alert. She didn't pull away when a cocky tongue licked a trail of wetness from her collar bone to the dip between her breasts.

Her breath caught in her throat at the utter softness of that tongue. Fluttering about her lips, so wet, so silky, and so velvety. She lifted upward, her lips, shoulders, and breasts, wanting that seeking wetness to taste her, savor every part of her, and swallow her whole.

Satiny lips.

They brushed her bra straps aside and kissed her shoulder blades. Teeth, gentle yet exacting, bit into her tender flesh, marking her. Damn. A wave of warmth raced under her skin at the combination of rough and soft sensations, the giving and taking an aphrodisiac, the kisses and bites causing her bottom lip to quiver. Rough hands startled her, coming out of no where, without the press of a body against hers. She gasped. Vice-like, they gripped her wrists, those hands, and positioned her own alongside her body. They peeled the bra from her bosom and sampled her nipples. She lay completely still, aching, throbbing.

The hands meant business, she perceived, like the tongue.

Under her chin, the kisses grew juicy and juicier, buttering her, slipping down her throat, the lips and tongue maintaining an unceasing, up-and-down stroking, the licking and sucking on the weak spot of her neck stirring a creamy churning between her thighs.

An exquisite need parted her lips, but she stifled a moan, understanding the command for silence. Then the tongue snaked to her lips, lingered lovingly. Gently, it ringed her groaning nipples in an enticing wetness just ahead of sudden pinches.

Somebody knew her well. Pinches mixed with kisses left her sloppy wet.

She closed her eyes, opened herself to a pleasing pain.

Feathery. Downy. The tongue redefined the contours of her lips, glossed them with desire, the luscious licks easing her into a pleasant weightlessness---with an abrupt bottom. She met it hard and fast when the pinches plunged, commandeered her clit.

Full and rigid, the tongue rolled itself at the sides, forming a piston, and drilled the cavern of her mouth. Her own tongue pulled back, flattened. But she opened wide, allowing the pumping tongue to pump her mouth and raise her heartbeat. Gradually, the surprise lessened, she tightened her lips around the thrusting organ and rode the frantic tempo it created in her veins. The mouth closed, open to lick her lips ravenously again, and then engaged her tongue in a slow sensual dance.

She imagined that teasing on her clit and her legs shivered.

But she dared not move a muscle that wasn't

already twitching. The hands appeared again. At her middle. As though to calm her. To regain a silken state of expectation.

Not so. Those hands were now reading the language of her pants as if reading Braille. In seconds, they ripped and unsnapped and yanked and jerked at the material, liberating her belly and pussy and legs. Then, without preamble or pleasantries, the hands lifted her, roughly parting her legs in a gaping, east-to-west arc. Her thighs sighed. Her pussy squealed in delight, large pink luscious tears shimmering atop its petals---it felt wonderful to be unclothed, unfettered, unrestricted. And when a long, thick, rhythmic shaft pushed headlong inside her flower, cleaving its sleek walls, pushing her clit hood backward, revealing the tiny root, a larger one pounding, throbbing wildly, plummeting deeper, veins shouting along its sides, easing in and out, throbbing against her swollen lips before nose-diving back into her honey, she flushed bodily and permitted her fingers to splay, to snatch air, to chance contact with the ass thrashing hers now.

A tongue was claiming her mouth and neck, the hands roughly keeping her in a position to render her ass lushly available, the shaft an oversized conductor's wand; someone was directing a jazzy scat throughout her pussy. She whimpered catlike, drenched in cum. A tantalizing tango jumped the firm flesh of her cheeks, and a smooth sexy rumba tuned her insides, where a beast of an orgasm surged. It spiraled deep within her middle, thrumming the bottom of her coochie, and imploded in a sweet satisfaction around the sides of a yet stabbing shaft.

Frenonia awoke restless and feeling out of place and sweaty on Thursday night. Her ponany pulsed. Her entire body felt thick with passion, as if someone had made love to her for hours, the heat of sex yet smoldering under her skin. Then, yawning, she remembered. She'd fallen asleep on the downstairs sofa, listening to Dinah Washington's haunting voice croon "This Bitter Earth."

She shirked dismissively. Masturbating in her sleep again. Horny as hell.

When she got up to restart the stereo, her gaze stumbled on J.T. inside a miniature frame dwarfed by her Alabama State University diploma on the mantle. How had it escaped the bottom drawer of the entertainment center? She'd ditch it tomorrow or…leave it be perhaps. It wasn't like she'd stopped loving him.

For all the good that love did her now, though, she pushed the play button on the stereo and returned to the sofa. The sun would be tossing her covers and climbing the sky shortly. So she reclined on her back and stared at the ceiling, confident her life wouldn't always be, as Dinah sang, *like the dust that hid the glow of a rose.*

Long after the music ceased, she couldn't stop the songbird's question from following her into sleep.

What good is love that no one shares?

Chapter 8

At Mt. Sinai Baptist, on Easter Sunday, a stone moved at her feet. Pastoria Roberts never saw it coming, never fathomed salvation to be as free as her next breath.

Right now, she was stirring in a cast iron skillet, the hot bubbling corn, creamy and yellow, fresh from the garden she and Booker McRae tended behind their Pine Mountain, Georgia, home. On the Kenmore's range, other pots whistled.

"How happen you got away from Atlanta without my only grandbaby? You know Trevor rarely misses an opportunity to visit his Nana, let alone on Easter."

Free looked up at her mother from the white, oblong kitchen table, where she sat mixing the ingredients for cornbread. "Rhonda planned an all-day, family outing at Six Flags for today."

"Did she mention why she's dissatisfied?"

"What do you mean?" Free sprinkled a teaspoon of sugar in the batter. "Dissatisfied with what?"

"Family tradition."

Pastoria rinsed and dried another cast-iron skillet and dug lemony-colored fingers into a can of Crisco, evenly smearing the creamy white lard around the skillet. Then she passed it to Free, who poured the grainy, yellow cornbread mixture into it and shoved the skillet into the Kenmore's gaping mouth.

"I don't think that's it. When she spent the day with me last Wednesday, we talked about her desire to create new traditions within her own family. She wants to deepen the quality of the time they spend together, is all."

"The way we're deepening the quality of our time now?"

Free's "Yes, ma'am" fell hollow and flat.

"I'd like to believe that, darling, but something tells me your sister is dissatisfied with me so she's making a statement by staying away from home, punishing me."

Free puckered her brows quizzically.

"Punishing you for what?"

"I have my notions, though I won't voice them without, at least, giving her the respect and opportunity to share what's eating her. I miss my baby girl. I miss us all spending time together: talking, laughing, cooking, shopping, and just being family."

Pastoria opened her spice cabinet and selected rosemary to season a pot of collards, turnips, mustard, and kale. The Goya all-purpose seasoning she sprinkled in the greens, along with pinches of Old Bay leaves and garlic, released a savory aroma that wafted up and began softening the stubbornness that kept her out of Atlanta.

"Why can't Rhonda change her life a little bit without being annoyed with anyone, least of all you? You're reading more into this than what is."

"Then why haven't you been home in a month of Sundays?"

"Okay, I'll be honest. Preoccupation with my own life, with the bookstore, and with my future plans to support reading and disadvantaged youth. Life, I guess."

"I love your spirit, baby. If our children read

more, they wouldn't have the time or the inclination to want to get into devilment. Breaking into folks' houses, killing, stealing, driving by and taking life like they could return it if they changed their minds." Pastoria sighed. "Honey, it's enough to make folks prisoners in their own castles," she said, before ending with, "But life doesn't stop you from calling me, now does it?"

"No, ma'am."

"My point exactly. Don't know the last time I heard from Rhonda, when I didn't call her. Trevor calls regularly. Am I still reading into her silence?"

When Free made no response, Pastoria conceded in a refined silence of her own, gesturing for Free to pass a chunk of salt pork in the center of the table. She deemed herself above forcing. Simply, she flowed peaceably in the river of life, accepting what she wanted along the shoreline, omitting the rest. In the pantry, she lifted a deep-dish peach cobbler she'd made earlier from a top shelf and placed it on a dessert tray to post near the dinner table.

Took her time and, fifteen minutes later, breaking their peace, said tactfully, "As a girl, Rhonda always held wrath. Slept with it. Whereas you'd speak up when you felt you'd been slighted, when you met antagonism, like me, but even now, a woman, your sister will nurture irritation until it virtually kills her. Haven't I taught you girls that what chases you, thundering and blaring, is---"

"An elephant."

"Yes, love, and once you turn to look it in the face, it's a what---"

"A mouse."

Pastoria nodded, moving precipitously between a teakwood cabinet and the table, stacking dishes to be used for dinner. Hands lost in suds, she asked Free about Sharmayne and J.T. With Free's edges starched, she figured to iron her out with talk of lighter subjects, as she pondered how best to revive another topic dear to her heart.

"Sharmayne's great. She's coming more and more into her own these days. She's finally taking responsibility for her happiness."

"Which is what every rational adult eventually, hopefully comes to. And J.T.?"

Free scoured, screwed up her nose. "He gave me grief when I shared my Techwood experience, and one thing leading to another, we had a blow-out. His jealousy, which irks me to no end, gets the best of him and infuriates me, I swear."

Pastoria dabbed the hem of a dainty white apron across her forehead. "Were you big enough to let him be right?"

"Let's say I gave him lots of time to be right." Free noticed her mother washing the expensive china. "No time for that now. Don't wanna be late for church."

Her mother continued rinsing the delicate plates and placed them on a clean, white towel to drain on the wide shelf of the storage cabinet near the sink. "And I'll not have my daughter eat from chipped plates and drink from jam jars on Easter Sunday. I am not taking the blessing of your presence for granted.

"Besides…" she began in a rush and then stopped in mid-thought—urbanely, to clear away the assorted spices, cans, dishes, and pans cluttering the table.

"Mother?" Free's voice hummed with sassiness left over from her teens.

"Besides, Frenonia, when are you and J.T. going to let me organize your grand affair so that I can invite the Sinclairs, the Roberts, the McRaes, the Thomases and half of Pine Mountain and Atlanta?" Her attitude shed its accusing nippiness, became warm and airy. "I'm itching to see my darling daughter in lace and satin, the prettiest bride that ever graced the red carpet of Mt. Sinai Baptist."

She awoke to the persistence of a silent foreboding. A foreboding that had suddenly come on her with the stealth of a secret, soundless on the wind, impregnating the atmosphere with an unseen angst. Booker sensed it also. Spoke it into the soft skin of her vanilla-scented neck. "Last night you slept fitfully, tossing and turning as if a witch were riding your back." Resolved, she forged on to church, anyway, beside her daughter. This Easter Sunday seemed no different from any other, except for the hurt absence of her baby daughter and her family, but the instant the piano player's fingertips alighted on the keys and an old hymn of dark clouds and rising storms roused a redemptive compassion on the air and hands clapped and feet stomped and Spirit moved from heart to heart and breast to breast, the hymn came alive in the Mt. Sinai Baptist congregation, and alive, too, in Pastoria Roberts' guarded soul.

She should have drowned long ago.

What saved her---kept her baby fine salt-and-pepper hair above invisible yet cold currents of river water that swirled about and around her, in bed, in church, in her high heels, giving her the volatile sensation of drowning---was an imposing pride. It kept her upright and undaunted in Booker's presence, in the outside world's eyes, and in the dark irises of her darling daughters, all of them, the two she had lain on her firm bosom—squirming, brown-skinned and curly headed—their little noses routing naturally toward her large tan nipples seeping the sweet smell of the colostrum, its richness loaded with protein and enzymes to strengthen their immune systems, all of them, that is, except one, the one whose mouth never knew her nipples, the one whose face would be known to her today, possibly by her name, but only by her eyes.

Seeing those eyes, for thirty years, she knew them in her sleep. They were one and the same with her eyes now. Inseparable. Another truth, she knew as well. The day would come when she would be called to put in an account for the breaking of the water.

The stone moved. It may have been the piano music. The stirred-up church air. Maybe even Pastor Ellis Menefield's thunderous command: "If you love Him like you say you do, leave those comfortable seats and come. Show whoever may look, that you, like all of us, got something God can know, already knows, that needs to be reconciled, hoisted from your bosom, from your chest, like a weight tugging you under—maybe for the last time. Let it gooo! Let it go!"

However the stone at her feet came to move, she broke free of her daughter's embrace that Easter at Mt. Sinai. With a surge of passion, her dancing, satin-textured, pale-pink pumps having practiced their part for most of the service, the matching two-piece suit mussed, a haze of salty tears in her eyes, Pastoria found herself an uncouth woman at the foot of the altar---head bowed, hat tilted, knees bent, lips imploring forgiveness; humbled before the Lord.

Behind her, on a middle pew, Free sat shaken. Why her mother reacted as she did was a mystery to her, although she speculated it had something to do with the Roberts' family secret, as clandestine as a married lover's gaze, that Pastoria, in all her perfection, had black marks against her, the likes of which, it was whispered, was too shameful to ever be known. Free speculated it had something to do with the new photo album under the living room coffee table, the album's last page vouchsafing the handsome face of a soldier in a yellowed photo, with the words, "To Pastoria, With Much Love, Earl," written in a flourishing scrawl.

Chapter 9

Rhonda stood in the Ida B. Wells High School's airy front office the Monday after Easter, staring at a pink slip, a telephone message from Free. She deliberated calling her right then or waiting until the end of sixth period, since she'd just opened her classroom door for her buddy Gail Johnson, whose personal-leave excursions were a must-hear.

Best to do it now, she conceded, dialing the number.

"Afternoon. The **WeAreFamily Bookstore and Coffeehouse.** May I help you?"

A perky voice rang with a joyous lilt.

"Hi, Reesa, it's Rhonda. Is Free within yelling distance?"

The girl chuckled. "Hey! No. How have you been?"

"Fine, outside of a few darlings who forget the way to school daily."

"I heard that. My moms didn't play that stuff. Your butt went to school or to the shelter, one, and that included the times when colds slapped fire in your temples. But Moms would give you a ride on those days. So you wouldn't die in the gutter and have her accused of child abuse."

Rhonda drummed a pencil on the counter. "Uh-huh."

"Okay." Reesa sensed she was hampering something important. "I'll tell Free you called. Have a wonderful day! Bye!"

Chapter 10

A reading jones. She'd had it as far back as she could remember, and even today, it was how she filled her waking moments between the hours and days that Victor was on the road, where he was now. Her living room was a haven of printed pages. Magnificent mahogany bookshelves spanned three walls. Two yellow sofas, a towering reading lamp, and pots of ivy were the room's furnishings. In this oasis, on Tuesday, Sharmayne locked out the world.

It was 5:45 A.M.

Anchoring herself, she sat cross-legged on the carpet, knees pulled up with the soles of her feet kissing. Head high, neck graceful and long, hands limp on the flesh of her thighs, palms open, back church-straight, she sat below the living room windows. Through fluttering curtains the dawn stroked her shoulders. Its fingers paradise, it relaxed her body, dark and unclothed and glistening with the massage oils she hid under the guest bedroom sink, far back against the pipes.

She closed her eyes.

With little effort, she emptied her mind. Releasing all thoughts of household chores done to the minutest specification of Victor Naylor's likings. Willed Free's break-up with J.T. to a distant corner of her mind. Took her foot and eased stubborn thoughts of Melba further back where she should've swept them long ago, where, with any luck, they'd slide down her neck and get lost on the heel of her shoes.

In no time she felt herself lighten, become as weightless as a feather. With the assurance that no one could see her, tucked away under the window's early-morning splendor, she marveled in her freedom, in her ability to sit nude, mind as open as her thighs, in her own space. With Victor about, she could no more manage to slip into solitude than not have breakfast piping, bath ready, dinner simmering, beer chilled, covers turned, or her body available for his desires.

She booted these thoughts, too, into oblivion with lightening quickness.

For a time, perhaps hours, she sat. Stark still. Then, there in the darkness, she heard the whispered gentleness of units not yet words. Serene, they allayed her with the music of the wings of a thousand butterflies. The air quivered around her. Vibrated. But suddenly, the murmurings vanished. Nothing moved. Spanish statue silent, she felt the rising of her bosom so subtle, her pulse so indiscernible, her breathing died down.

Calm descended. Another tranquil sensation enveloped her, and she realized a presence. To better receive it, she raised her palms. Her face turned upward, too, and her soul followed magically. Just flew on off. Floating up, up, upward, face brushing the vaulted ceiling, and, in a flash, she was free. Free of the confines of her flesh and bones, the living room, free of the house, the attic. Into the atmosphere she levitated, waif-like, spirit under a newly-risen April sun.

So this was how it felt.

To be without strictures. To be formless.

In her weightlessness, she wondered at the miracle of Being. She gloried at the majesty of all things without trying to name the trees, ancient and stately, in their age-old wisdom. She praised creatures large and small, from the bee to the elephant. Her adulation knew no bounds---no hate or separation or judgments; there was only Love---as her essence savored the breeze, the sun, the insects, and the freshness of an early-morning world. There was only perfection. Abundance. Budding, sprouting, reaching. All this she knew without senses, outside of her body there on the living room carpet.

A lifetime later, she perceived, "Come." The voice directed, inaudible enough to be the fanning of a single butterfly wing. "Come into yourself." Like air released from a balloon, she felt herself sucked back into her physical form. Through space she sank, the sensation filling her with a peculiar swirling that excited her limbs, cleared her chakras, and exhilarated every inch of her, plunging her backward with a blissful sweetness.

She dared not open her eyes until her spirits communicated.

"Go to the bookcase."

Obeying, she gathered her parts slowly, methodically, lovingly, and walked to the middle mahogany bookcase and pulled Marita Golden's collection, **Wild Women Don't Wear No Blues**, from a shelf. She parted pages she'd never read and, as though guided to satisfy a yearning, she sipped the sparkling champagne of Kesho Yvonne Scott's "Marilyn" from **The Habit of Surviving**. Eyes drinking in the black words on the white page, she read with a thirst that had to be quenched by someone who knew. On those ordained pages she met women who raised lamps and lit paths. She discovered women the likes of whom Victor Naylor never knew nor wanted to know. She was put in the mind of women like Frenonia Roberts. And Rhonda Butler. Sisters who were replicas of the woman she imagined Free's mother to be; women somewhat akin to Melba, although her mama reigned under the guise of piety.

Sharmayne met "*fuck-you women.*"

And she, like Kesho Yvonne Scott, was mesmerized, awed that such women lived right under her nose, and she never realized it until now. She knew, in that moment, that she would become a "*fuck-you woman*" to reclaim the girl who cowered within her. She'd coax that sistah to the forefront, have her stand wild and free before the world. Yes, she'd lay it all down to rise up with that lost sistah found. She owed that woman. Owed her a whole helluva lot more than she could ever repay for the years she'd crushed her, goaded her to the background, and slapped a mum's-the-word expression across her lips. She owed that woman, and she'd be damned if she wasn't going to start paying her back the minute Darling Victor---Free's nickname for him---trudged through the front door. For the first time, Sharmayne's mind cleared. The book yet open, she marched into her bedroom and plopped onto the bed, laughing. This time she read the entire essay aloud, the spoken words affirming.

No doubt about it; on her own terms, she would survive.

She placed the book on the bed head and flipped onto her stomach, her right hand finding a region of her body it washed then covered. That hand cherished no memory of stroking this moist sector, now dewy with wetness. Curious, one bold finger ventured inward, sneaking its way past the fleshy sentry positioned on each side of a zone, she'd read, that not only brought pleasure, wed lovers, birthed orgasms, but also sank ships, waged wars, and snipped lives. The finger, empowered and amazed, continued to explore. Wiggling backward and forward, it found a silky tunnel, the touch of rose petals in morning dew. Savoring the discovery though withdrawing shocked, it took a while to return fearless, to stroke away the belief that what she was doing was wrong. Nasty. Something left to dirty women with no shame.

But the drenched finger delighted in tantalizing this new conquest.

One by one, until they were four, the fingers dived. This time her ass rose to swallow the pumping pleasure, pussy tearing with each withdrawal, gaping wider with every entry. When the pumping quickened, Sharmayne rocked back and forth. The bed shook. Creaked. And scraped the floor boards. Breath rasped in her throat. Fire burned her veins, electrifying her flesh. She trembled bodily, experiencing a strange euphoria taking shape in the ocean she was churning in her earth. She'd never felt anything like it. What she knew for sure was the harder she rocked, the deeper she breathed, the faster her fingers pumped, the more a volcano roared inside her, had her screaming, moaning, humming, jabbering---until she couldn't stop, until she exploded, squirting a clear lava across the bedspread. "O goodness!" she whispered, thinking she'd shake forever, but her nerves, at length, sighed.

Outside the bedroom's opened windows, a white morning sun beamed. Under fluttering drawn curtains singing breezes baptized her. She didn't move to cover her nakedness. Rather, she allowed herself the simple pleasure of a light wind licking sweat from her skin, and at the rate it was going, she'd soon be smooched into a pleasing slumber.

Two hours later, to a chorus of insect and bird melodies, Sharmayne awoke a new woman, with new joneses. A long shower behind her, she had to be outdoors. To walk the neighborhood. To celebrate the first day of the rest of her life.

Chapter 11

Had one of them laps that didn't sit well, I suspect, the one with the head full of braids, blonde braids, did. Could tell it in the way she come in the rec room, cautious and alert, eyes shifty, ears perked, waiting for the littlest sign of trouble. Put me in the mind of a deer tipping through a plain of well-hid lions. Hungry ones. The kind you see on them nature specials, the kind be laid off on high rocks above a valley, their females somewhere belly low to the ground, just aching to strike out and chase a tuck-tailed deer across Kingdom Come.

Except this one--a doe, with enough hair to keep the dollar store in business for a year--bout turn and fight like a hellion if somebody give her cause for scare. With Miz Free and the other one in the rent office getting keys, I see it in the way she sit, too, her lap off limits, legs crossed and hands trying to figure, no doubt, how she come to be sitting in a musty, paint-chipped hall with too many chillen to shake a stick at.

But the other one different. Trailed by chillen, a female Piped Piper, her face shiny and happy, same as Miz Free's, both grinning as if they were in a television station receiving a winning ticket to a million-dollar lottery instead of keys to the rec room and the kitchen. They lugged food on colorful trays a knot of nine-ten-year-old boys was helping them tote. Miz Free seem not to notice the *don't-say-nothing-to-me airs* on the one with the off-limits lap.

I watch her join Miz Free and the other one as they turn the rec into a pot of gold under a banner with the words "Free Your Mind: Read" taped to the edge of one long table.

While Miz Free wiping and moving, she making introductions. The Doe got a pretty name. Reesa. She down at unrolling blue mats in front of three folding chairs and putting up a three-leg stand that hold huge storybooks. A classroom, I reckon. Good. All chillen could benefit from a lesson or two, I'm thinking, even on Saturday morning. The other one, whose name sounds like the word cordless, name Corliss. Kids circling her, arguing to hold her hand and help with the books she unpacking and the table she rowing with tiny crayon boxes and colored paper. The Doe announce she work in Miz Free's bookstore, the popular one her friend. Strange match. Stone opposites; one mad, talked outta her sweetness for a Saturday in the projects, the other sunshine, warming whoever stand in her rays.

"Pinky knowed you'd be here," I say, when Miz Free get around to asking after Mookey. "Said that's all he talk bout, his Miz Free coming back to read to him. Like he gone be the sole chile here. I suspect Pinky walk him down soon, if she ain't working, and if she is, then she bout have Short Dog get him here." I mention how Pinky say he got her reading before she leave for the Waffle House most evenings, got that **Jamal's Busy Day** down pat so, he recite it word for word, and will fool ya, you don't know better. He know all the stops. Turn pages like a champ, memory a deadbolt, locking in words like treasures.

Rec take on a different feel—a living-room feel—the second them gals start reading. Miz Free on a blue mat, legs crossed Japanese style, two little people squeezed in her lap, hanging, like the others, off her words, knowing they got to up and hit the mat in a page or two, so that two others can go to Heaven under Miz Free's heartbeat. She reading soft and low, then loud and dramatic, like she on stage, every now and then showing her group of eight chillen big, painted pages. Miz Corliss got her crew at the table, all seven, where she going step-by-step, peeping over the chillen as they draw their idea of summer. Miz Corliss head go down close to theirs. Real close. Close enough for her black braids to pour across little bullet heads and weeks-old top braids and ratty ponytails ain't been taught by Sunday's hot comb, them black braids at home across daisy-stem necks and bony shoulders, the scents rising from some had to be filling her nose with odors she bout ain't smelled since she quit playin' with rank puppies. Her closeness, though, made them chillen giggle and forget their interest in the donuts and orange juice and milk and sausage biscuits and fruit I done laid out pretty on flower-painted trays.

Miz Reesa.

She in a folding chair facing three mats of listenin' chillen, their faces empty cereal bowls ready for a second helping. She a good reader, too. Words leaving the page, taking shape round her, hunting tigers and eating gingerbread men, outfoxing devils and jumping on beds, cooking stone soups and searching for lost mamas. Yes, ma'am, them words softening her face, spilling down her lap and legs into brown and yellow and red and black bowls at her feet. Carrying them chillen with her to magic places. But that group of hers ain't slow. Techwood don't raise no slow chillen, though their schools might argue bout the slow that mean they don't add or subtract or spell well.

That bunch fast enough to know they outside the luck of the draw. Unlike the others. So they study Miz Untouchable. And follow them stories like bloodhounds at a coon fest. While they study her voice buttoned against the chill of raggedy play clothes, broken shoes, and no shoes. While they read her eyes zipped to uncombed heads, grimy cheeks, lent-lined braids, and wanderin' attention that end up at the food table. Being chillen, they ain't learned to cut their eyes at stares that snag and nip curious, little fingers and feelings. Like the older, tougher ones down the hall, hooping in the gym, whose eyes instantly seam-rip all stares. So they study Miz Reesa, until a short, skinny, serious boy with a round, nappy head, no more than six, if that, clothes outta the Goodwill bin, feet dirty, quit studying her. Without a mumbling word, he unbutton his legs and wobble to his feet, legs bout stinging from sitting still, head high, last night's pee probably itching his thighs. At her knees, he stop. Stop and read her, stop and see sunshine deep down in her, hidden way back under the distance from her brown face to his, stop and determine her lap might sit as well as his mama's. To see, he pull up on her jeans, timid, then seat hisself on that lap behind her book, and then make hisself right comfortable.

I could feel them chillen breathe one breath, waiting for Miz Reesa's face to vomit. They wait, ready to catch him when he come flying back to them blue mats. But her knee never budged. Pointed nose never flared. Hands never shoved. Only her mouth returned to life, and slowly, them chillen crept closer, like me, realizing a doe could graze with lion cubs after all.

Every belly full, including mine, when Miz Free go to filling arms with furry animals. Not only on account she big-hearted, but she and them gals organizing them chillen in the fastest program I ever seed. And that included Easter Sunday programs where the kids sing and shout and read poems and do everything, except preach. At the end of the reading, Miz Free's group tell what they liked bout what she read. Some giggle and find the cat done swiped they tongue; others act out the parts they like. That Miz Corliss has hers stand and explain their perfect summer, and Miz Reesa is lining hers up just as the rec door burst open hard enough to rattle the empty flower-painted trays.

A sweaty boy, chest pumping like he hooked to a machine, march in first.

"I told ya dumb asses they was having a party in here." He spy the food, then punch another boy pushing in behind him. "See. Coulda been got our grub on." He walking toward the table like the room empty, and I cut my eyes at him and get up to ask what he think he doing, but Miz Free beat me to it, moving quicksilver fast.

She in his face before he clear half the floor. "Good afternoon. Glad you could join us. To eat, you read." She point to the "Free Your Mind: Read" sign. "We got books for every palate, even yours."

That boy follow her finger to a table of books, spread and staked, little and big, hard and soft. Then he face her with a look so hot, it scorch me. Lips skinned back, sweat drying, he fanning thick black smoke over all us and direct his attention back to Free for a double scorch.

"Who you suppose to be---a book fairy? Ain't picked up no book since I thumbed a girlie magazine with pictures about as fine as the three of y'all."

Four other boys nasty laughter trickle in the doorway. Bringing funk and basketballs and teenage hunger.

Miz Free fan the air, too, and his disrespect. Say, "Understandable. Now's your chance to do something about it." She standing straight, staring the burn outta his flame. The smoke outta the room.

"Who I'm gone read to? Her?" He stuck on Miz Reesa. Walking toward her with his head cocked, smelling hisself. "What you wanna hear, Ma?"

The Doe ain't scary either. "Whatever you can read."

"Whatever you can't, we can teach you." Miz Corliss put her tit beside the Doe's tat, her face screwed in a *what-you-got-to-say-about-that* look.

That tickle the boy's funny bone. And the doorway's. And who could tell what woulda happened next, being I couldn't hear no whisperin' wind in that rec room with its barred windows locking out the day and locking in prowling lions. A good thing the nappy-head chile at the end of Miz Reesa's line got fed up and posted up in front of her, again, lips balled up and mouth poked out, like he done had just bout enough of the foolishness this older boy talking, holding up his show and looking at Miz Reesa too long, his Miz Reesa.

"Leave her 'lone," he said, growling low in his throat, voice a fist. A little one, but a fist all the same. He raise his hands and ball them to match his lips and stick out his bird chest. "Get out! Go away!"

Big Boy sell the baby a wolf ticket then. Scream, "What you say, squirt? Huh? Huh?" And make a swinging move like he might body-slam the chile.

That's when Miz Reesa snatch the boy behind her and press him close to her leg.

"Nobody's afraid of you. Not even this child. So go pick on somebody more your size and mentality, bully." Then she shoot Big Boy the meanest look, but it only left a grin on his ole hungry mouth.

That boy bent double, laughing so hard it probably hurt. I couldn't wait another minute, though; that laugh bound to turn ugly. Somebody get popped, I rather it be me instead of the chillen or our company, so I'm in Big Boy's face, fussing and easing his funky self backward toward his peanut gallery; they brows knit, wondering, I reckon, why Big Boy still quiet. Nobody there to stop him, he wanna act. Big Boy know this, too, and might've been ready when Short Dog walk in.

"Waz up, my dawgs?' he greet the basketball boys. "Where's the brawl? Who ya'll playin'?"

Mookey pulling on his hand, waving and shouting, "Hi Miz Free!" Them boys watch her wave and smile and recognize they fun over. They trickle backward, and Short Dog, scanning faces, his search ending with mine, smiling, sly as anybody's fox, want to know, "Hey Miz Too-Sweet, Mama say you gone keep Mookey today?"

Mookey waving at me now. And I'm waving and nodding.

Big Boy stop, read Miz Reesa's face, hair, body, clothes. Promise, "Next time ya'll come...I'ma read to you. All right?"

She roll her eyes, say, "Anything's possible."

Then Mookey fly to Free like his feet fit a limb, while his brother notice the food.

"That's all left?"

"If you read for it." Miz Free's voice is sweeter than the donuts.

"A paragraph, a page okay?"

She give him a thumb's up, and he pimp to the book table, followed by another boy. Big Boy and the others outdone, bounce angry balls down the hall.

The last box packed in her trunk and me in the front seat beside Miz Free, feeling like a hundred-dollar bill in a Mercedes, a car I ain't never examined up close, let alone sat in, Miz Reesa and Miz Corliss chatting with Mookey in the back---us wave to the handful of chillen left in front of the community center and ride back to 55 Lovejoy. A note on the kitchen table say Will at Preacher's. The 'partment stuffy, I open a few windows and invite the gals to come in, rest for a spell. We sit out in the backyard where it's cool, the trees spreading shade we can talk in. Listen, if nothing else, to Mookey chatter about first one thing, then another.

But that ole afternoon wind has a mind of its own, swirling gently round me, stroking and fingering the loose strands of gray peeking out from under my wig hat.

"A lap sits no better than how you take it" blow by my ears as Miz Reesa and Miz Corliss haul kitchen chairs to the backyard and before I see if they want me to cook a early dinner, Miz Free is already putting in a request for a story she and them gals can hold so I sit down and do what I know to do: listen and obey. And free my mind and talk.

Curtis Wilkes used to sit up 'side my daddy, near the fire, most every night God send, and smoke them lil tiny cigars. Sometimes he'd bring a tin of Red Man chewing tobacco to please my daddy, that is, if he wanted to stay longer than the customary hour after my granny served dinner and I washed dishes.

That's how it was with Curtis Wilkes.

Conversation passed back and forth 'tween him and daddy easy, like creek water in the summer when ain't no mess round to stir its bottom, sending mud every which a way, riling water moccasins and trouble. "Mister Sylvester, how the crops in the back? Time for plowing, I'm gone come bring my cousins from up round Tallassee, and we gone lend you a hand, get the job done in half the time." Course my daddy smiling all over hisself, pushed back in his Lazy Boy like Curtis Wilkes is God and nobody but Him and Curtis know it. Don't know which was brighter...the roaring fireplace or Curtis wide, handsome, shoe-leather black face, all that big talk flowing from his mouth.

By the time he figured out how he gone get the Studebaker rusting on the edge of the garden running again and where he can find paint cheaper than Sears catalog sell, that Curtis done started swooning my granny. "Miz Sinclair, this house be real pretty emerald green. Be a show to the world the quality of folks live here, your house be seen five miles coming or going. And I know you been talking bout tending a flower garden to rival Janie Mae

Whitlow's for a while now. Well, my oldest sister's middle gal work in Auburn, at one of them prominent whitefolks flower shops, and she gone save me the nicest selection of every kinda flower you can name, just as soon as they come in. I told my niece, I said, "Loreena, honey, Miz Sinclair is the sweetest soul under Alabama sun, can hear the future, too, and I'm certain she going to hear something wonderful bout a giving soul like you, so make Uncle Curtis happy and take care of the good sister." Wasn't nothing after a while...all the promises stored in our living room...so many my granny or Grandpa Hood should've heard how empty they was...except they couldn't hear a word bout theyselves or their folks. My granny nem went to leaving me home, with him, so's he could court me, being he had done got daddy's permission to marry me---I give him my hand.

That's how I come to sit in our living room, on Curtis Wilkes' lap. And it sit good, slap-somebody good, mind you, better than any lap I could imagine, considering I ain't never sat in a man's lap till then.

At fifteen, I was in hog heaven.

Here was a grown man, paying me attention, filling my nose with his cologne, thumping my body with his heartbeat. Sitting on his lap, I learned a man made different from a gal, learned a man could be compared to a fair ride, cause every time Curtis Wilkes, who had to be close to thirty at the time, strapped his arms round me---and I always been a thick gal, built like a woman, let my granny tell it...all soft and firm and ripe---and pressed me deeper into his lap, striking a hard up-and-down rhythm, a rolling grind, a bump-bumpty-bump motion, I be wet, soaked in my sweat and his at the ride's end. Curtis winded, panting, "Lil Mama, you marry me and come to my house; you can sit in this lap all day. This be your lap and your private ride. You be the envy of every gal this side of Lochapoka."

And I was. For six years.

During those years, some sad, some happy, most lonely, I grew from a gal to a woman, who never once lay in the same bed with her husband. Never slept in the same room. Every relation we had happened on his lap, which, when I think on it now, and laugh, our two chillen was lap babies in the true sense of the word. Those years I spent on that man's lap got to feeling like what it must feel like to be a inmate in the Lochapoka jail. Instead of getting passed food and water through the hole in the door, I got passed everything I needed to know to make Curtis Wilkes happy. He ride me, then get to whispering. Making me pregnant with what it took to be the prefect Wilkes wife. I can still hear his words, if I sit quiet, and don't let no wind in a shut room. The spill simple, went like this: "Stay outta my business, hand me every receipt for every dime I give you, never let me catch you in my room, keep these chillen and house spotless, and don't let me hear bout you in no man's face."

My twenty-first birthday, bout the time I got fed up with Curtis Wilkes' lap and rules, I started hearing the same things, eye-poppin' things, every time I walked outdoors or heisted a window.

"A lap sits no better than how you take it" was one; the others came in bits and pieces, bout my friend Janie Mae Whitlow, who was a class ahead of me in grade school. That wind, rain or shine, for days, worried me, hanging round my shoulders like fur, sweating to be told. But I dragged my feet, same as Grandpa Hood, when he heard things that wet his cheeks at dawn. The only difference, Janie Mae didn't know what I knowed to walk me down, make me tell. At least, until she flat pulled up in my yard one Saturday, as I'm sweeping the sand and feeling blessed for another day.

"Howdy, Sweet, long time no see." She big, with her fifth, I think. Shift dress tight, showing she yet hanging on to a womanly shape.

"Hey, Janie Mae. Life amazing, ain't it?"

"Could be, if ya life in order." She got her weight on one foot, then the other, hands anchoring her back. "Ain't come to stand long and I can see you busy and you can see I'm big. Us two busy women."

I looked up the road. The day was crystal clear---my thoughts wasn't.

"Look. I ain't never made time for bull crap, and I ain't going to make time for it now. What you got to tell me, to set my life in order? Sweet, I sense you done heard something bout me so spit it out."

Her matter of fact manner said she could take whatever she got dished. I liked that bout her, and it helped me serve her a familiar pot of beans.

"Your common-law husband holding court with every woman who turn his head, both of them...," I say, and the sigh she sighed told me she anticipated as much. "Your half-sister baby, due the same time yours, your baby twin." She looking sideswiped now. Hand go to the bottom of her belly, like the baby riding her bladder stomping. Like maybe she thinking bout whopping ass, since she and half-sister live on the same road.

The telling done, Janie Mae thanked me

politely, got back in her car, and down the road she go. Little did I know, we done helped one another. She took my husband, who I felt, had been sniffing under her hem for months, and she left me a helping of her strength, her quiet resolve. So the day he come back for his things, Curtis Wilkes met my daddy's snub-nosed shotgun in the front window.

"I give away everything in your old room, Mr. Wilkes." I got off his lap in my mind and told him, "If you got a problem with it, take it up with a lawyer, who you gone need anyway, being I already filed for divorce. Word on the wind, your lap got to grow some to be big enough for Janie Mae and her babies, and your wallet got to expand some for my two and who-send-ever else you fathered. So kindly clear my yard. Oh, and in case you ain't heard, Janie Mae's ex in the hospital with food poisonin'. Don't look too favorable for the chap, either. I was you...," I say, cocking the gun, "I'd learn to sleep with one eye cracked."

Then outside of his chile support, he died to me that day, and I been heedful of how a lap sits ever since.

Chapter 12

Pinky Taylor knew she ought to call home.

But first she had to roll Lewis Reynolds' bulk, ten times more burdensome when he was tanked, off her and search for her underwear and baby-doll dress she'd worn clubbing last night. If only she had the energy, a lazy mood heavy on her. Damnit! She'd forgotten to get up in the middle of the night and retire on the sofa. As lumpy as that old thing was, it outdid being mauled by an over-sized octopus. Whenever she forgot and awoke beside him, she got up aching.

Had half a mind to shove one bulging tentacle off her chest, where it pent her breasts flat. *God knows they're flat enough already.* She grinned inwardly at her flat, lemony-colored boobs swelling somewhat fuller where they rested against her upper abdomen. Couldn't hold a pencil again if her life depended on it. For a second, Pinky recalled the contests she and her teenage girlfriends used to have, vying to discover whose breasts were the highest, and the fullest. Looking back, she wondered if they'd really appreciated those shotgun titties, titties she, for one, would give a gold guinea to have again.

Lately, she scooped her breasts into her palms and strained to see them as sexually appealing, noticing their downward slope after Mookey. With Clemmy and Short Dog, they'd been undaunted. Rode her chest higher than the sun at high noon in those old Western movies. Maybe, she mused, when you're fourteen and sixteen and having babies, your body had trauma enough to undergo without worrying about dropping something as insignificant as little ole teats.

Lewis snored. In repositioning himself, one thigh rose unexpectedly, knocking the wind out of her. "That's it," she said, groaning. No longer caring how he cussed if she disturbed his slumber. If she didn't do *anything* outside of calling her kids, she had to do *something* that required her to get off her back, so she could get the circulation going in her listless body. Her bones hollered whenever she remained in bed past eight, weekend or workday.

"Lewis, get your leg off me, please. You know I got kids to check on. Can't help it you rarely check in with your other rug rats," she said, dispelling a disgusted breath, "and mine neither for that matter." She dug her heels in the rumpled sheets, scooting her body upwards, her dark pubic hair pulling against Lewis' knee.

"Ouch! Doggone it; I swear sleeping with your ass is pure-D hell. See, that's why I don't come over here as often as you be wanting me to. You get me over here and act like your brains seeped outta your ears with the wax. Get off me, man!"

This time she'd had enough. And he could do what he felt necessary, because she damn well was gonna get her butt up and get the hell back to 58 Lovejoy. She contended with the sleeping brother until she freed herself and tumbled out of the bed, she and a box of leftover pizza hitting the hardwood with a thud.

"Dog, Pinky, what the hell you doing?" Lewis shifted his body for the hundredth time, peeved she'd disturbed his sleep. "It ain't even noon yet. You keeping up ruckus, in bed talking to yourself like a crazy woman. And I heard that shit you complaining about---I don't make time for my kids and all." He yawned. "I got you to see about Mookey, and those other broads better keep keen eyes on my others." He shook his head."Women."

Not bothering to look up, Pinky tossed greasy slices of pizza into the Pizza Hut box and got to her feet and strolled into the kitchenette like he was talking to himself.

"By the way, has that Miz Free chick brought her fancy tail back over there, razzle-dazzling my son with her books and shit? What you know about her?" He sat up, waiting on Pinky to respond. "What kind of mother is you? For all you know, the heifer and my son could be on the back of a milk cartoon right now."

"What you mumbling about, fool?" She filled a garbage bag with excess trash from an overflowing container and reentered the bedroom.

"I got your fool, boo. You don't know shit about that bitch outside of the fact she drive a Mercedes and you don't know if it's really hers. Just gulliblc."

"You don't buy your son books. Hell, don't much visit the chile, so how you gone talk? My son is a handsome, likeable person; any woman in her right mind is slain by his charm."

Lewis looked at her and scratched his lower back. "Uh…like his ole man," he threw at her and laughed. "C'mon and rub my back."

Pinky ignored the request, countering, "I don't want Mookey growing up, making babies like they're trophies to prove he's a man. I'm raising him to be a man who loves and respects himself and others, especially women. Then, again, you wouldn't know anything about that kinda man, now, would you?"

"Nor would Short Dog." *That ought to hold her*. Lewis was good and pissed with her saltiness this morning, and after they'd had a crazy mad night of dancing and drinking and sexing. Shit, a woman could spoil a brother's good time without even trying. Here she was, falling her butt out of bed, and blaming him. Shucks, he hadn't *really* begged her to spend the night. She knew he had four other beds to fall into; four other complete and separate households in which he was a welcomed daddy.

The woman had better recognize. Nobody told her stubborn yella ass to get pregnant with Mookey, after nine years of being baby-free, although he'd kill anyone who dared harm a curl on his son's head. She knew what time it was though. Knew he'd already experienced the new-pappy syndrome, and knew it had lost its luster and lights.

"Bring me some water." His tone was conciliatory at the whim of his belly.

She stood in the doorway, the Sunday morning brightness from the room's windows setting her nudity aglow. A pout on her lips. "What's wrong now?" he asked. "And get your naked butt outta that window. Ain't you got no shame?"

Pinky sneered and crossed her arms, pressing them against her flat, stripped, taut belly. "Ain't you one to throw stones? Don't see you bucking to pull that sheet over your baby's breath."

Lewis chuckled and rose on one elbow. "C'mere. Bring all that sweetness on over here, girlfriend. Got some excess flava to whisper in your ear." He raked his fingers through the thick bushy hair, curly and dark, that grew on his broad chest.

Pinky just stared, then sighed. The brother was egotistical, carrying on like he hauled around a gold dick. But she had to give it to him, though…most times he had her feeling like she had a gold coochie. No. She couldn't discount that, although he could piss her off at the drop of a hat. Yet his sex was so good, she'd gotten hooked on fucking him and, although she'd thought her baby-making days behind her—at the prime age of twenty-five— after nine years of being without one, somehow she didn't find it the end of the world when she'd awoken one morning, four years ago, to a queasiness in her middle that spelled two things: another baby and an unfulfilled promise.

She had given her dad, as solemn a pledge as a sixteen-year-old could; she wouldn't bring another soul into the world until she was an adult. And it suited her fine not to recall he'd said "married adult."

"Make up your mind. You want something to drink or you want to screw?" The minute she said the words, the room seemed to close in on her. The poster on the left-hand wall displaying a bare-breasted Janet Jackson, somebody's hands concealing her charms. Another of Chante' Moore. To her left, a closet. In a corner, beside a window, a cheap chest of drawers. Pictures of Lewis' children gracing its top. Over the bed hung two paintings of robust sistahs, naked as she was now, posed as if they were freeze-framed in the midst of a fertility dance. Pinky laughed inside. Pictures of fertile women were the last things a man like Lewis Reynolds needed over his bed. An altogether colorless room, she mused, outside of the beautiful women—of which she was not one—

adorning his walls. In a flash, she compared Lewis' apartment with the tastefulness of Javan's house, the otherworld mystery of Omar's crib, and the quiet comfort of her father's home. Javan and Omar. Her other babies' daddies. Clemmy and Short Dog's.

She couldn't help but ponder why she allowed this one, Lewis, to take so much of her time, then seeing the fire flame in the man's light-brown eyes, she remembered and moved obediently toward his beckoning finger.

Life could wait. For a few more hours, at least, she reasoned. Short Dog knew better than to leave his little brother, and if he did, he had sense enough to walk him down to Miz Too-Sweet and Mr. Will's apartment. At fourteen, he still acted like he wasn't wrapped too tight. Needed Omar's influence, she knew, but what could she do when she and Omar weren't civil long enough to share a meal or a rump in the sheets, him badgering her about age and marriage. Hell, she knew she had embraced the big 3-0 last April, and was a skip and a hop away from 31 in another week. She didn't want him reminding her twenty-four-seven. When she got ready to change her status, she'd call the shots. Not some man with whom she shared a child.

But she didn't want to think about that now, not with Lewis twirling his hardness, stirring a mushy desire between her legs, making her nipples erect. At the moment, her coochie hummed. Longed to sing out loud. Harmonize. Lewis Reynolds could be dubbed a whole heap of things, but there was one thing for sure he wasn't: a minute man.

Pinky lay down beside the man and draped one leg over his butt and promised herself she'd call home, anew, the very next time she was on her feet.

Chapter 13

Rain fell in a torrential, afternoon downpour, pelting the windows and forming puddles in Free's front lawn. Thunder boomed in magnificent crescendos, and then rolled into low, menacing rumbles.

She wondered how many members of the *Daughters of Isis Book Club* would venture out on such a stormy Saturday. She wouldn't have abandoned the comfort of the bookstore to attend a book club meeting at another member's home, what with poor visibility, and an increased probability of accidents and low attendance. She sighed. Retreated to the kitchen to peep at the refreshments. The same, outside of the sweat tracking the glass pitchers of lemonade. She stole a skirting gaze at the clock, not wanting to see two. Perfect. Just now twelve fifteen. Members had more time to sit out the rain before hitting the roadways, while she made herself dizzy, pacing.

In the living room she lay on the black leather sofa. The television droned. Half listening, Free flipped from station to station before slipping into a light nap. A half hour later, the doorbell jarred her awake. Rhonda and her friend, Gail Johnson, huddled on the porch, stomping their shoes on the welcome mat.

"Hey, Big Sis," Rhonda said. "Thought we weren't coming, huh?"

Free hugged and kissed both women on the cheek.

"Oh mercy!" She inhaled the damp fresh

wind. "Your arrival brought a stick-up to the rain, which says ya'll good for something." The women laughed, and Free hung their light wraps in the foyer closet. "C'mon in, ladies."

Rhonda plopped into a yawning love seat near the window. Gail followed her nose to the kitchen. "Smells like potential in here." One manicured finger sampled the freshness of a powdered donut.

"What we touch…we eat, Miss Ma'am."

"Which I have every intention of doing, thank you," Gail called into the living room, stuffing the treat into her mouth. "What's on the boob tube?"

They watched the ending of a Lifetime special in a sisterly silence.

Within the hour, members began arriving; the appearance of each bringing a further clearing of the skies, Free's lawns refreshing and lush under the second-floor windows. When most were present— including newcomers, the club's count fourteen, Frenonia jokingly invited everyone, except Gail, who was already drinking, to partake of the beverages before the April discussion commenced. Most of the members hadn't come empty-handed, a buffet stretching the length of Free's counters and ending on the serving trays from her Techwood reading program.

"Alright, ladies," Free said, "with a show of hands, how many read E. Lynn Harris' **Invisible Life**?" Over half the hands in the room shot up. "Not bad. Any objections to discussing it before starting **Just As I Am**?"

A stout woman in her twenties tossed her head. "I didn't read it so I don't prefer to hear it discussed."

Reesa cut Corliss a slit eye, and her girl bum-rushed the invitation. "Why *not* discuss it? It's the beginning of the brother's story, revealing what went down in Raymond Tyler's life, explaining why he'd been relegated to dreaming about this beautiful place called Perfect. It also elucidates the unexpected lesson he learned during his senior year in college. Not only that, it helps us to better appreciate the characters, when we read background that makes what's to come clear. I say we discuss it." She shot Free a glaring thunderbolt. "What do you say, Madam Hostess?"

A slow smile crossed Free's face. Willie Mae had never been a favorite with her, and she admired the way Corliss had presented her rebuttal. Though she'd known the girl a short while, Free had enjoyed her participation in the "Free Your Mind: Read" program.

"So glad you could join us," she welcomed, then reverted her attention to the group. "Ladies, this is Corliss Hall, Reesa's classmate. I think she raises a sensible point. Understanding Harris' first novel makes our selection more enjoyable and may spark interest in others to go back and read it. Thus…all for discussing **Life**?" She raised her right hand and counted ten more. "Cool. Then it's **Life**, too." She bowed to Corliss. "Would you like to continue?"

The girl nodded. "I like Harris' style. It's conversational, provocative. He had me from page one, with that intriguing letter from Nicole Springer, the same girl, you'll remember, who offers Ray 'unspeakable hope' at the end of the story."

Rhonda licked her lips. "That's what I loved about the story: the romance at the core of both books. I do *not* waste time reading those formula romances. Ray may be different, but he *loves* the women in his life and of---"

"Please," Lisa, a lean leggy sip of vodka, interrupted. "Then how do you account for the way he dogs Sela and his beloved Nicole? Presenting himself as a straight man, knowing full well he's gay."

"Excuse me," Rhonda checked her, "but had you let me *finish* you'd have heard me continue, Of course he doesn't come out and tell them who he is. What woman would understand that---her man wanting to kick it with other men? I meant that he cares for Sela, tries to protect her, keep conflict out of her face. And *that* love isn't counterfeit."

Lisa shook her head. "The brother lied...to himself...to her, period. And that, my sister, is phony. When you conceal truth, you birth a lie."

"Yeeaah," Willie Mae and a round-faced woman sitting near Lisa chorused.

"Brothers like that," Willie Mae said, "are, as we all know, loaded pistols that ought to be registered. They be dealing with you, close-lipped, and exposing you to AIDS and all kinda stuff. Ought to be a law that protects the deceived woman and lets her nail his ass."

She sat back in her chair, arms crossed over her soft belly in a self-righteous smugness.

"Humph, he's as bad as Basil marrying Dyanna."

"Tell her about it," Willie Mae's round-faced friend, Melissa, piped up. "Raymond has sex with Sela before her wedding, licking her toes and carrying on all freaky and everything; I don't remember him warning her who he'd been with."

She yoked her neck and peered at Rhonda. "Do you?"

Changing the slant of the conversation, Rhonda broached the subject of the portrayal of Ray's family. How warm and close-knit they were. She commented on how she enjoyed reading about Mrs. Tyler being a third-grade teacher, who adored her students, noting how Harris made Sela a teacher and Kelvin a high-school coach. When she mentioned Kelvin Ellis, another Spelman girl accompanying Reesa and Corliss exploded. "Honey, that brother would have been mine, he was some kinda fine. But I'd have read his tarot cards coming and going. He wouldn't have slipped that bisexual rap by this homegirl. I'd have converted, exorcised, transformed, and blessed that brother, ya'll hear me!"

A few women laughed. Corliss shifted in her seat to stare into her friend's spirited face.

"Hold up, Freda. A bisexual man got rhythms you can read? Get serious. You can barely read the straight guys we deal with. But since you got an inside line on bisexual men, shed some light."

"Well…they still got a sweet streak, a way of talking that lets me know what the real deal is." She peeped at others for support. "Y'all know. It's a man's look, his walk."

Corliss dismissed the flimsy justification. "A close reading of Ray, Kelvin, Quinn and Basil Henderson shatters that. Fine, hard, sexy—they don't sound musical, look soft, nor act feminine. Hellooo!" She snapped her fingers upward. "Your heels would've been cooling in their faces, too. Just like Sela, Candace, JJ, and Miss Thang, Sister Diva."

"I heard *that*," Gail remarked, appreciating a

wisecrack when she heard one.

"My heart went out to Candace," Reesa spoke up. "Couldn't decide if she contracts AIDS from Kelvin or the guy she dates when she attends Spellman...the Morris Brown brother, who died with the disease."

Gail swallowed the last of her diet Sprite. "My guess, it's the Morris Brown brother, since Kelvin seems to practice safe sex and we never see him sickly."

"Yeah," seconded a skinny girl with her back to one wall, her legs crossed. "Maybe Harris is indirectly saying that just because Kelvin is bisexual doesn't mean he gives his wife AIDS, that heterosexual partners should be cautious, also."

Free agreed. "I like it that we're mixing details from both novels. So...who is your favorite character? How about you...uh---" she directed her inquiry to a tall woman comfortable in her Amazonian proportions, her face more shrewd than pretty, the green eyes large and expressive. Lips full and painted a soft bronze. She sported a low-cut, shiny, light-brown fade.

"I'm Nzinga Edwards, Gail's cousin." The voice came distinctive, musical and strong, overflowing with magnetism. "My favorite character—undisputed—is Raymond's friend, Kyle," she articulated slowly. "He's real, hides nothing, hurts no one, and faces up to what life hands him, while yet being positive. He teaches the others, gay and straight, how to be more accepting to the plight of the gay community." She paused, feeling clangorous thoughts filling the room. "I adore the way he characterizes bisexual men, as 'confused kids,' at the same time loving the most perplexed gay man of all, his beloved Ray. Kyle accepts himself for what he is, a gay man, not a claustrophobic like Kelvin, Quinn and Basil. Frankly, he lives truth. My favorite Kyle quote: 'God only gets mad at us when we come down here and pretend to be something we're not. That really pissed Him off.'"

Sharmayne dangled from this Nzinga's eloquent speech. Got velcroed to her lips. For the better part of an hour her dark eyes had focused on each speaker, yet they'd persisted on returning to this handsome woman, to perceive something she missed in the last observation. If she scrutinized any harder, the woman's large cat eyes would arrest hers again, the way they'd done minutes ago, and cause her gaze to slide downward, to her lap, where it marshaled the courage to rise and refocus on the contemplative book club. The strangest thing, it dawned on her she could stare at this woman forever and never weary of her captivating presence or her enigmatic voice.

Wanda Lynn, a short, spectacled woman, stuck in the Seventies, pursed her lips.

"Kyle is the most disgusting sissy, no, flaming faggot, in both novels. At least the other dudes had the shame to hide that filth. Hell, not only did Kyle not have any decency, and surely not before his mother—poor Peaches, messing around and getting pregnant by that bum, J.D.—Kyle makes me ill with the stupid shit he spouts," Wanda Lynn said, short of breath. "'Miss Everything and the Queen Bureau garbage and calling folks 'Bitches.' Homosexuality pisses God off, not that sacrilegious bullshit Kyle talks. My Bible says, 'If a man lies with his own kind, he should be put to death,' which is what we should do to all those weirdoes…every last one of them," she sermonized. "Nine times out of ten, they're child molesters and rapists anyway. We ought to line them up against a wall and hurl stones."

Free couldn't believe what she'd just heard, although she wondered who would broach the *homosexuality is religiously wrong* argument. She conjectured it would come from Willie Mae, the preacher's wife, not Wanda Lynn.

"I'm against that line of reasoning," Free said. "It's sick and unsupported. Gays are no different from you or me, except for sexual preference." She didn't mean to look at Sharmayne, but somehow, she appeared in her range of vision. "They should be free to lead happy, healthy, wholesome lives, just like you. Live and let live." Her nostrils flared and she took a deep breath. "There is a way to say everything, Wanda Lynn. And you might have omitted the profanity."

Wanda Lynn sat up in her chair.

"Oh bump that shit! Free, you walking the fence, that's what you doing. Either you for or you against the thing. No gray area on this issue in my eyes."

"I'm not surprised, and…I'm for a person's right to be true to himself."

"Then you're for freaks."

"So be it." Free almost spat on her, but the woman crossed her legs and looked away as though she were through with it. Though Free wasn't. "We'd do well to remember that Jesus also said, 'He that is without sin, cast the first stone.'" She paused. "Anybody to change the subject?"

"I will," Deandra, a petite, thirty-something

Daughter of Isis from its inception, spoke up. "But I have an observation. Our discussion has centered on the novel's men. But what of the sisters? It's interesting that Delaney is a lesbian, who is turned on to women by a boyfriend, who asks her to join him with another girl."

Luxuriating in the controversy, Gail dived back in the foray. "Yeah, Mr. Kyle, who has the dibs on everyone, doesn't read Delaney close. Her lover's visit blows him and everybody else away."

"Uh…huh," Deandra concurred. "That part's brief, as if Harris might not have known much about lesbians, me not sensing which woman was butch or fem."

What did these women know about lesbian stereotypical roles? Nzinga frowned and started to say so, but desisted. Studying the group, she spied the petite, cocoa-sweet woman's eyes awaiting hers, for the umpteenth time. Desire stirred, pricked her with a yearning to hear the sound of the mute woman's voice and to know her name.

"All the women are twins," Nzinga offered. "Sela and Nicole; JJ and Sherrod."

Rhonda considered her comment, brows drawn. "Uh huh. The lesbians are pretty, blowing the cover off Raymond's perception of dykes."

"Lesbians," Nzinga corrected from the sofa, sandwiched between Gail and Lisa.

"Yes, ma'am, lesbians. Sela and Nicole shine as gorgeous, pony-tailed divas, but JJ and Sherrod hit me as decent castoffs Raymond didn't care to write home about."

Gail tapped her chin with an index finger and chuckled.

"So where does that place the lady lawyer, Gilliam?" Reesa asked.

Corliss looked up. "In the same boat, on a higher deck than JJ and Sherrod."

"Checkmate," Reesa assented, laughing. "Thank you."

"What's your change of subject?" Free refocused on Deandra.

"Thank you. I realize it's getting close to chow time, but I wanted to know who thought what about the love scenes. Personally, my favorite is the scene with Basil and Raymond in the pool with those NFL bodies glistening and sexy."

"Oh, goodness! Jared making love with Nicole did the dang thang for me," Wanda Lynn joined in. "I can see myself rocking Homeboy now." She pumped her arms up and down and scooted her behind back and forth in her chair. "Lord, have mercy!"

Free bit her bottom lip, Wanda Lynn's comment inundating her with thoughts of J.T., whom she missed with a deep-down, hungry-for-his-touch longing. She wondered what he was doing on this wet Saturday...wondered if she crossed his mind...wondered if she yet co-starred in his dreams. She struggled to recall Harris' love scenes, her own sizzling memories too real to be ignored. Around her, women gushed, drenched in a sexual downpour from the novel's lovemaking episodes.

Sharmayne listened, yesterday quiet. She hoped she'd gotten away with experiencing one of Free's beloved book club meetings without offering herself up to praise or criticism. But a sudden tingling throughout her body knew otherwise.

"We've heard from everybody---good, bad, and indifferent—except for you," the Amazon outed her, that green gaze sinking into Sharmayne, the statement an unwavering question.

All eyes converged on her, propelling her into the center of the room.

"H-h-hello. I'm Sharmayne Cooper-Naylor." She arm-wrestled the urge to whisper and sought Free's smile; buoyed, her attention pirouetted to Nzinga's smile.

"I'm Free's guest, and this is my first book club meeting. My favorite love scene stars Raymond and Kyle in the opening of **Invisible Life**, because it's Ray's bisexual awakening. I love what Trent Walters and Raymond share at the close of **Just As I Am**. In his angst to find someone, Raymond embraces a lover who longs for the same thing he does: a relationship based on mutual love and respect. At the end of the day, isn't that what we all desire?"

Sharmayne basked in Nzinga's warmth, the intent expression on her gorgeous face frightening and thrilling, leaving Sharmayne vulnerable to falling, to toppling into the woman's spirit, arms, heart, words, life---a terrifying plummet. But she wasn't fighting. Wasn't afraid. She'd prayed for this moment.

"Yes," Nzinga said after a while. "And thank you." Her stare winged to the soft-spoken sister's small feet, where she didn't require words to know her larger ones would be at home there, and the Universe willing, the two would walk as one.

Chapter 14

"I'm here to get my woman back."

He lay on a relaxing cocoa-hued couch, hands deep in the pockets of his sweat jacket. From across the room he gazed out at a spectacular view of the Atlanta skyline from his therapist's tenth-floor, Piedmont Street office. Since he'd decided to get therapy, following his chef buddy Abdul Parks' advice, J.T. couldn't stop second-guessing himself. Kept hearing his paternal grandfather's words: "A woman got her place. It just ain't in God's or man's business." He knew it was crazy but he couldn't stop the words from skating through his brain and, lately, they skated with abandon.

"Women have landed more than a few men on this couch, Mr. Thomas."

"Yeah…but she ought to be here to get me back. She's the problem."

Dr. Anita Wallace sat nearby, legs crossed, white coat opened. She scribbled on a lined legal pad. "Is that true?"

J.T. clinched his teeth not to ask, What the hell question is that?

"Why else would I be here?"

"You'll answer that sooner than later. Meanwhile, tell me about your friend."

"She's hard-headed, opinionated, and demanding. Never listens to anything outside of her outlook on the world, which is gospel. Knows nothing about bending, she's so unyielding, so aggressive, at times, she makes me serial. When we argue, she pushes my buttons, and sometimes I'm seconds away from wanting to pop her. And she's a fighter. Cursing like a hooker with a gutter mouth. Bet her bookstore customers haven't witnessed that side of her."

"You ever listen to her advice?"

"Do I ever give her reason to check me?"

The smooth lake of Dr. Wallace's face rippled, then calmed. "Go on."

"Thinks she's superwoman. I'm like, 'Girl, stop closing the business at night, alone. You ain't God.' Think she listens? No, ma'am. But somebody could be casing her, studying her habits. Ain't nothing for a thug to wait in that freaking parking lot in front of her Spring Street business and bust her in the damn head for a dollar and fifty cents. That happened, hell, I'd pack my bags. Just lock my damn self up. That woman is my heart, and I can't stand to see her hurt."

"Oh but you must. And often, from what you just said."

Silence and the air conditioner raged. To hush them, J.T. said, "That's different. When I give her advice, it's not meant to be hurtful."

"Do you speak this advice in a lov---"

"Yes!"

Dr. Wallace repeated the question in the same calm tone. Her gaze buttonholed her new client, who, stilled in a moment of peace, shook his head no. She made note of his resentment.

"She doesn't address me with love when we fight. That heifer's mean. Especially when she's hot under the collar." J.T. took a cleansing breath. "I'm pissed when she shuts me down. Her not listening makes me belligerent. I'm her man. I know what's best for my woman."

"If she listened, how else would you advise her?"

Easy enough question. J.T. warmed up, hands snaking out of his pockets, arms folding his chest. His eyes crept away from the skyline and began swallowing the good doctor from her expensive black pumps, refined slacks, to the elegant white blouse under the jacket, a diamond butterfly at her throat and its match in her ears under a tapered chic cut.

"She needs to stop dressing like a teenager or a billboard for hollering men. Quit spending so much time with her girlfriend, who doesn't appreciate her husband. Next thing I know, she'll be talking against marriage---I mean, it's not like she sees it in a positive light. Her mother never married the man who helped raise her and her sister, and if that doesn't kill the dog, her sister's marriage wobbles along on three wheels and a busted dream. Sometimes I can only imagine what she thinks of me and other men in her private thoughts."

"And…is that it, Mr. Thomas?"

Silent, he studied his hands, scraped the bottom of his memory, and scratched.

"She needs to be mindful of driving that damn Mercedes of hers through the colorful parts of this town, pretending car jackings never happen. All of us don't live in the pages of the books she sells, where happy endings thrive. I could go hoarse saying it and she wouldn't blink but she's got to stay out of---damnit---Techwood Homes, calling herself befriending those people for the hell of it and helping them read. Them folks don't want to read unless it's to read how to swindle, beat, kill, steal, mug, and jack."

Dr. Wallace smiled and drummed her pencil's eraser on the pad.

"What attracted you to this interesting woman in the first place?"

"She's beautiful, inside and out. Loved her from the moment I glanced into her car in heavy, go-home traffic on I-20 five years ago. Drove up beside her and engaged her in conversation and heard that musical laughter, that magical voice, saw that showstopper face and the rest was history. She's big-hearted to a fault. Adventurous. Fearless in the darkest night. Loves her family, most anybody who enters her world and all children. She's health conscious and doesn't see life in terms of loss, always gain."

He censored the next thought then spoke his mind. "She's a dynamic lover, the best I've ever had. She craves my cooking. Laughs at my jokes and she aches for a good challenge, can roll with the heavyweights, while screaming, 'I don't want no trouble!' J.T. chuckled. "I love her." He stretched his arms. "Her name's Free."

Dr. Wallace pursed her lips and stared at the smile in J.T.'s eyes. "You'd have to love a woman named Free. Mr. Thomas---"

"Please call me J.T."

The therapist smiled, nodded, and cleared her throat. "Tell me, J.T., how you'd feel if you released every judgment you ever voiced about Free?"

"Well...I...err." He looked at the unblinking doctor. "Sensational."

"Now think back. Who in your formative years taught you to fear women?"

J.T. hung his head, said, "My grandfather," and repeated the old man's words.

"How would you feel if you buried your grandfather's advice instead of your love for this woman whom you are pushing away in your obsession to control her?"

"Relieved." The word was a mint on his tongue.

"So, J.T., why are you here?"

He was quiet for an eternity before he spoke. "I'm here to learn to love me, Dr. Wallace. To rediscover who I am and get that man back."

"And when you do, all else will follow."

Chapter 15

It come in with the birdsongs under the cracked bedroom window.

Had to. Didn't take it to bed with me, did, I'da told Will. See what he had to say bout it. Them words come soft like summer cream and baby skin and Will's breathing in the middle of the night. On a breeze only April can whisper, with her soft ways and light showers, it snuggled me and invited me to snuggle up under Will so it could slip in 'tween us, like our younguns used to sleep. I listened. Then I went back to sleep, hugging Will and the message.

At the start of the evening, as I'm rinsing dinner dishes, I take in a line of cars parked up and down Lovejoy. That Pinky Taylor the only woman I know who got more men in her life, at one time, than I'd ever want to deal with, after dealing with them others through the years and now Will Sinclair.

Kitchen clean, I step outside to dry my hands and see what else God has to see in a picture-perfect evening. Saturday sun hanging low and pretty in the sky with rows of clouds putting me in the mind of seeded Alabama cotton. "White, cloud filters, they the Almighty's way of stopping man's mess and smog from entering heaven." That's how my granny used to say it. Then rap music jiggle my mind and the evening breeze. Up the street, a car parks on the sidewalk. Pinky's oldest baby's daddy. Clemmy's father, Javan Reed. He never sits that car close to them others.

Sure enough, here they come. Clemmy's

moving graceful, grinning out of Pinky's face, its gingerbread color her daddy's. She in the get-up gals wear nowadays: baggy army pants, black bra-like top underneath some over-size vest, black baseball cap pulled low over long, stick-straight hair and, on her feet, boots. The kind soldiers wear.

I wave and head to the living room. "You going over?" I ask Will, a cigarette he rolled dangling from his lips. Been napping in front of our floor-model TV that keep up more noise than it's worth.

Wiping, arranging, and straightening up, I wait for his no. "Be still, 'oman," Will chide, head shaking, "before you give me heart failure." I laugh, pay him no mind. His whole system fail if I got still or left. "Her birthday today, Will, April 27th. She already invited us near bout two hundred times."

"Her daddy be branging his new lady. You be taking room the gal ain't got."

"Doubt that. I ain't seed him with a steady in a while. Besides, even if he brang a woman, it ain't the same. I'm the closest person she got to a mama. But I won't stay as long as them young folks. Be back directly." Will go to frowning, so I sweeten my tone.

"You be alright, sweetheart?"

"Sho. Tell the gal I say, 'Happy Birthday.'"

His mind in the past now. Zapped back to another birthday, years and years ago, that never stray too far from his heart. I make a mental note to tell Free the story one day, being she love stories.

In no time flat, I'm ready, wiped off and painted, wig straight and earrings screwed. "Oooh chile, you look so good!" I say, peeking in the bathroom mirror. Dress starched, with pretty flowers, making me skinny and cute, even if nobody notice.

Since I can't make rocks cry out, like God, I cry out, mouth full of my own praise. Before I go, I dish Will a plate of cornbread and collards for later, in case he get hungry.

I get there, Pinky in the center of her living room. Dressed in Nikes, painted-on blue jeans and a white T-shirt, her arms muscular, that dark silky haircut glamorous, one side longer than the other, looking like she want to purr. Could pass for Clemmy's big sister. All eyes staring, except Javan's.

"That's everybody," she announce, clapping, her gaze gentle when it fall on me.

"Miz Too-Sweet, where Mr. Will? Watching TV?"

I grin, bob my head. Ain't one to run off at the mouth round too many folks. Short Dog brang me a kitchen chair and I get comfortable, fold my arms under my bosom, and speak.

"How do?" I say to Pinky's menfolks and greet the chillen with "Hi, kids!" Speaking out the way, I rock without thinking, swaying my upper body from side to side, the chair wheezing softly. My eyes trail across the mens again and catch Mookey's eye and wink. He in Clemmy's lap, cuddling, not giving one iota about his Miz Too-Sweet.

"Take Mr. Will a piece of cake when you leave," Pinky remind me early.

"Okay!" she sing-song, snapping her fingers and lifting her arms in a high, wide, Diana Ross at the Apollo number. "Everybody catch up, I'll finish dinner."

Sherrie Ann Turner, Pinky's galfriend from the Waffle House, go to tossing enough straw-colored hair to whiplash a small chile. Sitting 'tween Omar and Short Dog on the sofa, she hush Omar's conversation bout statues he bought in the Sudan last year. "Hold up, babe," she say, spreading five fingers in his face, her concentration on Pinky. "Look, woman, how you gone lay out your own birthday dinner, uh? Ain't somebody suppose to do that for you?" Her blue-eyed feistiness cut into Omar. "Like you?"

Omar never know what to make of Sherrie Ann so he smile a Cheshire Cat smile.

His shyness tickle the tigress in Sherrie Ann, and she press a red-tipped nail into the dimple in his chin. "Help me get this woman's dinner on the road," she coo, flirt spelled clearly in her face and voice. Didn't bother her Short Dog giving his father a buck-eyed *Ask the chick what her problem is?* stare. And it didn't faze her to bat winks back and forth with Lewis Reynolds, whenever his ole sly fox-dog eyes corner hers. Sherrie Ann know the deal; Pinky done proclaim Omar Alexander a free brother, open to any woman, being she say she didn't want him even after he got her pregnant, on a fluke, fourteen years ago.

Pinky tap her foot, waiting on Sherrie Ann to crawl out of Omar's mouth.

I halt my swaying. "I'll finish dinner," I say.

"No, ma'am." Pinky giggle. "I serve you—in my house and yours." She backing Sherrie Ann up now. "And as for you, Miz Lady, yours is the last help I need, darling. I cook it. I serve it. Cause girrl, you know you a good disaster in the kitchen!"

Everybody laugh. "I been getting my own meals since my father taught me how to cook---right, Daddy?"

Pinky glowing with love and pride, beaming

at Mr. Taylor, a man so handsome he give me eye-aches. He sitting tight on the end of the sofa beside Short Dog and across from Lewis Reynolds, who looking plastic on a kitchen chair, wide-legged, one large hand on each thigh, gangsta cool, I reckon, as the chillen say. Mr. Taylor reflect his daughter's love. "Yeah, baby girl. Taught you everything you know about cooking." To listen, you'da thought he taught his chile to weave straw into gold, he so proud.

She start standing on a stepstool at the stove when she knee-high to a duck. Whoever he left her with—and there was crops of women through the years—Mr. Taylor made sure his baby girl full. Reckon it never crossed his mind her being lonely caused scarring, same as being hungry.

"Anybody help me, it'll be my daughter." Pinky hold out her palm. "C'mon, Clemmy, help mama do this thang right."

That gal spring up higher than a jack-in-the-box and hug her mama. They walk arm-in-arm to the kitchen. If Clemmy had her way, she be living in this apartment with her folks, but Javan'd rather meet Jesus first. Whenever Pinky reason with him bout it, she say Javan bark like a fool, telling her how he ain't raise that gal no thirteen years so she can end up in a Techwood unit, working a dead-end job, birthing babies by different mens, and going nowhere fast. According to Javan Reed, he rescued Clemmy when she was three and had no say in her future, swearing if she ever returned to Pinky, she'd be of age. By that time, though, he bout prayed she'd have enough sense to know better.

That Javan---*Lord have mercy, he so good looking*---favor Mr. Taylor to me. Javan sitting on the edge of the room's only arm chair like he scared. Sullenness a witch riding his back. The urge to rise and peep outside nagging him, although I ain't hear a car crank. Paranoid. His attention shimmy the room, jumpy eyes more at home on Mr. Taylor, than on Lewis and Omar. And I can't blame him. That Lewis probably take Javan for a punk, but Javan about know Lewis satisfy Pinky's urge to throw her dress tail up over her head and shake.

Him staring at Omar is a different story. Omar a soft man. I sense Javan's wheel's spinning and thinking: if Omar had asked him, he could've put him out of his misery and saved him some heartache by shooting him like a cripple horse in the road and told him Pinky don't hang long with soft men. She trample them, high heel marks on their backs identical to the ones under his shirt. The difference being, she disliked Omar Alexander and loved him.

But Javan Reed consider Pinky's love deficient. Just an empty checkbook.

He older than the other two, he and Pinky going on the same age. They was young lovers, high-school sweethearts, pushed into parenthood before their time, which Pinky had a lot of, especially unsupervised time. It allowed them, Pinky say, to experiment with they bodies, until at fourteen, once popular and pretty in his parents' eyes, when Pinky Taylor's tummy went to rising, she shot from 'a sweet girl' to 'that nasty whore,' and a motherless one, with no home training---just a hot mama a boy of Javan's upbringing should steer clear of.

Javan's eyes hard on me now. He bout thinking: Pinky ain't even got a real family, just this makeshift crew. Old rocking Black woman and white girlfriend short of a circus by one act. No matter to me, I love the gal. Pinky boast he finish school twice, and now a big insurance man with his own offices. Meanwhile, she unchanged. No college or trade school. No steady relationship after they split. Birthed more babies out of wedlock.

Yet in all the time he knowed her, my Pinky been as constant as the secret love I know he harbor for her. I see it all over him, hear it in his harsh words, and see it in his running feet. He just ain't discovered how to unfetter hisself, thinking he got to play God and protect Clemmy's future, his heart, and honor his folks' nonsense. Poor thing. Don't even see he trashing his own life.

Going on an hour later, folks chit-chatting and telling lies and laughing, Mookey pop in the room, screaming, "Mama say, 'It's time to eat!'"

The meal delicious, Pinky blow out the candles on her cake in the living room, where somebody forgot to tell a squealing, dancing Mookey not to ask. But he did, and his mama answer Mr. Taylor, like he asked. "The same wish I wish every April. For my mama." She slice a huge wedge of coconut cake and hand the plate to Clemmy for a scoop of vanilla ice cream. Then Pinky offer it to her father with the question: "Is 26 years of waiting long enough, cause if not now, Daddy, when?"

And that's when the meaning of the morning's message that come in under my bedroom window glisten and run down my cheeks, closing my eyes. I feel the words tremble in my heart: *Be the gift of Presence.*

I open my eyes then and Pinky's cake favor a fat, white onion and sadness gush inside me in waves, reviving memories of a birthday long gone. I look around the room. Only the menfolks dry-eyed, leaving Mr. Taylor, I know, to cry like a baby inside, too, wrestling the daddy-plaguing demon every man, including Will, know.

Chapter 16

May swirled into the city with her usual splendor and pomp, suffusing the air with the smells of summer. April, mindful of her sister's inevitable arrival, halted her interminable showers and lifted her skirts and, gracious, stepped aside. Free scintillated to see her go.

She posed in a full-length mirror and surveyed the short black dress clinging to her curves. She turned right, and then left. So damn sexy. Her bare, shapely, baby-oiled legs in black pumps made her undulate her waist, stomach a washboard, and shake her round ass in the heart-stopping way she danced when she wanted to short-circuit a dance floor. She was delectable in form-fitting dresses, let someone tell it. But damn, one minute she was a looker, the next, an exhibitionist.

Sharmayne had been right.

They *deserved* a girls' night out. For several reasons. She couldn't recall the last time she'd been dancing. Plus, she was excited about spending a night out with her girl, with whom she'd never painted the town. And she didn't mind owning up to wanting to read desire in the opposite sex. To forget a growing loneliness, she'd dance herself into an erotic frenzy and return home satisfied, if only for one night. Subsequent nights, she knew, would take care of themselves.

"Mrs. Cooper-Naylor, you sure you aren't looking for trouble tonight?"

Free smiled as Sharmayne slipped into the

Mercedes wearing a striking purple sundress, matching stilettos, silver hoops in her ears, and, on one wrist, a large silver bangle.

Sharmayne expelled a sassy puff of air. "I'm out to enjoy myself and the company of my best friend, who is—" she took in Free's legs, the black dress failing to conceal her thick thighs, "—the lady who'll trouble minds tonight. Thank you."

"Don't undermine your own allure, Missy. That wild, curly hair framing an adorable face. The purple regal. Your graceful little stride, an intoxicating mixture of softness and strength. You got it, girlfriend."

The Sunday-night traffic light, they headed for I-20 and downtown Atlanta.

"I saw the way Gail's cousin Nzinga turned your head at the book club meeting. She's smooth."

Sharmayne twirled a bangle absent-mindedly.

"Wondered if you caught that. You didn't say anything."

"What? You studied her from jump, and she had eyes for no one else. A blind person could've felt the attraction. Please."

"Girl, when we started eating, she---,"

"I know. Miss Madam walked up and offered you a sweating glass of lemonade, conversation and a come-hither smile. In front of everybody. I thought some of those good sisters would croak."

"Her eyes are unforgettable."

"Yeah, bet they spoke volumes."

The 30 and Up Club, a small, popular nightspot, formerly The Paradise Club, sat on the tip-top floor of the Hilton. The Mercedes pulled into an orange-level, well-lit parking spot near the hotel's exterior elevators. The women were silent as they stepped onto a conveyor, Free smiling at a wide-eyed, elderly couple, who mirrored her greeting. Inside the Hilton, she and Sharmayne basked in the admiring stares of milling men in business suits. In the lobby, they entered another elevator, this time, a glassed-in one, treating them to a lovely aerial view of the lighted city.

When the elevator doors reopened, they heard thumping dance music coming from a winding, carpeted corridor leading to the club's entrance. Free paid their entry fee, ten each, and they moved into a crowded, smoky, L-shaped space. Boogying bodies sweated in air awash in rotating colors from a hanging silver disco ball.

Free and Sharmayne paused near a well-stocked bar manned by two lady bartenders in cut-up white T's and flesh-revealing jeans. The warm air in the room caused butterflies in Free's middle to scatter and flutter. She took a deep breath and busied herself finding a table with a view, so she and Sharmayne could people-watch.

Sharmayne studied Free. "I know you miss him."

Free stared longingly at a grinding, lip-locked couple.

"At times I can't see straight for fighting memories. He was silly." She erupted in a jarring burst of giggles. "Always calling me his Black Woman, his queen. I dream about us making love all the time."

Sharmayne rubbed comforting spirals up and down Free's spine.

"You know the time away is vital to the relationship."

"Is it crazy I want him in spite of his…control complex?"

"Nope. It'll be okay. Everything's fine."

"How you know? Your spirits sanction it?"

"You could say that…since I feel it."

"According to Mama, I should live and let live in the interim. Oh, she's visiting Rhonda and me this month. Something's on her mind."

"Excuse me, ladies, how you doing?" A dark-skinned waitress with glittering sparkles in her eye shadow smiled down at them. "What are you drinking?"

"A strawberry daiquiri, please," Free said.

The girl chewed a wad of gum and grinned. "No sweet drinks, Precious Poo."

"Alright." Free laughed. "A Mississippi mud slinger."

The girl eyed Sharmayne.

"A glass of water, please."

She scribbled on a pad and switched a pair of itty-bitty hips to the next table.

"You never told a sister how you got Darling Victor to let you attend the book club meeting."

Sharmayne opened her mouth to say that Victor had not been home when she left, but a tall, slender brother, suited, with charm stitched into every seam, interrupted her. Compelling, he leaned over them, smelling scrumptious and favoring Denzel Washington. He glanced at Sharmayne, excused his interruption, and asked Free to dance. Sharmayne watched him watch Free all the way to a spot in the center of the floor. She had the feeling it would be a long night with ample time to stare at solo women or those in groups or with men. Despite most looked two minutes over twenty, she returned her attention to the dance floor and waved at her girl and continued feeding her woman-starved gaze to her heart's content.

On the dance floor, Denzel's look-alike got raw. Twirled Free as if she knew every nuance of his style, his rhythm, his body. He sparked long dry memories in her of how tantalizing hard male terrain could feel when she was pressed against places with the capacity to still her breath. She studied the ceiling and other couples and the lines of his expensive designer suit and tried not to inhale too much of his head-reeling cologne not to lose herself.

Two dances, the first slow, this one fast, her charmer was on his way to a seat at her table had the sight over his shoulder not gone and paralyzed Free. Made her miss a step, a whole breath, maybe three, the face-to-face encounter opiate in her veins. She gasped, desire igniting a fire deep within her.

She did the best she could to suppress an impish wink, seeing he'd caught a glimpse of her the second she devoured him. Yet he repressed nothing. His mouth formed a lush hello, and a dangerous surge of passion torpedoed through her body.

Denzel's twin's suffocating arms sent her whirling at that moment and when she refocused, searching the periphery of the dance floor, the vision vanished.

"Thanks for the dance." She barreled through the crowd, tossing the words over one shoulder.

"Can I come?" Denzel probed, but Free had already slipped on blinders.

The second Sharmayne saw her, she knew. Like a strange gust of wind in a closed room, no explanations plausible, she read what had silenced Free in her unhinged expression, in the black-dress-turned-nun's-habit, in the way she griped the table before plunging into her seat as if invisible palms shoved her down.

"Was he *with* somebody?"

Free opened her mouth, but nothing came. Not even a whine. All she could do was stare vacantly, so Sharmayne craned her neck and panned the crowd, searching for the unnamable.

Just like that, she spotted him. Decided they had to leave right then.

Sharmayne rose, downed Free's Mississippi mud slinger, slipped her purse on her shoulder, not knowing what she could or should do, short of feigning a hug, and thereby obstructing Free's vision. For a second, she considered hurrying Free along, arm-in-arm, brushing past the dancers, or acting natural and pretending she hadn't seen anything out of the ordinary. She prayed Free wouldn't look sideways, only beat a hasty trail to the exit. While she stood helpless and awkward, waiting for Free to catch up with her voice, Free caught a sumptuous eyeful.

Of an ankle-length, gauzy floral skirt. Of short feathery hair. Of a petite, birdlike slenderness. Of tiny shotgun titties under a red midriff. Of a pretty reddish-brown face, closed-eyed. Of J.T.'s right hand resting protectively on the small of a curved back.

With that, the world disappeared, and she with it.

Again, the crowd swallowed the twosome, Sharmayne reemerged, and grabbing Free's hand, she guided her through air so scathing it lacerated Free's heart.

Chapter 17

"**Who the hell** is Nzinga Edwards? And why the fuck is she calling here asking for you?"

Victor glared at his wife, brows furrowed in disbelief. It was bad enough that Free Roberts chick kept his phone ringing, not to mention adding another woman, with no man, no doubt, to keep her busy and out of *his* woman's nappy hair. Worrying him half to death whenever he was home. "This her third time calling in two hours. You'da thought the bitch got the message, me telling her you ain't here."

He rinsed the top of a Bud and leaned against the kitchen counter.

Brown plastic Winn Dixie bags brimming with groceries spilled over and under Sharmayne's arms. She raised a jean-clad knee to stop a bag with a jar of spaghetti sauce from crashing to the kitchen floor. Without a word, without so much as a glance in his direction, Sharmayne retraced her steps to the garage and listened to his questions in her head. Knew it was pointless to expect Victor Naylor to volunteer to finish bringing in the groceries, and she wasn't going to be cussed for asking.

"Sharmayne, either your ass is going deaf, or I'm already deaf and ain't realized it yet. I hear myself talking, and I know I ain't crazy. Keep piddling round here like you and them dumb-ass spirits home alone, see what I do." Victor dug inside a bag, fished out a six-pack of Miller Lite, and pulled a chair in the center of Sharmayne's route from the table to the cabinets.

She knew better than to continue ignoring

him, and him gulping beer like water. He'd chucked the last of the three beers left in the refrigerator. Ignored too long, he'd become downright ugly.

"Did Nzinga leave a message?" She asked simply, as if it weren't a stupid question, but what else was there to say?

The truth. The thought emanated like mist from a deep place within her. *The truth.* She felt the assertion, which did not startle her, accustomed as she was to retreating inside herself, acclimated to inner caverns of comfort. She acknowledged the words begrudgingly, at first, unwilling to confront Victor's nastiness this evening, so soon after a self-affirming week and weekend; escaping into her safe zone of motion, she continued to order and arrange food on the pantry shelves.

Victor wiped his lips with the back of his hand. "A message? Do you see one?"

He glared at an empty can, wondering if the beer had bypassed his stomach and jettisoned straight to his head, making him question whether or not the heifer had spoken. Hell, he laughed, he wouldn't take messages for her mama if she lived with them, let alone for her. His bloodshot eyes studied the outline of her slim figure. Mmmm. He rubbed his Johnson. Had he not been so damn tired, he'd throw her quiet ass to the floor and see how much hollering and talking she did then. But it was late, after ten-thirty, and he'd gotten in twenty minutes ago from a draining cross-country run. Tuesday morning a hop and a skip away, he'd eat and get some shut-eye.

Yeah. He burped, elected to stick it to her tomorrow morning.

"Now, bitch, don't fuck around and make me

beat that ass. Who is…is…this gotdamn Nzinga Edwards?" He offered Sharmayne an empty can; she ignored it.

Tell the truth; talk to him, the deep place reaffirmed. She felt the words loud and clear in her consciousness, deep down in her body. They reverberated upward with such shocking clarity until she pivoted and peeped into Victor's face. Maybe he'd heard. Staring, she saw he hadn't.

The longer the silence, the longer the suffering, the deep insisted. *True*, her spirits corroborated. *You must do what you are afraid to do.* The synergistic power of her spiritual voices coupled with her deep place swirled inside her, their force flooding her limbs and mind with light and energy. Thunder chilled her blood and stomped her bones. Sharmayne shuddered, the magnitude of the synergism overwhelming, and steadied herself to better feel the voices. *Know yourself. We are near, always,* the spirits confirmed. *A swallowed voice chokes. Release the pain.*

Heal thyself, the spirits commanded.

"I met Nzinga Edwards at Free's *Daughters of Isis Book Club* meeting."

Sharmayne spoke deliberately, though she had no way of knowing Victor was the type of man who shrank in the face of boldness, even as he belittled her.

She admitted to joining the group, owning they'd meet monthly, would be reading Campbell's **Brothers and Sisters** next. She dumped a pot of spaghetti into a white strainer, wiped a skillet clean and poured a rich red sauce. She diced mushrooms, onions, and garlic.

See how easy it is to take that first step, to begin telling your truth, to talk to him? the voice from the deep place attested. Its gentle prodding allowed Sharmayne to meet Victor's stupefaction with a smile, his hurling a can towards the trash with serenity.

"What's it gonna be next? You and Free partying?"

Sharmayne's lighthearted laughter plopped into the gently bubbling sauce with the thyme, rosemary and oregano. She felt herself growing light and lighter, too.

"How did you know? We went to The 30 and Up Club in the Hilton last night. You and Freddie ever been?" Her back to him, she asked the question with the same ease with which she sliced a small rectangle of butter and flicked it into the center of the steaming mound of pasta. "It's a classy little place."

Victor Naylor couldn't believe his own ears. The woman had lost her goddamn mind. Talking like she and Free had discovered a new church. His curiosity dictated he know precisely how far she'd gone. Hell, for all he knew, she might have been giving it up behind his back and the thought drove him to ask, "Ya'll bump and grind?"

"If the question is, 'What did we do?' we danced, bumped into J.T. and left."

"This Nzinga go with you…as your date?"

"No, though I'd have loved that. She's definitely enticing."

'En-ti-cing?" Victor conjured women in racy positions, akin to the ones he and Freddie sometimes gawked at on the VHS cassettes on the third shelf of his closet.

At the table, Sharmayne measured a teaspoon of sugar from the sugar bowl.

"Uh huh. So you wanna hump this Nzinga woman?"

Where his spit hit her burned. His nearness made her uneasy, made her wonder how far was too far to go.

The deep place reminded her, *He does not know you. Your testimony is healing. Let it free your pain and his.*

I AM, came forth from the deep. *We are,* the spirits spoke. *Speak.*

"Yes." Sharmayne thought to borrow his language. Say, hell yes, she wanted to hump the woman. For hours. No days. But she wouldn't bow to his level. Instead, she continued evenly, "She stimulates me. Mentally and physically. A natural beauty, she's vibrant and confident. Mesmerizing." She stopped speaking, feeling an invisible power move within her. "I'm thrilled she called me, in spite of you. And yes, I do intend to know her."

Had all her life been a red carpet rolling towards this moment, Sharmayne would have died a satisfied soul.

Victor, though, was far from satisfied. He'd heard enough for a man unaccustomed to listening. His right fist crushed another can. Eyes angry, fury spurned to life in his face; his features darkened with a palpable malevolence. This bitch had taken her life into her own hands with nobody standing between them to intercede on behalf of her inevitable ass-whipping. He shook with irritation, heart pounding. He knew she was unnatural, years ago, but he'd pardoned that, knowing also, how a good dick and steady income could transform a less-than-appealing woman---a mousy, nappy-headed, non make-up wearing, no dirty dancing, stiff, old lady dressing, clean-mouthed nun---into a tiger with a stripper's soul.

Yeah, that's what he got for trying to be a decent man, the Good Samaritan son, who took unto himself the woman his parents had given their stamp of approval for a God-fearing life. Told him how much they knew. They'd used him as nothing more than a ramrod to clean him out of their house and sweep her from the Coopers. He'd been shafted. But he would fix that right now. Yes, sir.

And he would have had Sharmayne not been doing some thinking of her own, for she had long sensed his brewing violence even before he had begun to move. Intuition warned her he was about to cut loose. Thus, she slipped up and forgot any peace she ever knew.

Stepping into his space, a thing she'd never done, tossed him off kilter, empowering her. Lightening fast, she grabbed an oven mitt and the handle of the scolding skillet and brandished it between them.

"What you wanna do, Victor, beat me?" She gritted her teeth, voice October cool. "Well, I tell you what, I'm tired of being afraid, I'm about to make Death the least of my fears. Okay?"

Piping hot sauce swilled in the skillet and Victor staggered and watched it, his eyes widening each time she waved it towards him to punctuate her words.

"You crazy, Sharmayne!" His breathing came hard and heavy. "Put that skillet down before you hurt somebody."

Sharmayne swayed, as if she were dancing.

"No, you only wanna play crazy. Right now, I am crazy." She thrust the skillet's contents towards him nice and easy, careful not to catch the backlash on her clothing or flesh. The air smoked where the sauce sailed inches from Victor's shirt, splattering the kitchen floor.

He leaned backward, voice quivering. "I done told you, woman, stop it!"

Then he made the mistake of stumbling towards her as though to bum rush the skillet, which, by now, he figured, should have been taxing her right arm.

Sharmayne drew back and heaved. Sauce seared his left elbow when he lifted both arms to protect his face and chest. The pain watered his vision, boomeranged his wails about the kitchen. Lit, Sharmayne danced towards him, bobbed away, and then flickered to one side: heated, glowing, hungry.

"Goddamn you, bitch! P-p-put that down or I-I-I---"

She slung again, and Victor howled, this time catching it on the right forearm, the pain driving him over the chair he'd placed in the middle of the floor, an enraged burning bending him double. He patted his skin. Scrubbed his angry flesh against his pants.

And though Sharmayne hadn't intended violence, she couldn't stop.

"You'll what? Come for a second helping? Well, c'mon. I got it."

But he couldn't move. Every part of him died outside of his weeping arms.

Witnessing the death, Sharmayne stepped out

on velvet.

She stood inches from his nose, as though daring him to spring. A disconcerting thing, he imagined he could see her thoughts steaming, like the stovetop, and the possibilities of the moment and the beer and the fatigue and the fear shut him down so sufficiently, he could barely think to breathe.

When she took her foot and shoved a chair behind him, Victor sat. He studied her, skillet rooted to her hand. How did she know that was half of what he longed for; some rest, a sit down? From her, the trucking, his anger, his friend Freddie. The whole nine. He watched her place another chair in front of him as if he were dreaming. He focused on her lips, on the skillet, and vowed to follow her to the end of this drama if it killed him, or her, one.

"I will not hide myself from you or anyone else ever again. I am who I am, Victor Naylor." Her words floated to him, peppering the spicy kitchen air and, seemingly, her chair floated further and further from his feet, making Victor speculate if he, too, floated, hallucinating. "I'm a woman discontent with being your wife. No, I don't intend to reside under your roof much longer. 'You pay the bills; you call the shots,' your favorite words. I've brought nothing to the table, you've reminded me, outside of cooking and cleaning and stiff, sporadic sex."

She eased her grip on the skillet and flexed her arm. "I understand. We want what we want in life, and no one should stand in the way of whatever that is."

To Victor's ears, her voice wafted in through a hollow tube, sounded so far away, until he felt eerie and sweaty under the stark kitchen light. Was she saying what he thought she was saying? If it weren't for the density of his cast-iron bones, his burning flesh, he'd have gotten up and bolted from the room.

"Thought I'd never be strong enough to say this," she said, "but in spite of the hurt and pain, I genuinely love you and wish you happiness. No. I can't and won't take your pain with me when I go. We do our own healing. Truly, I'd be remiss if I didn't say I'm sorry I wasn't honest when we married. I could've saved us both this moment."

Victor longed to part his lips to correct her. To tell her this moment wasn't all bad, as long as she stopped slipping backward through the elongating kitchen.

"Mr. Naylor," her tone softened, "I know your next woman will bring you joy, a happy home, and maybe, children. Whatever, I'll hold these thoughts for you, so treat her like the queen she'll be, when she appears. Nzinga Edwards is my queen; she's the woman I want to want me."

There, she had said it all.

Shock coursed through Victor's limbs anew. Everything had taken him unawares. Why was he being electrocuted? His head raced. Body throbbed with a deafening numbness. The futility of it all brought more tears. He never imagined missing her. He tussled to stop the terror of her leaving from invading his soul but he knew she knew he understood she was already gone and he was petrified.

Sharmayne respected Victor's presence in the house by not dialing Nzinga Edwards' number, until he got a call the following Wednesday to pull a cross-country stint. They had hardly spoken four consecutive words to one another since Monday night, their clipped communication civil yet strained. Victor kept out of her way, resorting to sleeping in the guest bedroom. Claimed he needed to stretch as sitting for hours-on-end in his truck was beginning to cause severe cramping in his legs, but Sharmayne knew he was hoping she would ask him back or offer to rub Ben Gay into his joints or change the dressing on his burns.

Right now the music of Nzinga's voice warbled in her ears.

"I'm too relieved to hear from you, my lady. That man of yours is a club-carrying Neanderthal. Is he often that sweet or was it just me?"

Sharmayne laughed. The sound segueing into the sensuous underside of a purr.

"Victor's pretty consistent. He's like that with everyone who knows me."

Sharmayne could hear Nzinga's teeth sucking, though not her expiration of breath at the way Sharmayne's laughter affected the reservoir that made her insides wet with anticipation of soft, silky, slick nothings.

"Does that reception include Frenonia Roberts?"

"Especially her. To Victor, she's my corrupter, his nemesis."

"You'd think he'd be used to her by now."

"That has no relevance to Victor. If he had his way, I'd be locked away forever. He's a Black Rumplestilskin, key in one fist and what he thinks with in the other."

"That so?"

"Yes, ma'am."

"So…how have you been?"

"Okay…I guess."

"Why are you guessing? My calling brought trouble. Told you. Remember?"

Sharmayne did recall Nzinga's unwillingness to call her at home in their last conversation, knowing she was married. "Yes, I remember. Well, Victor and I had a blowout, a showdown, a fall out. He wanted to know who you were, so I hedged until my…my spirits demanded I confront my fears. Please don't think you caused anything horrible. What happened was bound to happen and meeting you expedited it but I'd seen it coming well before I accepted the fact that I---."

"Sharmayne, you okay?"

Nzinga couldn't see the sort of bravery this woman had uttered or half-uttered in the professional women with whom she brushed shoulders, them owning, publicly, to listening to their spirits or admitting they even thought the word lesbian.

"Should I come for you? You can stay here as long as you like. Victor there?"

Here she was once more, buying stock in the community's adage: Women meet, nose dive into love, and move in the next week. But so what? She wasn't one to resist what she'd prayed for since her last relationship flew south.

"No. He's trucking for three weeks." She hesitated. "Nzinga, I told him I'd be leaving soon. I wished him love and happiness in his next relationship. I-I told him I wanted you to want me like I wanted you."

Nzinga closed her eyes and mouthed a Thank you, Jesus, before laughing and adding, "Well, you didn't lie. I wanted you from the moment I saw you. Pack a few things. I'll be there as soon as I can. Bye, baby girl."

Twenty-five minutes later, Sharmayne stood behind her kitchen curtains, peering up and down her street. The May afternoon pleasant, she expended nervous energy, trying to calm a maddening eagerness within her. She hadn't seen Nzinga Edwards in days, and she wanted to be cool when she saw her, wanted her stomach to squelch its giddiness, wanted her knees to remain firm. But as the minutes ticked and she ultimately caught sight of the white Camry pulling into the drive, Sharmayne's body betrayed her.

Her breath hinged in her throat at the sight of the tall woman striding wide-legged to her porch steps. Her neatly tapered fade hair-do glistened amber in the sunshine. She was stunning in a pair of baggy blue jeans and ribbed white T. The woman exuded a confidence that bespoke a rugged, in-charge quality that succeeded in weakening Sharmayne's knees.

She braced herself against the wall.

Nzinga grinned when Sharmayne opened the door. "Hey, lady, ready?"

She entered the foyer and glanced around the living room, her scrutiny ending with a quilted overnight case and a clothing bag. "Your place is nice."

Large green eyes promised how pleasant she planned to make Sharmayne's visit.

"This everything?"

Nodding, Sharmayne returned Nzinga's stroking.

Once inside the car, Nzinga, understanding

Sharmayne's shyness, did the talking. It astonished Nzinga how child-like and fragile she was. Yet there was something fiery, something resilient about her that awed Nzinga. She'd take it slow. The first thing she'd do for this doll woman would be to wash and comb her hair, massage and oil her scalp. Then she'd recite poems, until she could feel her loosening up, to resume the rapt talk they shared on the telephone.

But Sharmayne dumbfounded Nzinga.

When they eventually settled on Nzinga's sofa before a low-murmuring T.V., after Nzinga's tasty meal of garlic bread and salad, and Nzinga began talking about her love for her job as a Spelman professor, Sharmayne crawled into Nzinga's arms. She shut her eyes and took in the unfamiliar smell of the woman, and lay against her, listening to her heartbeat, where, minutes later, she slipped into a peaceful slumber. Nzinga, unwilling to wake her, to chide her for falling asleep too soon, contented herself with caressing the sleeping head and brushing her lips against a cheek soft enough to make her sigh.

Chapter 18

A creased-face clerk sat behind a glass partition cut in a semi-circle at the bottom, on the first floor of the bustling youth detention center. The rumpled navy-blue uniform the woman wore hinted the want of a long-awaited laundering; a lifeless ponytail hung across one shoulder, fatigue draping her like a shroud. The last thing she wanted to do at the end of a long day was look up at a pristine Black woman, probably unaccustomed to real work, not a hair out of place, red two-piece suit eye-opening, face pretty and shaded in tones of red.

"Who you here to see?"

"Jomo Wyatt."

The clerk's exhausted blue gaze strolled several lists. Not finding the name, she pushed back her swivel chair, calling to someone to her right. A louder female voice directed her to check the folder of recent arrivals. The clerk sighed and ran her hand across her head, catching weariness and stray hairs.

"When he get here?" Her scrutiny scaled the trim figure again, stopping short of the neck, where it got hung up on a gleaming herringbone necklace.

The Black woman clutched her fleeing cool. *How did she know when the boy arrived?* All the woman had to do was read and stop sizing her up or get her tired butt to somebody who knew. The line had begun to grow and rumble behind her.

"Is that question necessary if you have his name?"

Brown eyes held blue in a revolving tug-of-war. Then, to escape the unblinking brown, the blue strolled the lists again and stumbled on the name Jomo Wyatt.

"He's on the third floor."

The Black woman dropped a leaden "Thank you" and turned to go.

"Who are you? Need it for the records, got to know who's visiting the detainees."

"Rhonda Butler, his teacher from Ida B. Wells High."

"You bringing him anything?"

"Assignments."

The clerk's brows shot up. "Okay. You can go up now."

The halls of the detention center swarmed with people of color. Rhonda noticed whites stuck out conspicuously: from blue uniforms, behind desks, atop panels, in the waiting area. Unfortunate ones peered out of worried parental faces, akin to their brown and black counterparts, waiting, as she waited, to enter one of two elevators. Detainees were housed on the upper floors, where bars marred their view of the Atlanta skyline.

On the third floor, she entered a huge room filled to overflowing with more people. Some stood in tight clumps talking amongst themselves, as though desperate to be teleported to a more acceptable locale. Others conversed in small groups in low, hushed tones. She scanned the scene, searching for someone in charge. It wasn't long before she spied a brother in blue near a gate, a flock of visitors chattering around his desk.

Rhonda waited, scanning her watch, the Thursday evening disappearing as inevitably as the setting sun. It was already six. Big Trevor and Li'l Trevor would be eating dinner about now, and the thought of food made her stomach growl.

"Yes, ma'am?"

"I'd like to visit Jomo Wyatt, please."

"Yes, ma'am, no problem!" He riffled the pages of his pad. "Cell 37, one section back." Pointing to a barred holding pen, he added, "Behind this block." He studied the curve of her legs. "Been here before?"

"No." Rhonda mirrored his smile.

"Well, it may seem a little strange talking to Wyatt through bars and in earshot of other visitors, but you get used to it faster than you think."

"Thanks."

"Got to survey the contents of your briefcase, ma'am."

Rhonda opened her attaché case, and he browsed under and between the **Elements of Literature** textbook, new spiral-bound notebook, pack of yellow pencils and a tiny pencil sharpener.

"Appreciate it. I hated English."

Rhonda nodded.

"Wish I'd had teachers like you when I was in school, no telling where I'd be today. Bet your students love you, pretty as you are."

"They respect me. Anything else is a bonus." Rhonda let her smile ease into a check-yourself line.

"I know that's right," he said, unaffected. "Having these fellows we get in here in love with you can be a subject of major concern."

"If you don't mind, sir, I'll find Mr. Wyatt now."

"Yeah, sure. He's got nothing but time. Be

back there for two weeks or more."

Rhonda pivoted, feeling the guard's gaze hot on her butt and legs as she negotiated the crowd and, stopping within the barred enclosure, made her way slowly, reading the numbers over the cell doors. Behind the first block, she found Cell 37. Peering inside, she squinted under the hall's muted light.

"Jomo Wyatt." She pressed her body against the bars.

A Hispanic teen nudged a silent form sprawled on a bench built into the back wall of the cell. "Wake up, man. Somebody here to see you."

The form came to life. Stretched.

"Ain't nobody come to see me, man. Leave me the fuck alone."

"Jomo, it's me, Mrs. Butler."

"See...I told your dumb ass. There's somebody to see you. Get up."

The form rose, finally registering the gentle, female voice. *Why would Miz Butler care about where he was?* He'd told her not to look for him for a few weeks. Curiosity drove him to a seated position, then to his feet. That was her alright: in a red suit, briefcase by her side, unrifled, even in a hellhole like a fucking detention center.

"Hello, Mr. Wyatt. How are you?"

"Okay." He stared at her, happy to see a familiar face, ashamed she had to see him in jail. She was probably reading him, knowing he wasn't as tough as he let on, knowing he wasn't sleeping, that he felt insecure.

"Are they treating you right?"

"Whatchu mean?"

She ignored the tinge of mockery coloring his

question.

"Are you getting enough to eat? Rest? Exercise? Have you spoken with your Aunt Glory Mae? Are you allowed time to study?"

"Study." *She bugging.* "What I'm gone study in here, Miz Butler?"

Jomo laughed, thinking she meant well.

Rhonda stared at him, unoffended by his empty laughter. His locs were longer, more scraggly. He favored a lost poster-child. She could see a fine sheen of sweat on his face, sleep lines gummed into one dark cheek, and terror in his gaze.

"Delighted you posed that question, young man. You're going to spend the next two weeks catching up on your American Literature…for one thing." She pointed a red-tipped forefinger through the bars. "And don't give me any lip about not being able to do it because the guys tease you. They could only wish somebody cared enough to bring them a hello and a smile, believe me."

"Miz Butler, how I'm gonna study in here? You see how dark it is."

"It's well past six o'clock. Complete the work in the mornings."

"What I'm gonna say when these dudes ask me what I'm doing, cracking books?"

"Tell then the judge said if you don't, you're going down the river faster than a drug deal gone sour. Just don't tell them the judge is your English teacher."

Jomo laughed a pleasant laugh, and then parted his lips with another excuse.

"Put the rest in a suggestion box," Rhonda waylaid him. "You made the decision to rob that house or whatever you did to land in this trap. We're responsible for what we do in this life. You make your bed hard, you lie in it, until you resolve to take your life seriously and stop wasting the precious time God gave you."

A pout replaced Jomo's former cockiness, and slouching, he studied the cell floor.

"Yes, ma'am."

From the time he'd spent in Miz Butler's classroom, he realized you couldn't outtalk nor out reason her. The best thing he could do was take the book and supplies she was passing through the mail-and-food slot in the door and save his breath.

"If I can, I'll bring work from your other teachers, but don't hold your breath. You've been such a heel to the others they probably wouldn't throw you a lifeline in a flood. Lesson for tonight: Don't burn your bridges. You never know when you'll need to re-cross." Her voice sharpened and nailed him up straight. "You hear me, boy?"

"Yes, ma'am."

"Good." She reached into her skirt pocket. "Here's a twenty. Buy yourself a little something and call your auntie. Gotta go. Mr. Butler will be looking for me. Be good."

Jomo nodded, stuffed the bill into his pants pocket.

"Thanks, Miz Butler. I appreciate you."

"Act like it and get my work. Bye."

Short Dog watched the attractive woman wend her way through the opened gate and into the outer waiting area. Maybe she was his boy's parole officer or relative. She looked more like a parole officer, although he hadn't seen too many P.O.'s who wore expensive suits. He was glad she walked away when she did. He'd been on the verge of telling her to hurry the hell up, visiting hours sweating him like fever.

"What up, bro?" Short Dog grinned at a seated Jomo. "What your tired ass into tonight?"

Jomo ambled back to the bars and, thrusting a hand through, clasped his boy's palm.

"Nothing going down in here, man."

"Well, you the man. Shake shit up."

"You crazy? A niggah shaking shit up in here gonna be here for longer than a sensible mothafucker wanna stay. Me...I'm laying low...so low I can see my way under the door, dig? Being locked down ain't no good feeling, little man."

Short Dog rubbed the bridge of his nose with a contemplative forefinger. He'd planned to drop the word on Jomo how his boys wanted him to consider officially joining their ranks, with full status and privileges. Now Jomo was talking like a woost, as if he had regrets about what he'd done. If so, he wasn't the brother to give the 411 on how to map out stratagems. Maybe that chick was Jomo's P. O.

"Who that sister leaving when I walked up?"

"Oh, her...she my teacher." The truth couldn't hurt him or Miz Butler in this case. "Never get enough of worrying me. Can you believe she brought me work?"

Short Dog didn't say anything for a while. "That was cool, man. None of mine woulda come down here, let alone bring me sh-i-it."

"Yeah, well, I'm glad to see you, bro, but why you here?"

The younger boy swallowed. "This ain't the right time to peep you, man."

"About what? Visiting hours be over in a minute."

"Got to make my first hit on a house soon." Short Dog lowered his voice, uneasy, his words coming jumbled, rushed. "Got a little time but I wanted to start mapping the lick early so...so I don't wind up in a rat hole like this."

Jomo could barely see his boy's eyes. The darkness his cover, he longed to jerk Short Dog close to the bars, whisper that he didn't need to be hitting nobody's house, that all he was going to get for his trouble was a police record to add to his delinquent school rap, and his future would be bleak, a fucking rocky road getting rockier. He could pull his coat to the boys running with him now, too. Hadn't seen any of his in weeks.

He had to be strong, though. Miz Butler crossed his mind, her parting words alive in his head, in his pulse.

"Don't do it, man." Jomo gripped the bars, his knuckles prominent. "You map that hit and a rat hole is what you diggin'. Word."

Free knew Rhonda went to work on projects she initiated, but she never expected the scene before her. On Rhonda's dining room table, blue and white china graced a gossamer white tablecloth. The one Free bought her last Easter. Dishes of baked pork chops with candied apples, golden cornbread, glazed carrots, collards and smoked turkey, fried purple cabbage, tossed salad, and a chilling banana pudding made a spread so pretty, nobody thought to sit down until Li'l Trevor asked what they were waiting on. Told them his mama was hungry after cooking all night, and not to worry about his daddy, since he'd be golfing until dark sent him home.

Rhonda asked Mister Will to bless the table and they dug in, the clacking of silverware and the sounds of eating slicing the silence like switchblades. After her third plate, Miz Too-Sweet went to singing Halleluiah songs. She wiped her lips, praised Rhonda for delicious scraped-from-scratch cornbread. Said she would've enjoyed syrup and cornbread alone. When Trevor howled, she smiled and shook her head. Asked what he knew about good eating, being a hamburger might've made him holler. She took in what she could see of the house, again, while the others ate. Delightful. The kitchen spick and span, looking brand new. Even the garbage can sparkled. African art and bookshelves and a TV as wide as a wall in one room made her woozy. House like this, smelling like an inside garden, just naturally birthed chillen like Trevor. Just naturally bloomed success.

"I tell you the truth, gals," Miz Too-Sweet said after Trevor led Mr. Will to the back porch to hear him blow his harmonica, "if that young'un don't favor Pinky's Mookey, I'll pay for it. They say they brothers and nobody would question it."

She glanced at a nodding Free.

"You're right. I thought so the first time I saw Mookey. You gotta see him, Rhonda. He's Trevor, just quieter."

"Reeaallly," Rhonda sang. "Why didn't you bring them?"

"Pinky couldn't come no way. She working at the Waffle House on most days, even Sundays."

"Who keeps Mookey?" Rhonda asked.

"Me. I'da had him today, what with Short Dog running the street, but her gal's daddy, Javan Reed, let him stay with them this weekend."

"That was nice." Rhonda reset the table for ice cream and homemade apple pie.

"From what Free shared, Pinky has an extended family between her children's fathers and you and Mr. Will." She thought of Jomo Wyatt and his struggling aunt.

"Family is important in any arrangement."

"That's true, Miz Rhonda. That's why I tells Will I'm Pinky's mama, 'cause she ain't never knowed her real mama, and it done near bout destroyed her." Pinky's birthday party flashed across her mind. "But she young. And she doing the best she can raising her boys. And 'spite what my husband say---you know how a man can speak hard against a chile ain't his, 'spite all that---I baby the gal. Her and them chillen can always come find love with Miz Too-Sweet."

The older woman dropped her head and the sisters couldn't determine if she sobbed or sighed, so Free leaped up and gently rubbed the slumped back. A mixture of scents---rubbing alcohol, toilet water, soap and moth balls---filled her nose.

Through the living room blinds, the sun dangled low, a broken yellow yo-yo in a suddenly weary sky.

Chapter 19

Took Will years to accept it.

And sometimes I got my doubts bout how much he accepted what I heard that Sunday back in 1956, when the world was young and I was younger. At 24, I was a rose with stout thorns that nobody could blunt the tips of, don't care how they beat, banged or battered. I was a big gal with her feet flat on the ground. Come up outta two, not-so-happy briar patches of marriages, though each had they ten seconds of bliss, and I mean seconds, and those mighta been the ones I made, birthing and raising my chillens, who I haven't talked up till now, but I knowed they was on the way, what with me attending Pinky's birthday party and meeting Li'l Trevor and knowing how much Miz Free and, as it turned out, her baby sister Miz Rhonda, love and put a mighty lot of store by holding folks' stories. Them gals made me feel like I had a stash of gold nuggets and ought to be honored to share them.

So I told them the story.

That was the year my chillens was nine and ten. Following one another like footsteps and echoes. One couldn't do or go without the other, couldn't even get sick without the other laid up, too, laboring under the same symptoms, and let MaDear tell it, when she was living, they looked like fraternal twins---that fancy name for twins that don't come from the same egg. Truth be told, they come so close together I named them twin names. The gal borned first. I name her Lynnette. Sound French. And soft as she was, being she rarely hollered like a panna, whatever that was, which I reckon was something MaDear had growed up hearing her mama say. Then, a year later, here come the boy with the same everything only he was a boy so I call him Lynn, before folks I knowed went to trading off the same names to girls and boys. Now if Lynnette was quiet, Lynn was a shadow.

Voiceless.

Or so I thought.

But don't wanna harness the mule to the cart before its time.

That Sunday back in 1956 was special. Will Sinclair was to be my dinner date, after church. I hadn't entertained a man since I walked away from Buster D. Calloway and the Good Lawd Himself knew that had been too many years to toss a stone at. Took that year for me to understand how important another person's touch was to my soul, much less my body, and that person couldn't just be anybody, because I didn't light up for just anybody the way I glowed for that Will Sinclair. Plan was for him to meet me at the church, sit with me and the chillen, like a family, so I could feel how satisfying it was to be sandwiched between my man and my chillen, same as other women with families who studied me outta the corner of they eyes, blinking pity.

"The whole equation was mathematically sound," as Lynette could say. Add MaDear answering my question in a dream bout whether or not Will was "The One" to my soul's desire to be touched and the sum equaled, "Get to church on time, Li'l Mama. Opportunity knocks, and you either standing at the door or you ain't." As for me and my future, I was gone be standing at that door, at Calvary on the

Mount.

The February weather sunny and windy, that Sunday. Service bout living each day, as though it was the last. The singing soul-stirring. Calvary on the Mount belted hymns every Sunday and that morning was no different, folks driving in from miles past Lochapoka, Alabama, to be covered by Pastor Clyde Foot's sermons and our choir's singing. So when I stood on Calvary's concrete steps, Will grinning brighter than the sun, the chillen off chasing other chillen round back of the building where dinner was being served, I heard the wind whip the words: "In life, you cannot live, until you forgive." And I thought, Amen.

I smiled back at Will Sinclair and forgave Buster D. for ever looking at me and made a note never again to joke that the D. in his name was for Dirt Dauber. Right then, as far as I was concerned, it was D. for Darling. I forgave Curtis Wilkes for being born and forgave MaDear for dying in the night as I snored on the sofa in her living room. Then to be sure I ain't miss nobody, I prayed a lil prayer that I be put in remembrance of this moment whenever I needed to be showered in forgiveness for myself or anybody else from then on out. Little did I guess how soon that would be.

Will come to dinner and never left. Over crispy fried chicken and sweet potatoes and turnips and okra and cornbread that first Sunday evening, he talked and I listened; then I talked and he listened. He talked hisself up from my table, excusing the chillen from they chores, and talked me into the kitchen where we cleaned up together, never missing a crumb or a word. That was a first for me. I ain't never knowed no man to do nothing in the kitchen but pass through and give orders. We talked till we realized we didn't wanna waste time apart another moment, and I let Will talk me into sending Lynette and Lynn to Tallassee, Alabama, to my Cousin Rita the next weekend---never mind they ain't never been outside of my shouting range---and I forgot how to pray the following Monday. I swear, it's amazing how much a person can forget when the world come crashing down, cutting your flesh with shards of sky and stealing your breath with suffocating clouds.

Folks who ain't never knowed the sky to fall has no idea night can swallow day and the darkness last for months and the only Power to reach down and put the pieces of the sky back in its frame and set things right be Love.

I know.

For a good long while, I cussed and asked the Lawd why I ain't heard: "Keep your chillen at home. Be anxious for nothing. Much less a talking man talking separation 'tween you and your chillen, so's he can pleasure his eyes and arms with you." But I didn't. And I paid the price, my stout thorns busted. You hear me? Who'da knowed Cousin Rita and her boyfriend was fighting and she'd done put him out, saying she tired of him laying up on her, not working and eating up her hard-earned groceries? Who'da knowed he come that next Sunday, begging back, to have Cousin Rita yelling that enough was enough and he better clear her porch or she was calling the sheriff? And who'da knowed jealous Boyfriend gone pull a rifle and shoot through Rita's wood frame shack of a house and leave me and Will to learn how to love and forgive through a tragedy so sad I had to pray myself up in the morning and pray myself down to sleep at night.

Rita and Lynette and Lynn had a triple funeral. I made it through most of it with a towel glued to my swollen eyes. A year later, when I could see to clean out my chillen's bedrooms, I found my boy's journals under his mattress. Never knowed nobody in my family to be any thang close to a writer, but Lynn was. Evidence in pencil, scrawled out in one tablet after another, my boy's voice, even if folks never heard it much in life. The gift precious, I slumped to the floor holding it.

Through tears, I read:

Dear Bubba,

Hey! It's me, Lynn Wilkes. Got to tell you something Lynette and I can't tell Mama, being we never tell her anything outside of "Yes, ma'am," and "No, ma'am." See, we don't backtalk her out of love and respect, unlike some of the kids in my class who talk to their Mama any kind of way. Lynette and me love our Mama; we saw her struggle to get everything we got. Our MaDear used to say, "Honor your Mama and your days be long on this earth." We loved MaDear, but Lynette and me decided to honor our Mama even if our days run short.

I have dreams, like Mama hear. In my last one, MaDear told me Mister Will was Mama's third and last husband. In my recent one, MaDear didn't say nothing, because I didn't ask nothing. MaDear just rode up in a big long new car and got out and hugged me and my sister and held the door while we climbed in and sat on the backseat, smiling. Lynette asked me if Mama in the dream. If she was there, I told her, I didn't see her. Up front, beside MaDear, was this small man smoking a pipe and coughing and spitting out the window. His brown cap matched his jacket, old and shabby, like he'd been born in both and coming out of them would've been like peeling back his skin. I think MaDear called him something starting with an H. Maybe the dream has to do with Mama deciding to let us spend the weekend with Cousin Rita, even though Saturday is Lynette's birthday. No, Bubba. We won't say anything about this either, because Mama is grown. So, Bubba, stay put and I promise to tell you all about the trip later.

Your friend,

L

Lynn had done described his MaDear's daddy, my Grandpa Hood. They ain't never met him, since he died before I went to having chillen.

Won't lie, sometimes I wish my boy hadda been a chile who spoke up like Miz Free's nephew Li'l Trevor and didn't care one iota about putting pencil to paper to be heard. But I know that don't mean he'da met a different fate…and so young. Lawd knows I know His will be done, come hell or high waters, yet that don't soften the blow or blunt the cut. In life, you gone hurt sometimes, you gone meet Mister Heartache at the front door, I don't care how cunning you think you is at dodging his visit.

Question is, *When he come, how long you gone allow him to stay?*

The second I forgave me for what happened to my chillen and forgave Will for suggesting they visit Cousin Rita, I remembered that Sunday in February, in 1956, and the rose inside me, broken thorns mended, stood up under a shower of forgiveness and bloomed.

Chapter 20

Pinky inhaled, bowed her head, and dialed a number she dreaded. As usual, he answered on the second ring, as though starved to hear her voice.

"Hey, how're you doing?"

"Hello, Omar, I'm good. How're you?"

"Never better. And the children?"

"Good, good." She decided to jump right into things. "The school called, had me come in for a meeting today, with the whole damn administrative staff, from the assistant principal to the counselor and Taylor's teachers. They mean business this time. They've had it with Mister Man's fuck-ups."

"What has he done now?"

"Nothing's changed. Teachers say he ain't been in school long enough to complete assign---"

"Has he been leaving the house?"

"C'mon. I ain't crazy. Mookey don't walk himself to Miz Too-Sweet's in the morning. What that hard-headed boy does after he drops the baby off is a different story. Can't trust him as far as I can see him, and I wouldn't trust him then." She sighed, massaging her temples. "Anyway, like I was saying...the teachers can't help him if his raggedy ass won't go to class, thinking he's cool hanging out with a bunch of boys that stay suspend---"

"What are they charging him with? Chronic absenteeism?"

She fought not to get The Black Ass. "Will you stop cutting me off, please?"

"I'm sorry, baby."

Why couldn't he tell her something new?

"These boys. The counselor says they a part of some click, a gang, call themselves Black Sheep. Say over half of them been either suspended or expelled from the public school system so now they on the street raising havoc while folks at work. I'm sure Taylor is right there with them, trying to be bigger than the baddest."

Omar Alexander repeated his question when she fell silent.

"Their case airtight. Rude and disrespectful. Class and school interruptions. Skipping. Too many damn suspensions. You name it, he done it."

"So what's the punishment this time---a longer suspension?"

"Do you keep paying employees who do what they please in your art store?"

"No."

"Didn't think so. They want his ass expelled. And I don't blame them."

Pinky knew he tipped around asking her the question, what with him not wanting her to say what he knew she was poised to say. So she saved him the trouble, and pain, and said, "I think you should let my son move in with you, shoulda been done it. Change his world. Hell, get to know him."

"You know I would if…"

"If I came along with him, with Mookey."

"He hates being at my house, hates talking to me. Sometimes I think he hates looking at me."

"We hate what we don't know, is all." Pinky walked to the kitchen window and peeked into the courtyard at Mookey playing with some kids from the top of Lovejoy. She'd asked Taylor to stay in the neighborhood because she'd be leaving for work soon yet she hadn't seen his butt since he left hours ago. Now she'd have to burden Miz Too-Sweet again. Omar had started talking again, and she clenched her teeth not to tell him she had a lot on her mind. He'd already taken too much of her Sunday afternoon.

"Maybe this thing with Taylor indicates we ought to take a chance on us, Pinky."

"Omar---"

"No, hear me out. Please. I want us to be a family, a real family. I love you. You know I do. I love all of you; our son, Clementine and Lewis. Marry me, and we'll work as a family, as a unit. You'll see. I can provide for you, very well; you could quit the Waffle House and be home for the children. Taylor would straighten up. He's smart under that thuggish exterior."

"That sounds wonderful. Sometimes I pray I could do that and I love you but I don't love you the way you want me to." Not ordinarily the crying type, she walked about the kitchen as though to walk away from the urge to cry; Omar's softness, his love for her, hurt too much to be still. "Maybe daddy could keep Taylor a while."

"I don't care." He ignored her suggestion. "I can live with whatever love you have."

She sighed before admitting, "But I can't."

Silence reigned for five or ten minutes, until Omar decided to be The Man.

"I understand, baby. Let's not worry your father. I'll talk to our son and drag him over here if I have to. No matter what he thinks, he'll have no other choice. Either I'll discipline him or The Law will. Together, we'll work it out. It's never as bad as you think."

"No, because he's my child, and I never give up on my babies."

She exhaled, feeling the long fingers of fear and dread pried from her heart.

The sun showed out through the blinds of Free's capacious living room windows. Sunshine sparkled everywhere, transforming the street into a ballroom of beauty. Trees saluted, straight and suited, in shades of emerald green. The sky dazzled in turquoise. Clouds roamed pristine in neat blackbird bowties. Graceful houses posed camera ready. After watching the pageantry grow old, an elsewhere woman turned her attention to the comforts of the living room. Contentment thrived in the space, engulfing her in a quiet revelry.

Pastoria Roberts enjoyed visiting her daughters, but there was something special about Free's home, although she wouldn't admit it aloud, Rhonda's feelings easily hurt. Free's place didn't know the clamor of more than one pair of feet. It didn't ache with the weight of loving too many bodies, wasn't privy to the sound of slamming doors that stayed in the air, the tramping of muddy boots, the ingrained grim of too many fingerprints, until the weight of the living was etched, like an ingrown hang nail, into its walls and floors. Nor did it know the perpetual presence of a man.

She closed her eyes and let fatigue drain from her stiff limbs. There was a time when she'd have thought nothing of driving to Atlanta, shopping, eating dinner, and hitting Highway 85 South for the drive back to Pine Mountain.

But that was then and this was now.

She wanted to be in the talking spirit when Free came in from the bookstore and Rhonda from school. She hoisted her bags upstairs and dumped them beside the bed in the guest room across from Free's bedroom. After a shower and a change of clothing, she padded down to the kitchen and surveyed the fruit bin and jugs of juices in the refrigerator. She mixed the ingredients for a fruit salad in a large bowl. Growing up, the girls had always relished her fruit dishes. They didn't cook after a long work week and would be grateful for whatever. Not long after she placed three glasses on colorful place mats on the kitchen table, the doorbell shrieked at being rung at four in the afternoon.

"Hey, Mama, how was the trip?" Rhonda pecked her mother on one cheek and walked into the foyer. "How long you been here?" She smiled, checking out her mother's kaleidoscopic housedress and fluffy shoes. "You look cute."

Pastoria studied her baby girl.

"Hey yourself, Missy. The trip was okay. Congested, but okay. Everybody still hits the road on a Friday, I see." She stretched her arms toward her elegantly poised daughter. "Just got in. Give your mother a hug, girl. What's wrong with you?"

Rhonda filled her lungs with her mother's scent. Mary Kay. Same as she remembered. Redolent whiffs of Mary Kay cleanser, lotion and perfume. She shut her eyes and fed her starved senses. How she'd missed the woman, in spite of them not 'setting horses,' as her Grandmama Pearlie Mae, Pastoria's mama, used to say. Pastoria was the woman Rhonda searched for in the mirror, whenever she prepared herself to face the world. Whenever she styled her hair, made-up her face, slipped into a suit or dress. Pastoria was the woman she scorned, also, whenever she looked too hard.

"You're as lovely as ever, sweetheart."

Pastoria grabbed Rhonda's hand and led her into the kitchen. "You ready to eat?"

At the table, Pastoria handed her a wooden serving spoon.

"Ooh, fruit salad!" Rhonda squealed in delight and plopped down at the table, scooping slices of strawberries, bananas, apples, pears, watermelon and mango into a bowl. "But let's wait for Free. She'll be here any minute."

"Okay. How's my grandbaby?"

"He's fine. Talk about upset, the boy was upset he couldn't come, but I assured him his Nana would be spending time with us as well. Lately, he's been consumed with a science project. You should see him, Mama," Rhonda said. "He's genuinely thrilled with conceptualizing his plans and diligently plodding through the details." Her lips crafted a smile. "He's a little man. I love the way he questions me and Big Trevor about what we think of his progress."

Pastoria's enthusiasm rivaled her daughter's pride.

"He's just like you, always did love school. I swear you loved it better than eating. If you weren't doing schoolwork most afternoons and on weekends, you could be found deep in the pages of a book." Her hand found its way across the table and squeezed Rhonda's fingers. "See how all that studying has paid off? It'll be the same for Li'l Trevor, one day, too."

A light illuminated Pastoria's eyes. Fred

would've been so proud of his baby girl, seeing him, as she did, in Rhonda's face, hair and intellect. She discerned herself in the young woman's sense of style, in her single-minded manner of going after what she wanted. In her stubbornness.

The doorbell jarred her musings and her daughter's wonderment.

A tsunami, Free flung wide the door and her presence filled the room. She kissed her mother and sister and succumbed to an infectious Friday afternoon exuberance that soaked her clothes and drowned her cares. Standing unabashed in the kitchen, she stripped to a pastel bra and panty set and dived into a chair to grin at her mother and sister who shook their heads. When everyone's laughter subsided, Pastoria asked grace.

"Mama, it's good to have you here. Rhonda and I were just saying you need to visit more often," Free said through a mouthful of fruit. "And not because you please our palates either."

She winked at Rhonda.

Pastoria smiled and asked about her day and promised to visit the bookstore to see if she'd gotten any good books in lately. She shooed Free's hurt expression like airborne lint and winked at Rhonda, too.

Free giggled. She missed her mother's sense of humor.

"Alright, if you're planning to sleep under this roof tonight, girlfriend, you'd best be a good mama and not make silly conversation." They laughed, and Free shared Reesa and Sharmayne's hello.

"That's sweet. Sharmayne still seeing that woman?"

"Yes, ma'am. Please don't mention that unless she broaches the subject."

"Thanks for the advice, dear. Although I don't approve of that kinda stuff, I do know how to behave, since I taught you how to act."

Rhonda placed her fork on the table and cleared her throat. She'd been silent long enough. "So, Mama, what was so pressing you had to make a special trip to talk with us? I hate to squelch the merriment, but my men will be ringing soon, wondering if I've left. Didn't tell them I was spending the night."

"You always were exact," Pastoria said, thinking, *like your dad.* She stared off as though looking into yesterday. Then she shoved her plate aside and clasped her fingers together and slowly twirled her thumbs. "I came to tell you girls that--" her voice wavered, stumbled, and regaining its footing, ambled on, "—that you have an older sibling." Suddenly her throat itched. "Her birthday just passed, in April."

Free and Rhonda stared at the woman, then at one another. *Had Pastoria just denuded a secret that had tipped among them, sometimes silently, sometimes flamboyantly, for ages?*

Pastoria scrutinized the few berries left in her bowl. "Thought you deserved to hear it from me, in person, considering I've preached honesty forever." She paused to let her words jimmy a padlocked past.

"Wherever she is, whoever she has become, I know she's alive. I see her big brown eyes in my soul, those baby eyes I looked into when she was a newborn. They never left me. I know they search for a face, my face, and of late, I can't pretend they don't exist. Thirty-one years is a long time to pretend."

She flushed in an undressed shame, confession lessening her burden. The testimony hung in the air, like a cold puff of white breath on a wintry morning.

"Who is her daddy?"

Pastoria's perusal of Free's face expected judgment but unmasked a glaring curiosity instead. "A soldier."

Free's breath nearly chocked her then. "Your album."

"Yes. We were lovers...when your father was in Korea."

Rhonda couldn't make her mouth be quiet. "How could you do that?"

"Easy. I was lonely like many of the military wives I knew." Since she'd started, she might as well tell the whole truth. "Long separations tended to walk the short road to flings or good-byes, when you were young and---"

"Full of sap," Rhonda volunteered, standing up to Free's brutal stare.

Her mother nodded. "Yes, indeed, full of sap. We all were back then, and I've never been a woman to be without a man for any length of time. No. It's not that I needed one. I wanted one, and I've always received what I wanted."

That shut Rhonda down, though not for long.

"Why didn't you have an abortion?"

A bitter memory washed over her and she recalled...how her mother and Free had urged, no demanded, she have an abortion after she got pregnant six years ago. So what the question sucked sound from the kitchen and rendered Pastoria speechless. So what Free's eyes were stones, pelting her every-which-away. Her soul sat at the table like a natural woman, dumping its aches, as her mother had done, on the altar.

"Before I knew I was pregnant," Pastoria answered, "I was too far along."

"You…would've…had…an abortion…like Free?"

The words stung Pastoria and Free and left a mist in Pastoria's tone.

"Yes."

"Well, aren't I blessed I didn't listen to you and Miss Free here, huh Mama, or I'd have been plagued with guilt, with secret sin, too, huh? Had I been the fool you both thought I was…for marrying Trevor and making a go at raising a family, I'd have missed being your grandson's and your," she glared at Free, "nephew's mother."

Rhonda let her volume and tone scale the walls.

"You put her up for adoption? Why don't you know where she is?"

Pastoria cringed and sucked snot like a child. "I placed her in her father's arms and asked him out of my life." The truth wrung her insides, cabled them like steaming laundry.

"You mean you passed your firstborn to a man you fucked for a few months? How could you do that? Did you know him fewer months than you carried her?"

"Rhonda, that's enough. What the hell's wrong with you?" Free stood and pounded her fury into the tabletop. "No matter what she's done, she's still our mother, so remember who you're talking to, girl."

"Shut the *fuck* up, Free. Sit *your* ass down and put in an account for *the baby* you killed. At least Mama did have the decency to give hers to its pappy. Had he known, J.T. might have given his baby more love than you ever could."

Free took in a deep, slow breath. Anger and regret filled her lungs until they hurt. She clenched her fists and prayed for the strength not to tear into her baby sister. Their mother wasn't present, she might've tossed the chick into the backyard and stepped into an imaginary ring. When presence of mind replaced discord, she spat evenly, "I wasn't ready for being a mother, Rhonda. Why can't you *accept* that?"

"Whoever is? I wasn't ready for being somebody's wife, yet I was brave enough to push my boulder uphill. Why didn't ya'll accept that--" her eyes sliced Pastoria, "instead of making it seem like I coerced Big Trevor into marrying a stupid girl, sexing for the first time, who got herself knocked up, huh, Free?"

She leaned toward her sister, searching her balled-up face for the truth she alone hadn't brought to the reckoning table.

Under Rhonda's rock-hard resolve, Free receded. First in dribbles, then in waves. Her sister was right. About too many things she'd thought better left in a watery past. She couldn't force the hands of time and bring back the day she'd argued with Rhonda, adamant she get rid of the mistake above her bladder and forget starting a new life with a man she didn't love. But Rhonda had igged the advice, had dispelled her arguments one after another. The memory painful, Free lowered her head, willing it away.

"I'm sorry, Rhonda, I was wrong. You had a right not to be selfish, like me. Didn't have it in me to raise a baby alone, didn't want to give up the glamorous life." She sighed. "To sidestep his suffocating ways, I denied J.T. his baby." She almost cried at how devastated he would be if he knew.

"The truth might've made him a man minus the desire to suffocate."

Free lifted her head and faced her sister. "True."

"I'm sorry, too," Pastoria said. "Forgive me."

Rhonda sat up straight. Studied the top of her mother's bowed head. For the first time she noticed a thinning there, dime-sized and softly gray. Pastoria had never made a habit of apologizing. Tears fell inside Rhonda, and anger hammered a wall in her chest. She wanted to wage a second assault. But love leveled her weapons and willed her anger into a back-paddle to keep her from plunging over an unending waterfall.

"Ya'll hurt me, Mama," the baby girl inside her whined. "But I'm sorry for holding rancor against both of you, and especially you, Free, for looking down on me for giving my baby a family."

"I never looked down on you," Free rejoined. "I envied you…for having all of the things I didn't."

"What things? I envied you for being independent, self-employed and pretty."

Pretty. Free's head reeled. *Who was prettier than her beautiful baby sister?* And she said so.

Rhonda rolled her eyes. "Yeah, right. Try

telling that to a little sister whose big sis has always been the life of every party---" she fixed Pastoria with an incriminating smile, "---the apple of her mother's eye."

"I take that, too," Pastoria said. "With Free, I tried too hard to make up for what happened with your sister."

She reached out to her daughters through years of stale lies and waded through the stench of self-righteousness and asked what she'd rehearsed for months.

"If ya'll still love me, come on; we'll start again."

Rhonda bit her bottom lip, amazed their undeclared war had reached its end. *Should she accept a white flag now, or demand the two of them grovel some more, wondering how much longer before the baby girl announced enough was enough?*

She wiped her cheeks and watched Free. And railed against the stubborn heifer in her soul, who was able to hold a hurt until it ravaged her.

Then, without words, she accepted the truce, hugging her mother first. "I love you" in her mouth and "Forgive me" in her eyes, she and Free and their mother embraced, as though each were the other's lifeline. They hugged until they shared one heartbeat, as she and Free had done as girls, when wounded.

Outside the kitchen windows, Night swaggered up to an exhausted Sun, extended his hand, and danced her into the softness of his richly tailored tuxedo.

Together, the women eavesdropped as the two waltzed under the stars and Night finally lay Sun down, nothing of their rendezvous revealed outside of a pale-orange afterglow.

Chapter 21

Sharmayne's hair got so it knew the gentle touch of Nzinga's fingers better than it knew her own. Since the afternoon Nzinga had driven to Sharmayne's house and whisked her off in a white Camry to her fortress, Sharmayne's hair and Nzinga's fingers had become lovers, like the women themselves.

"Didn't know what you preferred for brunch," Nzinga said, setting a feast of a repast on the freshly wiped white gazebo table in her fenced-in North Highland backyard, a wilderness of magnolia trees, lush grass, and spray of bees and flowers. "Thus, I've prepared a sampling of tastes for your palate's pleasure."

Sharmayne's mouth watered, savory smells whetting her appetite.

There were waffles, vegetable omelets, fresh fruit, pancakes, maple syrup, hash browns, bacon, sausages and even a dainty pot of brewing chamomile tea.

"You shouldn't have." Sharmayne was outdone. And to think, they'd only known one another for less than a month, via telephone; yet in spite of that, Nzinga had unrolled the red carpet, a thing Victor Naylor had never done, would never do. She flushed, hands fluttering to her lips. "I'm overwhelmed. I feel so honored."

Nzinga sat on a sun-warmed seat across from the diminutive woman and smiled.

"That so. Before you dole too many accolades, taste a mouthful, and if it's yummy, I promise I'm yours for the heaping on of more praise." She speared a forkful of a fat omelet and brought it to Sharmayne's mouth, waving it slightly to release whiffs of its wafting heat.

Sharmayne parted her lips. Its flavor, like the aphrodisiac of Nzinga feeding her, ricocheted inside her mouth, snapping her thighs together under the round table.

The movement not lost on Nzinga, she unfolded a cloth napkin, fanned an insect, and dabbed at the corners of Sharmayne's lips. "Good?"

Sharmayne finished chewing, nodding her appreciation and amazement.

"Speechless, huh? That's a good thing." Nzinga tapped slender dark fingers when they reached for silverware beside a mirror-clean plate. "What of the waffles?"

"Oooh goodness! Fabulous and filled with blueberries." Sharmayne licked her lips. "They make me want to shout. To teach Women's Studies, must one know one's way around a kitchen?" She opened her mouth and accepted a bubbly brown, juicy sausage. The taste beat a drum roll in her stomach.

Next, Nzinga waited with a love offering of buttery, syrupy pancakes. "To love a woman is to be open to learning what stimulates her appetite."

Sharmayne's moistened lips agreed, her insides singing, mouth baby-bird wide. With a low, delirious sigh, she licked butter trickling towards her chin. And moaned.

"I could eat your cooking all day, every day." A darting tongue swept her lips.

"Do that again."

"What?" Sharmayne played ignorant,

knowing full well what Nzinga referenced.

"Lick your lips. That simple act rivals all of your generous compliments."

Nzinga leaned in close to better watch Sharmayne's pink tongue gloss those dark, berry-sweet lips from across the table, the mouth playful, her lashes batting under half-mask lids. Didn't admit that she, too, could eat all day and night, equally as ravenously. But she put no stock in telling, preferring instead to show the lovely lady, sooner than later. Right now, feeding her satisfied a long dry well-spring of passion she hadn't felt in ages, until now; the inclination to inhale another woman mentally, physically, and spiritually, not just smooch her, feel her up and wield her dick, overwhelming.

When Sharmayne had eaten to her stomach's content, she sat back and stared at Nzinga, concerned she hadn't touched a morsel of the delicious spread since lowering the fork. But Nzinga surprised her by half standing to kiss traces of crumbs from Sharmayne's mouth.

"How may I show my gratitude?" Sharmayne shifted in her seat, pussy purring, moistening her trembling thighs under her tangerine sundress. She prayed Nzinga didn't ask for assistance with the dishes just yet.

Patient, Nzinga got up and began clearing the table.

"Whatever you like, on another occasion. Consider this the professor's day off: it's our first full day together, set aside to shower you with welcome. I want you to either finish relishing your meal here in the sun or on the cool, screened-in patio behind you."

"What if I graced you with my company while

you worked?"

"What if you blessed me with your presence after your rest?"

Sharmayne recognized a treaty when she heard one and consigned herself to a cup of honey-laced chamomile tea and a soft corner of the pillow-stuffed patio sofa, where a light wind lulled her into a peaceful, mid-afternoon nap.

Inside the house, Nzinga cleaned the dishes and ordered the kitchen, then disappeared upstairs to the mistress bathroom where she lit vanilla candles and lined the vanity's marble countertop with bottles of sweet-smelling oils, shampoo, a white towel and black bands.

Over in the afternoon, Sharmayne awoke to jazz music and the scent of vanilla and followed them to the third floor, to Nzinga's shaded bedroom, the ambience soft in dancing candlelight. She glanced about, curious, wondering what this alluring woman was up to now.

"You a jazz woman?" Nzinga's voice floated in from the large, walk-in closet.

"Don't know, never indulged in music as much as literature."

"Darling, another treat to share with you. This is Al Jarreau's 'We're in This Love Together.' Like it?"

"Uh huh. What're you doing in there?" She fell back on the undulating bed.

"Handling my business, and hoping you can handle yours."

Sharmayne enjoyed the sensation of riding cool waves. "Which is?"

"Please come in the bathroom. Drape that

white towel about your shoulders. Then lean over the sink." With that, Nzinga emerged from the closet in a black sports bar and red silk boxers and stood wide-legged in the closet's doorway. The sight of her female musculature rendered Sharmayne breathless. The woman was her fantasy incarnate.

"Another treat?"

"Hopefully." Her voice roused a soft mewing in Sharmayne's pussy, the sound growing louder, more passion laced, with each glance of Nzinga's profile, the sloping biceps, broad chest, softly bound breasts, tapered waist, solid ass, tight hamstrings, her rough allure drowning Jarreau's beguiling sound.

When Sharmayne obeyed her, an instant heat dampened the seat of her panties. The meltdown, slow and slick under her short dress, weakened her knees. In the vanity mirror, she gazed up into Nzinga's stare. The woman pressed her silk-clad pussy into Sharmayne's soft ass, never releasing her visual clutch, even as she ran a stream of water over one amber hand, testing it before easing Sharmayne's curly naps under the warm flow. She watched as watery beads glistened and disappeared in the dancing curls.

Sharmayne sighed. Her body slackened, elbows loosened, neck dropped, as she gave herself over to Nzinga's skillful fingers swirling circles and relaxation in her crowning glory. A mesmerizing scent---macadamia---suffused the bathroom. Suds shut Sharmayne's eyes, the rhythm of the head massage matching the gentle bump and grind of Nzinga's shorts against her plump, up-turned ass.

"Good?" Nzinga wanted to know, for the second time that day.

"What's beyond good?" A moan rasped deep in Sharmayne's throat. "Whatever that is...that's what it feels like." Her ass cheeks quivered, begged for more contact.

Nzinga rinsed the macadamia-scented suds from Sharmayne's locs. One hand on her tummy, Nzinga straightened her and towel-dried her hair, burying her nose in the soft tangle of freshness. Sharmayne sighed, and Nzinga kissed her nape lightly, sweetly. Sparks of heat kindled another surge of wetness in Sharmayne's already soaking panties, the meltdown beginning to find its way under her panty's lace and down her thighs.

That Nzinga busied herself opening bottles of lavender, vanilla, and almond oils, dabbing dollops into her palm, as though she had no idea of the effect she was wreaking on her fueled Sharmayne's need. The combination of scents, Nzinga's warmth on her ass, on her back, on her scalp, electrified her. She gripped the vanity's ledge to remain upright while the smell of fired-up pussy ribboned the air.

In Sharmayne's eyes, Nzinga was a woman warrior. Green gaze direct, her demeanor demanding---Sharmayne resolved to give her whatever she asked.

"You are so beautiful," she whispered in Sharmayne's ear, working magic with the oils and black bands, styling thick locs in a pretty arrangement of twists across Sharmayne's head. Her lips, soft and warm, branded the damp neck and earlobes, as she changed Sharmayne's position to avoid stiffening her limbs.

Sharmayne's lips trembled. "And you...to me." Staring at Nzinga in the glass, she exhaled, her knees threatening to buckle when her bones disappeared.

"What do you think?" Nzinga's voice caught her. She washed her oily fingers and cleaned under her nails. Body yet intimate on Sharmayne's ass, she leaned around the smaller woman, busily drying the counter, as Sharmayne fought to admire her handiwork. Nzinga's wiping arm grazed a nipple straining against the cotton of Sharmayne's sundress.

"Oooh, oh God. It's more beautiful than I imagined."

Waves of need made her clit hum. What was left of her modesty dive-bombed to the tiled floor, and Sharmayne hugged the counter, her ass thrusting against Nzinga's pussy, nothing left to hide or fake.

That's when Nzinga did it. Dried her hands, swallowed the side of Sharmayne's face and ears and, supporting her weight in an Amazonian hug, snaked one hand under Sharmayne's hem and cupped her ass cheeks. Sharmayne cried out. Pleasure bolted down her arching back. Her ass in this woman's hand was home. Her heart raced.

"You're so soft," Nzinga murmured against her ear, stopping her heartbeat. Strong fingers fluttered over the satiny skin of Sharmayne's cheeks and then paused over her sphincter muscle, gingerly teasing it, her grateful, greedy hand floating back to Sharmayne's lovely bottom, where it squeezed and kneaded her hot, firm flesh. "Everything about you is velvety. I could stroke you forever." Nzinga's kisses wafted down her arms, back up to her nape, that tongue igniting her flesh with licks, boiling and ready.

The heat in Nzinga's mouth burned. One thigh rose, propped on the vanity, exposing Sharmayne's pussy. She sighed with the urgency to feel more of the woman on her skin, inside her, their flesh sweating as one. "N...zin...ga," she stammered, wobbly-kneed, "please."

Nzinga squatted, taking her time. She raised the sundress over the gorgeous ass. Pulling the panties to one side, she let herself be carried away at the sheer beauty of the pink folds of a passion flower glistening with wetness, soaking the shock of black curls trimming its swollen petals. "May I?" she groaned into Sharmayne's heady perfume.

"Please." Sharmayne stuttered, nearly hollering. Not caring how Nzinga entered, front or back, or together, as long as she entered.

Nzinga sucked the tip of one cocoa cheek into her mouth and, simultaneously, dipped one finger into Sharmayne's overflowing warmth, pushing up between the slickness of her sweet walls. Sharmayne's moans and Jarreau's "Blue Angel" and the flickering candlelight quickened Nzinga's slowly pumping arm.

"What're you hiding under this cute dress?"

Sharmayne's answer got smothered against the mirror, and, for the first time, she felt freer than she'd ever felt in her life. Flower splayed, filled with Nzinga's pumping fingers, then her thrusting fist, balled, tongue lapping across the pungent delicacy of her ass, Sharmayne's eyes rolled back, and she wished like hell she could unhinge her thighs and open them wider to quench this woman's thirst and satisfy her own hunger. Under Nzinga's onslaught, Sharmayne's body fell into the rhythm of Nzinga's fingers. She cried out in orgasmic delight after her pussy clamped on Nzinga's wrist, spastic. She'd never imagined being with anyone could feel this good.

Pinky stood under the **Pay Check Here** sign, wiping cake crumbs into her hand. She dipped a cloth in warm suds in a sink to the right of the cash register and swabbed the sticky counter clean. She surveyed the smudged glass of the pastry holder. Picking it up, she swiped outside, then inside the cover. Around her, evening Waffle House diners hovered over greasy plates of bacon, grits, cheese eggs and waffles. Other customers, waiting for an available booth or a counter stool, sat on black chairs lining the large glass window adjacent to the counter.

Unlike other days when she relished eavesdropping on floating bits of conversation, Pinky went about her responsibilities today blankly. She did things two or three times before she figured out she'd already done them. Again her hands sought refuge in the cleaning cloth, the foam comforting, and she scrubbed the counter until it squeaked.

Before long, her eyes no longer focused on any one thing or person.

They slid over an approaching girl, with a tattoo of a parrot fanning red and green wings vivid along the brown skin of her clavicle. Heavy breasts were hard-put to find reassurance inside a screaming tube top. Oblivious to the preoccupied glaze in the waitress's eyes, the girl barked her order. "Lemme have the cheese-n-eggs to go, a side of raisin bread, and a large cup of orange juice." She slapped a five on the counter. "I'm in a hurry," she roared, seeing the sister hadn't budged from her fanatical wiping.

When the waitress continued to take no more notice of her nor her gruff tone than if she were invisible, the girl bucked her eyes and digitized the joint, deciding, being the other two waitresses and two cooks appeared busy, to vent her angst on everyone.

"What the *fuck's* wrong with this bitch?" One stubby finger pointed accusingly at the wiping woman. The Waffle House, cranking to a stand-still at someone's sudden fury, turned to make sense of a bad situation. "Hey, y'all need to look in on this chick. She done cracked, and it's a good thing she's at this damn counter and not stirring shit on that hot-azz grill. Look-a-here, one of y'all, I gotta go. Shit!" Now she was screaming louder than her top. "Could I get some service right here, please?"

A teenager snickered in a booth near the jukebox. Everybody else was as silent as death, silent and alert. Like Sherrie Ann Turner, whose icy-blue eyes glinted crazy glints of madness. The pad on which she'd been scribbling a family's order in the rear of the restaurant thudded to the grimy floor. She walked past Jennifer, who continued placing condiments on the table she was serving. She spanned the grill area, the grease on the floor making her white work shoes squeal, and came to a halt beside her good girlfriend, who hadn't slowed one iota in her endless wiping.

Before the customer took her next breath, Sherrie Ann locked thick, ringed fingers in a mussed head of braids. From the grip Sherrie Ann had on her, Miss Girl realized, intuitively, suddenly, that fear came in many forms, one of which she least expected, that of a wild whitewoman who whispered: "This cracked bitch is my friend, my family, and if you so much as look at her again like you don't take her for anything but the good sister she is, I will slit your muthafuckin' throat. You can think I'm calling your bluff, but be smart. Take time to see it in my face, hear it in my voice." Sherrie Ann's face was a loaded gun. "You from the street; I'm from the gutter. Recognize a real cracked bitch who ain't got shiiit to miss. I give you my word, hoe. My word."

Sherrie Ann let Miss Girl feel the strength in her grip. "No cheese-n-eggs for you today, Ma. Not in here anyway. So hit the door."

She loosened her grip on Miss Girl's astonished braids and watched her back away, shove open the glass door, and narrow her eyes, before storming into the day.

At her departure, the Waffle House breathed and returned its attention to plates of congealed food. Bernie, a quiet waitress with shiny red curls piled high on her head and a missing front tooth, dropped what she'd been doing and moved toward Sherrie Ann and asked, "What was that all about?" David, a bald cook with muscles bulging under a white T-shirt, towered over Bernie. "You know her, Sherrie Ann?"

Shaking her head no, Sherrie Ann wrapped her arms around Pinky.

"Only thing I know, she ain't likely to forget me." She rested straw-colored curls against Pinky's head. "Bernie, I'm gonna take her to the back a minute. She's been having it rough lately." She considered the cook. "Dav, I'll run her home, okay?" Not waiting for his response, she eased the wash cloth from Pinky's fingers and led her to double doors at the end of the room marked **Employees Only**.

"It's alright," Sherrie Ann began softly, lowering Pinky onto a large cardboard box beside her chair. "Everything's going to be okay." She smoothed damp hair back from the warm cheek. "Girl, sometimes life is a storm, a vicious sucker of a storm that'll rip your guts out, you let it, and toss them back at you. And in this storm, honey, everybody gets rained on---sometimes---hard and long.

"Half the time I'm drenched, soaked clean through to the bone; I been where you at, girlfriend." She laughed a quiet laugh and stroked Pinky's hands. "Kid bent on traveling the superhighway to West Hell. Better-paying job, like a golden carrot, always outta reach. And Good Lord, pray I forget the worthless men, trying to put foot where the sun don't shine, sending me through hoops and changes, for a little bit of give and a whole lot of take.

"I been there, honey." She pulled Pinky into her side, rocking her in a comforting, back and forward motion. "But a better day with a better man and a better job will find me. It's a matter of time."

Pinky listened to the familiar voice cutting through her erratic thoughts. It was something to hold on to, something to steady her feet on sinking sand. But her shoulders persisted on disappearing inside her body, tension heavy on her limbs. Although it was her habit to hold herself rigid, braced against the demons of her existence, she longed for a slipping away, like the simple relief after childbirth. And Sherrie Ann, perceiving Pinky's longing, continued to massage her back, intent on buoying her up past sorrow.

"What's happening is, you're going through the darkest part of the storm, babe. It's scary. But the key to survival is keeping your eye on the light, that flicker of hope at the end of the tunnel." She pressed each joint in Pinky's spine. "You see it?"

Pinky nodded, fighting to see beyond her troubles to somewhere else.

"Taylor gone, run off when I told him Omar coming for him."

"Let God work with that one." Sherrie Ann didn't bat an eye. "You keep looking for the light; see it for Mookey Man and Clemmy and that old lady, Miz Too-Sweet. You gotta see it for the future with someone other than that---" she couldn't stop it from coming, "---mindless Javan." She bit her lip. No woman in her right mind oughta be wishing on a star for the likes of a Javan Reed.

"When I go get Mookey, I ain't going back no more. Tired of him using me."

"Pinky, girl, that's what I'm talking about. I know you see it now. You gotta stay focused on letting it guide you out of the madness, because," she wondered if she should say what sat on the curve of her lips to say, then reneged, then blurted it anyway, "because it's going to lead you to your mama. She's out there, looking for you."

She hugged her sisterfriend to her bosom again, tighter, trusting what she promised didn't prove a lie. Praying it wasn't.

"You love someone as hard as you love your mama, she gotta come. Gotta."

Pinky latched onto two words that succeeded in hoisting her up from the day's downward spiral and yanking her into the storage room. She felt her friend's breath in her hair. "My mama..." she parroted, childlike.

"Yeah." Sherrie Ann sighed softly. "Your mama."

Chapter 22

"**What've you been** doing with yourself these days?" Dr. Wallace took the ballpoint from the pocket of her jacket and sat down. The usual white legal pad rested on her crossed thigh.

J.T. sank into the familiarity of the chaise lounge, ready to loosen his tie and talk.

"A few things. Treated myself to the Fabulous Fox to see the Pointer Sisters in 'Ain't Misbehavin'."

The therapist smiled. "Good you're spending time enjoying you."

"Met someone, been spending time with her, too."

"Mmmm. That always changes the landscape. Wanna talk about her?"

"She and a group of her friends came into the Marriott to dine one evening, her party spending money like it bubbled up from the bottom of a magic well. Champagne and wine flowed all night. After the dinner, one wanted to meet the chef so I came out, sweaty and amused, and met them."

"Bet that excited them."

"They got all giggly and chatty and flirtatious. One tripping over the other to keep my attention. But a small girl, with a seductive smile, quietly reeled me in. After the others hugged and tipped me, then filed out of the restaurant, she lingered long enough to present her information on a perfumed card outlined in roses."

"A charming beginning."

"Uh huh. I called her, on a lonely night in April."

"Rebound sex can be painful so tell me loneliness didn't take you there."

"Not them. At first I was sensible. We made a date to view art and listen to evening jazz at the High Museum."

"That should've been wonderful."

"Right up to the second I slipped into a daydream, staring at this huge painting."

The doctor smiled. "There are many provocative paintings throughout the High."

"In the dream, I was about to touch her fingertips, about to break my arm in an effort to lean forward far enough to grasp her wrist, to brand her with the intensity of my grip, you know, to make her feel how much I miss her. Want her beside me. My fingers were frantically reaching…feverishly stretching…straining for her."

"I know which one you're referring to."

"The painting or the woman?"

"Both." Dr. Wallace met his grin with a friendly eye-wrestle, penning him neatly.

"In the dream, I was nude, we were naked, and I was reaching in desperation. In the painting, one figure reached easily, kinda languidly, a forefinger limp, sorta pointing towards the other, a woman, a naked lady leaning towards him, too, her white fingers fixed on her lover's yearning."

"That's an excellent description. This new someone…this small girl. Tell me about her."

"She's a recent Emory graduate, with all the leisure time in the world to fill her waking moments. Doctor parents sustain her well-padded accounts. Shopping, entertaining, traveling, and hanging with her girls flesh out her days."

"So what else have you done together?"
"Fuck."

J.T. knew it was arguable. But he didn't give too much of a decent damn anymore. He would see the woman this day, even if it meant disrespecting the one sitting up under him now, on the seat of his old sky-blue Buick. He could smell whiffs of her perfume and feel the curvature of her soft, unrestrained breasts in a crop blouse and the taut slope of her thighs in low-slung blue jeans, she sat that close.

"Why can't I go in there with you, Junior Thomas? Isn't like she hasn't seen us together." Donna Lorde crossed her arms and poked out her bottom lip. "What messages are you trying to send the bitch anyway? That you want her back? That you'd rather beg with your presence than with words? That you aren't satisfied with a more beautiful, wealthier, younger, educated woman? That you're jealous of that niggah the bitch was with at the club? Tha--"

She was on a roll, but before she avalanched his pride, J.T.'s thumb dug into her windpipe while his other fingers walled the back of her small neck.

He looked into her face. Without removing his fingers, only letting up on the pressure, he stared at her, beyond fabricated innocence, across a lackluster polish, through nights of screwing her, over his prayers that she be the one to free him from loving Free, past the petite features and stenciled brows, into hazel pools, until he stared at a possessiveness he never expected to come eye-to-eye with in a woman.

"You aren't trying to hurt me, are you?"

"Don't ever call her a bitch, Donna. She's more lady than you'll ever be."

He released her neck then and pulled the Buick's keys from the ignition.

"Oh, well, listen to you, Mister High and Mighty himself. How would you know anything about a lady? You never talk that shit when you sweating over me, dripping funk in my eyes and trying to take up residency between these legs, your pistol shooting its cum anywhere I'll let you." Her nose crinkled as though she could smell his attitude.

"I'm not going to argue. Stay in the car and wait until I come out.

She wasn't trying to hear that. "Since when did you start reading anything besides recipes?"

Blotting her out of his mind, he got out of the Buick and slammed the door. Had he stayed a minute longer, he'd have heard her growl, "Shut up and get right, nig-gro."

The cool air fortified J.T., steeling his frayed nerves the minute he stepped inside the bookstore. Around him, people leaned together, stood off to themselves, or sat in rows of folding chairs. Others peeped down from the coziness of the **Coffeehouse**. All were drawn to a soft-spoken, animated, biscuit-brown woman, whose braids hung to one side of her chin, the rest of the do swept back into a delicate knot at her nape. On the ample fabric of her varicolored skirt lay an open book.

He eased inward, excusing himself and nudging past folks on the outskirts of the audience. Best to cloak himself in the crowd. He calmly glanced about without moving his head, not wanting Frenonia Roberts checking him out while he searched for her.

There, up front, on the fringes of the hushed book signing, he registered Free's girlfriend Sharmayne sitting beside a tall, attentive woman. He stepped up his scrutiny.

The crowd applauded in unison when the author stopped reading and adjusted her vision to their presence. "And that, ladies and gents, is the first chapter of my novel." She informed listeners Atlanta was the first in her 10-city book tour, and standing to bow gracefully, she glanced to her right as the audience cheered and whistled their gratification.

Then Free emerged from the right, a perspiring bottle of water in one hand. She presented it to the writer and smeared the bottle's wetness into her palms. J.T.'s heart felt like crowing but he dared it to bray any louder than it already was or he'd have to leave. And since his heart couldn't permit him to exit without communicating with her, heart to heart, a thing he needed same as he needed his next breath, he willed her attention to his presence behind a seated, elderly couple.

"Thank you so much for being such a considerate audience. As always, we appreciate that. And now the floor is open for questions, comments," she smiled, "and praise."

J.T. fixated on her straight, sleeveless cream dress showing off her shapely figure and those damn legs; there was no doubt in his mind he'd follow them to the ninth circle of hell and beyond. Her hair was longer. His mouth salivated, and his hands ran the length of his jeans. He clamped his teeth to stifle the longing to touch that mango-colored skin, skate his fingertips through the thick auburn hair. After all that he'd gone through, was going through, he wanted her still.

Engrossed in Free's presence, J.T.'s second sense kicked in and reminded him he'd promised Donna he'd be out in ten minutes. So he stepped up his program and courted Free's gaze. And Free, skirting the bookstore and beaming a 'Don't be afraid to speak up' smile, glimpsed a rakishly grinning J.T. a row from the back of the audience, waving nonchalantly near the bookstore's entrance.

But had she known who would be bold enough to speak up, eventually, Free might not have beamed so radiantly.

The air in the store vanished, his presence leaving her statue stiff, again. Her lips parted, mouth dry, eyes holding the man she missed, the reason passion had gotten up and walked out of her life. Outside of him and her, the room emptied; her love lay like alms, a testament to her devotion, at his feet. And he lifted that love gently, reverently, gratefully, a contender winning in the face of odds, within a hair's breadth of defeat.

The audience, forgotten, looked from Free Roberts to the stranger in the rear, at Free, and back again, and then, at the bookstore's entrance.

A young woman's entry bashed the spell. Glaring about, she discovered him behind some old people.

"JUNIOR THOMAS, you said ten minutes, goddamnit, now let's get out of here! DAMN!" She hated to whine. "It's hot out there. WHAT WAS I SUPPOSED TO DO, HAVE A HEATSTROKE?

Cutting the bookstore a 'What ya'll looking at?' stare, Donna looked towards the makeshift stage, got a clear eyeful of Miss Mama with the project name—Shameka, LaKeesha, Shakira, Frenonia heifer, and with a toss of her head, switched back out the door.

Chapter 23

Free and Sharmayne walked into the dark coolness of the small, empty restaurant. With many of the tables unoccupied, they were grateful the bustling lunch crowd J. R. Cricket commanded throughout the week and on weekends had come and gone. Across the street, The Varsity's parking lot had emptied, too.

Under a stick-straight blonde bob that reminded Free of Mary J. Blige, a waitress, butterscotch cheeks plump and rouged with fine traces of gold powder, lifted thick spidery lashes and scolded the two women with a sneer. Overly gold-smeared lips puckered and asked saucily, "What kin I get for ya'll?"

"A chicken salad and a large glass of water with lemon on the side." Sharmayne wasn't that hungry.

The girl scribbled on her pad, shifted her weight under a greasy uniform, and folding one arm across her distended girth while fingering her chin with a gold-tipped forefinger, communicated bodily an unmistakable *Can it be that difficult?*

Free took her time ordering then, intently perusing the menu until she settled on chicken fingers and lemonade.

Sister Waitress huffed away, her nurse's shoes squeaking angst.

"What's with these waitresses and their nasty attitudes?" Free raised her voice as if to summon the girl back so she could cut her down to size, and then request the manager. "Why do Blackfolks treat one another so badly sometimes?" She'd had it up to her eyeballs with one too many gold-lipped sisters with chips on their shoulders for one afternoon.

"Maybe she's tired of being Black or maybe somebody told her she had a few more pounds to lose before she could pull off a successful Mary J. Blige."

"Better yet, maybe somebody should tell her to fire her beautician."

"Maybe the last table ticked her off." Sharmayne laughed softly, placing her pocketbook in a nearby chair. "Besides, you've had enough foolishness for one afternoon. Can you believe that prissy missy? Coming in shouting like she was at home. And cussing!"

"That's what he gets for dating a child." Free screwed her nose and stared towards the entrance of the restaurant at one-way Spring Street traffic. "He claimed I dressed like a teeny bopper, which is what he's got. Said my mouth was trashy when he pissed me off, and again I say, 'Isn't that what he's got?' Ironic, huh? Seems he isn't controlling her any better than he tried to control me." She sighed. "Damn, Sharmayne, talk about complaining---he cut the fool about me acting my age, and here he's dating a girl. Do you hear me? A girl."

Free raked her hands through her hair and pulled it back in a nervous flourish.

"Why the hell did he come? To torment me? I swear, I wish he'd stayed away."

"That's anger talking. You're disappointed J.T.'s girlfriend came in and made a scene, but before she appeared, girl, you both were hypnotized. And it was obvious J.T. hadn't meant for her to come in. Seeing you, poor thing, he overstayed his promise, and Li'l Bit came in to show her tail."

The sound of J.T.'s name sent shivers through Free's body, doused her in instant heat. She knew Sharmayne's interpretation was accurate, at least where she and J.T. were concerned, but that didn't assuage the hurt in knowing he was spending his days with the hussy. Who reeked of being spoiled. And rich and unaccustomed to men forgetting she was the Queen Bee. If that's what he desired, she wished him well; though she'd thank him, however, to leave her the hell alone. A hussy that bold might provoke her to heed the whisperings of a bitch in red stilettos sitting on her shoulder and make her get up and whip that narrow ass one day.

"It's easy to see he hasn't learned much since we separated, huh?"

Sister Waitress placed their orders on the table, but this time, her "Okay, ladies, kin I get you anything else?" came light and cheery.

Grateful, Sharmayne smiled. "Thank you. I'm good."

"No." Free, distrustful of a quick fix, resumed her conversation as if the waitress had suddenly vanished. "Each day, for these three, going on four months, girl, I'm thinking more and more that we may not make it." She unrolled her silverware and examined the fork and willed herself to eat, animosity having squeezed its way into her gut and put her hunger on the run, though the food boasted an appetizing aroma.

"I wouldn't say J.T. hadn't learned anything. On the contrary, I'd say Girlfriend is teaching him quite a bit. For starters, it was obvious he missed you, so much so he had the chile sitting in a hot car, waiting, while he visited his girlfriend's---"

"Ex-girlfriend's." *Why couldn't she stop saying his name?*

"Okay, excuse me. His ex-girlfriend's establishment. I'd wager her purpose in his life is to show him what a gem he had in you. And---"

"But," Free interrupted again, pointing at Sharmayne's untouched food, knowing how slow the woman ate when she started talking.

"No buts. Listen." Sharmayne paused to nibble her salad. "Did you see the nasty look J.T. shot her? Had it been loaded, he'd have sprayed half the room."

Nodding in agreement, Free recalled the look and changed the subject.

"So how's life and love with you? Nzinga ready to host the book club meeting in our premiere lesbian household? The *Daughters* are already buzzing with the idea of such a preposterous notion. Worried cootie juice in the sofa might stain their clothes."

Sharmayne guffawed. Pictures of Willie Mae and Wandra Lynn tipping around, grumbling, sniffing out a place she and Nzinga hadn't made love flashed across her mind and she fell out again.

"We'll make it. Nzinga insists the route to their hearts is via their stomachs, so food will flow like a cascading waterfall. We do everything together, cook, run, shop, bath, read. Yes, ma'am, she has me exercising, us jogging through her neighborhood in the evenings. I adore every moment with that woman."

"Oooh, it's like all that, uh? And so soon?"

"I don't choose to get caught up in time and its limits anymore. Nzinga's forever doing something to make me feel loved and cherished. If you've ever had someone pamper you, say cook for you, and feed you, and make love to you with an unsurpassed tenderness, then you know what I mean. Most times she makes love to me with her mere presence, no touching, just us being in the same room. I imagine her kissing me, soft and wet, and I ache for her touch, her stroke. The mind's amazing. She sends me, as that old song says, 'Babee, yoouuu send me, honest you do.'"

"Sounds like you're happy." Sharmayne's description brought J.T. to mind, made Free bat her lashes to clear her head. "You glow when she's near, I'm talking scintillate. Would've been nice to have her join us for lunch."

Sharmayne smiled. "She had a class. One more thing, I didn't know making love could be...exhilarating...as rejuvenating as it is. Girl, it's the next best thing to breathing."

"Amen. Especially when good sex is scarce. I don't want to ever live without it."

"Loving Nzinga teaches me I don't ever want to live without passion."

They ate in a ruminating silence, tasting only the blessing of their thoughts.

Sharmayne was the first to speak. "Listen, girl, I've been meaning to question you about the jobs available out there for women like me, women who have been stowaways with absolutely no job experience to speak of, women who need to pay for a divorce and become financially solvent while doing so. Please tell me you know of something before I begin pounding the heated pavement and circling the Classifieds."

Sister Waitress squeaked over to the table and smiled. "Dessert, ladies?"

"None for me, thanks." Sharmayne patted her waist. "More water, please."

One brow rose comically. Giggling, the waitress bobbled her head, one finger dramatically indicating her own middle. "Not a problem. And you, ma'am?"

"The check, please."

"I'm sorry about the way I acted. Somebody said something rude and I took it out on ya'll." She placed the check face down on the table with a handful of peppermints and pirouetted, tossing, "Have a sweet day" over her shoulder. 'Thanks, De'ja' was scrawled on the bill's back.

Sharmayne peered at the name. "That was sweet of De'ja."

"No, honey, she probably heard me or remembered we might not be tipping, but let's go back to your interest in a job. Did Miss Edwards intimate you need to help win the bread? We haven't been talking as much since you moved in with her."

Sharmayne smeared a water spot with her napkin, appreciating her best friend's concern. "Two days ago I broached the job issue with Nzinga, but she said I ought to forget about getting one. Says she can take good care of me, far better than Victor Naylor ever could in more ways than one...and she can and does---" she peered at Free's elevated brows "---but I've been gently telling her I never felt whole in that relationship, for a number of reasons, dependency being number one. As a matter of fact, I don't ever want to be dependent on anyone, ever again. Somehow I get the feeling Nzinga thinks my getting a job will take something away from us. I keep telling her I lack nothing, that she satisfies my every whim and need. She scratches me before I itch, and that's how I like it. Except..." her voice trailed away.

Free said nothing, only waited patiently.

"I'm not a kept woman; I know I can pull my own weight."

"I admire that, girlfriend." Free reached in her purse and fished for her wallet. "You can always work with me in the bookstore until you find something more profitable."

An animated ponytail whisked across Sharmayne's back.

"Okay. We'll job hunt together then, maybe go online and devise a creative resume. Something."

Sharmayne pulled a twenty from her billfold and placed it on the bill.

"What's the update on your mother?"

Sharmayne waved at a waving De'ja and followed Free into a steamy afternoon, Spring Street traffic burping fumes and exhaust, as it raced towards Interstates 20, 285, and the 75/85 junction.

"She's coming back for another visit, to search for my older sister and her ex-soldier. Rhonda and I promised we wouldn't do anything until she returned. And no, she hasn't any leads, only that the rumor mill has it that he lives here. I'm glad. That secret was such a burden for mama to carry alone."

On Thursday at the end of the school day, Rhonda slipped into the head counselor Mrs. Garcia's office and took a seat near the window. From their small talk, she gleaned the woman knew next to nothing of this suddenly-called meeting.

With Mrs. Garcia immersed in a pile of PSAT scores, Rhonda courted silence and let her thoughts drift to her mother. Her week spent, Pastoria returned to Pine Mountain without sharing her intentions on how she'd go about finding her ex-soldier and their sister.

"Afternoon, ever'body." Glory Mae Wyatt's deep-south greeting skidded smack into Rhonda's thoughts. "I 'pologize I'm late." She stood in the doorway, out-of-place, waiting for an invitation to enter the office. When Mrs. Garcia greeted her, she sat in the seat nearest the door.

A sparrow of a woman, Glory Mae Wyatt looked from the counselor to the teacher and plumped an unwieldy purse onto her lap as though it were an unmanageable child.

"I 'pologize fah callin' dis meetin' so last-minute, but I had tah take quick action. Ya see, my male friend and Jomo cain't see eye-tah-eye, like I done tole Miss Garcia the las' time we talked. They fights a lot, ober any li'l thang. I cain't unda'stand it. Seems a man bein' grown could look ober what a chile be sayin'."

Glory Mae Wyatt spoke directly to Rhonda, the darker of the two women, and in that, the most familiar.

"I knows y'all got plenty tah do so I'ma jus' gone say what I came to say." Her short thick hands took up a nervous condition, fluttering over her purse straps, winged to her collar, hovering above a threadbare spot in her pants, and flitting about, eased the pocketbook over the hole before she continued. "The boy ain't got nobody but me. His Mama, my

206

niece, in prison fah drugs and she gone be there a while, I hear, same as Jomo's daddy, her boyfriend. And now they baby headin' down the same road they on. If Jomo stay wit us, Miss Butler, he gone tie up with my man and he gone try to hurt the chile sump'um bad, showing the boy who boss, who pay the bills and who carry the weight round the house. When he wanna be, that man mean as these here pit bulls folks be walkin'."

She spoke as if the listening women didn't believe her. "My man has it in him, 'cause I done seed it." There was no need to admit she'd felt it, too.

"And since I loves my nephew, and since he done promised me he gone do betta, I gotta ask you, Miss Butler, if I can pay you a li'l sump'um fah Jomo to stay wit you till I'm able to get him in the Job Core program or youth camp or sum'where?"

Rhonda, surprised, opened her mouth to say she couldn't possibly make that decision, and definitely not without her husband's input, but Glory Mae Wyatt's next spill silenced her.

"Jomo say you the only one who care about him here. He the one begged me tah come, tah ask you. I tole him, Miss Butler," she went on, no longer aware of Mrs. Garcia's presence. "I said, 'Jomo, dat lady got her own fam'ly tah deal with and cain't be saddled wit us, wit you.' But naw, he steady tellin' me, 'Aunt Glory Mae, she dif'rent. She love her students, and she love me, too. Ask her, she do it.'"

Seeing Rhonda mute, Mrs. Garcia got up to impose order on an up-ended conference knocked off its base, and Glory Mae Wyatt fell silent in the heat of their reaction, then said, "I unda'stand, baby. You caint' do it---you just cain't do it. We all do what we cain. And goodness knows, you already done more than yo' share as it is. And I jus' wanna thank you for that."

Glory Mae rose to go, bowing and thanking the women for their time. But Rhonda Butler gazed into the older woman's eyes and blocked her exit. In a glassy silence, she heard her purpose clearly.

"I'll do it, Miss Wyatt."

Mrs. Garcia stepped around the desk. "Mrs. Butler, I don't think you should--"

"Tell Jomo he can stay with us." The counselor the last of her worries, she hardened her resolve for the greater battle to come, Big Trevor angered when term papers and weekly tests trailed her home, snuffing their already tendered time.

"The school year is almost over, Mrs. Butler," Mrs. Garcia insisted. Then to Glory Mae Wyatt, "Besides, isn't he still in the detention facility?"

Glory Mae Wyatt and Rhonda Butler stared at the counselor. What Glory Mae knew was what Rhonda suspected. The woman had never dealt with the heartache of a problem child, had never had one dumped into her lap, had never reached out to one through prison bars, had only, like Rhonda, witnessed someone else's woes.

"If Jomo can abide by the rules of my home, he can stay as long as he needs to."

For there to be no mistake, Rhonda reiterated her position with Mrs. Garcia pent under her resolved irises.

Chapter 24

The Saturday afternoon of the next *Daughters of Isis Book Club* meeting, the *Daughters* had difficulty latching the gates of their mouths. Sidelong glances shifted to steadfast stares, storing gossip about their hostesses and the oddity of their female-plastered world. Behind arched fingers and affected vivacity, the women settled into Nzinga Edwards' sun-splashed living room, the gentle radiance of June struggling to purge the room of a persistent prating that sprang up like weeds.

Unlike Free, Nzinga predetermined food would be near at hand throughout the meeting. She'd set out plates of spicy meatballs, assorted cheeses, multigrain crackers, purple grapes, diced fruit, buffalo wings, three salads, and a heaping tray of corn.

"Being we'll be double discussed," she said, "the least they can add is we had some damn good food, hey baby?"

Sharmayne had stared at her, as she stared at her now. The woman could be pushy sometimes. From her post in the archway of the kitchen, she watched the sun's rays get caught in Nzinga's fade, the white button-down shirt and jeans complimenting her noticeably handsome allure, a characteristic Sharmayne adored.

Nzinga's visual caress fluttered along her cheekbone, and Sharmayne sighed, lost in her touch.

When she crossed the room, though, one hand rose self-consciously to her softly curling wilderness. *Was every eye in the room trained on her?* In her head, someone asked how so dark a woman dared to adorn herself in bright purple, then, to kill the dog, go and leave her naps uncombed, the hair twisted in spirals across her head. She glanced about. Under the music of Nzinga's voice, the blessed assurance of Frenonia's presence, and the familiar regard in Rhonda's smile, Sharmayne straightened her back and remembered she was beauty incarnate and volleyed her woman's affection with a slow, sexy smile.

Nzinga glowed, opening the floor for discussion from her seat on the blond hardwood. Her glance, like Free's, roved to Corliss, who, ever eager, sat up and toppled into talk.

"Plain and simple, ladies, I loved the novel. My sole disappointment--its length--all 476 pages. In **Brothers and Sisters**, Bebe Moore Campbell created a world I could've lived in for 500 more pages." Animated, Corliss sprang to her knees from a seated position on the floor. "Of course, I didn't expect anything less from Sister Campbell, whose **Sweet Summer** and **Your Blues Ain't Like Mine** enchanted me."

Her eyes swept the room. "Anyone else read her other books?"

"Here we go again." Willie Mae yawned, stretched, and eyed the ceiling.

"I concur, the sister is tough," Free spoke up. "**Blues** made me a fan for life."

Thick dookey braids in a chin-length pageboy softly framed Corliss' dark face, her smile appreciative. "In **Blues**, I admired the humane way the blacks and the whites were portrayed, especially the whites directly responsible for Till's death; fate doled its spoils to everyone, not Bebe, as a sword-welding writer, divvying up Hell to pay for the atrocity committed."

"Can we," Willie Mae growled, "stick to the book we all read? Gee, we put up with that stuff at the last meeting. I don't know about anybody else, but I don't have the time to read more than one book a month." She crossed her arms. "Humph, all us ain't students with personal time." She sat back on a kitchen chair and rolled her eyes.

Corliss and Gail glared at Willie Mae, their comments primed for blood-letting, but Nzinga, the consummate hostess, had a nose for spiraling smoke, a skill perfected in her classes.

"So...let's circle the room telling what we liked about the novel first. And don't forget. Be specific." She grinned at Deandra. "We'll start to my right."

Deandra perched on a sofa, her sandaled feet scissoring air.

"Ooh, Nzinga, you start. I'll listen for right now."

"No problem." Nzinga smiled. "I was crazy about Esther Jackson. Homegirl was intelligent, kind, attractive and sharp-tongued. By the novel's end, I knew she'd excel beyond her old position at the bank, whatever the future held. She was level-headed, success-oriented, and--"

Suddenly Deandra forgot about listening. "What? That chick was a childish, snobby-nosed heifer, who despised Brother Man for having the wrong j.o.b."

"---and multi-faceted," Nzinga finished, ignoring the small woman's interruption. "Esther was a *real* person, more *real* than many of us."

Snickers trickled through Wandra Lynn's fingers.

"Yeah, I know what you mean," Rhonda acquiesced. "Not only was she all of what you initially outlined, Nzinga, but also Esther..." and she glared from Wandra Lynn to Willie Mae, "...fell for the wrong men, snubbed the interracial couple next door, booted Hector for LaKeesha, and wanted Humphrey because he smelled successful."

"Precisely!" Nzinga popped her fingers. "Humphrey had a grab bag full of problems Esther would've had a time dealing with, from that domineering mother to that ghetto sister and her teenaged, going-no-where-fast son."

"Yeah, but he owed them," Reesa added. "They couldn't help being poor. The sister...remember...had a story of her own. Her mother slighted her for Humphrey."

"Don't think so, girlfriend," Wandra Lynn said, scratching her scalp and yoking her neck. "Nobody told her to marry that poor man and birth all them children. Nobody stopped her from going back to school after the marriage hit the rocks either, and I'm pretty sure 'Humpty,' as his sister's boy called him, might have willingly paid for it."

"Willingly, I doubt," Gail said, "but true, 'Humpty' might have loaned her the money for the abortion. Let's shift the subject a minute, though. I kinda liked Tyrone my damn self. Brother Man was fine, had a banging body and gorgeous booty, a serious set of ethics, and a level head. Charming, he was a considerate lover. And most importantly, he possessed the instinct to survive in tight-ass situations."

Gail waited for someone to whiplash her, so she could verbally beat them within an inch of their tired lives, but no one touched the critique, her tone advising them to think before they leaped.

"Undoubtedly, Cousin," Nzinga conceded. "Tyrone was Esther's man, with his T-shirt-selling behind." She laughed, recalling Tyrone's entrepreneurial spirit. "If he were a dyke, we'd be married." She and Gail fell out and an ominous silence coiled in the room, until Lisa's comment revived the crippled conversation.

"I agree," Sharmayne said. "Mallory was similar to Esther. For starters, both made unwise decisions when choosing lovers." Her voice boasted a confident stride. "Take Hayden, Mallory's married heartthrob, who never intended to leave his wife; then look at Mitchell, who sailed in and out of Esther's love life with impunity. Both men left havoc in their wakes. Esther and Mallory were prospects for a friendship made in heaven, although they had to work through Mallory's whiteness, which left them estranged, at times."

"Good points, Sharmayne," Reesa praised.

"Yeah, baby, we can't discuss the novel without comparing those ladies."

Nzinga's gaze was so balmy she may as well have gotten up and kissed her.

The *Daughters* ate and recorded the tenderness between the two, and in the remaining hour and a half of the book club meeting, the discussion was a garden snake, winding its way over various topics from Mallory's sincerity about Humphrey's sexual harassment, Kirk's insanity and crime, pages and pages of the book's unbroken paragraphs, its "excessive descriptions," as some called it, LaKeesha's portrayal, which all deemed beautifully authentic, to Preston's son's affinity for brown sugar and for Humphrey, the backdrop setting of Los Angeles and the Rodney King riots. Even Willie Mae admired the novel's message: we all need to get along: Korean, Black, white, Hispanic, rich and poor alike.

By the time the tail of the conversation glided back towards its beginning, pleasantly stuffed, the women trudged to their cars, hushed exchanges about the brow-raising bond between Sharmayne and Nzinga venom-less. Which didn't say, though, that parts of the meeting wouldn't make for savory, leftover chats.

When Pinky went to get Mookey from Javan Reed's secluded East Point mansion, Clemmy passed as much of the day as possible under her mother. After dinner, she sponged and rinsed the last plate and passed it to Pinky, whose face shone under the light of the recessed fixtures in the white showcase kitchen. Outside, the night was genial and cozy.

Angelic. That's how her mother looked.

Clemmy swished the sink clean and wiped the counter, rinsing her hands under a lukewarm stream. She still couldn't believe her mother was 31. That meant her mother should've been a relic, though when she pictured her girlfriends' mothers, Pinky looked more like her older sister, as some people commented, whenever they made treks together into downtown East Point.

"Look outside, Mommy," the girl whispered, standing on her toes to bring her cheek to Pinky's in the kitchen window. "We look like sisters?"

"Absolutely."

Pinky savored the velvety softness of her daughter's cheek. The texture of the skin anchored her, kept her in the present, instead of displaced in the outer reaches of her mind, alone, where she'd begun to spend quite a bit of her existence, sitting or standing in one spot or lying on her bed, her body stuck, like a stereo's needle in a deepening groove, habitually executing whatever task she'd undertaken before her mind abandoned it. In that state, she was oblivious to time and place. When she disappeared, she conjured a facsimile of her mother, same as her daughter entreated her to peer into blackness so that she could better envision their likeness. Staring into the night, their reflections lucid in the windowpane, Pinky watched a sun set in a woman who favored her and a younger carbon copy of the woman.

In the window, their fusing faces were one.

"Our skin is different, huh, Mommy?"

"No, not *that* different."

"Mine is brown, Daddy's color. Yours is yellow, with a high shine underneath, like there's a sun inside you. I'd rather have your skin, Mommy."

The fusion in the windowpane frowned.

"Don't talk like that, Clementine Reed. Your skin, like my skin...and hair," which she knew the girl would mention next, "has done nothing good or bad for you to place one color over the other, one hair texture over the other. It's all the same in your mama's eyes. You hear me?"

Pinky's tone struck a nail in the girl's joy.

Yet in her musings, Pinky's mother reincarnated in her image, and since she didn't favor

Earl Taylor, she had to favor the nameless woman she adored.

The reflection of the younger version nodded. Then giggled. And the older replaced her sternness with a closed-mouth smile. They continued like this, until Mookey tore into the kitchen and interrupted their revelry, his round face captivated by their strange play each time he witnessed it.

The kitchen ordered, the way her father liked it, Clemmy grabbed her brother's hand and her mother's and led them upstairs to her bedroom, where the three retired, Mookey to watch "The Simpsons" and mother and daughter to play Scrabble. Clemmy, like her brothers, nurtured a proclivity for entertaining herself, yet she relished the opportunity to match wits, her father not a man for idle play.

Before the night felt old, Clemmy and Mookey showered to be ready for church on Sunday morning, the alarm clock on the cherry wood nightstand beside her canopied bed flashing 10:30 p.m. Javan Reed could be coerced to see a situation from divergent angles at his daughter's encouragement, but missing church services to hang out with her mother and half-brother was not one of them.

Later, they giggled over cups of lemonade with Pinky, who made a game of identifying rappers and singing groups on the walls of Clemmy's bedroom. For each one she identified correctly, which weren't many, she received a kiss on the cheek.

Then Clemmy poked her own cheek out of the covers for her mother to smooch.

"Good night, Lewis Earl. Good night, Mommy." She kissed Mookey's cheeks, her mother kissed theirs, sister and brother snuggled into the bed's cloudlike softness, and Pinky longed to have them, with Taylor in tow, happy and secure, in a home of their own, on a beautiful, tree-lined street called Lovejoy.

***

Wet from the shower, she slipped into a lacy white gown with elegant flowers scattered along the scalloped bodice. Delicate. She'd caught it on sale, in Perimeter Mall, and saved it for an occasion like tonight. The last time should be special. So when she thought the children were asleep and wouldn't make out her footsteps past their slightly jarred door, she tipped down the hall to Javan's master bedroom.

Hopefully, this time would be different--- she'd be appealing, desirable. In her dreams, Javan stood at her door, gently rapping, and twisting the knob, quietly letting himself in. He kissed and embraced her. Pulled back the sheets and, after a long moment admiring her taste in sleepwear, mesmerized by her supple womanliness underneath, his mouth fell on hers and, this kiss far sweeter, he touched her soul. Every time. His lips sucked her neck, his tongue in her ears, driving her to pant his name, draw his mouth to her delirious nipples, the white lace abandoned. Leave her soaking.

She ached for him to want her without malice, without her invariably offering herself up to him, like a whore in heat, as he'd whispered one night, his fingernails gouging her flesh, when she'd have died a thousand deaths for him to touch her delicately. "You come to me so unashamed," he'd said through clenched teeth, his handsome face contorted, the luminosity of the fringed bedside lamp making a cameo of his features, rendering the moment strangely, sadly magical.

She neglected to hear the hateful words, and imagined that he cared about her, this last time, the sweetness of her body and the pureness of her love possessing the power to cure and change, endear and enamor.

And he lay awake in the night, waiting for her to come.

He'd tried to be gentle whenever she entered his room, but judgments always slipped in behind her and took a seat on the bed, on the chairs, on the windowsill. He did his best to fend them off. But their voices were loud, their recriminations stinging, persistent, familiar. Most times he wanted to kick himself for being weak, in a sick way, for this woman. So he punished her instead. Now, kicking back the covers of his king-sized bed, he looked down at his dick bent towards his tangled mass of pubic hair, the veins along its side pulsing, its head purple with need. Rigid, it bobbed, calling for a woman with no future to part her thighs over the one-eyed drill, so he could bulldoze her, heedless of passion, which he didn't have time for anyway.

In lamplight, he offered his hand. Desire rose in him like a fountain. Then before it bubbled towards his heart, it receded back the way it had come.

Pinky stumbled to him anyway, her body wet under the lace, thighs already smeared. The thought of his nearness set a lioness on the prowl, the attraction to him raw, primal. When she reached the bed, Javan embraced her roughly, and she tumbled across his broad, slightly hairy chest. She devoured his scent, a musk that brought another chute of wetness down her thighs.

"You come so shamelessly," he snarled low in his throat. "I'm not responsible for what I do." One hand clasped her wrists, the other slapped her butt cheeks solidly, then softly, surprising her, and she began to whimper. That behind of hers made him holler, all solid and round, tambourine tight. He meant to make it sing while he put a stinging on it. The sound of each lick made the next harder, sink deeper into the beautiful flesh. The riff of her moans became lyrical, and his bongo-playing palms beat a blues melody across her butt that made him shudder, it was that sad.

All of her white was worrisome. "Why you got on this mess?" Mad, he rose up and flipped Pinky, trying not to wrench her arms in his passion. She bounced onto her back. They exchanged looks. He liked the shock in her eyes. It empowered him, and yet clasping her hands, though they'd have remained bound had he released them, his grip mesmerized her.

Right now, his free hand was slapping promiscuity out of her coochie. Popping it rhythmically. Steadily. Her head rolling from side to side, Pinky's moans stained the bedding, and her thighs widened of their own accord, as though her joints knew springs, instead of ligaments. With each smack to her ruddy-colored pussy, she flattened her mouth into a fervent line not to cry out, her body moving up toward his receding hand, as though magnetized, anticipating another blow to tender flesh. She buried her face in a pillow to take it: the want, the stings, his hand, the heat. And he was bent on giving her what he thought she wanted, this woman---clout, slap---with three children by three different men. He'd give it to her alright. Hand soaked in her wetness, he reached down and spread her swollen, grape-red lips, mining her juices and mashing the flesh between his fingers periodically as though to make a sweeter wine.

When he got enough of spanking and reveling in the way she lay so motionless for his pleasures, his tool thumping, salivating to be inside her, he pushed ten inches of hammer into her furnace and pounded mercilessly. Insane, his hands stalked her terrain, grabbing and stroking her thighs, dipping and digging. Atom-bomb temps steamed her insides, and she breathed hard, he harder. The pounding satisfied a yearning deep within both, and hurtled them over a precipice, where Javan Reed plummeted to her breasts, exploding with her in a climax of her desire and his lust.

Rough, he bruised her back against the mattress, until he shriveled and slipped out of her body, indicting, "Whore." But this time she sighed something that sounded like, "You the whore, your folks pimp you for their happiness." Her lashes flickered. "No more your whore." She said it so, so low, Javan couldn't be sure she said anything at all.

He darkened the bedside lamp. Since she favored the color white, for whatever inexplicable reason, he didn't want her gown lighting the hall with enough light for his daughter to know what he did with her promiscuous mother in the still of the night.

Had he known their coupling was already memory, Javan Reed might not have bruised Pinky's heart. But asked judgment the hell out of his head, heart, and home.

Chapter 25

Disquietude and dread befriended him. Took up with him for weeks now, like old friends.

Victor Naylor opened his front door to a resounding silence. He didn't have to shout her name and walk through the bellowing rooms to know she wasn't there, but he did both anyway. Action steadied him. He entered the kitchen. She'd scoured it of everything, even smells. "Shar-maaayne!" The inside of the refrigerator tattled, much like the unanswered calls when he'd phoned home in Colorado and North Carolina. He walked inside the pantry and found a can of whole stewed tomatoes and a half-empty box of macaroni among the olive oil, crackers and oatmeal.

When he tired of the mocking house echoing her name, Victor washed his hands and boiled and drained the pasta and then, in a small sauce pan, sliced the stewed tomatoes over the unappetizing concoction.

Was it possible she was gone?

He ate, his head churning with thought. Leaving the dirty dishes on the table, he sought refuge in the living room, where, in his favorite chair, he imagined what he'd say when she walked through the door. From shopping with Free…most likely. He picked up the phone to call Freddie but changed his mind. Freddie might say the unacceptable.

Exhausted from bouncing on the lumpy seat of his tractor trailer, he climbed the stairs with wooden legs, gripping the banister, heaving his weight upward. He undressed slowly. The bedroom whined and he knew why, though he needn't have opened her drawers and stared at the gaping space in the closet where her clothes had been. No shoes neatly arranged on the other side of the door. No make-up tiered on the vanity. Not even the latest books she was reading on her side of the bed.

"Shar--maaayne!   Sharmayne? SHAR...MAYNE!"

A cold shower revived his faith, and he sprawled across the bed in fresh boxers and a white T-shirt he'd found in his underwear drawer. With bleary eyes, he bore holes in the vaulted ceiling, bewilderment closing in on him like a lizard with addiction in her veins and infection between her legs, stalking a truck stop for peace in a stranger's arms. His body cried out for a few measly hours of real slumber, but his mind mocked louder than the mocking house, louder even than roaring silence.

He still couldn't believe it. His woman had snapped, had allowed those freaking spirits to uproot shit in her touched brain. An unnatural heifer. She and that...that...damn dyke were probably laying up lapping and feeling on one another and bumping and grinding and doing whatever else made up their bullshit love.

When Victor couldn't take anymore of the ceiling, the white stucco flashing subliminal images of women having sex, he flipped onto his stomach and pressed his forehead on his crossed arms and gritted his teeth to keep from crying.

How the hell had loneliness climbed down out of his truck's cab and walked its ass into his house like he wasn't Victor Naylor? Behind closed lids, he strained to remember who he was. Amused, his mind took pleasure in the knowing and reminded him what others thought of who he was, too.

On a recent run, a fellow Georgia trucker stopped at his table. Over a dinner of liver, side salad, rice and gravy, and rolls, they shot the breeze at a stop in Charlotte, North Carolina. Victor did most of the talking, guffawing at his own jokes, while he shoveled food into his mouth, and kept the Mexican waitresses tickled at the play in his eyes and the dollars tipping from his wallet to their palms after he'd palmed them enough to understand, "No mas" and "Muchas gracias" and "Le gusta?"

The trucker's mustache fluttered over thin, gravy-stained lips. "Victor, man, you talk a lotta shit about that woman of yours. She cain't be as bad as you raggin'."

A penetrating blue gaze dribbled over Victor, unafraid of the result of his unsolicited advice. "Ever have a decent word to say about the old lady? Ain't half careful, man, your lady be done packed and left you with a big-ass, gapin' hole smack dab in the middle of yo' heart, and you, my friend, ain't gonna have the ready resources to repair it. Keep talkin' that yang, Homeboy." How he pronounced 'homeboy' ridiculed Victor's ears for hours afterwards, male laughter at an eavesdropping table curdling his hunger.

Now, bile in Victor's stomach spawned the notion that although he rarely had anything pleasant to say about Sharmayne, surprisingly, he did love her and found her physically appealing. He vowed to fill the house with purple hydrangeas and lilacs and find her, wherever she was, and invite her home.

The Friday after he'd been home for one

week, disquietude and dread caught up with him in the form of a tall, officially pressed sheriff, who served him papers that brought tears to the back of his throat before they stood in his eyes and overflowed his heart with shards of a woman he never imagined he'd miss in a thousand years.

Passion lived in Nzinga's fortress, Sharmayne's spirits knew.

Lying on her back, arms splayed in sleep's helter-skelter repose, Sharmayne awoke gradually, mind and body yawning, like the morning, every inch of her instantly desiring a replay of last night's love-making. She luxuriated in the beauty of her magically changed life, and in the way it, like her body, had come into a wondrous wakefulness. Her toes snaked the width of the cozy bed, already knowing as they slithered, the object of their hunger was up and about. Skiing into the warm indentation left by Nzinga's body in the waterbed, her toes ached to caress Nzinga's ankles and feet, one of their favorite pastimes.

Her arms settled for cradling a starched pillowcase, sweetly redolent with the vanilla scent of Nzinga's body and hair. Sharmayne lay under baby-powdered sheets, listening to another Monday morning symphony.

A flush of water, a cascading waterfall, segued into the padding of feet to the vanity, where a pelt, pelt, pelting simulated the music of morning rain.

After the pelting, whining cabinets creaked and an electric whir followed a soft sucking of teeth, and then gurgled liquid wafted to her ears. Spurts of rain masked footfalls into the walk-in closet. Then, almost imperceptibly, there was the quick click of metal on metal and a soft slap of leather against skin.

Unless Sharmayne muffed her ears, Nzinga couldn't camouflage her coming.

Would she ever get enough?

"Good morning, sweetheart." Nzinga grabbed a handful of sheet and yanked it from its tucked-in neatness at the foot of the waterbed and slid her hand underneath the cotton, aiming for Sharmayne's ankles. The tiny woman squealed in delight, flailing her arms and straightening then drawing up her legs and skating them out of Nzinga's grasp, their foreplay making her 'it' in a heated game of tag.

"I heard you coming. No fair!"

Nzinga marveled at her raven's heightened nature, at how perfectly she fit into her muscled embrace. "You hear everything?"

Sharmayne giggled, sheets above her head. "Uh huh, but I'm not sure what you did in the closet."

"Got a shower gift from me to you. And a promise, you'll never be the same."

"Life-altering, huh? Might have to think about that one."

"Abandon thinking. The objective is to feel. And feel deeply."

With heavy rains still falling, the squirming bundle fell limp, listening, as Nzinga crawled the sheets and squatted over a humped back, cocooning it, and when she did so, a thickness between the cleft of Sharmayne's ass made both women shudder. Nzinga lowered the sheets and breathed in the macadamia-perfumed locs. She stroked the frozen shoulders, a purple and beige strap-on, custom-made, fitting perfectly on her washboard waist. Nzinga tapped it against the guitar-shaped curves of her woman's body. Dark and delightful. The phallic saluted, its cool, bulging head startling Sharmayne.

"Not frightened, are we?" Nzinga kissed the back of Sharmayne's hands. When Sharmayne shook her head no, thick locs sweeping her shoulders, Nzinga cupped the small chin, and turning it sideways, gently kissed the mouth, sucking her bottom lip. She caressed the neck, the hair, the shoulders, before savoring the sensual delight of a handful of beautiful breasts. The nipples chocolate raisins, Nzinga tasted and nibbled them, until they melted on her tongue.

Sharmayne sighed. Her lashes black butterflies, like the bevy swarming about her heart, making her flesh glow with a sweet heat washing over her entire body, from the curls of her nape to the back of her thighs, every inch of her alive with throngs of quivering for Nzinga's kiss, for the way she was drawing every drop of flavor out of her, her pussy weeping to have Nzinga finger it, kiss it, and now fuck her with a dick bigger and more colorful than any she'd ever seen.

Nzinga's fingers massaged her spine, soothing her. Though her heart was beyond soothing. It throbbed with a frenzy that doused the jet skin in a spicy sweat. Everything about the woman made Sharmayne feel good. Flat on her back now, Nzinga above Sharmayne, their breath in the other's lungs, the women embraced.

"You…go-ing…in…to-day?"

"Not before you receive my gift."

With kisses slipping down Sharmayne's spine,

her pussy purred prettily, and she gave herself over to being carried to wherever prisoners of love were taken at dawn.

Nzinga stepped into the tub and, maneuvering just enough to permit the cold stream to shock her body first, gradually eased Sharmayne under the deluge, the water beading clear crystals down her back. Sharmayne whimpered and went baby-soft against smooth, strong flanks, their bellies kissing, with shapely midnight calves encircling firm golden hips. Soapy hands, silky and sensuous, lathered Sharmayne's body. Nzinga, gently penning her against the shower's cold tile, moaned and stroked Sharmayne's waist, back, and thighs. She wiggled in excitement, the cold and the heat commingling, taking her to the mountaintop to be baptized in Nzinga's kisses.

Skin soggy, Sharmayne struggled to maintain a slippery grip on Nzinga's towering slickness. She tittered, slipping and sliding, thighs eventually tiring. To keep her from falling, Nzinga anchored Sharmayne's weight with her hipbone, the upward motion sending shivers of liquid heat to her hidden pearl. Exhilaration bathed the delicate woman, and she moaned against Nzinga's shoulder, teeth nipping the skin over rippling muscles. Desire and wetness melded their flesh, pellets of water powerless to squelch a smoldering building towards a second coming.

Sharmayne gasped.

Nzinga was lifting her up and down, slowly, playfully, and she reveled in the sanctity of her ass in Nzinga's palms. She kissed her lover's neck and lips as she felt a saluting stiffness kiss her own drenched pussy. "Hold on, baby. Tighten your arms around my neck." Nzinga's murmuring against her ear made her shiver, and she clamped down on the Amazon, the shower's tile aghast at her back. Sharmayne let out a soft shriek and leapt for joy. Nzinga was sliding the purple and beige wand into her body. Tongue flickering over her nipples. Fingers thrumming her clit.

And Nzinga's gift filled her, and she rode it, and Nzinga rocked her, and she cried. It was true.

She belonged to Nzinga, and Nzinga to her.

Nzinga bouncing and fucking her to a variation of rhythms, their energy mounted, sending them into exquisite titillations, one filled, the other filling, until they imploded, together, in a spell of lights and colors and heat and emotions.

"You okay? Didn't hurt you, did I?"

"Only if you can make it hurt more...I'd like that."

Nzinga laughed. "I can handle that."

Sharmayne lay prone in a puddle of moisture. She wanted this woman, Nzinga Edwards, to love her however she wanted, as long as she loved her passionately.

Understanding, Nzinga planted a kiss, like an African planting a holder's post, on the curvature of Sharmayne's lower back. Then she plucked the CD's remote from rumpled sheets, where it often hid, like Sharmayne and a book, and, pointing the remote towards a glassed, ivy-adorned, mahogany case, pressed a button and released her personal brand of fuck-me melodies, the first the crooning lushness of Me' Shell Ndege'Ocello's aphrodisiac, "Stay."

Then Nzinga began to play her again, a

maestro, this time laying Sharmayne on her belly, unaware she was, of how thoroughly she decamped all memory of Sharmayne ever lying under Victor Naylor, the memory, something that gnawed at her, sometimes, whenever they were in the company of men. But her insecurity dissolved, always, in the love in Sharmayne's eyes. The woman couldn't imagine a world outside of Nzinga's kisses, kisses potent enough to have her, as she was now, climbing their waterbed, a sumptuous morning glory vine creeping toward the sun.

"*Who* do you love?" Nzinga murmured into the side of Sharmayne's neck. "*Who* loves you?" Her breasts sighed against Sharmayne's back, her pubic hair tickling the gentle rise of the ebony buttocks. She reached for a plush white towel on a chair and dabbed it along the soft darkness of her lover's body. Their fingers laced spontaneously, and Sharmayne basked in Nzinga's aura. A magnet, she pushed upward, slowly, arching her back, signaling Nzinga to rock with her against the cool sheets. The ceiling fan whirred rhythmically. A fine mist of sweat formed on Sharmayne's upper lip and, as the music they made sizzled, her face against the sheets, rivulets of moisture glazing their skin, causing suction kisses and, remembering the shower, their tempo sliding from light to momentum, she fastened her perspiring arms about amber forearms, her backbone hot against Nzinga's bosom, and the smack of Nzinga's dick easing into her became a never-ending symphony.

Nzinga's body commanded her, and Sharmayne couldn't think straight to entertain the question lodged in her locs. She prayed Nzinga wouldn't stop, but when Nzinga's crescendo smashed her dazed pearl into the mattress, her body's honey sweetened the grateful sheets and she lost the power of speech...again.

"Who *do* you love?" Nzinga trilled, low, no threat to Ndege'Ocello's soulful "Who Is He and What Is He to You?"

Sharmayne heard her and felt her and submitted. To a point.

She allowed Nzinga to play her skillfully. Teeth clamped, she suppressed what Nzinga aimed to hear and went with the drumming in her ears a while longer. Complete submission would come, inevitably, as it always did; but for now, she bit her bottom lip, prolonging sweet release for them both.

Nzinga had it like that. So she rotated slowly, until she faced her and rained a flurry of moist, tantalizing kisses on her face and neck, breaking Nzinga's meditative pose above her. Slowly, methodically, Sharmayne pushed herself into Nzinga, their rhythm a slowed bongo that picked itself up and up, past Sharmayne's elevated legs, and empty cat, then pounded faster, then beat harder, working itself into a steady, frenzied backdoor thrashing. In no time, Nzinga had her dangling over the edge of the world, right where she wanted her.

By the time Nzinga rescued her, breathing hard, and trembling, Ndege'Ocello had graciously stepped aside for the rock-n-roll sass of Melissa Ethridge, whose plea "Don't You Need?" suffused Nzinga's insatiable need to taste Sharmayne's nectar.

"Who do *you* love?" Nzinga took a rare pearl between her lips. She massaged slender thighs before tossing them over her shoulders. Her tongue lashed a chocolaty clit, lips sucking greedily, mouth consuming sugary vulva lips. Her fingers, thermometers, gauged Sharmayne's internal fire.

Sharmayne couldn't control it. She clawed at the sheets. At Nzinga's back. At her hair. At the soft valley between her thighs and hips. Until a scream roiled up from her. Head back, throat exposed, Sharmayne wafted towards a tongue that refused to take silence for any answer and, tensing with satisfaction, knew again the masterful musician Nzinga to be, her sonorous melodies coming from Sharmayne's pores and pussy.

"Who do you *love?*"

Sharmayne couldn't deny her. Forever.

"You!" she screamed. "Oh my god, you! I love you, Nzinga!"

Lips parted, like her thighs, both screaming their pleasure, the small body writhed in flames of liquid fire.

"I love you, too, baby girl." The Amazon cradled her, their heartbeats one.

Neither woman cared a single iota about the unbridled passion slipping under the raised windows of Nzinga's fortress into the calm of their North Highland neighborhood.

On the inaugural Saturday of the *National Black Arts Festival*, the sky was periwinkle blue. It shimmered with an invisible heat that reflected off the asphalt in the Greenbriar Mall's parking lot and volleyed it up the bare legs of crowds of festival-goers. Pinky and Sherrie Ann weaved their way through bands of folks heading towards the mall's entrance.

"Honey chile, you betta drag your behind on."

Sherrie Ann had to admonish a tarrying Pinky, who sashayed leisurely, hips and thighs seductive in blue-jean shorts. A white crop top inches below her bust, glittering white flip-flops on her feet, without jewelry or make-up, Pinky was at home in her sensuality. Her A-symmetrical haircut had grown out, and the curly bob that replaced it now threatened to bouffant into something resembling the unconquered territory on Sherrie Ann's straw-colored head.

"It's hot as hell out here!"

Pinky snubbed her, stuck a finger into her mouth as if to vomit. "What's the rush? There's so much to see at these events, I love them."

"C'mon, woman, before I have to cuss---some of your cousins stepping on my damn feet like they crazy and no apology to speak of."

They cruised up the right-hand side of the mall corridor and jockeyed through a knot of kente-clad sisters engaged in a reunion and stopped to admire a display of hand-crafted, hand-painted, resin dolls. Arrayed in elaborate traditional costumes, with braids and soft wiry halos as hairstyles, the dolls were miniature girls and women.

"Bet Clemmy would love one of these little ladies." Pinky examined a placard claiming the dolls as Sandra Blake originals. "I should put it on my credit card." She peeked at another, searching for a price tag. "Girl, it's a hundred and twenty-five dollars!"

Sherrie Ann frowned and gave her a look of disbelief.

"Now, I know you didn't come way over here thinking these folks traveled further to permit you to rob them slap-happy blind. They done sweated over this stuff, and can't hand it to you, for peanuts."

"I know…but…"

"Honey, unless Clemmy came out and said, 'Mama, I want a Blake doll,' I say you ought to encourage Homegirl to check in with that stuff-shirt daddy of hers and let him shell out his greenbacks for this doll." All the while Sherrie Ann spoke, she guided Pinky backward into the milling crowd.

"Would you buy one, seeing how much you collect all kinda sculpture?"

"Yeah, if one could sing and dance and feed my fish and jump up and scratch my big butt when it itched. Uh huh. I'd buy one."

Pinky laughed, cut her a *Girl, shut-the-hell-up* look.

"Okaaay! I'd buy one if I really wanted it; they are nice dolls, but don't make a decision just yet; you might see something else that catches your eye."

Stopping a few feet ahead, she peered left then right, before pivoting right and plowing towards a dazzling exhibit of African-American sculptures, the first in a long line of exhibits running the length of the mall's main thoroughfare.

Pinky stared at her girlfriend's departing back and shook her head; the woman's living room was buried beneath wood carvings and masks and figurines. But she couldn't worry herself with that nonsense, not with the mouth-watering aroma of yogurt, candy, and popcorn assailing her nose. Though the last thing she needed was extra weight in all the wrong places. So she checked herself.

Then she meandered down another section of the mall, pausing now and again to finger multicolored ceramics, photography, more clothing, books and jewelry. When she'd purchased a set of seven-dollar copper bracelets for herself, a storybook for Mookey, and an unusual bangle, wide and silver, for Clemmy, she drifted back into a throng of shoppers and, stopping before a partially unoccupied bench, plopped down and crossed her legs and people-watched.

She marveled at the beauty and diversity in the predominantly Black faces and stared at the hairstyles---afros, cornrows, serious weaves, Senegalese plaits, dookey braids, straight wraps, pressed do's, twisted locs, natural and permed, and wrapped and kufi-crowned heads. *Did the brothers always rival the sisters in clothing and headdress, many decked in loose-fitting, cool-looking African chic?* After twenty minutes, she got up and looked around for Sherrie Ann.

Tucking her possessions under one arm and surveying more displays, she resolved to catch up with her talking girlfriend a little later. Right now, something was telling her to peep at one final exhibition.

Paintings mounted in ornate frames, metal and wood, hung from a draped contraption behind a black, velvet-cloaked counter. A tall, good-looking, dark-skinned brother stood behind the counter, talking with a short stocky woman in a flowing dress. He was handing her a large bag Pinky knew whatever was inside she couldn't afford, so she wended past a clump of teenagers with British accents scrutinizing a painting of a wearied black man leaning against a wall. She cocked her head in contemplation. *What had drawn the kids' spellbound attention? Wouldn't have been Taylor staring at that picture, but maybe*

Clemmy. What looked like a nude sister painted in effulgent pastels, bringing to mind watercolors she'd purchased for Mookey, jumped out at her. She grinned and shook her head. That would be the painting her Taylor would deem tight.

Continuing to browse the exhibition unaccosted, Pinky floated from painting to painting, which seemed to oppose one another, watercolors now, brilliant with varied hues, and then charcoals, muted with subtlety, and always of familiar Black faces. Scenes. And emotions. One painting, no, a series of paintings, beckoned her, summoning her to communion with them, the intimacy of their women, common African-American women, some young, some older, alive with the pain and joy of living in their features and bodies and personalities. She studied the sequence of eight paintings, positioned in a thoughtful combination. Astonished at the familiarity of the exchange between the images and her, she was transfixed, remembering, instantly understanding something of what could've reached out and held the teens rooted in their footsteps before a simple painting.

The women whispered.

Of secrets from her childhood. Of loneliness. Of longing and the compulsion to be wanted. Brown and black and hazel gazes stared back at her from breathing, still faces; faces that soundlessly chuckled at her tomboy appearance when she accompanied her daddy looking any kinda way; faces that bided her scoot back on a sofa and thumb a magazine while Earl Taylor's speechlessness screamed under modest moans; faces that glowed over plates of beans and cornbread and salt pork and invited her not to nurse the food but eat it; faces that censured her whines and apprehensions when fast afternoons faded into slow evenings and tumbled into slower nights; faces that favored the wintry beauty of Grandma Taylor and Miz Too-Sweet; and most poignantly, faces that connoted specters of a face that might've resembled her own.

"They tend to wrench you right up out of yourself, don't they?" a disembodied voice intoned behind her, startling her. "One woman told me yesterday they're the very semblance of her mother and aunts---until it's uncanny."

Still under the womanly spell of the paintings, Pinky nodded slowly without turning to recognize the speaker. "Yeah, like they're casting spells. The more I look, the more I see things I didn't notice a second ago. And the strange thing about all of them is I know them, I really know them, but then again I don't."

The voice hummed and she went on. "These women was all I knew as mothers when I was coming up. By the same token, I didn't have a mother, I mean, not one there every day, you know, cooking breakfast, fixing lunch, kissing your boo-boos, going to PTA, fussing you out, sticking up for you, and tucking you in at night." She crossed her arms and outlined her lips with one forefinger. Lost in the pictures, she swallowed rising waves of bitterness and blinked back corrosive tears.

"Hey, it's all right." An unexpected hand on her shoulder soothed her. "I have happier paintings that might lighten your mood. Sorry my ladies conjured such melancholy memories." The phantom of the exhibit, his voice crisp and up North, pointed a well-formed arm to frames of dark children carousing on a corner block.

The admission turned her head. "Your ladies? You painted these?"

"Afraid so, but I hope that doesn't mean you'll be flying away now?"

Why would she?

It was the tall brother she'd seen chit-chatting with the woman when she first approached the exhibit. He smiled, his face suspended above hers. He was disturbingly handsome, the kind of fine Sherrie Ann would say, deserved some pussy on looks alone. She couldn't arrest her gaze, couldn't thwart her body from wanting to flutter into his arms, her heart positive he'd be a flawless fit in her embrace.

"Hi," he said, still smiling and appreciating what he saw and reading the undisputed language in her eyes. "I'm Grant Johnson, the guilty visiting artist whose work has profoundly wrecked your morning." He chuckled.

They shook hands and he imprinted her features on his painter's retina, where he'd keep them, until he sifted through the images of beauty there and brought them out of safekeeping for memorializing on canvas. "So nice to have affected you, Miss---?" he hesitated, leaving the unfinished question dripping on the air between them, a balm.

Fragrant and inexorable.

Like her presence.

"Taylor." She offered her prettiest smile and her hand. "My family and friends call me Pinky." Invisible, the balm oozed along the surface of her skin, its aroma intoxicating. "Nice to meet you, too, Grant Johnson, the man with two last names."

"As in General Grant, sometimes, too."

"Ain't never met no real-live painter."

The admittance plummeted through the balmy sweetness between them and reverberated a timbre a brother like this one wouldn't want to get used to; the flatness of her tone and the childishness of what she'd said upsetting her, making her wish she could magically ingest the words.

"That's perfect. Never met a real-live princess."

They laughed. And he walked her around his kingdom narrating back story for his work. And she reigned in the sun of his easy talk and possessive nearness. And they exchanged explosive glances. And the episode of their love played out in their heads like a movie.

Then Pinky bumped into time. It was already past 1:45 p.m. on Grant's gold Timex. She remembered she'd promised Miz Too-Sweet she wouldn't be late getting back so that she'd be there when Free brought her and Mookey and Mr. Will back from a festival event at her bookstore. She thanked Grant for his time.

"The blessing was mine," he said. "Thank you for being…here."

She turned to go, and then spun around to hug him. "See you."

"Hope so." His words were more prayer than parting.

Chapter 26

Later, when Pinky got in from the mall, she heard the front door creak and hurried **to** lather her body one final time before stepping out of the shower. She pulled on a white terry cloth bathrobe and wrapped her moist tresses in a blue-and-white striped hand towel.

Couldn't be anybody but that gotdamn Lewis Reynolds or Taylor.

Down the hall, she came face-to-face with her son.

"Look at you." She pinched her nose. "Been by a mirror lately? You looking too much like what any self-respecting alley cat would have the decency not to bring home."

"Ain't like the streets got accommodations, Mama, when you ain't got funds."

"Well, get used to it. Seem to me, you bent on a future with more of the same, the rate you going. Enough young brothers in public looking raunchy without you adding to the list. Just throwed away. Too pathetic for words."

Pinky shook her head and grimaced. "C'mon in the kitchen, and tell me where you been, boy." She spoke softly, fanning him forward with her hand.

"Ain't seen you in days. Guess you smelling yourself, thinking you a man now, huh?"

Short Dog sulked as if he were five.

"Aaah, Mama, it ain't like you missed me."

He dropped into a chair at the table. An excruciating itch developed low on his belly, and he resisted the impulse to claw the area under his mother's scrutiny.

"Boy, stop talking nonsense. If I didn't love your bad ass, I wouldn't have gone up to that school to see about you before the other kids got out for the summer, since Lord knows you dismissed yourself weeks prior to June fifth. What you be doing every day?" She didn't wait for the answer he searched for on the ceiling, out the front windows, down the hall. "Baby, what's wrong with you? Don't you know whoever you running with in those streets ain't gone be down with you when the going gets tough? What they doing for you anyway, besides nothing, Little Man? You look like you been rummaging in somebody's garbage pail some damn where."

Short Dog was mute.

He kept one sneaker atop the urge to tell his mother that his boys were doing more for him right now than she or his daddy ever did. But he didn't. He might've reminded her that she couldn't even see how much better off they'd all be if she'd just stop fucking around with no-good-for-nothing dudes like Lewis Reynolds and Javan Reed and get with his old man. Maybe he'd cut his crew loose, and be the little man she longed for. Hell, she'd lived her life. Was still living it and dancing by the beat of the drummer in her own head, not his, not Clemmy's, not Mookey's.

So, fuck it; he was doing his own thing, too.

Nobody ever listened to him no way. After all, a niggah like him---he'd often informed his boys, who frequently needed reminding he was a real man, too---was going to get his, no matter who got trampled.

"Where's your mind? I'm telling you things to help you, not hurt you, and you're sitting here daydreaming, not paying me any attention. What did I just say?"

Short Dog hunched his shoulders and rolled his eyes and held his head to one side. Gazed up at his mother through long lashes. "Sorry, Mama."

She softened when he said that and reached out, motioning for him to submit to a hug, a blessing to settle any dispute in his mother's reasoning.

When he was younger it could, but now, at fourteen, it wasn't enough. But since he loved her, he knew he'd come whenever she offered an embrace. Although he smelled like a monkey, he succumbed to her hug and tried not to cry, a thing he couldn't help doing when she hugged him. A tear fell, and he focused on getting a shower and changing into clean rags. He sniffled. Wiped his face on his mother's robe.

"When the last time you seen your father?"

Pinky held her breath against his smell and rubbed his muscular shoulders. "Bet you ain't seen hide or hair of the man."

Short Dog remained tacit, secretly enjoying his mother's freshness.

"Baby, promise me you'll either stay here at night or go over your dad's house."

As she held him, he longed to beg her to visit his dad, and he'd honor them both by spending more time with Omar. Dreams of being at the center of a real family crept up on him like a thief in the night, in his quiet moments, but he never wanted to blatantly disrespect his mother so he said, "Okay, Mama."

"Okay, Mama, what?"

"Yes, ma'am, I'll come home."

"Thank you. Mama don't want you to wind up

headed down a one-way street."

She kissed him gently on a grubby cheek. And his stomach growled.

No, she wouldn't want that. 'Cause that might mean Lewis Reynolds and me would be traveling companions.

Pinky released him and asked offhandedly, "Where were you when it poured?"

Short Dog hunched his shoulders diffidently, mumbling something even he couldn't understand. His mother responded with a raised-brow sigh and began chattering, picking up Mookey's books and toys, rehashing her morning at the *National Black Arts Festival* and telling him she had to get to Miz Too-Sweet's to see how his little brother had enjoyed his day.

Short Dog's gaze trailed his mother from the refrigerator to the stove to the pantry. He sat and flicked on the radio which promptly emitted the mellifluous voice of Rachelle Ferrell singing, "You gotta believe…you gotta believe in me."

He got up and leaned on the counter, wholly interested in his mother preparing a grilled cheese sandwich and dicing a red apple and pouring a glass of milk.

"Go wash your hands."

In the hall bath, he washed his face and hands and cleaned under his nails and reentered the kitchen. He bowed his head, said grace, bit into the sandwich. He didn't know if it tasted good because his mother prepared it or if he was simply starving.

While he ate, Pinky cleaned the kitchen then disappeared inside her bedroom. When he heard her door slam, he breathed deeply and his head sank to his forearms, his thoughts a mad jumble.

Jomo sensed Mr. Butler's presence before Trevor, seated across from him, peeped up from the desk to serenade his father's arrival in the doorway of their bedroom. Since his first night under the man's roof on a humid May evening, there was something lurking behind every comment Mr. Butler made, resentment in his glance, gruffness in his gestures when Jomo ventured too near.

It was now June, and Jomo was yet trying to understand.

Would he have willingly shared the closet of a bedroom his Aunt Glory had been able to give him with another person? Hell yeah, he'd be resentful. But he couldn't reason that argument too long in justification of Mr. Butler's actions, considering how Mr. Butler was a big-time dentist, for crying out loud, had a bad-ass crib, cars for everybody except the kid, who'd probably, no doubt, get his own on the afternoon of his high-school graduation. Comparing that to where he was coming from, which was no damn where, Mr. Butler should've be ashamed of his sorry-ass attitude.

Despite Mr. Butler's behavior, Jomo delighted in having a little brother, someone to look up to him. He took pride in helping Trevor with his science project, staying up late into weekend mornings, overseeing the little dude while he shaped flow charts on the effects of air pollution. He loved assisting with the reams of research Trevor lugged home from the Etheridge Elementary library. In no time, Trevor's notion of a futuristic air pollution monitor was built.

Mrs. Butler and her sister—Aunt Free, the only ones who noticed, appreciated and praised his efforts---counted. But even when the little dude won the school competition hands down, and Mrs. Butler raving on and on, praising his influence, Mr. Butler was uncompromising.

Try as he might not to overanalyze the situation, Jomo understood the man's position. He was a stranger to everyone outside of Mrs. Butler, and he'd have to confess, straight up, in the pathetic time he'd passed at school, fighting with her and later loving and respecting her against his usual intention, he was sure glad she hadn't argued that she didn't know him that well her damn self to be letting him into her home.

That Mrs. Butler, she was something else.

She was the closest person to a mother he'd ever known, aside from Aunt Glory. And he'd do almost anything, no anything, for her. All she had to do was ask, and she really didn't need to do that.

Which reminded him. Mrs. Butler asked that he eliminate profanity or not use it in the house. He promised her he'd honor the latter and contemplate the first, considering she didn't ask for much. The house rules were simple: help Trevor clean the bedroom daily, assist with the household chores, complete homework early, attend school regularly, be home for dinner, and be home before midnight on weekends.

No hanging out during the week.

When he thought about it, merging into the Butler family hadn't been a beat down, thanks to Mrs. Butler, nor had it been a bed of roses, thanks to Mr. Butler.

He got up and lowered the volume on The Notorious B.I.G.'s "Big Poppa" and waited until the father-son chit-chat ceased, and then he shifted his weight in the chair to greet Mr. Butler. His "How you doing, Jomo?" held about as much warmth as a fine girl turning her head, knowing she'd heard him holler.

What did Mrs. Butler see in the man?

Yeah, he looked decent, but he wasn't all that. Jeez. Why couldn't he be cool and giving, like his wife? Instead he was identical to Aunt Glory's man---hard-hearted, selfish, and domineering. The blessing, they both showed him the man he wouldn't be.

He turned around in his seat, resumed his position bent over his American history textbook, and scanned the boring reading. He had to do well on all of his up-coming finals for several reasons: one, his American history teacher wasn't especially fond of him; two, he was behind in everything and was working double time to play catch-up; three, passing grades were a major clause in the deal he'd cut with the school and Mrs. Butler; and most importantly, four, he wanted Mrs. Butler to know that he was down enough to make good things happen so that she, his Aunt Glory, and Aunt Free could be proud of him.

That was why he'd canceled the profanity that trekked across his mind whenever Mr. Butler appeared. Why did the little man have to look like Mrs. Butler spit him out single-handedly? Just because he wasn't fortunate enough to live with his dad and mom, he'd be honest and continue to work overtime trying to assure Mr. Butler that he wasn't as foul as the animosity that wrinkled Mr. Butler's nose.

Thus far, his overtime meant buying a leather belt. He'd given up sagging three days after he moved in. Though sometimes he couldn't erase the memory of Mr. Butler's voice blaring through his bedroom door. It was as if he and Mrs. Butler had taken their argument out of the privacy of their bedroom and put it on blast throughout the house.

"What kinda shit is this?" Mr. Butler had yelled. "Why didn't you teach the boy how to dress before you brought him into our home? Next thing I know my son'll have his pants hanging down around his tail and a handkerchief on his head, huh, Rhonda! What kinda negative influences you got in my son's face, right under my nose?

"You can't save the world! How many times do I have to tell you that? All you're doing is playing with fire, hot searing fire, and if you aren't careful, not only will you be burned, but you risk bringing harm to my only son as well."

No matter how hard he tried to go deaf, fighting back angry tears burning the back of his eyes, he couldn't make out Mrs. Butler's response. He remembered the knockdown drag-outs he and Aunt Glory's man put down. All because of his presence. Shit. Seemed he didn't belong anywhere, except with Short Dog and the boys.

He drummed his pencil on the desktop.

But hell, he'd put those dudes out of his mind. They were trouble. They were the reason he'd ended up in the detention facility; rolling with them, he'd always be headed for somebody's jail.

"How can you all do homework with racket going nonstop?"

Jomo's gaze stumbled to his history text. *Damn, didn't he have something better to do?*

"The music helps us study, Daddy." Trevor

chewed the tip of a pencil. "I know because I always get my work right when Mama checks it, after Jomo reviews it first." He grinned, swinging his black and white Nikes, grazing Jomo's jean-clad legs with every swing. "Jomo's helping me with my math assignment now."

"That a fact?" Mr. Butler was amused at the child's enthusiasm.

"Yeah. You don't like rap, Daddy?"

Big Trevor's gaze skirted Jomo's back, the teen's head askance, his posture poised in inquiry, too. "It's not that I don't like rap, son, it's just that I wouldn't want you---or any other kids---glamorizing the profanity, violence, and misogynistic themes that come up in most rap music, that's all. And I especially don't want you listening to that loud music when you're supposed to be concentrating."

"What's misogynistic?"

"When rappers say unkind things about girls and women in their music," Jomo explained matter-of-factly.

"That's right." Mr. Butler cleared his throat. "So son, how's the math coming?"

'Great! Jomo's teaching me the times tables and explaining fun ways of understanding the word problems I used to hate. It's cool having a big brother, Daddy!"

Mr. Butler peered at the teenager with kindled interest.

So the kid had smarts. He was thankful for small miracles.

"Want me to turn it down lower or off, Mr. Butler? Whatever you say goes."

Even with the dark mop of corded hair

hanging just above his brows, giving him a roguish quality, sincerity glowed in the youthful, sepia-colored face. Gruffness imploded within Big Trevor. After several weeks, he didn't know why he treated the teenager like an ex-convict being rehabilitated in his home. He knew his attitude pissed Rhonda off, leaving her unable to separate the difference between why she constantly fussed with him to be nicer to the teen and why she moved to the edge of the bed at night, nearly executing a balancing act, whenever his leg ventured close to hers.

"Just turn it down a little, son," Big Trevor heard himself say, the word 'son' surprising even him. He never dreamed of calling the kid son. Ever. But now that it was out, the word cemented the three together in a tangible sense; causing, as it did so, Li'l Trevor to study his father quietly, realizing without knowing that something good had happened; the word floated between man and teen like a prayer, and in that instant, Jomo Wyatt would've attempted the spectacular feat of righting every wrong he'd ever committed.

He shot up and flicked the CD's sound button to a faint volume. When he rejoined Trevor, their eyes rose to a beaming smile that abruptly appeared behind a now grinning Trevor Butler.

"Love you, darling." Rhonda's whisper tickled her husband's right ear. "Thank you."

The current between them rendered Big Trevor bashful for a fleeting moment. Recovering quickly, he moved his head and brushed his wife's cheek with a kiss.

"No, thank you, baby, for another opportunity, as you would say, to choose love." He averted his attention to the watching boys. "Should have known you dudes wouldn't be radiating that kind of affection at me."

"Aaaw, daddy," Trevor said, giggling. "You jealous?"

Big Trevor laughed, stepping out of the doorway and pulling Rhonda to him.

"C'mon, guys." Rhonda playfully shoved her husband and winked at a shame-faced Jomo and an amused Trevor. "I need to break up this male thing. Before I know anything, my sole respite will be the kitchen." She snickered. "Dinner's ready."

Miz Too-Sweet saw him first. She eyed him eye Pinky well before Pinky stood over their table to note her and Mookey's order. Flitting about, Pinky saw to it that she and the children and Sherrie Ann had seats and were comfortable. Then she elbowed her way back through the crowd, Clemmy close on her heels, to brave the counter.

The Varsity was crowded for a Monday, but not so crowded Miz Too-Sweet didn't spy the tall slender man, looking like money, treeing Pinky. The look called to mind a hound dog that had chased a coon to the top of the highest pine, the dog spitting fire, boldness in its standing hair.

If there were two things the old woman knew, she was, for one, daggum sure she could still read that hungry look in a man's eyes---didn't matter she hadn't seen it directed at her personally in not nary a man's eyes since Will's nature had simmered years ago; what mattered was that she had on her freshly wiped glasses behind which she could yet see to see---and, two, she was for absolute certain Pinky Taylor needed another man making admiration over her about as much as she needed more holes in her head.

Somehow, though, she was positive he'd strike a beeline straight for their table, which overlooked The Varsity parking lot and Spring Street. Down below, Miz Too-Sweet watched young folks swarming everywhere, so many flies, buzzing from cars to small knots of other young folks and back to leaning on the cars and each other, just bees in the breeze.

For a second, Short Dog crossed her mind.

Hopefully his stay-in-the-street, wet-behind-the-ear self wasn't getting into too much trouble with his grown behind.

Her attention shifted from the scene in the parking lot to the bodies around her, bodies she knew would've had Will's head spinning and swimming, had he come with them. After a while, her attention lighted on the dark-skinned young man, stretching his neck over the crowd, straining to keep his eye on the children's mama. Right now, Mookey, little bronze legs swinging to beat the band, face resting in cupped palms, those nut-brown eyes shining, smiled his pleasure.

"What you grinning at?" Miz Too-Sweet gripped her purse to her ample bosom and mirrored the child's happiness. "Are you a li'l-tee-bitty boy or what?"

Mookey recognized the opening to their familiar game, and grinned.

"Yes, ma'am! I'm a li'l-tee-bitty boy, and I'm happy because I got my Miz Too-Sweet with me!" He sang the words, as though they were a childhood ditty, his voice growing louder the closer he got to the word 'me,' and reaching 'me,' he threw his head back, arms up, and let his voice rip toward the ceiling.

"Sh-sh-sh, Mister Man. You got to hush that fuss, you ain't at home. Us got to be mindful of where we sitting, folks everywhere, looking and eating."

Miz Too-Sweet skewed her mouth to one side and sucked her false teeth, tickled.

At that moment Mookey startled her. He pointed a finger toward her left shoulder. "Here comes Mamaaa! And she's got lots of food!"

Miz Too-Sweet liked to have squealed herself; she was tired of listening to the growls rolling up from her own belly. Hadn't realized how hungry she was earlier. She watched as Pinky, smiling like a movie star, rested a red tray heaping with food on the table. Pinky passed her a large Pepsi and a plate of golden, crispy onion rings and a weenie overflowing with chili. It smelled so good Miz Too-Sweet almost licked the aroma right off the air.

Clemmy set one of the trays she was balancing in front of her brother, then slipped in a plastic chair beside her brother and leaned over and rubbed her nose against Mookey's cheek.

The girl was dressed in jeans that stopped inches under her navel and a white off-the-shoulder blouse---the same outfit her mama wore. Javan Reed had dropped her off on Saturday so she could spend a few days with her mama before mid-August, when school started.

Miz Too-Sweet giggled. *Bet the gal did some serious whooping to accomplish that.*

Once Pinky and Sherrie Ann got seated, she bowed a gray head, the others automatically following her lead, and asked grace.

"How you enjoying things?" Pinky loved seeing smile lines soften the old lady's features.

Miz Too-Sweet grinned in response and bit into her chili dog.

"Mookey Man good while we gone?"

Pinky glowed with maternal love, asking this more of her baby than the old lady. Mookey bobbed his head, mouth stuffed with onion rings, ketchup smeared across his top lip. He and Miz Too-Sweet shared conspiratorial winks.

Not five minutes into their meal, Miz Too-Sweet saw it again. She saw him shove his hands deep into his pant pockets. Saw the hunger in his look grow hungrier.

And finally, saw him politely excuse his way through a drove of people on a straight beeline right up to their table.

He decided to walk. Despite being unlucky in love, he walked out on the tenuous ledge of chance and leaped. Again. The decision took him all of twenty minutes.

He'd been studying the group since they'd entered, knowing instantly that she was 'The One.' She was unforgettable. From the moment he'd first laid eyes on her.

"Good afternoon, ladies…oh, pardon me." He grinned at the boy. "And gentleman. Please excuse the interruption." He slipped into his Teddy Pendergrass voice. "Had to come over and say hello." His gaze swept the party and hurried back to Pinky's face. "It's Miss Taylor, isn't it? And do people still call you Pinky?"

She recognized him instantly.

He stood there, rooted, praying he wasn't predestined to smile down into yet another pretty face he could love effortlessly, into a face that might never return his tenderness, into a face that, for whatever reason, always loved someone else. Life had doled him a different hand this time, though; he could feel it. Her aura foreshadowed it, in the twinkle in her big brown eyes, in the way her parted red lips intimated desire, and in her extended pause, implying she remembered something about him she hadn't realized she remembered until now. But he'd go slowly this time, real slow, honoring all that was communicated between them...even if he had to do it long distance.

"They do, if people still call you Grant."

He smiled and laughed royally. "You remembered."

"Still painting?"

"Can't not. With me, it's more my life's pulse."

He got stuck watching her mouth. "Been thinking of you...often, even tried calling but you're unlisted. Don't want to prolong your lunch. Wonderful seeing you again."

Pinky could feel him receding, but he was a tide she needed to lap her a lifetime.

"You're not interrupting, I was about to ask you to join us." She raised one hand ceremoniously. "Forgive my manners. Dunno what I was thinking. This is my oldest, Clementine Reed. We call her Clemmy." He bowed to the teen. "And beside her is my youngest." Pinky giggled. "He's Lewis Earl Reynolds; nickname's Mookey." The room fell away around her, and she went for broke. "I have another boy. Taylor Alexander. He's fourteen."

Something told Grant Johnson to stay, not allow appearances to fire his feet.

"This is my good girlfriend, Sherrie Ann Turner."

He bowed at the scrutinizing girlfriend.

"Beside Sherrie Ann, last but never least, is our adopted mother, Mrs. Sinclair. We call her Miz Too-Sweet."

"My pleasure."

Thank God! How incredibly lucky he'd thought to grab a dog at The Varsity before heading back to the Alliance Theatre where his art was on exhibit in the lobby. Even as he reached into his wallet for a business card to pass down the table, the thought of a young single woman with three children by three different men begged his heart to be cut out of his chest and handed to him. But he wouldn't begin with doubts.

No. A woman that attractive and sweet had to have been with other men, but...no, there'd be no getting hung up on the butts. The ball was in motion now.

Silence following the introductions, Miz Too-Sweet glanced at the stranger's business card. *Free ought to get his number, too, being he was a painter.* Then she looked at an enraptured Pinky, rising and looking around for a chair.

"Oh no, can't do that." Grant arrested her effort with an airy caress.

"But thanks for the offer. Gotta get back to an engagement."

"In Atlanta long?"

"Only if I'm spending time with you."

She considered his card. "Great! This your

cell?"

"Yes. Call anytime. Maybe we can grab a bite to eat..." his eyes skirted the table, "...and take everybody to the zoo, a movie, dinner or all three."

"I'm sure we'd...they'd like that. Maybe they can see some of your art, too."

Their eyes cuddling, Pinky poked at her cold greasy onion rings; any other time they'd have turned her stomach. She considered her children, Mookey down at gobbling his meal, Clemmy staring up through long dark lashes, another mommy-daughter secret between them. Miz Too-Sweet was studying this stranger while busily cutting up her chili dog and pouring ketchup on her onion rings. Chin on laced fingers, Sherrie Ann's attention pin-balled from Pinky to Grant, amazed at the tendency beautiful people had to find one another anywhere.

"Hey, that gives me an idea! Kids and paint is a surefire winner, and I've missed the workshops I used to offer school kids in my hometown."

"Where you from?"

"Down 85 South. Tuskegee, Alabama."

"You're kidding? Three hours away, and I've never visited the Carver Museum."

"Not a problem. I'll sign up to take you. We'll make a weekend of it."

"Promise?"

"I'd leave you my heart if I could make it to the parking lot without it."

Everyone, even Mookey, laughed.

"One question before I go, Pinky---What's your given name?"

"Pastoria."

Grant repeated the name. "That's the most

beautiful name I've ever heard. It suits you."

"Thank you. I kinda like Grant myself."

"That's good to know. And I grant you may like me more for an afternoon of your time. I'll grant you three wishes every hour, and if they're rare, I'll write grants to obtain them. Don't take me for granted…and miss the time of your life."

Pinky laughed. "Enough, enough, your request is granted, I'll call."

She was grinning, they both were, they all were, and in that instant, he saw himself taking her to Tuskegee and introducing her to his clan as Pastoria Johnson. And for the first time ever, he wondered what it'd be like to adopt a woman's children and call them his and possibly share his last name with more than their mother.

The good feeling the thought engendered walked him to her side, made him extend his palm, and when her fingers floated to his, he brought them to his lips and kissed her hand. It was soft, incredibly soft, and softer even than any hand he'd ever kissed.

Chapter 27

"**Ya know, doc**, I don't know why Black folks—at least quite a few of the ones I know---forge a brick wall against seeing a therapist when their worlds spin outta orbit. For years, I was the same way, thinking seeing one was double crazy. It was like admitting to the world your ass was nuts, and two, you had to pay somebody to learn the good news."

Dr. Wallace chuckled and shook her head. "So true. Too many of us labor under the notion that therapy is solely for whites, as if we're acclimated to hard times. Got genes to combat the inner workings of the mind when it goes for a walk on the wild side, dragging you along for the ride."

"Pretty much."

"So, J.T., you ought to have a bit of knowledge to share about what life has taught you since last we talked. Learn anything new about yourself?"

"Have I? That's all I've been doing lately...getting to know me, and the first thing I'll say, which you'll be happy to know, Dr. Wallace, is I like me, love me, actually."

"With that said, I'd say you're definitely on the road to reclaiming self, and..."

"...everything else will follow." Junior Thomas sank deeper into the chaise lounge, crossed his legs at the ankles and entwined his fingers in his lap. Smiling, he couldn't help adding, "It reminds me of church, and the preacher saying if you get right with God, as in 'Seek ye first the kingdom of heaven,' almost like that's our primary purpose for being here, and then whatever we desire or need finds our front door."

"It's closer than almost, sir. It's the bottom line."

"Yes, ma'am. One thing I've learned is jealousy is a motha. Only thing I figure you can do with it is let it make you better or get you mad enough to do something constructive."

"You jealous?"

"I used to be wildly jealous, but right now I'm referring to the Green-Eyed Monster in somebody else's eyes where it's easier to analyze. Donna's forever comparing herself to Free, always asking me if she can screw me better than that 'old lady,' and Free isn't even thirty."

"You've got to remember, Donna is what, twenty-three? In her mind, Free is an old lady and an ancient one at that."

"Yeah." J.T. laughed. "In my mind, there's no comparison. Donna's insatiable appetite could never sex me into forgetfulness. However good she is, being with her doesn't hammer memory from my dreams. May I be frank?"

"And when have you not been?" Dr. Wallace tapped her pencil against the pad.

"Okay, just don't want you to feel disrespected."

"No need for apprehension. I've listened to far more graphic, sir. But thanks."

"Donna Lorde and I shared the type of sex that some women mistake for the Fourth of July; it feels great on the surface, where you're raw and ready, banging and biting, and many times the delusion of love can be spawned from flying sparks, which, the morning after or a month after, proves passionless, spawns instead the birth of custody battles and disappearing dads and why-he-ain't-no-good and she-shoulda-kept-her-knees-closed blues."

"You're one of the best male communicators to ever grace this couch."

"Thanks, doc."

"But did you ever communicate your feelings to her? To save you both time and trouble."

"Kinda sorta."

"No, okay. Let's continue."

"Making love with and to Free is the elation of a dive in a sparkling lake in the freshest of mornings, feeling the utter magic of slipping into the water, that reminds you of slipping between her legs and being marooned on the beach of her body, all soft and toned and sweet-smelling and sleek and it's not that you don't wanna go crazy and bite and stroke and fuck, but it's a different desire to go ballistic. It's where you go far deeper, and with a reverence, to please, to adore, to love."

"If everyone could make those distinctions early on, we'd have fewer relationship catastrophes, but we learn at different rates, at different times. And it's all good."

"I've learned where jealousy and envy exist, a healthy, wholesome union cannot. I've learned love, true love, has no desire to possess. It gives of itself freely, without expectation; one presents, as a gift, one's love to another, no ulterior reasons to speak of. I've learned that I adore everything about Frenonia Roberts, even the traits I said I wanted to change. Learned I've forgiven her for having an abortion she thought I didn't know about."

"An abortion?"

"A couple of years ago, after we'd been together for two years. We never talked about it, of course, but now I know she figured life with me would've been hell if a baby were added to the picture. And she would've been right, too. I was crazier back then."

Chapter 28

Yes, ma'am, she killed the dog.

Almost like the time she and the gals come for the "Free Your Mind" reading program but on a grander scale. That Miz Free done outdid herself and got every unused space around Techwood packed with folks and a lot ain't even from this community.

Me. I'm sailing from one event to the next, tickled and making sho I see and hear everything and everybody. She calling it "A Celebration of the Arts," a leftover off-shoot of the *National Black Arts Festival*, what done come and gone, but this Miz Free's brainchile geared just for us. Ain't that something? These youngfolks can do a heap more today than we could in my day, 'cause I still can't get over it, though wind don't lie, said she gone be a blessing to many and I be hog-tied if that ain't true on this here July Friday. I'm in the rec, sitting in a corner watching the gals, Miz Reesa and Miz Corliss, who grabbed and squeezed me, when they laid eyes on me this morning, like I was family. Made uh ole lady feel special. You'da thought I was on vacation instead of right here in Techwood and they wasn't at that women's college they attend across the city.

I like them, they sweet. The Doe, Miz Reesa, precious.

Don't know what got into her the first time I met her but she sho didn't return with that 'Stay outta my space' spirit. And that's a blessing, got everybody loving on her today, same as they loving Miz Corliss and everybody in Miz Free's party, which go for the adopted ones, like Big Boy, who done left his basketball and peanut gallery somewhere, and he plastered to Miz Reesa like he uh strand in her plait.

At the moment I study Big Boy plugging up a T.V. and another gadget, a VCR maybe. Chillen on blue mats, the same ones they brought before, patiently waiting for some kinda movie to start. Miz Reesa shuffling through a bag, pulling out tapes every so often. Then I see why they off in a corner. The chillen watching a video on dance with skinny Blackfolks, men and women, from what I can see, leaping across the screen, flying without ropes or wings.

"Hi, Miz Too-Sweet! You wanna join us?"

Miz Reesa grinning and waving, calling the chillen's attention to me in the back, near the doors. That helper of hers grinning, too, all muscle, mouth and hormones.

"Oh no, ma'am. Miz Too-Sweet just glad to be here, taking in everything." I wave at the chillen, who waving like they in a parade. "What ya'll watching?"

"It's *The History of African-American Dance*. We're going to talk about the film later, and Deondray and I are going to show the children a few dance steps, then the children will share their favorite dances with the group. Right, children?"

Good Lord. Ninety-nine voices go to clamoring at once and near bout drive me outdoors where it's sunny and warm and peaceful.

"That's so nice. Be back around when ya'll gets ready to cut a rug." The chillen find that hilarious and Miz Reesa tickled, along with Big Boy, who can't seem to keep his eyes off her; she right cute in faded jeans with holes at the knees and a tight pink T-shirt with 'I love AKA' in a big heart. If I remember correctly, it's a college group she say she pledged recently, this semester, I think.

"Alright, Miz Too-Sweet, we'll be looking for you!"

"We miss you, I'll come find you, okay!"

Big Boy shout this, arms muscular and folded across his chest, black shirt tighter than hers making him bigger than big. Amazin' what the birds and the bees can do for a person.

"Okay, Pumpkin," I say, "I be here." He go to grinning and look over at Miz Reesa for the signal to turn on the T.V.

I get up and head to where Miz Corliss got her space sectioned with a semi-circle of chairs, and she and a hive of big and little girls sitting on mats facing one another. Miz Corliss is holding a huge book of rich pictures of Blackfolks with braids and roped hair, what folks call dreadlocks. She's reading and pointing to the large glossy pictures. The girls bobbing they heads, following her. A slew of white foam heads, under blonde and black wigs, long and short, lined up at her bare feet. I wave at her, not to interrupt; she gone teach her chillen how to braid or twist or lock. I smile at that one. She gone find some of these chillen bout workshop her when it come to braiding and fixing hair. I slip up and take uh seat around them, somebody might go to work lifting this wig and braiding the tender gray strands I got left---do and I'll end up dancing the gig in Miz Reesa's section.

Next, I mosey on to a set of older kids and youngfolks and nearly fall out, just drop clean to my knees. Miz Free done used the number I give her from Pinky's new beau and got him to come out to

Techwood Homes. A real-live painter who done stayed after the *National Black Arts Festival* done gone. Talk about killing the dog.

Here he is, Lord have mercy, with a display of his work, a collection of paintings, framed and unframed, step up so pretty, I can't help but stay awhile. I try to make myself invisible while he do his thing. I tarry from picture to picture, "portraits" one of the chillen say, and I'm knocked off my feet. Out the corner of my eye, I detect he done got more handsome than the last time I seed him. Can see why his name in Pinky's mouth more than any of them other menfolk what court her; he something else, though she ain't mention he uh genius. Shame my Pinky went to the Waffle House, what with all this excitement going on. She always missing out. But if God be God, ain't no such uh thing as missing nothin'.

There Mookey. Since Short Dog ain't here, Clemmy musta brung him. How come he at the front, like Mr. Grant need him to hold, run, grab, while he talk. But he sho is doing his share of listening to Mr. Grant---and everybody else---talk about how and when he painted his art. They listening so close, you'da thought he was preaching the keys to the Kingdom. Miz Free shoulda invited the local preachers so they could see how folks can pay attention so, they sit on your bottom lip to hear everything.

Mookey wave, and I wave back, careful not to encourage no talking.

All these giant pads of drawing paper and boxes of pencils and crayons and charcoal for his crew, I reckon. Uh huh. Stacked paints and brushes off to the side, beside his pretty pictures. The minute I walk up on a group of pictures of different black women, eyes and mouths familiar, like you looking at the lady next door or your cousin in the back pew or ya aunt at the stove, I think back on what Pinky told me after she come way from Greenbrier Mall with Sherrie Ann.

"Miz Too-Sweet, you shoulda seen them, the pictures this gorgeous man painted. They breathed, just climbed outta the frames and hugged you." Never thought I'd see them, but God is good cause they here. I looks at them, they looks at me. Then I go to thinking of Aunt Judy and Aunt Josephine and Cousin Carrie Bell and Diane and Baby Everlener and Grandma Pearlie Girlie and Sophie Mae and Ida and Dorothy. They all come back, one at a time, visit in a flash of memory, and step aside for the next, polite memories. I'm happy, feeling blessed they here, too. Course I ain't seed some in years and others with the Lord and a few might call if Hell froze over.

Then Mr. Grant's voice change, and the group go to stretching.

"Trevor Butler, come up to the front, son."

Oh, he here? Got me. Miz Rhonda's baby ain't shy a bit, shoot up like a rocket, standing beside Mr. Grant, grinning.

"Everybody, this is Miss Robert's nephew, an artist in his own right." He smile at Li'l Trevor, who waving and speaking and talking like he a politician.

"Tell us, Trevor, how you came to art."

"Well, I have always loved art, everything about it, from the way the pencil or crayon feels in my hand to the way it glides on the paper. When I draw, I feel real good, almost like I can do anything, leap tall buildings and do everything that superheroes do and more."

Chile had me tired. Wondered when he gone catch a breath, but he keep going.

"My Aunt Free and my Mama said I can be anything I want to be now and when I grow up, so I believe them, which is why I am an artist today. You peek inside my book bag, which never leaves the house without me, you'll see what I'm working on at the moment. Comic books. Last year, it was animals." Li'l Trevor put his hands behind his back and balanced on one leg, leaning into Mr. Grant's side.

"What medium do you prefer?" Mr. Grant ask.

"Charcoal and pencil and paper. Watercolor takes too long to dry for me."

That chile is some kinda smart. Got it honest though, with a schoolteacher mama and doctor daddy and aunt like Miz Free.

"Thank you, Trevor. You may sit down now."

"Thank you, Mr. Johnson, for the opportunity to come up." He batting those long dark lashes, same as what's on Mookey's face. "May I ask a question?"

"Yes, sir, little man. Fire away." That impress Mr. Grant.

"People are very important to you, from the larger than life faces and the smaller ones. They're really nice. But why did you paint all those women---" he pointing to the collection near me, "---behind Miz Too-Sweet? Who are they?"

Ooops! There go another dog.

"Good question, Trevor, thank you. Let's see, where do I begin?" He clap his hands and stroll across the front of his group and look from me to Mookey to the others. "My mother died when I was very young. I never knew her. Grew up with a loving father and two brothers, I'm the baby. My father never remarried, and though he brought a few women into our lives every now and again, he tried to make sure we knew something of our mother. There were her pictures, repainted and framed from old snapshots. My favorite is of her at a World Fair, holding my oldest brother's hand and he was pulling away, pointing to a man in a hat selling cotton candy.

"My dad gave us the baby quilts she made. He saved things she valued and presented them to us, to choose and keep as heirlooms. I got her wedding rings. And dad recorded her, saying good bye. So in a sense, I do know her." He smile. "To answer your question, I painted those women to channel my love for her. I painted them to honor those women who came to love me in her absence."

Everybody clap then and I take myself on before I require a towel, my eyes go to streaming when I holler. That one, he's going to be good for Pinky. A man love his mama, and she dead and gone, he will sho honor that woman---my Will a living testimony.

The rec's kitchen claim my attention now. The smell say somebody putting they foot in baked goodies. I tip to the door, pull it open and peek inside. Fan blowing on a handful of girls, some rolling dough, others sprinkling cinnamon and brown sugar, dicing fruit and pouring lemonade and chilling water. A young woman with a light brown Afro and apron tied over her jeans is supervising.

"Hey, ladies! How ya'll?" I ease on in. "Ya'll bout to cause a riot."

"Oh no, hi! I'm Bren Mason, Free's cook at the **WeAreFamily Bookstore and Coffeehouse.**" She wipe her hands and come over to shake mine. "You just come in? I don't remember you when Free made introductions."

She pretty, like the rest of the Free crew.

"Yes, ma'am, I just walked in the door. What ya baking?"

"Cinnamon rolls my grandma used to bake. I wanted a light menu because of the heat, nothing heavy or everybody'll be sleep immediately after lunch."

I agree and then look at her closer. She sweating like it's raining. Use the towel on a chair to dab at her forehead and head and then wash her hands.

Right then the door swing open...hard.

A chubby li'l gal chewing gum, stomach high, say, "Mama, ready for me now?"

"Your taster?" I ask.

Miz Bren nod, eyes bright. "My baby. Say hi to Miz Too-Sweet, Dahlia."

She give me a hi and get back to the business of whether or not her mama ready to let her taste the rolls. When Miz Bren give her a corner, she chew, make a serious face, then shake colorful beads across her head. "Yes, ma'am. They're greeeaaat! Bye!"

She gone, I leave too, the space hotter than a second menopause.

On my way to the rooms down from the gym, I pause to see what's going on in there, and they's two women, a tall light-haired one and the other short and dark, sitting Japanese style, hands up, thumb and forefinger touching, heads bowed. They in uh circle.

More adults than chillen in the group. Look to me like they praying, though the stand-up sign say "The Art of Meditation." Everybody could do with a bit of that. Music right peaceful, guitars, I believe, or harps, one. Whatever. I go off in there, I'm sleep.

I get on to the last two rooms, before the exit door.

A man and woman in the one on the left, talking to another older group. While I'm peekin' in the glass in the door, Miz Free come in through the back exit door.

"Hey, Miz Too-Sweet, what do you think? Did we bring it?"

"Absolutely! Ya'll did more than bring it, ya'll killed the dog!"

Miz Free break out laughing, trying to keep the sound low.

"Well, thank you, ma'am! It took the support of quite a few people, financial and otherwise, but love made it happen." She peep in the window I just got out of.

"Those are Reesa's parents, Dr. Eddie Lee and Marion McMillan. I still can't believe they're here! That's an empowerment workshop. A part of his business involves making people believe in themselves. They just flew in from Hawaii."

"Wow! I keep wishin' everybody could hear all the other folks."

"Oh, don't worry. The groups will rotate after lunch."

I shoulda knowed she'd done figured out that detail.

"C'mere, Miz Too-Sweet, let's go outside a minute." She take my arm and before the door open, I hear drums. Bongos, beatin' soft and low. The light mid-July breeze burdened with heat but I don't mind, I'm glad Techwood getting some of the blessings others been enjoying for years.

Off under a tree, in the shade, a teenager with dreadlocks and a red T-shirt down at playing the bongos. With his shirt sleeves rolled to the shoulder, the muscles in his arms just gone to town jumping up and down and rippling and rolling. The li'l neck yoking, he feeling every beat, done felt every emotion them drums wailing.

More teenagers on mats, they eyes closed, swaying to the beat.

"He's Rhonda's new son, Jomo Wyatt. A student she took in at the close of the school year. I just learned he was musically gifted and taught himself to read music. I took him to his aunt's to get his bongos."

"Sho would like to meet ya'll mama, you and Rhonda. Ya'll some special gals."

"She's in Atlanta for a while. I think I can handle that!"

She thread her arm through mine, and us head back inside.

"The couple in the gym, Nzinga and Sharmayne, are my friends, Sharmayne, the shorter of the two, is my best friend. They're teaching the art of meditating."

"I saw that." I point to the last room opposite the McMillans. "Who in there?"

"Rhonda and her best friend, Gail Johnson."

"Any relation to Mr. Grant?"

"Don't think so. But you'll appreciate this workshop." She lightly touched my arm. "Come on, let's go inside."

Miz Rhonda stop talking immediately and introduce me to the group. She go to talking bout her sister Free and how she was enchanted with the stories I told her, then she inform the folks if they got older relatives or people in they lives, they need to cherish them. That's when I notice Clemmy off to the side, waving. I grin, wave, too.

"So…everybody, now that we've heard Gail and me read short memoirs from different traditions, we want you to interview somebody in this group now and be able to retell the story to the entire group, to honor the sacred in our stories." Miz Ronda get up and walk among the class and encourage them with her smile and nearness.

"Gail, why don't you help get us started? Who are you going to interview?"

The woman light up and pop her fingers like a chile and choose uh man, half sleep, bout Preacher's age. She sit down beside him, run her hand down his shirt sleeve. He start grinning, too glad she noticed him, and they go to whispering.

Seeing it's simple, others get up and choose folks to chat up. And I'm heading for the door when Miz Rhonda waylay me, looking like a snapshot of Free.

"Miz Too-Sweet, do me the honor. I'd like to spend some time with you, quite a good bit of it---the rest of the summer and the fall---because I'd like you to join me in launching my writing career as I capture the exciting story of your life."

She fall outta focus for a minute. Can't help but wonder if she pulling my old legs, but she look serious enough. No laughing. No moving on to someone else.

"Me? My life? A book?"

"Yes, ma'am! We all have at least one book in us. I wanna start with yours."

She bring her fingers together, like she praying.

"Think about it. No rush."

Now if that don't beat all, I'da said she done killed the meanest and biggest of all dogs this morning, but when reporters from **The Atlanta Journal and Constitution** came later, trailed by folks from a television station pushing cameras, I quit counting the number of dead dogs in the Techwood Homes Community Living Center Project. We was on the map, done made the news without a cop, a murder, or a mugging. Tell me God ain't good. And even if I don't see nothing like it again, I done seed this one!

Devilment on the night wind howled worse than zombies in a horror flick. The roaring drove Short Dog off his boy Tank's back porch an hour ago, when a late rain chased the party indoors, Tank's folks in Mississippi, gambling.

"Git yo' ass up offa me and bring me another beer. Got me dry as a gotdamn desert, you laying on me like a fucking heatstroke." Dog growled, knowing chicks at Tank's crib expected and respected tough talk and rough rides from the homeboys who fell through. Her inebriated softness crowding him where they'd fallen after they couldn't grind against one another a minute longer, her high on, too. The music was thumping, kicking nasty rhythms and nastier rhymes.

Damn. The booty was inviting him to crawl up in this bone's drawers.

He'd checked her out the minute he and some of the boys, heads yoking to Bone Thugs-N-Harmony's "Tha Crossroads," had busted up in the joint, a plain single-family house with a one-car garage. Clean, full, and feeling alright, pressed black shorts hanging low, revealing the elastic band and white cotton of his Fruit of the Looms, a white Tommy Hilfiger shirt with bold red and blue strips, his head freshly washed, twists the length of a nursing bitch's paired tits standing like miniature antennas across his head---Short Dog felt it. For sure, for sure. He'd finally collected the fragmented chips of his life and was on his way to cashing them in for more than he'd been dealt amongst his chosen set.

The homeboys had been testing his manhood for the past couple of weeks and months, fucking with his head, trying to make sure he was worthy of their inner circle. Tank nem had him on the brink of a mothafucking nervous breakdown. Had him skipping school and staying on the streets and executing silly shit, just to keep up with the program. But he counted himself lucky. They hadn't demanded that he cap somebody---just drive by and pow! Another niggah gone.

Now he could move up to the final test. Once this burglary bullshit Tank was planning for him went down, he, Taylor Alexander, the infamous Dog, would be good to throw. Whenever. And wherever. A full-fledged member of the crew.

The night slipped in under a slightly raised window and fluttered a twirling skimpy sundress with hips gyrating over him. He could see how plump the cheeks of her ass jumped when the booty moved. Slowly, sensually, it mesmerized him. His teeth could almost taste what it'd be to nip at that behind, basketball tight, supple. When he could bring himself to gaze past the fluttering hem of the dress, he noticed the pout. Cute. It was blowing smoke rings down on his crown, puckering and promising, offering up peeks at her cooch, minus panties, which he could tell feeling her up while dancing.

Yee-aah! Bet that mouth would look pretty around his stick.

He slid out of his black shorts. The Looms followed.

She palmed her boobs, hands floating around them and tweaking the nipples. Tossed her head back in ecstasy, weave jiggling on the curve of her sculpted ass and bounced it inches above the teenager's flagpole. He nursed his beer, and that ole wind blew across his hardness and he asked, "Hey, Slim, who you know up in here? You ain't got a man in one of these rooms, do ya?" When she shook her head no, he pumped himself and, giving her that L.L. Cool J. thing with his mouth, guided her down.

The music slowed, slow-drag slow, and he rotated his hips into her whirling behind, her body balanced over him, feet still in black stilettos, hands on her taut thighs like she was on stage, about to climb a pole.

He tingled from his head to his crumpled toes curled up in his sneakers. And she hadn't even gotten started yet. He pumped up towards paradise, easy and slow, then fast and hard. He clenched his teeth. Couldn't be screaming like no bitch, not with his boys drinking and popping the honeys.

She was raking her fingers through his locs now, butt floating up and down, her nails skimming his scalp as if to ask, Am I riding you like I got a man up in here?

He read the look, desire painted across her features clearly telling him he'd be well within her wishes if he slid her ass to the carpet, whipped that piece of a dress over her braids, rode her like an urban cowboy, and after they'd both popped a nut, catch some z's. Without disconnecting from him, she maneuvered until she faced the dance floor, her back to him, and he woke up out of his revelry enough to put an S in his back before sweat went to flying and that cantankerous night wind tired of drying the perspiration from their bodies and meandered down the hall.

"Niggah, git up and put yo' shit on," came from somewhere in the back of his head. As if through fog. He shook his head, groaning, wiping sleep and streaks of beer from his lips. Then stronger persuasion came. The toe of Tank's boots caught him in the side, dislodging his breath. A razor-sharp tone finished clearing the fog from his brain. "C'mon, we gotta roll. Yo' sorry ass done got as buck as these other fools humping these bones without raincoats. Ain't caring how fine they is," he said from a great distance above the fourteen-year-old, "a roll like that could cost you the rest of yo' young-ass life, homeboy. Now hurry up. Ain't got all night."

Outside, the July night hailed the boys with a welcomed coolness, draping itself around their danced-out, cloudy-headed, sex-scented, smoky forms. Sitting in the rear of the red jeep, between two dudes, Short Dog fought to claim his former camaraderie, but he suddenly knew himself to be a boy on an island, alone. Motionless, he clenched his fist and hid his nervousness, mentally punching hell out of the bitter taste of fear coating his tongue. It settled thick and palpable in his gut, like the fishy taste of castor oil his mother once insisted he take whenever he came down with a cold.

The power of memory compelled him to drag his tongue slowly along his top molars. Had to shake the fear, damnit. For himself. For his reputation. For his rightful place in the only world that mattered.

Before long, the jeep took a right, then another, leaving the forlorn Saturday night freeway behind. South Park Drive, in a ritzy garb, lay ahead, a bejeweled Auburn Avenue lady, winding her way down a quiet, curvaceous street, boasting shady trees rising from white bricked circles in spacious sidewalks and majestic lawns. In the jeep's headlights, fancy structures moonlighted as mailboxes with the names of the moneyed. They crept along slowly for a while, spotlighting everything, creeping as though they had no destination, but then Tank turned off the main street suddenly and pulled into an immaculate driveway, the jeep's engine dying.

"Go ask if somebody you looking for live there," he said to Short Dog, more with his eyes than words.

"Who…who should I ask for?"

"Quit sounding like a fucking owl and hell…think. Try Norman. Norman Bates." Laughing, he almost backhanded the little squirt for masquerading as a brother, asking what he should do once he gave the phony name. *Idiot.*

He dreamed of a more seasoned, big-money set in his twenty-year-old wisdom. Not this measly young-ass bunch he attracted. But he had to walk before he crawled.

Devilment in the night air, drowsy, got behind Short Dog and spurred him gently to the steps, then egged him up, one at a time. He paused, tried to peek into the two-car garage, to no avail, soft white curtains in place.

Tank watched him knocking from the jeep. "Bet he don't even know that bitch he all the time bragging about own this shit. Probably think I chose the crib at random."

No one home, Short Dog, secretly elated, climbed back into the jeep. He said nothing, only aware of his racing blood and a forgiving breeze.

Pinky was immobile.

As a girl, she'd become familiar with a burdensome something that lay across her bosom and weighed at the edges of her smile, leaving her, as a woman, motionless. Same as she was doomed to be before certain men, Lewis and Javan, two, whose power left her standing and watching, exactly as she was doing now, standing and watching her youngest squirm from the pleasure of being tossed and caught, she and her son, tossed and caught in Lewis Reynolds' large, insensitive hands.

"My man, my man! What you been up to? Huh? Huh?"

Lewis Reynolds had eyes, momentarily, for his boy, whom he continued to thrust upward, along with his booming voice, both bouncing of the ceiling and walls of the apartment.

"You growing like weeds, dude. Must be eating all your food like a good li'l mack daddy."

His voice made Pinky cringe. Listening to him was having two of Lewis in the space, so loud a voice rare in her home, now that she and Mookey were without Taylor and the loudness that followed him, too, like a shadow.

"You miss your old man? Glad to see your pops?"

Lewis waited for Mookey's laughter to subside, the tossing rendering his speech nonsensical. Watching him, Pinky's lips trembled. She tried to keep from chiding Lewis about tickling the child until he had difficulty catching his breath, but this was Lewis' way of making up for some-timey visits.

"That's enough, Lewis. You gone choke the boy carrying on like that."

Mouth set, she pivoted and headed down the tight corridor towards the kitchen. He was bound to want something to eat first. Knowing his gaze pierced her back for checking him in front of his son, she'd said it anyway, and the burdensome something across her breasts steadied her, straightened her back.

Behind her, Lewis eased his son to the sofa, controlling the urge to shout her name and promised the boy he'd return before trailing Pinky to the kitchen, where her shapely, denim-clad rear-end in the opened refrigerator made him forget what he planned to say.

He stopped himself from going over and grabbing her around the waist and pulling her into his groin. Didn't know when Mookey might come down the hall seeking Kool-Aid or a snack, though she knew he'd come to play with both of them, especially her. There'd be plenty of time to check her reprimanding tone later.

He sat in one of the four kitchen chairs and stuffed his long legs under the toy table. It killed him the way it rested on his knees. Heifer didn't have sense enough to get a bigger table after all this time. He refocused on Pinky, and then glanced about the kitchen. Inside the microwave, a casserole dish circled in slow motion, while a small pan of dark-green broccoli waited its turn on the counter. The savory smell of macaroni and cheese suffused the apartment, and Lewis, mouth watering, was pleased he'd decided to visit her and not one of his other women. That Pinky could wear out some food, and him, too; his thighs opening and closing involuntarily, eyes hot on her as she opened a can of Ocean Spray cranberry sauce.

Yes, he could even forgive her for not having any meat, calling herself being so gotdamn health conscious, when all it got down to was her skimping on the food bill. Depriving his son of proper nourishment. Licking his lips, and one hand disappearing under the table, he determined to overlook that, too.

"So what you been into, Miss Lady? Long time no hear."

"You got a phone. You ain't call, guess you didn't wanna know, huh?"

"Oooh! So it's like that? What's got you so up-tight? Ya home with the Saturday off. I'da thought you'd be chilling, not finding fault with everydamnthing. What, somebody piss you off at the Waffle House? Sherrie Ann find a new running partner? Miz Too-Sweet or her old man die?"

Lewis Reynolds got up to wash his hands and returned to his seat.

Any other time his comment would have pinched a nerve. Her being so sensitive about people near and dear to her. Interesting. He studied her as she slipped a baking mitt on to pull the piping-hot dish from the microwave. In went the broccoli. On the table she placed cranberry sauce and breadsticks, then rinsing a plate and silverware and a glass, she placed these before him, along with a folded napkin.

All the while she did these things, Pinky chaffed. *Why the hell did she bother to serve this man like he was somebody?* Who he was, after all, was a guy she'd screwed and slipped up and screwed again and with whom she got some kind of a relationship going and couldn't break it off. Then she'd woken up one morning pregnant with another baby, the only beautiful outcome of her having known a Lewis Reynolds and any of the others, in the first place.

At least he, as with all of her children's fathers, had thought enough of his child to give his name. What did it matter hers remained the same. For the names, she thanked God, even though her children had come home from school---at different times--complaining about somebody laughing at how nobody in their family had the same last name.

"So...you wanna small talk? Okay." Pinky stilled herself, leaned against the counter, and wiped her forehead. "When the last time you been to see your other children? See them as often as you see Lewis Earl? Probably. Why would they deserve any different behavior from a daddy holding onto being a lifetime bachelor and father-of-the-year? On numbers alone."

She didn't mind that he'd begun eating, as long as his ears functioned.

"How your women friends? Can't remember the last time you laughed about what stupid thing one of them did or said; guess you telling them what a stupid ass I am now, huh?"

Her laughter filled the kitchen, while the lemonade she poured tinkled the cubed ice in his glass. Cartoons blared down the hall. His stomach sighed, and she knew her meal was lulling him into peacefulness, was making it easy for him to listen to her without rancor.

"You satisfied racing between four women. Know you ain't jealous 'cause I ain't called you in a few days. You really come over here to check things out, like I'm a chick in your stable." She made a sour face. "Well, I'm not. Oh, and something else, hope you didn't come to get any either. That's all we seem to do when you come this way. I'm not your whore, ho, or bad girl." Why hadn't she said such liberating words sooner? "I'm your son's mama." She smiled, feeling blessed, as though she'd been baptized.

"That's it...from now on, Lewis. I'll feed ya, I'll feed most anybody, but I'm not fucking you anymore."

She didn't know where the words were coming from. They were filling her mouth as though they were stored somewhere, waiting for the precise moment to be spoken. She didn't know why they'd come on this Saturday afternoon, of all Saturdays, without a warning to speak of. And she surely didn't know why her eyes had abruptly pictured Lewis in the same light as Javan or Omar; the most she could say for him---at one time---was when she was with

Lewis, skin to skin, she enjoyed him and felt he honestly relished being with her, too. Yet, strangely, since the night with Javan, most importantly, what she did know was that being with her former men friends wasn't enough anymore...not since she'd known Grant Johnson.

"That niggah must have put some good shit on you, got you talking outta your head. What he do---go down or something? You know he ain't staying long, once he see how fucked-up you really are. Yeah, I'll give the niggah credit. You fine and all, but fine is as fine does, huh, baby? And your fine ain't done a gotdamn thang, too much, has it? Other than produce kids."

He took a sip of lemonade.

Her back to him, she swabbed grease from the stove top and grinned.

"My new friend, he makes me happy and high without aid of drugs, dick, or dough. You do that for a woman lately?"

"So what? You found another pussy you used to in Javan and Omar. Have you noticed I'm the only real man who comes around to see about you?"

She placed the dirty pots and pans in the sink, sponged the table and counters, and began washing the dishes. While she worked, she sensed the burden on her bosom teetering, just downright wobbling dangerously, and threatening to tumble. A London Bridge falling down. She thought of Mookey and giggled to herself. The more she worked, the more she spoke, the more confidant she became.

Out of the hall closet she grabbed a broom and dust pan. Swept the kitchen and went to whistling, careful to sweep away any speck of dust around

Lewis' chair, as though her intent was to sweep him out of the apartment and out of her life, and all the while smiling, as if she were merely reporting what Mookey had done that day.

"Have you ever taken your woman and her child to dinner and a movie? Now that's my new idea of sexy."

"Your new stud better not meet your oldest son or he'll be booking up faster than a thief in a Buckhead house with a security system."

"It's gratifying getting to know a person first and then anticipating sex. Change can be thrilling, don't you agree?"

The second the words left her lips, the burdensome something toppled clean off her bosom, and with it gone, she rose like yeast in bread, her soul expanding beyond the dimensions of the half-a-handful space, the swelling exploding the windows and cramming her joy into every nook and cranny of the spic-and-span kitchen.

Didn't matter what Lewis said after that, she'd discovered she could fly.

Chapter 29

The morning outside Rhonda's bedroom window was temperamental. Same as it'd been for days on end. Having had all night to decide the next day's weather, here it was cutting the fool, at six o'clock on a Wednesday morning, daybreak teetering between the grayness of a pending cloudburst and the hint of sunny skies. Behind the cottony puffs camouflaging the heavens, periodic shafts of light beckoned Rhonda's attention.

Big Trevor rolled over, his lips seeking her cheek.

"Morning, Precious Pooh. What's on your mind?" He gathered her into a bear hug and smothered her face, neck, ears and throat in kisses.

Rhonda lost herself in a shower of giggles. "Good morning yourself. How'd you sleep?" She let herself fall back against his barreled chest, eyes appreciating the morning outside their large, softly draped windows.

"With you beside me, sensational, as usual. You didn't. What? Still worried about Mother being here? It's only been two days."

"Mother? Are you talking about Pastoria Roberts?"

"Yes, ma'am, my mother. Did you know she's an amusing conversationalist, who makes the best cinnamon rolls this side of paradise?" His nose sank into the warm musk of her skin under the neckline of the nightgown. "Shucks, the woman's a genius…and after all, she did make you, too, right?"

She burst out laughing, him tickling her

underarms and along her sides.

"Yes, yes, your mother's a genius, I agree, now quit!"

"Okay, Precious Pooh, but the only thing that's saving you from me is Mother's rolls, my 8 o'clock appointment, and our date tonight. Understood?"

Rhonda grabbed a king-sized pillow and bopped him on the head and, screaming okay and giggling, nearly fell off the bed, Big Trevor a beast with a pillow. Down the hall, Li'l Trevor and Jomo heard the fun and dashed into the room. Instantly, they both armed themselves and joined in the pillowed fray.

Minutes later, everyone fell across the bed, exhausted, breathing like they'd pent a tag team of National Wrestling Alliance champions, and laughed until their sides ached. Then Big Trevor headed to the shower. Li'l Trevor and Jomo cuddled beside Rhonda.

"What are you guys into today?" She ran a hand atop both their heads.

"I'm taking the new comic book I'm working on to Mr. Moss' store."

Rhonda frowned and looked at Jomo.

"I'm sorry, Mrs. Butler, you were sleep when I got in last night. But Mr. Moss said if it's alright with you, Trevor can help me with the inventory and shelving today, since he thinks Trevor is the smartest little kid he knows."

"Oh. Okay. How nice. So it's an early Wednesday, huh? Well...Dr. Butler has promised to take me out tonight and---" she moved to hug the teenager, who finished for her, "I'll keep the little dude occupied. Grandma Roberts can do whatever she wants, too. We'll mind the store, right, Trevor?"

The two shared a conspiratorial smile, while Rhonda hugged them both.

"Gee, I love you guys."

"We love you, too."

"We got a question apiece," Trevor said. "Mine is, 'What's the secret of summer, Mama?'"

Rhonda pursed her lips and furrowed her brows and scratched her head and said, "Whatever God reveals it to be...once you ask."

Trevor massaged his bottom lip in contemplation, and then looked at Jomo, who was reaching for the phone on the night stand. "May I call Aunt Glory? Gotta make sure she knows I love her, too."

He dialed the number and Glory Mae Wyatt's cheery alto filled the room.

"Good mornin', Aunt Glory! It's me, Jomo, your favorite nephew! How you doin'?" He looked at Rhonda mouthing, "Tell her we love her, too."

"Hey, my big baby boy! Aunt Glory loves you more! You stayin' out of trouble and mindin' Mrs. Butler?"

"Yes, ma'am. Mrs. Butler and Trevor have a shout-out for you."

"WE LOVE YOU, TOO, AUNT GLORY!"

"Oh good Lawd, I loves all ya'll, too! A woman could walk to Heaven and back on all that love this mornin'."

Jomo talked to her a minute more, up-dating her on his new job and his new grandmother, excitedly rehashed the Techwood Homes program and his bongo performance before hanging up. He and Trevor had a breakfast engagement.

***

In the kitchen, Rhonda let out a deep sigh and hummed. Stared at her mother, who was bending over the table staring intently at an opened residential phone book.

"Mornin', sweetheart. Hungry?" Her eyes sparkled behind red and black reading glasses. On the air, the eatable aroma of cinnamon rolls filled her nose.

"Good morning, Mama. Having any luck finding Earl Taylor? Which ought to be the equivalent of hunting a needle in a den of junkies, huh?"

"Let's hope it won't be that severe. I counted 40-to-50 possible choices."

"What if he's not in Atlanta? If that's the situation, Big Trevor has ProPhone on the CD Rom on our computer. It'll give you a listing of every Earl Taylor in the state."

"That's a blessing, though I hope I won't need it. Honestly, I think he's in Atlanta. Earl, if I remember correctly, wasn't the moving kind." She studied her daughter's disheveled appearance. Hair looked as if it had fought every vain attempt to lay it low, and her old green housecoat might've been snatched straight from the hamper. "Why you up so early? Don't tell me you're already tired of summer mornings in bed?"

Rhonda wanted to say yes, but your presence in the house makes me mindful of things that typically wouldn't warrant minding but thought better of it, not wanting her words to be misconstrued for a meanness that wasn't intended. She stalled, like the murky morning muddling the view from the bay windows.

"Sit down. Let's clear the air, honey. Okay? I'll be around for longer than a weekend; I'm right tired of all the tippin' and shushin' you've been doing. I wouldn't halt my routine if the shoe was on the other foot. Let your family be who they are. And the same goes for you."

Rhonda sat while her mother rose and washed her hands and dropped the oven door, withdrawing a long silver pan chockfull of big-as-your-fist cinnamon rolls.

"Strange...Big Trevor hasn't changed his spots. He enjoys my company."

She placed two rolls slathered with butter and a glass of milk before her baby girl.

"Mama, it's not that I haven't been enjoying your presence, it's that I know how you are about noise and stuff out of place and running kids."

She bit into a chewy mound and let her gaze skim the potted ivy to the phone book to the stove top to the tile, everywhere except her mother's exacting eyes.

"I'll buy that for now, but you know there's another issue tippin' somewhere. Don't sugarcoat anything you want to say regarding me. What? You thinking I'm here putting in time with you first so I can speed on over to Free's?"

Pastoria grimaced. "For all I know, you could be trying to figure out what the hell I'm doing trying to find a daughter I've seen only once and, here I am, haven't even clocked enough hours to shake a stick at with a daughter I've raised."

Rhonda nodded in agreement. Continued

savoring the delectable delicacy.

"Really. What makes you want to find her now?"

"Love. Regardless of how long she's been gone, that doesn't change the fact that she's my firstborn, your eldest sister. I've forgiven myself for committing such a---"

"Heartless act?" Rhonda suggested.

"It seemed the right thing to do at the time. I was married, my husband away, and there I was pregnant. Had I kept the baby and your father miles removed, writing me love letters daily, the knowledge might have killed him---he loved me that much."

"How do you know for sure it didn't kill him?"

"Perhaps there are some things we'll never know."

"Then why did you do it, Mama, knowing how hard he loved you?"

"Loneliness and...my own passion for conquering men, I guess." Pastoria sighed. "God has a way of bringing things to be reconciled down front and center stage. I can't get on with my life until I reconcile this deed with my child."

"Has it ever crossed your mind she might hate you? Your abrupt appearance in her life, after all this time, might be more painful than healthy."

"Yeah, could be, but I feel she wants to know me. I love her like I love you and Free. Besides, I think everybody and everything wants to be with its own mother."

Rhonda couldn't believe her ears. "No, Mama, I beg to differ. I say you're in love with the idea of knowing you have another daughter whom you want to need you. And if my sister loves you, she is simply in love with the notion that she, too, has a biological mother. Somewhere. That's it." Her spread hands said, "So there."

"Okay, see it any way you desire. The bottom line is, I want your sister in our lives."

Pastoria's jaw tightened, the table vibrating slightly from her shaking foot, and Rhonda knew she was riled. But she didn't light up.

"How is Booker taking all this?"

"Like your daddy might have taken it, quietly, sadly."

"He loves you, too, just like daddy did."

She watched as her mother's face took on a mask-like quality, almost as if she were tired of these questions leaving her naked sensibilities unprotected before this womanchild bent on dragging her emotions across the table and laying them bare amongst uneaten cinnamon rolls. "You dog the men who love you. Tell me…have you ever been dogged, Mama?"

In Pastoria's silence, Rhonda reminded her she didn't want it sugarcoated.

"No, I've never been dogged."

"Ever loved a man?"

Did she detect sarcasm? "In my own way, I loved every man I let into my life. Maybe some women are destined to be loved more by the men in their lives than they can love them in return."

"What was so good about staying with Free as opposed to staying here? Did I ever unknowingly mistreat you, say something you didn't appreciate, make you feel unwelcome? Or is it that you wanted privacy and felt you couldn't have it here?"

Anxious to dispel the cloud of resentment above them, Pastoria thought about her response and bit her bottom lip and willed herself to be as honest as possible.

"I apologize for purposely looking to stay with Free, Rhonda. She didn't have a man in her home, nobody else to deal with when you wanted to watch TV or sit in a corner or read the Bible. There was nobody to watch you and make you feel like everything you touched and ate belonged to him; being with her was like being single, nothing but peace and solitude, although it goes without saying I dearly love my grandson."

Rhonda considered her mother's words and glimpsed a pleading in the older woman's beautiful, aging face. Drawn by this pleading, Rhonda's hands reached out, fragments of brunch sweet on her tongue again, and stroked her mother's soft, thin-skinned hands.

"I appreciate you admitting that. And I realize it took a lot for you to say what you said. You were right. I'd been wondering why you'd chosen to stay here."

"I'm staying because I love you, baby girl, and you and I have back quality time to recoup. Plus, me and my boys have too much fun, never a dull moment."

Mother and daughter smiled a girlfriend smile.
"Think Free knows?"
"If she doesn't, we'll tell her."

Rhonda grinned, and following Pastoria's lead, stood and walked through cleared air between them and stepped into her mother's embrace, savoring another Wednesday hug. Midas strokes streaked the sky a pale gold outside the kitchen's bay windows, the sun, exhausted but bright, finally breaking through the barricade of dark clouds it had battled all morning to herald in an afternoon aflame with the beauty of mid-summer.

***

Free called daily. At the end of the week she asked her sister if the next book club meeting could be held at her home. The proposal sat well with Rhonda and Pastoria, the first had never hosted the gathering, and the latter had never attended a book club meeting.

"What's the selection?" Rhonda wheezed as she cradled the receiver on her left shoulder and lifted a ten-pound weight in her right hand.

"Connie Briscoe's **Sisters and Lovers**. Read it?"

"No, girl, bought it from you a while back, remember?"

"Whatever. What's new on your end of the world?"

"Been swimming in some much-needed me time, though a sister's catatonic from watching skin flicks. Don't need to ask what's new with you. You missing Junior Thomas, Miss Thang. Go on, admit it."

"Some darn kids knocked on my door recently in the middle of the night, banging like fools," Free said, evasive. "I didn't answer. Peeped at them from the blinds. I'd gone to bed early after reading, just lying there meditating. Thank goodness they didn't wake me out of sleep; I'd have been on my way to pressing my security's fire alarm since they roll up super quick."

"Lost. Kids are forever roaming the night, girl, looking for other kids and something to do; too many out in the world with nobody making time to love them and see to it they stay out of trouble."

"Thought about that." What she didn't add was that she did miss Junior Thomas, and if that knocking boy had gone to twisting on her doorknob, she intended to unsheathe the insurance she kept in a drawer in the base of her bed and ask forgiveness later.

Chapter 30

Warring spirits. Two black funnel clouds heavy with cold rain and charged with static electricity, Sharmayne and Melba swirled about one another and grew black and blacker and showed no signs of waning, their guileless dance becoming more and more frenzied in the small white house supported by cement blocks at each corner. The Cooper farm, nestled on the right by woods and creek water, open fields on the left, and a chicken yard and fenced-in garden at the rear, faced a long recently paved rural LaGrange, Georgia, road.

That same road brought Clyde Cooper's only daughter home, but after a week and a half, it had to take either Melba or Sharmayne somewhere and fast or the house would implode, their fray squeezing the life out of his last nerve. The verbal sparring nerve-wrecking, he was out-and-out tired just watching them, and he didn't give a good hoot who the gal was sleeping with, long as she was happy.

What could he do? Melba's brassy spirit was bent on breaking the back of a will she'd miscalculated as weaker than her own.

Clyde brought his pipe to his berry-black lips, thin under a thick salt-and-pepper mustache, tastefully offsetting the gray spliced blackness of his full head of tightly curled hair. Spirals of Red Man tobacco fumes floated up past his narrow face and suffused the room with a smoky aroma. Right now, legs crossed, he listened to carefully targeted crossfire.

"Sharmayne, you still talkin' crazy like I ain't

been hammerin' away at the emptiness in yo' head for a whole doggone week and better, girl." Melba's voice was strident. She sat with her back in the living room doorway, busily cleaning collards, popping the large fanlike leaves free of dirt and occasional worms and slicing away their thick stems. "A woman made from man's rib, she supposed to be happy with him, she bone of his bone, and I can't see no other way. How some woman gone make you happy anyway, as much as womenfolk be scratchin' and keepin' up confusion when two or more of them together?" She tossed a collard stem onto a growing green heap on her right.

Her daughter sucked her bottom lip into her mouth and inhaled deeply. "Mama, life isn't worth living if you don't have someone, male or female, with whom to share happiness and love. Why can't you accept that Victor doesn't do that for me? He brought me pain. Every day of my married life, pain. Who do I thank for that? You."

"Don't blame me you made sin yo' bedfellow, no, ma'am."

"Who else is there? God?"

"If I hadn't done my righteous Biblical duty-"

"Biblical? We're not living in Biblical days."

"The Bible cover Biblical for me as in then and straight through now. So. And you, I suppose you woulda found a man on yo' own, huh? You couldn't talk about anything outside of finding somebody's job. When I was yo' age, Sharmayne, I had me so many li'l boy babies crawlin' round, you coulda broke a leg trippin' over 'um. Now here you still without child to cry or die, talking about bein' happy with a woman." She shook her head sorrowfully. "Uh old maid, that's where ya headed."

Sharmayne checked the deep-dish mac-n-cheese and hen baking in the oven. "Which is what, turns out, I'm going to be anyway, Mama, except I pray to be an old maid loved by another old maid, a couple, like you and daddy, living and loving one another into tomorrow."

"Come get these greens and dump them in water and bring me that squash, please." She wiped her rough hands on a damp white cloth. "Stop comparin' you and that woman to me and yo' father. It ain't the same. Period." She selected several large squash, laid them on a paper towel in a plate, and began paring the tawny bumpy skin.

They quieted for a spell, intensely aware of the other. Sharmayne monitored the water in the steaming pot of green peas and okra on the stovetop. Everything smelled appetizing, looked good.

Without lifting her eyes from the squash, Melba asked, "You sure you don't wanna use that straightenin' comb I left on yo' dresser? You'd look more like the Sharmayne I raised insteada some wild-by-the-head heifer been throwed away." She gathered the batch of pared squash and placed it in a casserole dish and motioned for Sharmayne to rinse it at the sink. "Course you about can't comb that tangled bird's nest all clumped like somebody's ole matted wig. It's a wonder Victor let you stay as long as he did…head wookey and dense as them woods outdoors."

Sharmayne frowned, hands on her hips. "Mama, Victor didn't leave me or put me out. I…left…him."

"Ain't nothing to be proud of. Now I know

why I been sick lately. The Good Lord punishin' me for yo' sin, the sins of the daughters, but I hope not." She got up to beat eggs for the casserole. "Can't believe the Lord brought me this far to leave me sick 'cause you done committed uh 'bomination. We gotta answer for our own sins."

"Nzinga is a wonderful, beautiful person. She's super smart, caring, and friendly."

"So is your friend Free, but you ain't layin' up with her, is ya?"

"She teaches Women's Studies at Spellman, the women's college in Atlanta. She loves the arts and exercising and enjoying life and reading and..." she broke off, her voice tiny and soft, dubious, then more convinced, "...and me. The woman is all I've ever wanted in a mate. We're happy. What else matters? If you were to meet her, give her a chance, you'd like her."

Melba's brooding face glared warmly in disbelief.

"Well, do Jesus. Don't understand you anymore, girl. Just told you I was sick knowin' about yall, and here you is still talkin' about me meetin' her. Why would I wanna do that? Bring that taint in my house. Bad enough you here. You done lost yo' mind, that much I do understand. How long you think this woman gone offer you a free ride? How long it be before she open her sinful eyes and see what you really are---a fallen woman, without a man, a job, or uh ounce of common sense. Look at you...a wannabe virtuous woman. In purple."

Sharmayne said nothing, just stared into her mother's vexed face.

Above them, funnel clouds corkscrewed.

Stinging water and crashing thunder loomed from one. And through the raging storm drenching the kitchen, one kindred spirit desisted, its winds calming gradually. Fingers of falling light found their way through a jet cloud, burning it marshmallow white. Under the shafted paleness, the women continued to cook in a safe routine, executing one task and then another. Their silent fury discordant, the noise drowned the ringing of the living room phone.

After dinner, Clyde could barely contain himself. He resettled into the comfort of his Lay-Z-Boy before the television and trained one ear on any sound coming from the road. Throughout the meal, which had ballooned his stomach to the size of a four-month pregnancy, he smiled as he chewed, the odd behavior prompting Melba to wonder aloud if he'd lost his cotton-pickin' mind, and if he had, that made two of them. Him and his daughter. It was all Clyde could do not to inform his wife she stood a better chance of losing her mind, in a few short hours. To salvage his thunder, over dessert, he'd eaten and grinned and marveled at his only girl for bucking all that Melba had mapped out for her and eaten and grinned some more and was astonished that he, too, welcomed the gall to go against his wife's undisturbable grain.

Dishes cleaned, kitchen swept, Sharmayne kissed her father's sable cheek in route to her bedroom to read Briscoe's novel, quietly choosing to forego the television's Thursday night line-up. She'd left Melba in her bathroom, sitting on the tub's edge rubbing a lime-green liniment into her ankles, knees, shoulders, and elbows. Every joint in her throbbed uncontrollably. "All that daggum salt in the cornbread---what with Sharmayne's heavy hand" she'd said to no one in particular after the meal.

At ten to nine p.m., a jumping eye drove Sharmayne out of the pages of **Sisters and Lovers** and redirected her footsteps to the living room, where her father sat, unmoved.

"What's wrong?" Clyde blinked and raised one brow. "Can't sleep?"

For the life of him, and after years of living with his wife and daughter and their spirits, he couldn't get over their strange sense of knowing things. So, years ago, he'd stopped trying to understand why their energy force hadn't seen fit to take up with him or any of his boys, opting to leave them, in the women's safekeeping.

"Eye jumping," Sharmayne answered matter-of-factly, gently walking around his chair and plopping onto a circular sofa. Her eye accurate, she didn't want to be caught in bed. Country folks had a tendency to visit and expect everybody in the house to come out of hiding and say hello and exchange small talk, didn't matter if they hadn't come to see her.

Clyde ignored her knowing. "Feel like watchin' T.V.?"

"Okay." She perched on the arm of his chair. "You think Mama'll be okay?"

"She fine. In there rubbing herself with that liniment. Smell gets in yo' nose and next thing you know, you got sinus problems for weeks. Go check on her. Make sure she knows we wouldn't mind her company." He winked, adding, "Long as she brings a blanket to cover that perfume."

In her parents' bedroom, Sharmayne found Melba peeking into the night through closed blinds. Like a fly in butterfly, her attention was riveted on a car that Sharmayne could now hear---under the barking of the dogs stretching to life under the house---humming to a standstill practically below the window. There was something familiar about the car's sound, but the medicinal essence of rubbing liniment swabbed her usually keen senses, tossing them off the second she'd stepped into the room, and asked, "Expecting somebody, Mama?"

"Naw," Melba said, still peeking. "Don't look like nobody I know." She pivoted to face her daughter. "Tell your father to turn on the porch light and look out."

When Sharmayne returned to the living room, her father was posted in the front door shrouded in soft amber light, screen thrown wide, comfortable with whoever was traversing the dirt yard to reach the steps. "Hey, how you?" he was saying. "Glad to see you made it in one piece." Then, "Hey there! Move out the way, Welfare! Nobody here to see you." He stepped onto the wooden porch, the screen clapping shut behind him. "Here, let me get that for yuh," he obliged someone Sharmayne couldn't see, held the door with a tan suitcase in his right hand, the screen door held wide for…Nzinga!

Seeing her, Sharmayne froze. Her tongue cleaved to the roof of her dry mouth. Her speech suspended, a wooden expression set her face, and her breathing slowed. *It couldn't be, could it?* Yet there she was, glowing, the look on her face communicating, "Peace be onto this house." The irony of it all stunning, Sharmayne remained tacit.

Then, suddenly, she was being drawn effortlessly inside her lover's eyes, her father---his focus volleying from one to the other---becoming more uncertain the longer the women visually embraced, his caller in the flesh, bewitching his daughter from across the room.

An imposing funnel cloud behind Sharmayne quickly dissolved Nzinga's claim on her soul, and raging with a renewed fury, barreled into the center of the living room, animating the stilled scene. "You can close the door now, Clyde. I'd say you done let in enough without the rest of the flies joinin' us." With that, Melba brushed by her daughter to get a better look at the smiling brazenness responsible for snatching the purple from her child's crown. She scrutinized the tall slender frame in rumpled jeans and silky red blouse.

Lips a faint red. Hair short and mannish, but attractive and curly. Skin light, bright, and damn-near too close to white. Smooth though. Great big ole light eyes staring back into hers with confidence and done drove way out here from Atlanta, alone, at this hour. As opposite from Sharmayne as night from day.

"Who call you?" Melba quizzed reproachfully.

Clyde secured the lock on the front door. "She called me." Unable to recall the correct pronunciation of the woman's strange name, he said, "Miss, this here's my polite and gracious wife Melba and you already know Sharmayne." He passed his daughter the suitcase and disregarded his wife's noisy "Humph!"

"Leave it outta the walkway there and come sit down, girl." Melba said this more for Clyde's hearing than Sharmayne's. Slowly bowling a sneer down the hall towards Sharmayne's bedroom, she added, "If she stay, she won't be sleepin' in there no way."

Clyde winked at his statue-stiff daughter and beamed like Nzinga had handed him a new tin of Red Man tobacco. "I reckon you can put it in yo' room, sweetheart, now or later. That don't matter," he said softly, waving his wife out of his line of vision. "What matters is this is our house and if I say a person welcome, she welcome, and if she grown, she can sleep any damn where she please." He threw a frown at Melba, shifted gears, smile intact, and bowed to Nzinga. "Have a sit-down. Rest yo'self. How was the trip?"

"Thank you, Mr. Cooper. Hello, Mrs. Cooper. Hi, sweetheart. Missed you."

"Hi, Miss Edwards, it's lovely to see you again, missed you more."

Nzinga blew her a kiss and took a seat on the circular sofa, redirecting her attention to Mr. Cooper. "The trip was shorter than I expected, being I've never had the pleasure of stopping in LaGrange. From what I could see at this time of night, it reminds me of Opelika."

Sharmayne scowled when Melba pulled up a chair, ready to hold court.

"How happen you up and call Clyde outta the blue?"

Nzinga grinned like she'd been patiently awaiting the question since she arrived.

"I missed your daughter more than I ever imagined, Mrs. Cooper. The house was so lonely without her, I had to come. Felt like I was beginning to come apart at the seams."

"Goes to show, most of yall unstable, that much is true, I see."

Nzinga's eyes twinkled. *This old lady was hilarious. But it'd take more than nastiness to run her away from the woman of her dreams.*

Clyde sniffed and glanced down at his wife's bare feet. "Might wanna slip on a pair of light socks to keep the night draft off yo' ankles, honey, and to keep the liniment close to yo' skin, where it'll do the most good, instead of fumin' up this room." Retiring his pipe on a small glass ashtray, he pointed the remote towards the television and pressed one channel into another.

"So, you from Opelika, huh? Can't say as I 'member any Edwards; I usedta go through there all the time when a cousin of mine lived up 'round that neck of the woods back in '75, '76. Born and raised there?"

"Yes, sir." Nzinga liked Mr. Cooper more and more. Had a smooth style of operating; no fuss, no sweat. Chatting with him on the phone earlier had given her no indication of his unpretentious wit and down-to-earth nature.

"Heard tell you a college teacher."

At least the girl was a talker, that husband of Sharmayne's, all he ever wanted to do was drop her off, get in the wind, and pick her up without so much as slowing his car long enough for him and Melba to walk her to the road and wave bye.

Melba shook her head, Clyde and Nzinga's fast-liking embarrassing. "I'm sure you sho nuff love what you do, what with all them womenfolks 'round at that all-girl school. They know you like that?" Her right hand surfed from right to left.

"Oh, yes, ma'am, I'm out at work, and I do enjoy my teaching position…" she smiled, sharing a vibrant smile with Sharmayne, "even if I complain about the long hours dealing with the paperwork. Overall, it's rewarding, especially since most students are serious about pursing a higher education, and it pays the bills. Outside of a multi-book publishing contract and a movie contract, there's not much more I could ask."

"Try askin' the Good Lord for some salvation, deliverance from sin, and the desire for a man. Don't forget the Bible also say 'the love of money is the root of all evil,' and I do not think it smile on women teachin' either."

When Melba flared her nostrils huffily and strode into the kitchen, Sharmayne rose, too, her spirits plummeting to the hardwood, but Clyde bobbed a forefinger, and she resumed her seat.

Unperturbed and jovial, her father and Nzinga launched into a conversation about his plans for the farm next summer, the John Deer tractor he aimed to buy, and the possibility of Nzinga learning to operate it.

They laughed agreeably over the drone of the T.V., when Melba, now in white socks, reappeared in the living room.

"Honey, bein' you standin', what say you offer us something to drink like the good Christian woman you are, before you forget all the hospitality lessons in the Good Book." To halt her protests, he proposed she open that new jar of cranapple juice for everyone and be certain nothing out of the way fell into them. Sharmayne rose, and he waved her down again. "Your mama know her way 'round that kitchen. Besides, she know I'm teasin', because no decent Christian woman would stoop low enuf to put something in her guest glass." He grinned at Nzinga. "That stuff only happens in the movies, ya know. So..." he drawled, "how long you stayin', Naw-ziin-gah?"

Sounds of a grumbling Melba rinsing glasses, pouring liquid, and slamming the frig door floated in from the kitchen. She stomped into the room with three jelly jars of crimson-colored juice, passing two to Sharmayne, the other to Clyde.

"I figure to leave tomorrow, late. I took Friday off, but we have a book club meeting this Saturday." She turned to face her lady. "Haven't forgotten, have you?"

"I'm nearly finished." Sharmayne's gaze asked, Did you start?

"So y'all meet to talk over books? Ever meet to talk about the Good Book?"

"No, ma'am, the books we read tend to be contemporary works by African-American women. But the notion of reading the Bible isn't far-fetched, although I can see some of the sisters fussing and making judgment calls over their conflicting interpretations of different passages."

"One verse they wouldn't need to fight over tell Christians---" Melba emphasized the word Christians and glowered at her husband, "---to flee from sin, no matter what form it come in, 'cause the Devil come to rob, steal, and kill those that love the Lord."

"That's true, honey, and it also admonishes women to submit to their husbands, like they submit to the Lord, so I know you won't find no argument in fleein' on to bed with me now, would ya? We done near 'bout talked Nah-ziin-gah to sleep, so c'mon here." His grip on her elbow firm. "Ain't feeling well, are ya?"

The women were silent studies, listening to Melba complain all the way to her bedroom off the kitchen, her last words being, "I bind up that wickedness…" Sharmayne knew what followed: Melba was sending Nzinga's love, in the name of Jesus, back to the pit of hell from which it had come.

Instinctively, she knew, too, Nzinga's presence anchoring her, combined with her father's cordial checking of her mother's rudeness, that a fight was rarely necessary, when one knew, unequivocally, the battle was already won.

Chapter 31

The soulful sound of Phyllis Hyman's full-bodied jazz wailed throughout Free's house, the day Sharmayne drove to LaGrange to spend the week with her parents. Without her friend's attentive ear, Free wallowed in sadness and hid what she was feeling from her sister and mother, choosing instead to drown herself in Phyllis' plaintive woes about finding love that made the wrong seem right---the right somehow never quite right enough. Like Phyllis, she ached for the want of happiness, of fulfillment, and songs about love gone wrong pacified Free's ache. Made it more bearable. Every time thoughts of J.T. crossed her mind whatever she'd been thinking was erased, leaving her empty.

She stood before the CD carousel in her bedroom and studied the singer's sexy image on the **Prime of My Life** disc cover. A well-manicured hand poised atop a honey-colored, vast bosom, adorned in silver, Phyllis was the epitome of a woman in the prime of life, accomplished professionally, self-assured, provocative, her large smoldering eyes and full, fuchsia-painted lips, a covenant of owed love. Free liked gazing at the picture; it simulated the daily perpetration she executed at the bookstore.

Cool, calm, collected Frenonia Roberts.

A woman confident in who she was, a woman with Phyllis' polished exterior---and the sadness, too, and the confusion and open-mouthed expression like the one on the flipside of the CD; the one with the chin-lifted, bosom-clutching, cheek-grasping, eye-clinched demeanor, as though the singer were suspended between a farrago of feelings. Between gratification and gloom. Which must have bordered more on gloom given the article on the sister's suicide in **Essence** a few months back.

Poor Phyllis.

She hadn't been able to hurdle whatever was happening in her life. Hadn't been able to sidestep life's sorrows and just, as she crooned, "walk away."

Free propped the CD cover against a mirror and returned to preparing for another Monday morning. She was drowsy although she'd already been up and about for awhile, and now she was running behind. The red digital numbers on the clock face read 8:45 A.M. Ordinarily, she'd have been halfway to the bookstore.

Deftly sorting through numerous garments in her walk-in closet, she selected a rich maroon, ankle-length broomstick skirt, flat gold sandals, and a silk, gold-and-maroon shell. Jewelry, gold and dramatic, like the chain draping her waist. She sprayed oil sheen on her hair, ran her fingers through her grown-out Cleopatra do, and sprayed dashes of body mist on her shoulders, wrist, and upper thighs. As she dressed and smeared bronze lipstick on her mouth, the words to **I Can't Take It Anymore** resonated throughout her body, racing her pulse and kayaking the winding course of her veins. When she leaned over the vanity to accentuate her eyes with mascara, she stopped short, listening to the music and staring.

At whom was she looking?

The old Frenonia?

Free couldn't be sure it was she. Hadn't seen the sister in forever, although she'd missed her, but, at times, she'd felt her standing in the shadows, waiting.

Old Frenonia took nothing lying down, unless it was a rendezvous with her man. No, that woman contemplated what she wanted and set about devising plans to procure it. She lived in the only time she'd ever have, in the now, not pining over next month, next week, or next year. Walked fear down whenever she sensed it rearing its scaly head and embraced its spine-chilling nature; counted it all joy for another opportunity to stare dread down only to discover herself the victor where the illusion of defeat hovered, the walking out on a limb, amongst the lions, reminding her she was alive.

After all, wasn't she the one who buoyed Sharmayne up when she nudged open the door of her lady-loving closet? Didn't she go against J.T.'s grain to love her new Techwood family? Who encouraged Rhonda to be there for Jomo when Big Trevor roared? Didn't she hold the door open for the one man for whom she'd brave fire and brimstones…if he asked her? Wasn't she supporting her mother in finding a daughter whose father, if found, too, might pose a decision with the potential to break her stepfather's heart? And didn't she survive the lean business years with a lioness' ferocity, even as the bookstore strained to remain afloat?

Then why the hell didn't she dial the number yesterday?

"Hey, Reesa darling, it's Free, who has just remembered she is free!

"No, you're the one, sounding bright and bushy-tailed before 9 A.M. Stay off whatever you're drinking or bring it in for me to dispose of. And no, you're too young to forget you're free.

"Listen, I've got some vitally important

business to handle for the next few days…as in I'll see you on Wednesday. Uh-uh. Everything was never better, just coming to my senses about something…let's say, J.T. related. Yes. You're such a smart little girly, so hold it down for a sister. Love ya! Bye!"

She disconnected the line. Then she called her sister's house, hollered at her mother and Rhonda, who were more bubbly than usual for a Monday morning, too. Next she called the Marriott; Chef J. Thomas was scheduled to clock in before noon.

"Good afternoon, ma'am. Table for one?"

Free surveyed the Marriott's main dining hall, nearly filled to capacity with the city's corporate crowd, who could afford a palatable, well-priced buffet or menu. Colorful chatter drifted over artfully arranged meals. Across the space, large windows offered a sunny view of pillowy clouds floating across a turquoise horizon.

"Yes, thank you." She gave the girl a broad smile, feeling incognito behind black Jackie Onassis sunglasses and a wide-brimmed straw hat, her auburn hair tumbling about her toned shoulders.

The girl glided through the diners, turning heads with the sensual sway of curvaceous hips and a seductive patron on her heels, both women gliding as though the floor were a runway. They paused at the perfect table before scenic windows.

"Your waitress will be with you shortly." She handed Free a menu and left.

Free took off her hat, fluffed her hair, put the glasses on her head, and hung her purse on the back of her chair. A middle-aged woman arrived to take her order.

"Ma'am, we don't have ox tails and purple cabbage." She scrunched her nose.

"True. But please do me the honor of passing the order on to Chef J. Thomas."

A slow look of understanding sifted across the woman's face. "Yes, ma'am."

The minute he heard the news, J.T. walked over to Abdul Parks in the bustling, steamy, noisy, industrial-sized kitchen. "Aaaw, man, she's here. Here! She just sent our love code."

Parks wiped sweat from his face and neck with a white cloth from his pocket. He towered over bubbling, savory-smelling vats and giant skillets, supervising a team of sous chefs. Around the kitchen, pastry chefs bustled, busily designing varied confections, while other workers prepared fresh green salads and garnished a queue of dishes.

"Who? You got a new lady already? Damn, bro."

"No, dude." Laughing, J.T. came out of his chef's coat and hat. "Kevina says an attractive lady just came in and asked for me and ox tails and purple cabbage."

"None of which is offered on our menu, the last I looked."

"Frenonia Roberts is well aware of that, also, and she loves ox tails and purple cabbage, my oxtails and purple cabbage, and me, okay. Let's say *my* attractive lady has finally realized *she* can't sustain *her* Junior-Thomas sabbatical a moment longer. So today's *my* day."

"How long has it been?"

"Four months, two weeks and one day.

Today."

Parks grinned, slowly realizing he'd be holding things down for an hour or more.

"Guess going to see Dr. Wallace paid off, huh man?"

"You got it! Once I got *myself* back, everything else, she claimed, would follow, and she was right. I enjoyed seeing Anita, and if I never said thanks for your suggestion to see her, I'm saying it now. Thanks, my man. She was precisely what I needed."

"So what you gone do besides clear this camp?"

"Hear her out." He grinned rakishly. "Honor her treaty."

"Why don't you invite her upstairs to the room you use whenever you work late? Talk there. I'll send up treaty food, light and tasty, and hmmmm…a bottle of her favorite wine…which is?"

"Plum wine."

"Done deal."

He and J.T. shook an intricate, inside handshake and pounded the other's back before ending their show of friendship with a testosterone embrace. "One more thing, Parks. Nearly forgot with the thrill of having my Blackwoman in the building."

"Shoot."

"If you ever see or hear of me wanting another woman other than Frenonia Roberts, don't care how desirable, wealthy or smart this woman may be, I want you to whoop my ass. And if I buck up and propose a fight, I want you to get your brother with the muscles bigger than mine," he fell silent and looked Parks in the eye, "and let him help you hold me down, and together, y'all can whoop my black ass."

Parks guffawed, reaching for J.T.'s white jacket.

"Man, get out of here! Never keep a lady waiting, especially not when she comes for you. I'll play it as though you won't be coming back, so don't feel rushed or obligated to return."

When J.T. emerged from the Marriott's kitchen in black slacks and a white short- sleeve sports shirt, when his eyes found hers and he grinned that heart-stopping grin, when he strolled to her table and pulled up an unoccupied chair and sat down, Free felt a current of attraction plummet from her heart straight to her ponany. Boomerang back up to her chest and splay outward, stimulating her nipples, and then nosedive to her clit.

They exchanged a subdued greeting and he stared, promising he'd prepare her request for their evening meal. She concurred. Caught up with her fleeing breath and smiled broadly, unable to think of anything sensible to say, to ask, for fear the scene taking shape in her head might fall from her lips.

He required a moment to take it all in.

They licked one another visually, sensually, seemingly for hours.

She didn't know why she was tripping. He probably sensed the materializing scene in her face, no doubt could describe it better than she was seeing and feeling it, so, after a while, she allowed him to help a sister out. Whispering if they might speak in private, since obviously she had something personal on her mind, he stood and reached for her hand, and she nodded. Wobbly-kneed, she followed him through sticky stares to the door.

As J.T. slid the key card in the reader of a door on the seventh floor and stepped backward for her entry, a spray of red roses on a wooden tray boasting wheat crackers, cheese, grapes and plum wine regaled her from the center of the king-sized bed. He marveled at Abdul's fast handiwork.

"I love the balcony on this room because it overlooks downtown without the traffic fumes." He gazed at her naked biceps, fingertips longing to glide her arm, their sidelong looks sending shivers to dance along the other's spine. "Let's take this party outside, shall we?"

Free dumped her pocketbook on the T.V. stand before stepping onto the balcony. She seated herself at a leaf-etched, wrought-iron table.

"How did you know I'd stop by today? It's Monday!" She puckered her lips in mock anger. "This intended for someone else?"

"No one else whose name isn't Frenonia Roberts. Wait a minute, baby."

He sat the tray on the table and reentered the room. Meanwhile, every nerve in Free's body quivered at the magnitude of such a coincidence.

Had he been feeling the same?

"Here, darling, for your hands."

The sound of his velvety voice pressed her bottom to wrought iron. Each time he spoke, addressing her affectionately, she wanted one thing: to be one with him, breathless and sweaty, their lips locked, her thighs taut around his waist, those gentle, engaging, creative hands on her skin, everywhere at once.

She wiped her hands on a white, microwave-heated face cloth. "Thank you."

His smile a dazzle of white in deep-chocolate, looking at him, she realized they needed to talk, but desire kept strangling her thoughts and pelting her pussy with love taps. So she focused on the birdsongs, the afternoon, and her blessings.

"You are and have always been and will forever be devastatingly beautiful to me. God, how I've missed you."

He took the seat beside her, plucked a claret-red grape from a juicy bunch and brought it to her lips, which parted slightly, and he watched that mouth, those teeth accept it, before offering another.

Her breasts shifted under the silky gold and maroon shell. Thumping palpitations arranged an aria of her breathing, as if she was sixteen again and the guy for whom she'd been starry-eyed telephoned.

"I-I've missed you, too, J.T."

He grinned, leaned into her and placed his right hand soothingly over her heart and murmured against her scented auburn wilderness. "It's okay, you can deep breathe." His lips savored her cheek. "I can feel your heart throbbing. Here." Standing, he maneuvered her to an upright position and caressed her back. "Match it to mine. Hell, I've waited too long to have you keel over from a heart attack."

She giggled. He fed her another grape. They resumed their seats.

"I've missed you with an ache that explains why absence makes the heart fonder."

Free vowed not to touch the curly black hair yet, but simply say what she must; not to lave another glance on his chiseled chest, an aphrodisiac in her veins; and not with the essence of his nearness soaking her panties.

"I know what you mean. I've come to understand so many things in your absence, lady. Primarily, I understand the urge to control someone you love is death for a relationship, can only lead to a walking away. Yeah, you love and the need to protect what you love is as natural as breathing, but dominating what is cherished says you intend to mold and reshape your lover in your own image---says the beloved requires fixing, as though something is wrong with her.

"And anytime you find yourself reshaping someone, you might want to look inside yourself..." he shifted his gaze from Free to a colorful dragonfly taking an ease-dropping break on the arm of his chair and continued, "...examine yourself to peep your own flaws. See, if you can't appreciate your lover for who she is, your next decision ought to be to step. It's only now that I understand why it was imperative that you showed me to the door. How else was I going to get it?" He hunched his shoulders and fed her a tiny wedge of pepper jack cheese on a cracker. "Baby, honest to God, I never want to control anything you don't ask me to."

Free waited, respecting his silence, and fell in love...again.

"Ya know, had an opportunity to view the control issue from another angle." He gave a peculiar little stumbling laugh. "The...uh...girl I'd been seeing---"

"The one who came into the bookstore, the one from the club?"

"Uh-huh. Donna Lorde. She had her notions

about controlling me, and subjected to that type of behavior, I realized how I drove you to the point of anger with…uh…what I'd put you through. It's a wonder you put up with me as long as you did." His tongue glossed his bottom lip, commanding Free's attention. "I'm sorry."

"I forgive you."

"Thank you. I appreciate your forgiveness. It means everything to me." Another scorching grin. "Oh. I realized I love your manner of dress. So feminine, sensual. What I faced was how jealous it…uh…how I chose to be jealous thinking that other men would see you and be attracted, too. Fear in the thought made me a mad man. Yet…I had to come to the realization that if I trusted you and loved you, with the confidence of a brother who knows his woman loves him, then jealousy served no purpose. So…" he drawled, pausing to offer her a goblet of plum wine and the ball, "your heart slowed down long enough to share?"

Free was none too anxious to begin, her prepared script sacked and her mouth suddenly a sand pit, its dryness recalling a recent dream of black feathers floating from her lips. She searched her heart for the most euphonious way to hang her scattered thoughts on the lifeline J.T. tossed her. She sipped the wine to calm her nerves and then offered J.T. a grape. The touch of his lips jig-sawed her mind.

Should she put it out there?

"I've learned that…no matter how much it hurts…honesty is the sealant for any relationship. It's hard to admit, so bear with me. Please." Downcast eyes, a pleading tone, and left-over shame begged his forgiveness; involuntarily, J.T. moved to comfort her, but a manicured hand stayed him.

"A couple of months after we met...I...got pregnant...and had an abortion." She paused, bowed her head and then leveled a direct stare at him. "At the time I didn't think we'd known one another long enough to be anybody's parents and I was too selfish to love anyone but myself and I wasn't mentally ready to be a mother, let alone an unwed--"

A dam crumbled in her resolve, and J.T. closed the distance between them. For the second time, he stood and took her into his arms and then seated her on his lap, arranging the pleats in her skirt. Gently, he soaked himself in her face and hair, smeared the lotion of his kisses into the back of her hands.

"You left your physician's letter on the dresser one morning, under something, and," he hedged, "sorry, but I read it. That being the case, I didn't discus it with you, just let it fester, and got what I deserved. What good would have come out of it, knowing and waiting for the bottom to drop out? Now, finally hearing it from you, it dissolves any ill will I'd harbored."

"Oh God, I'm sorry, J.T." She swallowed a sob. Sighed heavily.

He cradled her head. Her hair felt silky, welcoming his fingers. With a forefinger, he outlined her profile, the finger skiing off her nose and exhaling at the softness of her lips, and then surfing her neck and clavicle, it skimmed down her front to trace her fingers resting in her lap. How he'd missed every inch of the woman!

"I forgive you, Frenonia. I love you."

Impressed, she listened, grateful, as he

explained what his therapist said about forgiveness preceding healing and how the past---once revealed---needed to be left in the past so they could look to a future minus the desire to conceal anything from the other.

"Our future babies will know nothing but love, in a union I've dreamed about. I want them to know the sense of family my parents raised me in." He squeezed her tight, engorging himself with her natural scent.

"Our babies, they'll be much like Li'l Trevor and Mookey."

"This Mookey, he's from Techwood?"

"Yeah, Pinky's baby. Remember?"

"Of course. Never heard you talk about her though."

"Haven't met her yet, can you believe that?"

"Yup. I saw what you spearheaded for Techwood on the news. It was awesome, you're awesome. I was so proud of you, and you were even more gorgeous on camera!"

"I'm going to run out of thank you's, Mister, you keep this up."

"Mookey's mouth motorized like Trevor's?"

Free took a jab at his shoulder. "That is not nice, Junior Thomas."

"Sorry, sweetheart, just kidding. Fact is, I miss the little dude, also."

J.T. glanced at his wristwatch and excused himself, saying he needed to take care of something. He disappeared inside the hotel room and returned with an armful of blankets, tossing them over the balcony's railings to obstruct their table from the street. In minutes, he softened the table with several pillows and a green and beige comforter.

"Girl, I've had enough of this talking. It's time for some jazz."

He lifted her onto the table and stared into her eyes, his hands raising her shell to unclasp her black bra, the action freeing soft riffs of melodies from Frenonia's throat. The mango-hued mounds jiggled in his grasp and, with his eyes holding hers, his tongue stiffened and tap-danced over one light brown jelly bean of a nipple and then the other. He sampled the sugary areolas, teeth gently nipping, until the jelly beans became miniature party hats.

When Free sighed, music bubbling up from her belly, a fountain of moisture between her legs made her panties uncomfortable, and she wiggled about, her ponany singing the blues. To keep from falling backward, although J.T.'s mouth was hotly relishing her left breast, the right clasped in his palm, she gripped the cushioned table edge and felt congas beating in her veins.

With the afternoon breeze on her belly, the insects scatting, the traffic humming, a flurry of sensations strumming her insides, Free's thighs parted. She arched her back and let her head fall backward. Her lips trembled. Long dark lashes beat her cheekbones. Her mouth opened and closed as she watched J.T.'s tongue flatten and lick the underside of her breasts, then suck as much of them as he could into his mouth, then tease her with his teeth, then taste her in spiraling strokes.

She knew he meant to do it. He was the only one who could. Make her climax simply by making music with her breasts alone. A sweet sensation began in her middle and spread to her ass where it rose to pluck her thighs, rendering her movements jerky, sandals been off, long broomstick skirt skewed, her hands flopping, gripping, doing the best they could to anchor her. Gracefulness blew over the balcony. An enticing wind played a scale of love notes over her heated flesh, she parted her lips to scream, but J.T., having tuned up months ago, popped a thumb between those painted lips. She began sucking, and a wet scream slid down his wrist.

Moans filled the air. Drifted down to the street, but they couldn't stop.

"Hmmm." J.T. groaned against her cleavage. "God, you so sweet."

When J.T.'s taste buds were somewhat satisfied, he leaned her backward until she reclined, body enmeshed in pillowy softness. He ran his hands up the naturally crumpled material of her skirt, noting the tremulous thighs. The skirt slid smoothly up her exquisite legs, exposing the slight hair and shapely curves that made his Blackman press against his slacks to experience the jazz they were composing. But he'd finish composing the full score, later. He had other plans, but right now he'd slurp Free's honey, and make her hum a slow sax solo under the reed of his tongue.

With the skirt up past her black thongs, he admired the intoxicating picture of her nakedness, plump and supple, and skated his fingertips along her inner thighs. *Lord, have mercy!* The woman was irresistible. He lowered his head and her legs sprang open so he could inhale her luscious mound and sip her juice through black lace. Kisses slithered down her curved thighs. Got drawn back to her passion-swollen ponany. Tumbled towards the plumpness of her hips. Peppered up from her thongs and the scream Free fought hard to control wailed out and rode the July breeze. Beside himself, J.T. eased the thin seat of the panty aside, kissed her clitoris and, delicately parting her labia, mined her with a thick finger while savoring her sugary sweetness.

"J.T.! Oh goodness! Mmmm! O my God!"

But he couldn't help her. She was on her own. Too far down the table, he kicked caution to the wind and thrilled to the sheer taste of beautiful, clean, savory, plump, inebriating mouthfuls of female delicacy, his jazzy funk, a repast for which he'd salivated in his dreams. Was she really here, under his tongue? He pulled up to the blanketed table and gingerly pulled her squirming body closer, not to miss a taste of her cream.

His tongue speared her licorice, lyrical walls. Dark hair curled in a streak of wetness. Under her moans, he sucked her snippet of joy hard. Until it wept.

"Wish I could photograph you now." J.T. said the words with her fragrance in his nose. She listened and moaned. Purred. Then her pussy sang another long, wet solo. With Junior Thomas conducting her body's orchestra, Free experienced balcony-rocking climaxes. Satisfied, J.T. rained kisses across her ass and sat back and sighed.

As she recuperated, he rubbed her feet until her breathing returned to normal.

"Listen, you lovely, lusty lady." He kissed her kneecaps. "Take a shower, a nap, and I'll send up a snack later, whatever you want. Watch some T.V. Don't worry about clothes. I'll send an outfit so you can join me for dinner here later tonight."

He grinned, wetting his lips. "I'll be your chef, as usual."

Chapter 32

Pastoria waited for the perfect opportunity, Monday afternoon with nobody around, to call the last two of the seven Earl Taylors listed in the Atlanta white pages. With Li'l Trevor calling himself working with Jomo at Mr. Moss' corner store, Big Trevor at the office, and Rhonda off on her new writing adventure interviewing an older friend, she was drenched in excitement and anticipation.

Though she never knew him to have a middle initial, she'd noted forty chances of finding him in the E, EA, EO, E Ray, EL, Earl, and one Earlie Taylor listing. She knew she'd been stalling, underneath fierce determination, afraid of hearing his voice again. Afraid of what they would and would not say. After thirty-one years. And although she wouldn't have admitted it to anyone, this man, Earl Taylor, was the only one who had, as Rhonda put it, "*dogged* her."

Crow. He made her eat it, by never breaking, never returning to her arms, with his heart and their daughter in tow.

She dialed the first number, her finger shaking. The line rang twice, then what sounded like an elderly white woman twanged, "Missus Eh-rull Taay-lor speakin'," and Pastoria apologized and disconnected. The next three didn't answer. She stared at the notebook's page of numbers and inhaled deeply and clenched her molars and selected the sixth number. Once she exhausted the last three, she made a note to ask Rhonda about that CD Rom she'd mentioned earlier.

Pastoria caught her breath abruptly. Bosom heaving, pulse thumping, just galloping, she felt it slow suddenly, short of stopping. Her nerves gave a violent lurch. If someone didn't pick up soon, the ringing reverberating in her soul, the others would come back to find her, phone in hand, sprawled on the carpet, gone.

"Hello?"

She exhaled and closed her eyes. Years washed in on her, bringing with them memories she could touch, the voice seeping into her pores like a sweet balm. Patti LaBelle was right. Love never died. Although she hadn't been strong or selfless enough to continue loving him so many years ago, she had, she knew, always loved him.

"Earl?"

"Yeah? Who's speakin'?"

"Pastoria. How are you? Catch you at a bad time?"

Silence bellowed. Under it, she could hear erratic heartbeats, could hear Earl Taylor's sporadic breathing. She said nothing for a while, supposing they both deserved time to absorb the shock of hearing one another's voice.

"Well, I'll be. Excuse me. Hearin' your voice knocked the wind outta me. Usually, I see things comin'. Never expected to hear from you in this life. Had to hold onto my senses for a minute."

"So how you doin'?"

"Okay, if okay constitutes a job, a roof over your head, fam'ly livin' and breathin', and a man in his right mind. How you been doin'?'

"Can't complain. It's been good." She paused. "Hope you don't mind I called."

"Mind? It's not so much that I mind as much as I'm stumped on why you'd call. But I'm sure you've got your reasons, and we'll cross that bridge in due time. You in Atlanta?"

"Yes, but not living here though. I'm still in Pine Mountain."

"With that guy? The one I heard you were with...Booker?"

Pastoria swallowed. "Yes. Booker McRae. You married?"

"You're the only woman I'da married. If the question's, 'Are you seein' anyone?' Yeah. A man gotta keep livin', right?"

"Guess so."

"You Mrs. McRae?"

No, because he wasn't you, damn you, he wasn't you. "He's a good man and I cherish him for all he's done for me over the years but I---"

He cut her off. "But you never really loved him...like you never really loved anyone."

The statement a question, it floored Pastoria and left her wounded. When the shock and hurt and truth of his venom coursed through her, as potent as a drug, she cleared her throat, parted her lips to speak, and then shut her mouth. Silence reigned once more. Minutes later, she whispered, "That's untrue, Earl Taylor. I did love you, more than you'll ever know. Back then, I was young and careless and used to having what I wanted from men. My feelings were the only ones that mattered. What did I know about loving a man, let alone a baby? Nothing. All I knew was people said I was exceptionally pretty and if I wanted something or someone, pretty was more than enough to get it.

"As for Booker, well, I'll always care for him. He helped me raise my gir---," she faltered, thinking of the baby girl she'd seen but once, and silently praying nothing had closed between them. "Forgive me." Instantly, the notion occurred to her she'd said the words so often in the past few days, it'd become a benediction.

She could hear him taking in stabilizing breaths.

"There is nothing to forgive," he said forgivingly. "You've got two, I've heard."

"Frenonia owns a bookstore, and Rhonda is an educator. Both live here. I'm a grandmother, Rhonda has a six-year-old." She said nothing more, preferring to listen to his reaction. When he, too, settled for listening, she went on, "It's been a long time. Do you believe time really heals all wounds?"

"Sure," he owned. "I'm healed."

"Somehow I knew that."

"Yeah, and you wanna know something crazy? Raisin' her was the best departin' gift you coulda given me, 'cause she look a spittin' image of you, like I ain't had no part in makin' her at all. And lovin' her was lovin' you. Took me damn near thirty-plus years, but I done it. Learned to live without the one I loved, y'know, like that song Gladys Knight sings. Every time I hear it, even today, I think of you.

"And the craziest thing of all is I'da been your fool, same as Booker, had you popped your fingers and called my name. Me and my baby girl woulda been there.

"She like me. Kicked to the curb and no better off than a burlap sack of unwanted puppies but she loves you to this day, Pastoria." His tone bittersweet, he couldn't hold his peace once he'd opened his heart. "And she ain't seen your face. Though she have and just don't know it. Every time she look in the mirror, she seein' your face, and don't know it. Yet she loves you, same as I do, as if you'd been there every day of our lives."

The sour words curdled Pastoria's emotions, a reminder of the lives she'd carelessly damaged, and the magnitude of what he said causing her to leave bite marks in her bottom lip, uselessly fighting back tears. A loosing battle, but she fought it anyway.

In the end, she listened to Earl talk and eventually reeled under the meaning of his simple words: *they'd never stopped loving her*. Damned river water in her soul burst, and Pastoria was unable to wipe the tears away fast enough, before the next surge of sorrow and regret engulfed her.

Earl felt her pain and let her cry.

"I sent for you when my husband got killed in a military maneuver. I waited. A long, long time. You never came or called, so I kept your army picture, the one you signed. Figured your silence meant I'd missed my chance and hurt you too deeply and you considered me unworthy of our daughter's love, so I never tried again."

It was Earl Taylor's time to be outdone. Her admission stout. And to think he'd stayed mad with God over the years for not hearing his prayers, not bringing her back to them.

"Who you send word by?"

"Your friend, Bo. Bo Stinson."

"Never got it." And it didn't surprise him. Stinson had carried a flaming torch for her, too, like half of his other buddies.

"Oh my God." She twirled the phone cord around her fingers. "You think we could've made it?"

"Anything's possible, if people...love one another."

"Do you think you could---" she stopped and licked at the salty tracks of tears above her top lip, inhaled, and began a bit more steadily, "Would you consider letting me meet her, Earl? I know it's a lot to ask, but I need to see her. Her eyes...they haunt me."

"I can't see why not. She grown. Been pinin' for you anyway, askin' for you ev'ry birthday, since she was a small girl. She got a girl of her own now and two boys, and still she asks for you."

"Oh my goodness!" The thought of her and Earl Taylor's grandbabies painted a big smile across her face, and she flat lined the phone cord into a long beige line. "The birth certificate has her as Pastoria Taylor. I looked for her first, without ever telling her sisters her name or that I was trying to find her. Somehow, trying to find you helped me face the past."

"Don't know. She's never listed her numbers; guess she's private like that."

"I'm happy you gave her my name, in spite of what happened."

"Pastoria, I love you, have always loved you from the moment I saw you, in bobby socks and that hooped skirt, and me dressed in Uncle Sam's uniform. You were beautiful. And life blessed me that day. The only name I'd ever give my female child is Pastoria, even if you'd never conceived our baby girl."

Free had to give it to him, Junior Thomas was

a keeper. Here she was sitting at one end of a grand table draped in a white tablecloth in the Marriott's private Peach Blossom Room on a Monday evening. Dressed in a sparkling white, spaghetti-strapped sun dress, delicate white stilettos on her feet, with a classic white bangle on each wrist and white whoops in her ears (he'd requested that she style her hair in an upsweep for dinner, sending up bobby pins and reminding her she barely required lipstick), she looked extraordinary. And felt like Miss Universe.

"Why so huge a table? Will dinner be a feast? A banquet?"

She was fishing, but J.T. didn't mind. About now, the woman could say and do whatever she pleased, even disappear, if that pleased her, too.

"You might call it that, my love, but dinner will be served shortly." He gave her a wink and a grin from the room's doorway. "Comfortable?"

"Exceptionally. Did I kiss you yet? To say thank you for all this finery?"

"Nope. There will be ample time for that mushy stuff later. Right now practice smiling and glowing without spoiling your gown," J.T. suggested before leaving again, her jaunty, "Yes, sir, Chef Thomas," at his back.

Twenty minutes later, as she was on the brink of strolling to the bathroom to keep the blood circulating in her legs, Rhonda and Big Trevor darkened the ornate room's doorway, and absolute shock shaded Free's countenance.

"Hi, guys! What are you doing here?" She got up to hug her sister. Before she could ask after the boys, Li'l Trevor and Jomo pimped in, decked out in Sunday attire and shining shoes. "Goodness! I should've known J.T. was cooking more than he let on." She closed her eyes and took in Big Trevor's expensive cologne and complimented his choice of colors. He was dashing in a linen, golden rod, button-down dress shirt and matching baggy slacks. She raised one brow at her sister. "Girrrl, don't allow this man to the restroom unescorted. Preferably Li'l Trevor or Jomo or both. We don't want no trouble. No, ma'am."

Everyone laughed. Then the boys smothered her in hugs and auntie kisses and darted outside, saying they had girls to see and others to meet. Meanwhile, Free chatted with Rhonda and Trevor. Her gaze patrolled the door, waiting for it to open at any minute; something telling her J.T. had only just begun to surprise her.

"I'm so grateful Miz Too-Sweet was on your path. You were right. Her stories are amazing! Did I tell you we've started spending a few afternoons together, her listening to my stories and commenting with that one-of-a-kind, country-folk wisdom; me bowled over by the scope and depth of her experiences. I love her and writing about her life, and our readers are going to love her, too."

Trevor whispered in Rhonda's ear. Whatever he said made her lean into his broad chest, girlishly, cheek up-turned for a smooch.

'That's my baby," he said, bouncing a diamond ring with a miniature golf ball on his pinky. "Her teaching days are numbered! You mark my words, Ms. Roberts."

When Rhonda nudged his underarm with her elbow and tittered, Free nearly gagged. Until, that is, Miz Too-Sweet and Mister Will strolled in, Preacher close on their heels. Awed in spite of being sufficiently galvanized for one evening, Free did more than gag. She practically fainted, and would have had J.T. not warned her about spoiling her dress.

"Okay, that's it! Where's Junior Thomas?" she shouted, rushing to hug the older woman, smelling florally sweet in her yellow hat with a swathe of lace on one side, her dress a medley of yellow and cream flowers. "Oh my god! Mr. Will's here!"

Mr. Will hobbled into her embrace, mindful not to stub her toes with his cane.

"The little lady here told me if I wasn't ready by the time she walked out the door, she wasn't cookin' fah the next two weeks runnin'." He chuckled, glanced at Big Trevor and Preacher. "Don't take no genius to know I be dead fo' then. So here I be."

The men guffawed, all except Preacher, who laughed with his eyes.

"Uh man's gotta eat come hell or high water," Mr. Will said to a chorus of amens.

Free enveloped both men with a bear hug and introduced the threesome to Big Trevor. It was apparent from their warm exchange that Rhonda and Mr. Will and Preacher were anything but strangers. And before Free could question Miz Too-Sweet about who brought them to the Marriott, in glided Pastoria, possessively holding the hand of a gorgeous gentleman with splashes of salt-and-pepper through a mass of black curls. Taller than she was, he complimented her more than any man she knew.

"Hello, everyone!" Pastoria smiled a beauty-queen smile, complete with the finger fluttering and kisses blown around the table. Free couldn't recall the last time she'd seen her mother look so youthful. And radiant.

"Seems everyone has met Earl except Free and Trevor."

Trevor stood. Free turned to stone.

'This is Earl Taylor, my eldest daughter's father."

"Hello!" Earl grinned. "My pleasure."

Pastoria glowed in a rich red dress with a wide white belt under her breasts.

"Dr. Trevor Butler, Rhonda's husband and Li'l Trevor's father. And Jomo's new dad."

"Trevor is good, man," Big Trevor said with a friendly tone.

Earl released Pastoria's hand, and the men shook hands.

"My entrepreneurial daughter, Frenonia, whom we call Free."

Pastoria's hand fluttered in Free's direction as if she were a grand prize in a showcase on the television show, "The Price Is Right." And in that instant, Free knew that her mother had always loved this man, contrary to what may have transpired to separate them for thirty-one years. *Love could not hide itself from itself.*

When he reached for her hand, she could no more stop herself from hugging him than Pastoria could stop fleeing thoughts of Booker McRae from evacuating her heart.

'It's a joy to meet you. Since your mother called me this morning, she's painted these beautiful scenes of her girls, though they fall short in the beauty of your presence."

He looked from Free to Rhonda. Both sisters beamed scintillating smiles.

"Okaaaay!" Free giggled. "I like this man, Mama." She pointed to two seats on her left. "Do me the honor of being seated here, please."

She glanced around the table with an overwhelming joy emanating from her core. Rhonda and Big Trevor sat to her right, and beside them, Miz Too-Sweet, Mister Will and Preacher. Counting two seats for the boys and one more for J.T., and noting three more seats, she gave Pastoria an inquiring expression. "Mama, where's our sister?"

Her mother shifted her gaze to the door. Saying nothing, she exchanged a knowing communication with Rhonda, who nodded, peeked at her watch and studied the door. That's when Grant Johnson emerged in the doorway. By his suited side was a sexy, spittin' image of Pastoria Roberts.

"Hi!" the couple said simultaneously, a colorful Barbie and Ken.

"To my knowledge," Pastoria was saying, "everyone knows Grant except Trevor; thus, Trevor darling, Grant Johnson, a visiting artist, a painter, here by way of the *National Black Arts Festival*." She winked at Grant. "Grant, my son-in-law, Dr. Trevor Butler."

And while they shook hands, she added, "And this is my eldest daughter." She and Pinky shared a conspiratorial happiness. "Tell them who you are, sweetheart."

"Hi, Free and Big Trevor!" Her smile rivaled the Peach Blossom Room's expensive chandelier. "I'm Pastoria Taylor, and I am so blessed to know everyone."

A teenager in a cute blouse and tight jeans stepped around the couple and waved.

"Hello! I'm Clementine Reed, Pastoria's only daughter, and Grandma Pastoria's only granddaughter. My other brother Taylor Alexander isn't here, he's fourteen."

The room filled with laughter, Free leading the applause.

Jomo's brows furrowed. *So this was Short Dog's family? How lucky could a brother be?*

"And I'm Lewis Earl Reynolds, and this is my mama and big sister!" Mookey exclaimed. Then, upon seeing Free, ran to her and dived in her lap. "Hi Aunt Free, you look pretty! Mama says you're my auntie now!"

Everyone laughed and began talking at once, joy circulating the huge dinner table. When Chef Junior Thomas walked in and bowed, silencing the room with a wave, while directing Li'l Trevor and Jomo tacitly to their seats.

"Good evening, all!" Applause resounded; faces glowed. "I have called you together because I figured you needed to know one another and for my own selfish reasons. You see, I need you here to witness my special occasion and to break bread with me to seal the deal. In Greek and Roman mythology, one wasn't a brother until he'd broken bread with another. So help me with that momentarily, when my chef buddies and I serve this repast of ox tails and purple cabbage and steaks and shrimp and salmon and salads and buttery rolls and potatoes and vegetables." He inhaled, stopping to wag his finger at Li'l Trevor and Jomo. "Pay attention, gentlemen. I'll let you know when to salivate."

A toastmaster without a podium, J.T. waited for the laughter to recede before continuing. "Don't know how I did it, if I did anything, as God is the Alpha and Omega of every story, because on my own I couldn't have pulled off what has materialized on this divine Monday. My sweetheart and her sister and mother finally met Pinky, a woman they've wanted to know and love since forever. My man Earl reunites with a woman who has reigned supreme in his dreams."

More applause.

"Mmmm! I'm getting good at this talking thing. You agree, sweetheart?"

"Here, here!" Free shouted. "To my heart, the guest speaker! And chef!"

The room erupted in more applause, and J.T. lifted his hands for order.

"The food, folks, the food. Gotta land this plane before she lands me."

"Amen," Preacher said, and Free and the Techwood crew lost their breath, and then hollered loud enough to make J.T. flash the chandelier lights.

"One more minor thing, my beloveds---"

"Sorry, Chef Thomas, but Sharmayne and Nzinga aren't here," Free bemoaned.

"No, but I'm certain you'll do a fabulous job bringing them up to par on the phone tonight, wherever they are," J.T. checked her. "Now, if I might continue."

Pinky looked at Free and frowned playfully, as if to say we'll get him later, girl.

But J.T. missed that. He was too busy wading into the middle of the most important part of his speech, after beckoning his buddy Chef Abdul Parks into the room, and strolling towards the head of the table where Free sat watching him, starry-eyed.

No, he wasn't---was he?

"In the presence of family and friends, I, Junior Thomas---" and he dropped to one knee, humorously straightening the sleeves of his white jacket and reaching a hand in one pocket, and Free's mouth opened and Mookey applauded in glee and Junior Thomas finished, "I never want to be without this woman, so I'm asking her on bended knee to be Mrs. Junior Thomas, to stand beside me and join me in living our dreams and raising our family and cooking our meals and loving this family." He looked up at his best man, Adul Parks.

Parks handed him a shimmering yellow diamond engagement ring.

"I do, sweetheart!" Frenonia jutted her hand forward, and J.T. slid the ring on.

Preacher couldn't take it, again unhinging his jaws for a shaky, exuberant "Amen!" His fist came down on the tablecloth, shocking the gathering with the sudden sound and the craggy music of his unusual laughter vibrating the orange air of the Peach Blossom Room.

"Now can us eat?" Mr. Will asked. "He up now, and I'm dead."

Miz Too-Sweet elbowed him softly and cut her eye at Preacher and frowned.

Free and J.T. laughed around their kiss, and for the umpteenth time the room exploded in more laughter and commotion. Toasts went around, dinner was served, hugs sweetened the air, and other Marriott guests poked their heads in the room to discern the origination of so much love and gaiety.

Chapter 33

That Saturday, Pinky stood in the doorway of her baby sister's brick home, smiling apprehensively, though proudly, at the sight before her: a living room jam-packed with women, of every color, on sofas, chairs, and even the carpet. It amazed her they'd come with the sole intent to discuss the novel nestled in her purse.

"Hey, sis, c'mon in! Glad you made it!"

Rhonda kissed her cheek and hugged her, the smell of delicious food lingering about her hair and red and white Delta T-shirt. Pinky stepped into the foyer, smiling, and waved, while Rhonda greeted Miz Too-Sweet and Sherrie Ann with warm embraces.

"Everybody, this is my big sister, Pastoria Taylor. Isn't she beautiful? We only found her last Monday evening, but I…we feel we've known her all our lives."

When Rhonda introduced her companions, Free bounded down the stairs where she'd been putting the finishing touches on several gift baskets. "Hey Big Sis, I've missed you!" She and Pinky hugged and giggled, Free too elated to have a sibling older than herself, too tickled to honor her with love and respect. Pinky beamed, watched her enfold Miz Too-Sweet and Sherrie Ann in her arms.

"Will Mama be back before the book club ends?" Pinky thanked a girl with braids for giving up her chair to recline on a floor pillow.

"Don't know, honey," Free owned, shaking her newly trimmed do, "ever since she reunited with your dad, they've been inseparable."

The sisters traded a knowing expression and hugged once more; they, too, had been catching up since J.T.'s surprise, engagement dinner, although there didn't seem to be enough time to wade through the years and sate themselves with the highs and lows of the other's life.

"Hi," a woman said, emerging from the kitchen. "I'm Sharmayne. It's an honor to finally meet you."

"Free's best friend," Pinky remembered. "My daughter spoke well of you and another lady coming to Techwood with Free's cultural program."

A tall woman approached them, draped a chiseled arm across Sharmayne's shoulders and kissed her on the cheek. "I'm this one's humble half, Nzinga Edwards, and we've heard nothing but 'my sister Pinky this' and 'my big sister Pastoria that,' since Free here called us this past Tuesday...about sunrise."

Sharmayne and Nzinga traded hugs with Miz Too-Sweet and Sherrie Ann.

"Hi, Nzinga," Pinky said, "Pretty name. Different."

"Thanks. It means the central source of beauty or the alluring captivation of a sensual woman. Can also define a manipulator who uses her womanly charm and beauty to control her surroundings." Nzinga bowed, leaving Pinky enchanted by her handsome, rakish appeal.

"She's more the latter significance of her name, love," Sharmayne rejoined, and Pinky giggled.

Rhonda feigned a playful deafness. Free politely placed a hand to her lips. And Nzinga, nonplussed, went on, "Actually, my goddess, Nzinga of Ndongo, of Angola, was a West African warrior queen, whose discipline and military strategies defeated the Portuguese. Mind you, legend has it no Black Angolans were kidnapped and enslaved during her reign." The smacking sound of her lips against Sharmayne's jaw drew more soft giggles from Pinky.

"Interesting." Pinky glanced around the cute couple to observe two women giving their seats to Miz Too-Sweet and Sherrie Ann. Somehow, she felt more than heard the *Daughters of Isis* inhale. Could only imagine what they were thinking about Miz Too-Sweet in her shapeless, floral print number with a thin white belt at her middle, dingy white pumps, greasy bare legs, and large ole-timey earrings and, mercy, of Sherrie Ann, a shapely white girl, blonde, in jeans with a blouse tied above her pierced navel, those grinning blue eyes sweeping every detail to get busy with later.

"Is the family reunion over?" Willie Mae crossed her arms under her bosom and slouched in a computer chair, feet swinging. "Not complaining, 'cuz I'm above that now, but who needs movies with ya'll around."

Laughter bubbled up like a fountain and the book club meeting got under way. Pinky listened raptly, recording everything. The characters did sound amusing, though she couldn't relate to half of them.

It was only when one woman's retelling of Beverly sucking on a bone and Charles saying he wished she'd suck him that way, did Pinky, forgetting her shyness, giggle aloud. Infectious, the sound swept the women up on a tide of relating and connecting; laughter surging from woman to woman. The hymnal music baptized Pinky with an instant friendliness that began thawing the slight discomfort she'd felt upon entering the room and replaced it with a light veil of warmth, inviting her to study the conversation closer.

She hadn't read the whole book, but **Sisters and Lovers** seemed to be about three sisters---Evelyn, Charmaine, and Beverly---who lived in Washington, D.C. Just then two similarities between her life and theirs occurred to her: she had two sisters, and Free's best friend was Sharmayne, though she didn't know how Free's friend spelled her name. The thought brought a smile to her lips. Evelyn, the sister with the money and good job and lawyer husband and two kids, didn't interest her.

The girl had no problems. Was worried about some woman named Wanda taking her man. If Wanda didn't have any money, she couldn't do anything for Evelyn's husband no way, since her pussy 'bout couldn't start a law firm, let alone break wedding vows.

As for that other one, that Beverly, Pinky half-liked her. She admired a woman who could take matters into her own hands, and a nine-inch blade, to drive a point home to Vernon, a trifling man, like Lewis Reynolds and Javan Reed, who thought they could trample women. Unlike Lewis, Vernon had potential and money. She might've hung in there with him, too, as Beverly ended up doing.

When the conversation got around to Beverly dating a white man, who turned out to be a junk collector, with whom Beverly had considered having a test-tube baby, Pinky almost laughed again; but she didn't want Sherrie Ann to take her laughter the wrong way, so she bit her bottom lip and let her eyes poll the living room's Black art.

Who she respected and wanted the women to continue discussing was the sister named Charmaine. Now she and Charmaine had much in common. For one, they were horrible at picking men---or she had been in the past. Charmaine had to shake Clarence same as she was shaking Lewis and Javan and Omar. Pregnant, Charmaine was raising her small son, Kenny, single-handedly, and she was a single mother of three. Trapped in a dead-end job, Charmaine still beat her time, the Waffle House the bottom of the employment barrel, though it was honest work. Yep, they could've been sisters.

But in spite of the shit they waded through, both had hope. Charmaine, the *Daughters* had said, returned to school at the end of the novel, and her sisters had her back for the new baby coming. As for Pinky, God had blessed her with someone beyond her wildest dreams; someone better than wonderful, in Grant Johnson.

Knocking at the front door jarred Pinky's thoughts and the discussion.

Rhonda opened the door. Pastoria and Earl walked into the foyer, holding hands, a teenager jaunt in their step and the unmistakable allure of rekindled love in their faces.

"Hello, everyone." Pastoria looked lovely, a glamour girl straight off a World War II calendar, except for her sleeveless yellow umpire-style dress.

Earl Taylor grinned and squeezed Pastoria's hand.

"Hey, Mama!" Free sat up and began dancing in her seat, popping her fingers.

Rhonda kissed them both on the cheek.

"Hello, Mother!" Pinky chimed,

complimenting her taste in sundresses. "What's up, Dad?"

That did it for Willie Mae. "Could somebody pass the popcorn, please? Damn."

***

Nzinga rested her head against a high-backed sofa and eased her sandaled feet onto a cushioned footstool, the living room peaceful and air cool. Jeans abandoned, she sat in a light blue muscle shirt and bikini-cut underwear.

Sharmayne gazed at her admiringly and sighed. The woman was a heaping Dairy Queen sundae with a boatload of cherries and mounds of whip cream. She placed a frosty pitcher of lemonade and a plate of fresh-from-the-oven macadamia nut cookies on a low table before her sleepy woman.

It was going on ten. A muted white essence emanated from the soundless T.V. In the corners, orange, pumpkin-scented tea candles spiced the air from the bottom of large glass flower vases. Shadows loomed. Tongues of light slipped under the cracked kitchen door, heralding the aroma of freshly baked cookies and the hum of the refrigerator and palpable grunts of the shifting house---a scene both women knew and loved.

"C'mere, honey, and sit with me for a minute. We'll wash dishes later. You're always doing something special for me. Here---" Nzinga insisted, pulling Sharmayne onto her lap, a spot the moving woman adored. "Lemme rub your feet."

Sharmayne balked. Then desisted, giving herself permission to be pampered, although she felt more gratified giving than receiving. Nzinga's hands, strong and soothing, massaged her shoulders, and Sharmayne closed her eyes, relishing the tantalizing tingle in her feet and legs, and leaned in closer to her woman's warmth. Good feelings enveloped her, reminding her how fatigued she was; she and Nzinga having remained longer than the others to assist Rhonda and Free with clean-up.

Bending her toes backward then forward, and then wiggling each, Nzinga massaged the soles of her lady's feet as though she were caressing a long-awaited gift on Christmas morning. Sharmayne moaned.

"And to think I thought our book club meeting was the most eventful next to meeting you at Free's." Her light eyes cuddled the curve of Sharmayne's chin and lingered a bit too long on the shape of her perky breasts. For a second, she had to make her thoughts behave, for what they craved meant no more talking, only hunger and desire and surrender. "That sister of theirs is attractive."

Sharmayne reached over and selected a cookie and brought it to Nzinga's lips, only to snatch it away. "Uh huh, I saw you shamelessly flirting with her, and if that weren't bad enough, she responded as if women flirted with her 99 times a day."

"You've nothing to fret about, my precious. You have no equals, living or dead."

Sharmayne giggled softly. "I could tell by your actions."

"Stop it, love bunny! Shouldn't I be nice to the in-laws?"

"There she is, Queen Nzinga, undefeated!"

Sharmayne shared a bite of her cookie, dabbed Nzinga's lips with a napkin, and nestled into her side.

"Who'd have guessed Frenonia's sister was living right here in Atlanta? I'm still flabbergasted. It's the stuff novels are made of."

"True, but wait! I loved Free's presentation of gifts. That was too cool. The next time we host the book club I'm going to continue the practice."

"Who all got them? Miz Too-Sweet got one for being the youngest in the house. Corliss and Reesa received one each for being the most overzealous to talk. Willie Mae was honored as the sweetest *Daughter* and Lisa the mental instigator. Talk about irony."

Nzinga scratched her temples and hugged Sharmayne and bribed her with promises for another cookie. When Sharmayne bit one and popped the remainder in Nzinga's mouth, the sugary delight melted on her tongue and rendered Sharmayne a kiss on the tip of her nose and along her clavicle.

"Sherrie Ann got a gift, too…for giving the most interesting take on interracial relationships. Said she was living for the day when lovers could love without the trappings of race, sexual orientation, class, wealth, health, etc. Girl broke it down."

"Uh huh, the *Daughters* looked at her as if she'd grown two heads, too."

"But Free's mother knows how wonderfully heavy it is sometimes to love someone," Nzinga was now saying in a solemn tone. "A mesmerizing woman, Love drives you, commands you, until you have no will of your own. Your life may as well be a check passed to a beloved daily. Brings to mind that Emily Dickinson poem, 'I Gave Myself to Him.' The lines 'Sweet debt of life, each night to owe, Insolvent every noon' kinda sums up the situation. When we love, we owe of ourselves."

Her voice faded into a reassuring caress in the dark room. The Amazon delicately guided Sharmayne's locked head to the curve of her neck and shoulders. Between forefinger and thumb, she twirled the springy curls and brushed their fuzziness across her lips. Vanilla and lavender shimmied up her nose. Fingers laced, their connection filled the Amazon's belly with butterflies.

"I love you, lady."

"I love you more."

"Before we go upstairs, darling, I've an announcement."

Sharmayne walked her fingers up the front of Nzinga's shirt. "I'm all ears."

"You've an interview with the director of the museum at Spelman so we'll begin role-playing skills for a successful interview tomorrow. The position, which has potential for growth, is administrative assistant to the director. Do you think my queen could be in professional attire and ready to leave with me on next Monday morning, about 7:45?"

Sharmayne stiffened. "How long have you known about this?"

"Since Friday." Nzinga cringed, playfully dodging fanning arms and kicking legs. "Didn't tell you because I was waiting for the perfect moment. You'll be wonderful! You speak beautifully, and you're one of the most organized people I know."

She couldn't even play mad with Nzinga. "Oh my God! It's happening." She clapped her hands, infinitely grateful and kissed Nzinga's mouth. "Oooo, thank you, thank you so much! What would I do without you?"

"The check I owe." The tip of Nzinga's nose brushed the smooth darkness of Sharmayne's cheek and inhaled her naturally delectable scent. "I have some paperwork I need you to sign upstairs, in my office, regarding your lifetime account at the Nzinga Edwards Bank and Trust Company."

"Mmmm. Shall I swear my love, trust and check-cashing loyalty forever?"

"That'll be a sufficient start, yes, ma'am."

Chapter 34

The following Friday, Pastoria couldn't cease an internal trilling since Earl Taylor sat down across from her and stared a hymn into her heart. Nor did she want to. Throughout their meal his dark brown eyes attentive and conversation charming, while visibly pleasing Pinky and Grant from the smiles on their faces, she and Earl's closeness only served to compel Mookey Man to exert serious signs of four-year-old jealousy. Didn't bother him his rival was the coolest grandfather he had.

Pastoria gave Earl 'the eye' halfway through dinner, so Earl, winking, cheerfully redirected some of his attention to his grandson.

"Grandma, is the building really turning or is the city turning?"

Pastoria giggled. "No sweetness, the floor is turning, and the city appears to be moving, but it's not. Amazing, huh?"

Mookey giggled, too. "Hope we don't fly off over the other buildings."

"Me, too, Mr. Lewis Earl Reynolds. Did you tell your grandfather what Grant told you about the name Sun Dial?"

The child shook his head and stuffed more chicken fingers into his mouth. When he swallowed and gulped another mouthful of his soda, he wiped his mouth and sat up.

"The sundial is like a watch on your arm, Granddaddy."

Pinky beamed with maternal love. "Don't forget how it works, Man."

"By shadows. When the sun zooms," he explained, using his hand as a rocket, "it makes shadows, and people told time by the watch in the ground."

Earl raised his eyebrows in mock surprise.

"Thanks, professor!"

The dinner over and the group assembled in the Sun Dial's parking lot, Pinky beside Grant, who was dialing Rhonda's number on his cell phone, and Pastoria and Earl leaned on the hood of Grant's champagne-colored Jaguar, Pastoria's head filled again with a renewed refrain of the trilling she'd enjoyed every time Earl Taylor's eyes buttonholed hers, except now the trilling had progressed to a wild chorus of cheeping and chirping and tweeting and twittering. And she, listening to the music in Earl's smile, knew she was headed for trouble when Pinky's voice, louder than she'd ever heard it, pushed through the trilling.

"Mama." She popped her fingers. "Mama!"

Her father looked at her as if she were loosing her mind.

"Excuse me, but Grant called Rhonda's and nobody picked up so they must still be at Six Flags so you can stay with me tonight, if you want, and Grant can take you to Rhonda's tomorrow."

"Thanks, Sweetheart. I'll stay with you next, but I was going to ask your father to take me to Free's since I promised her I'd help with our all-girl sleepover plans. She ought to be up. She and J.T. should have talked themselves to heaven and back by now."

"No fair," Earl complained. "Why can't the guys be there to protect ya'll?"

Mother and daughter frowned, rolled their eyes. Pinky gagged on a forefinger.

Pastoria held Pinky in her arms and kissed her cheek. "I'm so glad you and the guys were able to double date with us. We'll work on getting that oldest grandson of mine to stay home sometimes."

Pinky bubbled over under her mother's soft, moist lips. "Maybe you can help me remind Taylor he isn't a man yet."

"Definitely. Either that or we'll send him to a boot camp somewhere. I don't play with little boys who wanna be men too soon."

"Can you stay with us all next week?" Mookey wanted to know.

Pastoria blew out a deep breath and tossed her laughing daughter a kiss. "I promise." Then she hugged her grandson. "Bye, Nana's li'l man."

She kissed the top of Mookey Man's sleepy head and propped him up in the Jag's passenger seat to await his mother's lap. Waving good-bye, she kissed Grant and reached for Earl's outstretched hand.

Inside Earl's old but well-kept Ford pick-up, Pastoria's body sighed and became one throbbing pressure point, as though it had suddenly come live, truly alive, for the first time in years. Colors, even night colors, vibrated. An orchestra of melodies sprang up in the moving night coming in soft and sweet through the truck's windows.

At a traffic light on Peachtree, Earl bent towards her and murmured something, the sight of his lips inches from hers mindboggling. "You welcome to stay with me, too. And I'll still take you to Free's in the morning."

Those lips still made her skin pant. She gazed

at them, tingly inside, and then turned her head to take in downtown strollers laughing and talking in crowds on the city's sidewalks. *Did the city ever sleep?*

"Thanks. I'll pass this time, though it's tempting." She sighed. "You give rain checks?"

"Only to you."

He felt twenty-one again, the one woman he'd ever loved yet causing him to want to run marathons when he didn't even trot; she still made him want to howl under a full moon in a starry night.

To keep her mind from being swept back through the years to relive how divine she'd felt being with this man, sitting near enough to inhale his touch, in another car, in another era, Pastoria talked up elaborate storms that filled him in on what she knew about getting to South Park Drive, although he'd already gotten the directions from Grant.

Somehow, Earl understood. He wasn't a man to follow a yarn all the way around the world and back just to sneak up on the truth staring him in the face from the outset. So, before steering the truck in the direction of I-20 and 17 South Park Drive, he parallel parked in the perfect spot off a side street flowing into 10th Street near Piedmont Park and dispensed with the small talk of their revelry and set her former question, redressed, into her lap for safekeeping.

"Lovers in the park at night. Reminds me of families in Calloway Gardens at dusk, so beautiful to see people together, happy."

"Ree."

His pet name for her jimmied a locked door deep in the chambers of her heart. She thought she'd never hear it repeated in this life, ever, so she'd treasure-chest the memory under the seeping sand of time and forgot its location up till now.

He said it again.

Her lungs lost their capacity to rise and fall under her still bosom.

"In answer to your question: Did I think we could've made it if ole boy hadda delivered the message after Roberts died?" He had to know where she was to better determine his strategy. Life was happening for him, and he'd honor it even if his heart was slivered and scattered along the street like confetti.

She nodded, her forehead furrowed.

"And I said it didn't matter 'cause I'd gotten over you?"

Pastoria stared at him. His words sent shockwaves to her heart, another phenomenon she hadn't imagined happening again.

"I lied. I'm willin' to try. With you. Now."

Pastoria was mute. Could do little more than peer across a sudden divide at Earl Taylor, at Booker's hurt, at the possibility of a different life, at the Unknown.

She couldn't not say it. "What about Booker?"

"What about him? I feel for him, honestly, but a man knows when he's living on borrowed time, and with that, he can't settle for less than what he wants. Vice versa, a real man wishes the same for others...even if it means...even if it feels like...somebody you love is walking away. Which would you want---someone being there outta pity or love?"

"Earl, I-I---" Pastoria checked her watch. It

was going on 11:20 P.M.

"I know, we gotta go. Free's probably wondering what the hell is going on with us. But, Ree, time ain't never wasted, contrary to what folks say. Time's precious, so you take all the time you need to answer. I want you. I love you. We can be happy together, with our growing family."

That was when Pastoria presented the best answer she had: she brushed her lips across Earl Taylor's mouth and lingered there, their kiss exploratory and long and tender; she kissed him with the passion of a woman who'd waited thirty-one years to slip into the arms of a man she'd kissed a million times in her dreams.

And when she pulled away, he could taste her sugar in his skin. *Did the kiss mean yes?* He couldn't be sure. She'd smashed his heart before and handed him every precious piece, although he wouldn't change a thread of the tapestry of their past.

"May I sleep on it?"

"Do anything you desire. I'll always love you."

He cranked the truck and gazed into the darkness beyond the streetlights. Looked in his side mirror for pedestrians and on-coming traffic and maneuvered the truck down St. Charles to Ponce de Leon.

"Joo-moo! Joo-moo!" Rhonda hollered the name, hands cupping her mouth as though she were screeching through a bullhorn, not caring if her screaming irritated a knot of teens sauntering in front of her as she stood in the entrance of Dee Jay's Diner, a restaurant whose atmosphere, food, and music recollected the days of poodle skirts and penny loafers. One of the teens, a walking heap of clothes, looked around as if he half expected to see a trained monkey leap from the crowd. When the teens finally passed, drifting like they fully intended to remain at Six Flags until sunrise, Rhonda hollered again. "Jooomooo!"

Behind her, Big Trevor's unsolicited retort brushed up against her back. "That boy can't hear you, woman; all these other bodies absorbing your words. Leave the kids alone and come sit down."

She didn't pay him any mind. He'd thrown in the towel, letting the kids go for it. She watched him plop down on a cushioned pink booth near one of the diner's large, opened windows, a plate of greasy fries, onions rings and two char-grilled burgers with ketchup dripping every which-a-way, the center of his attention.

But Rhonda wasn't having it. By her watch, she could spit into midnight, Saturday morning seconds off, and Li'l Trevor didn't need to be up too late. She didn't give a decent rip if it was August. In a few short weeks he'd be back to getting up at 7:00 A.M. And her problem was, she was good and exhausted, meandering from ride to neck-and-back-arresting ride, loosing her voice screaming beside Big Trevor, who behaved like he and Li'l Trevor and Jomo were instant compadres, fighting to decide who got to choose the next attraction.

After tonight, she didn't care if she never saw another rollercoaster ever again, and one on a brochure would be too soon. All she knew was she had to get some sleep before she drove to Free's, in a few hours, to help her plan their sleepover, her idea, to acquaint the women in the family with one another, including Miz Too-Sweet and Sherrie Ann, Gail Johnson, Sharmayne and Nzinga, and even Glory Mae Wyatt. Besides, she couldn't have her mother back from her Sun Dial dinner sitting at the house alone, twiddling her fingers until she and the guys crawled in like teenagers who'd conveniently forgotten the way home.

Hands back on her hips, the wide tail of the starched kente dress swirling prettily in the glare of the park's streetlamps, Rhonda shot Big Trevor another *I can't imagine why he's playing deaf* look.

She wanted to move, and badly, but something stayed her feet.

A stone's throw away, across a small, lit square, she caught sight of Jomo engrossed in conversation with someone, to whom he periodically shouted, off near the Looney Tunes U.S.A. restaurant. She was sure of it. Then minutes later, she was certain. Li'l Trevor trotted out of thin air to flank him, a midget sentry, pants baggy under an oversized T-shirt, same as Jomo's.

She tried her luck with Li'l Trevor. On the third bellow, he turned, searched the thinning pockets of people, spotted his waving mother, and began tugging Jomo's shirt bottom, garnering the older boy's attention before he shuffled off in the opposite direction.

Rhonda shook her head, her mouth skewed to the side in annoyance, and watched her son jog towards her, already talking.

"I'm not interested in that. What kinda stuff you and Jomo think you're hatching, staying away so long, talking about you'd be back in a minute." Her tone assured her son she meant what she said so he'd do well to shut up and march ahead of her piloting forefinger.

"Where have you been and where did Jomo run off to and who was he so darn preoccupied with he couldn't hear me whooping like a crazy woman? Everybody else in the park heard me except him." Rhonda's finger directed Trevor into the pink booth beside his grinning father, who immediately asked him if he'd had fun.

"Never mind that, Trevor Butler. I want this little boy to answer my questions. He and Jomo were up to something, and I want to know what it is."

Li'l Trevor peeped up at his mother through long dark lashes. He hadn't realized he and Jomo had been hatching a diabolical plot, as she made it sound, just because they'd backtracked to do a repeat performance of the coolest rides.

The child gazed at his father for silent support, grinned sheepishly, and said, "We rode the Big Six again; you know, the Viper and the Ninja and the Scream Machine." A grin the width of the theme park stretched the length of his face. "Remember, Mama?"

"Yeah, yeah, and how," Rhonda relented, still peeved.

"And how what?" he asked, basking in the glow of the rides' mere names.

She sighed and watched father and son savor what looked to be a delightful snicker. "Back to the question, son."

"When we got off the Mine Train and I wanted to eat at Looney Tunes, Jomo said cool and that's when we started walking from---"

"Hold it, little boy. You left the Mine Train to

eat at Looney Tunes. Then what?"

"I had to go to the bathroom and Jomo waited. When I came outside, he was talking to somebody named Dog. He was with some more big kids. Jomo didn't let me get near them. When you called me, he told me to go on and tell you he had to hollah at some dudes."

Li'l Trevor's smile asked Big Trevor for the liberty of a few soggy fries.

"Somebody named Dog?" Rhonda smelled trouble. "Did this Dog have a last name?"

Li'l Trevor shook his head and laughed, greedily licking ketchup like he hadn't eaten a morsel all day.

"That's it, Trevor." Rhonda had heard more than enough. "Let's go. Don't ask me how I know, call it a woman's intuition, but we gotta go. Now!"

"Look, Precious Pooh, Jomo is a young man with a good head on his shoulders. He's not about to do something stupid now that we've helped him get his life back on track. If he hasn't been courting trouble up to this point, what makes you suddenly sprout Avenging Angel wings? Do me and our li'l man a big favor and eat the rest of this burger. It's better than I thought."

Rhonda didn't hear anything after the part about sprouting wings. She was up and maneuvering through the crowd like Moses parting the Red Sea, one thought in her head: Jomo was heading toward something for which God hadn't let him get this far just to have somebody's Dog lure him away from them now. And Big Trevor, when it dawned on him she was serious as sin, snatched his son up by the arm so fast he nearly disconnected the tiny joints trying to keep up with the glint of his wife's gold kente dress.

In hour-like minutes, he snagged a flicker of the dress, fleetingly, in a tight cluster of excitedly talking people pushing in on one another to see something off in the grass near huge trees under the heavy tracks of the Mindbender. Whatever the something, several Six Flags security guards wanted to see it, too.

"Everybody move back! Give us some clearance!" a burly officer shouted.

"I'm looking for my son," Trevor gunned. "That may be my kid in there!"

He fell in behind the white shirts as they barreled deeper into the underbrush beneath the ride; eventually, what he witnessed, in the attraction's bright lights, in the grass, lying against Rhonda's gold-gone-scarlet bosom, dropped his temperature as swiftly as a ten-minute tour of a walk-in deep freeze. And before he could intercept his son's curiosity, he felt the little body go limp, become a paralyzed softness across his shoulder.

Loud rap filled the red jeep with a distinct presence. Under it, something thrashed against his rib cage, the rubber of the jeep's radials striking the asphalt, heedless, as was the heart-stopping panic inside Short Dog of patrolling police cars. With the taste of warm blood filling his pulpy mouth, a need to spit frightened his swollen lips. He longed to allow a little spittle to seep from the corner of his mouth to mingle with the dampness of his already bloodstained T-shirt. His traumatized tongue---the only part of his body boasting movement---canvassed his mouth from top to bottom, inspecting his injuries.

For a split second he forgot the pain and thought about his mother, but then the pain returned with a vengeance and he couldn't recall climbing inside the jeep where he now sat crumpled between two of the boyz. Knew he must've been knocked unconscious in the beatdown. And, bit by bit, he bribed his mind to replay the events of the last couple of hours.

Was he dead and demons favoring the boyz were ushering him to hell?

The harder he bribed himself to recall, the more his consciousness clung to the present, and for long agonizing minutes he couldn't determine if hyped voices were inside or outside his head. But as long as those voices remained voices and didn't metamorphose into fists, he'd analyze the situation from a crawl-space behind the intense throbbing his body had become and count his blessings.

But just when he was getting used to the rhythm of the speeding jeep, it slowed all of a sudden and rolled almost soundlessly through the calm darkness of a familiar neighborhood and crept to a standstill a car or two away from a streetlamp.

"Damn, how much dumber you think a muhfucker kin get, blabbin' our business like uh punk bitch!" The dark face glowered from between the front bucket seats. "Oughta break off another piece of his monkey ass, at least till I get the satisfaction my knuckles hollin' fah. Gotdamn!" angry lips snarled, addressing teens crammed in the jeep's interior, one in the front, three in the rear. "Still can't believe the shit, and I heard it with my own ears. I'm gon' try not to shoot his ass before the smoke clears."

Short dog tensed.

"Naw, man," a quiet brotha, hands on his knees and body held serene, as if he were in church, warned in a calm baritone. "Mad as you is, you gone really hurt him. One near-casualty chalked up to us tonight is cool, though the dude took the beatdown like a for-real brotha. And got in some serious hits, too."

Short Dog trained his eyes straight ahead.

"Word. That mothafucker woulda fucked somebody up one-on-one."

"Humph," Tank scoffed. "Nobody told him to come runnin' his Rambo-lookin', ig'nant ass up in our business no way. Chump been watchin' too many bad-boy flicks and not knowin' what time it wuz, he come close to lights out...fah good."

"Yeah, and I thought he was gon' freak when you slugged Motor Mouth here," the thin-voiced brotha in the passenger seat added. "His eyes went bright. Might as well have hollered 'Round One!' cuz the niggah went to puttin' down big time."

Tank and the others howled then, but the serene dude suspended the good times with the precision of a snub-nosed rifle halting a mocking mouth. "Something tells me Homey ain't know that niggah would know what he knew, and check it out. Li'l Shawty back there never mentioned the house digits. It was like the brotha was a magician, pulling shit outta the air and crap."

"Betcha not-uh-one be tellin' nobody ta'night tho." The sneer in his eyes made him menacing in the lamplight. "C'mon, niggahs," he said, hyped and ready, gazing admiringly at the well-spaced homes on a manicured South Park Drive. "Got business to handle, and dis li'l sucker need all the energy he got left tah do what he gon' do up in this camp, ai'ight?"

The boyz echoed his "ai'ight," and then a hand shoved Short Dog, panic in his eyes, out of the jeep and onto the asphalt. Bending low, they expertly negotiated the night until they faced their rendezvous point.

The impressive house was just as they'd last cased it, only now, through the side window of the garage, Tank spied a second car beside the Mercedes. It slowed his roll but not for long. A thirty-eight jammed in the waistband of Tank's underwear, drawn blood and drink downed earlier---all went a long way towards overlooking unanticipated details in a planned program.

With the hands of the bedroom clock ticking quietly towards midnight, Free snoozed naked, legs straddling J.T.'s left thigh, warm breath rasping gently in the crook of his neck. Overhead, the ceiling fan's exhalations licked their bodies. The left-over languor of lovemaking glistening on her mango-colored skin.

Now she awoke jarred, a dream she'd been having persistently annoying.

J.T. patted her butt and stroked her back, his fingertips teasing her skin in long, soothing strokes. His breath fluttered her hair. Kisses drifted through her curls to her cheeks.

"Bad dream?"

Free sighed, snuggling into his comforting presence. She pressed herself against him bodily, loving the feel of firm male pecs on her breasts, the delight of his tight waist and those granite legs. One palm floated to his chest, and he automatically flexed, the muscle jumping spastically. She giggled. Down below, she admired the curly black hair sprinkled lightly below his navel leading to a thickly curly briar patch, the nestling place for his slumbering Black Man, the hair continuing down chocolate thunder thighs. The man was exquisite, and the totality of her---mind, body, and soul---missed him terribly.

"Been having it for nights now." She kissed his shoulder. "But it's not frightening now that my baby's here. Nothing in a dream or reality can make me sweat with you near, lover."

"Oh, so you been sweating without me? Should've called me. You know I can't have my lady afraid, I don't care if she did walk my ass to the door."

Her face nuzzling his armpit brought his laughter, her giggles infectious.

"Everything happens as it should." He rolled her on top of him and palmed her ass with both hands and bit her shoulder. "Tell Big Daddy your dreams."

"I can't talk with the BlackMan yawning and you bouncing my butt."

"Sorry, ma'am, my apology." He slapped her behind before his hands drifted to the sheets. "Okay, how's that?"

Free inched higher up his chest, the heat of the BlackMan's breath incinerating.

"In the dream, I'm talking, usually, in a jolly mood, and just like that I part my lips and plush black feathers come floating out of my mouth, making me the cat that swallowed the canary."

"Haven't been fibbing to me about anything, baby, have you?"

He corkscrewed her hardening nipples.

"Quit, I'm serious. Sometimes I awake fighting for breath. I assure you, the feeling isn't cute."

"Well, now that you've accepted the adventure of being Mrs. Junior Thomas---or are you using Roberts-Thomas?"

"Hmmm. The latter is impressive."

"I'll hold you, the future Mrs. Roberts-Thomas, and give you my very breath, if necessary."

His hands encircled her waist and slid her body lower as his lips sought hers. Pressing her ass into his groin, rocking her with his lower body, he relished her wet tongue. Aroused, the BlackMan caught a sweet whiff of Free's ponany and shivered, rising slowly to military stiffness. Before it could throb and thump against her heart-shaped ass, the door bell shrilled.

"Ignore it." J.T. had a renewed rhythm and he wasn't about to stop for anyone other than God but the doorbell chimed persistently and Free was already reaching for her robe.

"It's Mama. Earl is bringing her after their date."

"She has a key, right?"

She leaped off the bed. "Maybe she forgot it at Rhonda's."

She made sure the robe was snug before taking the stairs, yelling, "I'm coming! Hold on!"

Pressed against the front door, she blinked and focused long enough to discern she didn't recognize the shadowy figure on the porch, the movement of her hand iced on the cool doorknob. Then, she inhaled and took a step backward---an ear-splitting peal rang out. Her flesh burned under the robe. The invasive sound of consecutive, flat-soled kicks assaulted the door, and Frenonia sank into a warm pool of unfamiliar darkness.

"Oooh shiit, Freee!" A deathly chill brought winter to J.T.'s feverish, passion-heated skin. His senses went into full alert, and he perceived what was up instantly.

A home invasion. And Free downstairs? Oh, hell no!

In the darkness, he found his pants on the carpet near the bed, yanked them on, and grabbed the phone, dialed 9-1-1. Knowing time was essential, he growled home invasion and South Park Drive and slipped the mobile phone into the waist of his jeans. He squatted, opened a wide drawer in the bed's frame, snaked a hand inside, and retrieved a forty-five caliber handgun, Free's insurance. He checked its chambers. It was loaded.

An ominous silence invaded the house. He prayed for mercy, for his woman and for the fools kicking in her front door.

Flicking off the hall light and crouching low, close to the baseboards, J.T. moved with ninja stealth, practically sailing the stairs in one bound. The front door trembled and complained on its hinges, and he knew it wouldn't hold too much longer. Quickly, he negotiated the bright living room until he reached the light switch, shrouding the room in sudden darkness. By the door, Free lay stark-still. Her lashes flickered. He knew she had been hit, from the bloody mushroom on her right shoulder. He crawled to her side, prayed moving her didn't jeopardize her life. Hopefully the bullet only grazed her.

The door groaned and held, making J.T. grateful for its density. Gently, gingerly, he eased Free deeper into the living room. Kissed her motionless mouth and brushed auburn strands from her damp forehead, the cherry-red stain appearing harmless.

J.T. pulled the mobile from his pants. The 9-1-1 operator yet on the line, he whispered, "Send an ambulance. My fiancé's been shot. Hurry."

What he didn't say was, if he could help it, there'd be no cause for rush with the other ambulances.

Then he ducked. A bullet shattered the window to the right of the violated, angry door. Covering his head, he crawled close to a sturdy arm chair and posted up, the location offering a perfect position for his range of fire. Whoever crossed the threshold tonight would be within a wingspan of Heaven.

Calm showered him. No call to waste his steel, even though he'd slipped a handful of bullets into his pants pockets. The police would be there soon. He'd wait, make his rounds count.

Whoever it was wasn't too smart. No silencer. Her neighborhood wouldn't abide August fireworks long. Somebody had to be calling the police.

His fingers wandered over the handgun, its coolness tempering him. The boots kept contact with wood, until, in a fraction of a second, the front door gave one last grunt and ceded to the night's heat and soles; the jarring force of the deed spewing falling figures into the foyer.

J.T. aimed and fired, plugging the biggest of the three in the chest. Twice.

"Goddamnit, the mothafucker's gotta piece!" a husky, gurgling voice said. "Where the bitch? She shot me!"

J.T. watched the figure stagger in the muted glow of the streetlamp.

Instinctively, the others hit the hardwood. A bullet whizzed somewhere near the sofa's other side, and he aimed again, hitting a smaller, crawling shape. Another scream pierced the night.

J.T. unloaded a third time. In the fray, two bodies scurried over themselves and dashed back to the door, abandoning someone trembling and moaning in practically the exact spot Free had fallen. A peewee. But Big Boy squeezed off disoriented fire, no one thinking to take his gun. The smaller body jumped. No longer a threat, Big Boy breathed sporadically, creeping backward, pulling his bulk towards the porch. J.T. let him go. He sighed, glad the intruders weren't men, experienced men. The night stilled. He registered whimpering from the bleeding form on the floor. Abandoned, his crew had run off without him.

Were they gone? Grabbing a flower vase from a nearby end table, J.T. hurled it towards the door and a shot rang out, then two, from the porch, through the opened door. A crouched figure passed a window. Cast an eerie shadow.

"Get dah hell outta here! Niggahs turnin' on they lights and shit!"

"Let's book, Tank," someone huffed in short breaths from the porch. "Dah Man be here in a minute."

J.T. inched a few paces around the sofa. Strained to get a picture of how many other kids were outside. Another shot caught him off guard, shattering a living room windowpane, the missive missing his head by a hair. "Shit!" He froze at an agonizing moan riding the air from where he'd left Free. Fear cudgeled his heart, but J.T., flipping like a large agile cat, shouted, assuring Free he was okay, and, seeing shadows looming behind smashed glass, he surveyed the doorway and what was left of a window, before discharging a third time.

And this time a shadow fell. Hard.

The thud thundered in his soul and, waiting instinctively, he realized the drama ended with the music of dazed utterances and running feet assailing the stairs. Waiting a few minutes, and stepping over the quietly moaning figure, gun reloaded and held in front of his body, both hands on the weapon, J.T. cautiously reconnoitered the porch. In the night's quick silence, he realized there had only been one gun. With several clips. Where J.T. dropped him, a heavy youth, looking older than the one in the house and another moaning on the steps, lay crumpled on the porch, the handgun smoking in his palm.

J.T. knew Big Boy was gone, several streams spewing from the lake of his body, soaking the porch boards with memory. Upper body inclined over the banister, he watched two sinewy figures sprinting, heads thrown back, running down the middle of South Park Drive. A thorough check of cold pockets uncovered a key.

Probably to the red jeep parked beside the lamppost.

When he re-entered the living room, the

distant wail of sirens followed him. Shaking his head, he kneeled down near Free and stroked the side of her sweaty face, the delicate features crinkled in pain. They looked at one another gratefully, lovingly. He trusted his lips to memorize what his vision treasured---the hair, mouth, cheeks, ears, nose, throat, breasts, arms and back, anything that anchored him deeper in the moment.

Standing there, he slipped into the past anyway and reeled under a simple truth, one of his father's favorite expressions: "Although the Black man gotta be twice as good as a white one to go anywhere in this society, servin' in the Korean Conflict taught me I'd rather go down fightin' for this country than any other country in the world. 'Cause the sin here beats what I don't know somewhere else."

J.T. shrugged.

Enervated; enlightened. That was his father's truth. He'd rather lay it on the line for Frenonia Roberts, simply live to be there when she called, than for any other woman, anywhere else. The night taught him they could rise above any perceived problem that came against them.

Gently, he stroked her pulse, asked, "What you doing, Li'l Mama?"

Her smile was weak but present. "Help me to the one near the door, please."

"The police will be here shortly. They'll worry about him."

She managed to shake her head and push a request up past the pain in her shoulder. "Please."

He scooped her into his arms then and eased her down beside the moaning boy.

Watching her, he softened when she reached out and stroked the teenager's locs, resting her palm on his trembling cheek. Something in her knew him in spite of the darkness.

"Put his head on my lap."

J.T. adhered to her command without protest. While he cradled Free, she stroked the fallen boy, who calmed instantly under her touch. His breathing puttered, and they knew he was clinging to whatever was left of the life seeping quietly from wine-colored corsages on his chest and abdomen.

"What about that one?" She indicated the crumpled form on the porch.

J.T. sighed, closed his eyes. "Don't worry. He can't roll over, let alone get up. I'm just thankful I was here tonight." He inhaled a deep breath and said a silent prayer and shook his head. "Had I not, you might've shot the door off yourself."

Gurgled giggles drifted up from Free's lips, although her gaze watered and her lips mouthed, "Kids."

"Kids my foot!" J.T sneered, dark brows puckered, nose scrunched. "It's kids like that, armed and breaking in folks' houses; turning into men doing God knows what. Something's got to be done, 'cause Lord knows I didn't want to shoot them." He pressed the back of her hand to his heart. "Damn." He inhaled her precious scent. "Could've lost you. Forever. Can't take anymore chances like that, Black Woman. We gotta hop that broom and fast after you get a tune-up. Or hell, we can do it on your back. I'm inventive!"

Soundless laughter floated from Free's mouth and rained over the boy's head.

Then the phone rang.

Then, police and ambulance sirens filled the night, and the teenager whimpered. Free said a prayer for goodness and mercy to follow them all, and thought she heard J.T. greet Pastoria somewhere above her head.

Then, her lashes fluttered and the last thing she remembered was unimaginable pain and police swarming the porch like army ants.

Chapter 35

Wasn't nothing but love.

Though Short Dog left here as sure as my name's Miz Too-Sweet, he was supposed to, being God ain't in the mistake business, like Mama usedta say. Us can't leave before our time no way. Just that some folks' time long, others short, by our measure. By the Lawd's, it's the same. Perfect. He upstairs and down here, controlling everything, not man, who creating ruckus more times than not, and goodness knows, if it was the other way round, this world be in more of a bind and a pickle.

So much done happened 'tween now and the time Free walked into my life, holding us and my Mookey in the palm of her hand. I tell you, can't nobody write a drama like God. Yes, ma'am, the Lawd can script some happenings.

Who'da thought this of a total stranger, though ain't none of us true strangers. We just ain't had the pleasure of meetin' one another until we meet. Anyway, here come this lady outta the March night and who she turn out to be---Pinky's sister. If that didn't beat all! Hallelujah!

Done heard tell of a lotta things, one being, what you searchin' for is usually right under your nose. That seem stale, if you done heard it a thousand times, but in this case, I saw it get refreshed before these old eyes, and I thank the Lawd I did. Pinky ain't have to leave the city looking for her mama. The woman drove up from where she live in Pine Mountain, Georgia, the home of some kinda famous gardens, where she say she gone take the lot of us.

Pinky's daddy Earl Taylor drove the mama right over here to Techwood Homes like he been driving her to their daughter every day of they lives.

Now ain't that a shout and a run up the church aisle for you?

I can barely get Mookey Man to spend a sacred minute with his Miz Too-Sweet no more, what with him clamoring to get to his little aunties, Free and Rhonda, and his "Nana," as he say, 'cause Pastoria like her grands to call her Nana. That's the new grandma these days, though Big Mama and MuhDear and Grandma and Grandmama good enough in my day. Things change. From one day to the next, one month to the next. Life is a blanket of colorful patches. The changing shades of love, I reckon.

Us buried Short Dog not too long ago.

The boy put away nice, Pinky's new boyfriend, Grant, who I like near bout as much as she do, foot the entire bill, only letting Earl and other fam'ly buy flowers. Say that's why he in his woman's life---to lift her burdens.

That li'l fellow was strong, though, hanging on for a few hours in ICU, which was colder than death, you ask me. Yes, ma'am, he held on till Omar came and stood beside his mama. Was one of the onliest times I ever knowed them two to hug. It broke my heart. That was the one thing Taylor wanted, to see his parents love one another, or at least, act like they did. But, I got a choice: to holler or to smile, and I choose to smile. It's a blessing the chile took that sight on into paradise with him; it coulda been worse, like drowning in blood on his auntie's floor.

Mr. Thomas bullet and that of that demon

what spearheaded the whole affair found in the boy's body. Paper called it a home invasion gone foul. Yet, that Tank boy was somebody's chile, too, in spite of his hard head. Bet he fell like a horse, he the biggest one in the paper's pictures. That third boy made it. But how bout them other two tough rats didn't know enough to not hide under they mamas' skirts?

If Short Dog couldn't stay, I'm sho glad Jomo did. Course he still at Grady Memorial, making good progress and talkin' more and more each day, even if he cry a lot 'cause he say he tried to save his friend but he was outnumbered in a fight he still l' up from. Say Short Dog's crew had they eyes on his Aunt Free's Mercedes for a decent spell, wonderin' what business a lady like her doing in Techwood. I can hear them now, probably talkin' bout, "She   ruising' for a brusin' over here, so we may as well gone give her one." Insteada praising God for bringing her here and the blessings of her outreach programs. Nope, I ain't gone harp on that, it happened, he gone, Edwin "Tank" Jackson, and that's all to it. Some things ain't for us to know. I tend to leave God's business to God, and lean not unto my own understanding. All I can do is listen and reckon with my own business.

In the midst of death, there's life.

That's a fact I been living long enough to spout with authority. When Mr. Thomas called Rhonda the day Free visited him at the Marriott, and he decided to run down here and meet me and even rode over to the Waffle House and met Pinky and invited us all to that fancy dinner I will never forget, I knowed wedding bells was on the wind. The wind don't lie. Them bells was ringing sweet and high, too.

It mighta been in the Marriott water.

But they yet looking for the church to 'commodate the big affair: Mr. Thomas and Free, Grant and Pinky, and, get this, Earl and Pastoria. Tell me God ain't in the script-writing business. Not only that, Free's friend, Sharmayne and her lady friend, that tall one with the off-color name, they gone have a commitment ceremony, a new-fangled something women who love women call a wedding. Next thing, Will be talkin' bout when I'm gon' remarry him, or, as Free say, renew my wedding vows. Tickled me. My vows ain't broken, torn, shred, scraped, or old, so I'll let young folks be young folks.

Pinky and her daddy forgive Mr. Thomas, say you can't halt God's will.

Sad as it is, Short Dog ain't gone; he here in Spirit, with our changing fam'ly. Yes, ma'am, us fam'ly, the whole lot of us, from Preacher to Jomo to Sherrie Ann. Oh, and let me not forget that Miz Glory Mae Wyatt, that's Jomo's li'l aunty---she in our circle of love. Met her at Grady, when she come to see bout her great nephew, and Lawd, was she grateful he survived the whopping them boys put on him, no matter his lungs collapsed, like Javan Reed and Lewis Reynolds' heart collapsed when they learned love done found Pinky.

Had to call the Law on that Reynolds, who went to cutting the fool like that gal cheated on him to get with her new man. Despite that, she stood by her word, told him to gone visit his other women and chillen, who miss and need him. Reminded him not to be a stranger, long as he's law-abidin'.

And how bout that Rhonda.

She something else, too. Me and her got us a growin' manuscript. Us meet, either she come to

Techwood and sit in the yard with me or she come get me and Will and Preacher and us sit in the yard with her and I speak into a recorder, just as happy as a fly in buttermilk, telling the stories of my life. Still floors me. Yeah, everybody got a story, just that I got 999 more than most folks.

Seem life done called me out and asked me to live and live more abundantly, as the Bible say, 'cause I done experienced a heap of living. Attended my first book club meetin', the *National Black Arts Festival*, participated in Techwood's first Outreach Programs, and better than all that, made Free's all-girl sleepover at her house. If I could win uh award at the book club meetin' for being the youngest, I can attend uh all-girl pajama party. Us had all kinda fun. Popped corn, watched movies, movies watched me, eat, laughed and discussed one another's lives, played games (I like Checkers), and eat cinnamon rolls, which Trevor made from scratch, calling it "the secret of summer," say God reminded him what ingredients to gather and he went to work with Big Trevor and Mr. Thomas help (since Mr. Thomas is a chef, wonder if he really made them). Whoever made them, they eat delicious.

Us even painted our nails, which I ain't done since Jesus was a tot, and loved up on Pinky, who doing the best she can holdin' up after loosin' her boy. I know. Loosing a chile ain't no easy thang, I don't care who holdin' you up.

But she gone make it through the storm.

Us all here to support her, and be her shelter in the wind, her palm leaf in the noon day sun, her umbrella in the heavy rain.

All things work out, so I don't get hemmed up

in fussin' and fightin' bout nothing, since it don't matter in the long run no way. *Fact is, Love call, you come.* That's it. Don't need a fancy degree to understand it: Everybody come forth to love and be loved in return.

But then, what do I know? I'm just Miz Too-Sweet, Will's wife.

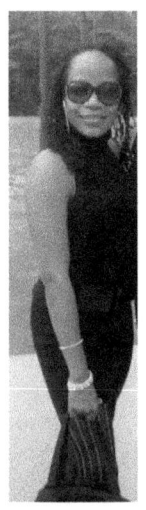

CLAUDIA MOSS is a writer/speaker/performer who currently calls Atlanta, GA, home. She is the author of *Dolly: The Memoirs of a High School Graduate* and *The Wanda B. Wonders* series (*Wanda B. Wonders Speaks Her Mind, Wanda B. Takes the Cake* and *Wanda B. Sings the Bailout Blues*). Readers should visit Amazon for her coming releases: *Soft Tsunami* (a poetry collection) and *Not Without Passion* (a novel). She blogs at www.claudiamoss.wordpress.com.